Ross Klatte has given us a robust novel which captures the political and social turmoil as well as the drug-addled opportunistic sexual muddle of the 60's and 70's. "Too young to be a beatnik, too old to be a hippy", reckons Tom, taking a break from newspaper writing in Chicago, a would-be novelist and spurned husband. He searches for Angela from Oaxaca, across America and over the border to a back to the land commune in British Columbia. Angela reclaims her moral compass, rejecting a charismatic commune leader (I found myself cheering her on!) and Tom, a decent man at heart, rediscovers his Minnesotan farm boy roots. Raunchy, soul-searching, authentic--this is the real deal.

—Caroline Woodward

According to mythology, those who came of age in the Sixties and early Seventies thrilled to a magic-carpet-ride of sex, dope, and cheap thrills. But in *Waiting for the Revolution*, instead of celebrating Woodstock, Janice Joplin, and the romance of marching on Washington, author Ross Klatte plunges us into the pain and confusion of those who narrowly survived turning on, tuning in, and dropping out. Part spell-binding love story, part expose of the true cost of rebellion, this skillfully written novel evokes a world of Hippie communes, partner-switching, bad drug trips, and social experiments gone wrong. You want a vivid flashback? Try *Waiting for the Revolution*.

—Ken McGoogan,
whose latest book is Searching for Franklin

The 1960s were an era of social experimentation and social change, but as Ross Klatte's poignant novel *Waiting For the Revolution* grippingly chronicles, heartbreak and loneliness were by no means eliminated as a minority of young people try to fashion a new and better world. The novel convincingly shows how, despite the Sixties' life-enhancing optimism, even those individuals at the forefront of change could find themselves bewildered and hurt by the era's evolving morality as it affected relations between men and women. The plot unfolds in counter-culture enclaves in Mexico and BC's West Kootenay, where, as the main character notes, his fellow seekers "were all refugees" from not only the conformity and repressive strictures of 1950s America, but from the old culture they carry inside.

Klatte deftly portrays his characters' twists and turns of thinking as they try to achieve in their daily lives "some saving integration with the natural world, some happy accommodation to the complexities of human relations. Some grand righting of all the wrongs in the world." The author's consummate skill with words lets the reader feel what living in a time when the goal of building, together with like-minded others, a more humane society seems almost within reach, even while old values—both within the characters and in the larger community—still have power. *Waiting For the Revolution* shows how the Sixties' aims and legacy of peace, love, justice, fairness and respect for nature must be realized by people who are far from blank slates when they adopt these causes . . . people very much like ourselves.

—Tom Wayman, author of *The Shadows We Mistake for Love*, and recipient of BC's 2022 George Woodcock Award for Lifetime Achievement in the literary arts.

Waiting for the

Revolution

A Novel

Ross Klatte

 FriesenPress

One Printers Way
Altona, MB R0G 0B0
Canada

www.friesenpress.com

ISBN
978-1-03-918888-4 (Hardcover)
978-1-03-918887-7 (Paperback)
978-1-03-918889-1 (eBook)

1. FICTION

Distributed to the trade by The Ingram Book Company

For April again,
and for Will and Alicia

Acknowledgments

I owe many thanks to Jennifer Day, who did an encouraging reading of an early draft of this novel, and especially to Nicola Goshulak, who did both content and line-by-line edits of that early draft, including the helpful suggestion that I cut my then closing, tying-up-loose ends section of the novel, leaving only the final chapter.

And I owe my deepest thanks to Brittany Peters and the editors at FriesenPress for their help in the publishing of this novel.

Part One

Mexico and the US, 1970

Chapter 1

In Puerto Bonito that morning, after another of their exhausting, hurtful quarrels, Thomas Weber left his unhappy wife in the village's one hotel and went ahead to the only restaurant in town. He'd ordered *café con leche* and a breakfast of *huevos revueltos y frijoles refritos* and was sitting at one of the half dozen tables, shaded from the heavy tropical sun by the tin roof over the open dining area, when Angela appeared—with Richard Sullivan, "Ricardo," their new friend. They were walking very closely together and Sullivan was talking intently to her, his head under his straw hat bent confidingly toward her troubled face.

"Hi, honey," Tom said carefully as they drew up to him.

"I'm going out to the Plantation this morning with Ricardo," Angela abruptly told him.

Tom didn't say anything.

"We're catching a ride with Charlie."

The Plantation was an abandoned coconut plantation a couple of miles down the coast. They'd been introduced to its long, empty beach, its encampment of international hippies, by Richard, shortly after their arrival in Puerto Bonito. They'd met Richard their first morning here, been charmed by his friendliness, his eagerness to show them around. He was an old hand in Mexico, a merchant seaman who, between voyages, lounged around Puerto Bonito or out at the Plantation until he ran out of money and had to head up to one of the Gulf ports and ship out again. Like most of Puerto Bonito's gringos, he was a doper, stoned most of the time. He'd kept *them* mostly stoned since they got here.

"Do you know what you're doing, Angie?"

He supposed it was a cliche to notice she'd never looked more beautiful.

"I *have* to do this, Tom," she told him. "We *both* need to get away from each other for a while."

"No," he said. "It's just *you* needs to get away from *me*." He'd known this was coming; he'd waited for it. "How long is a while?"

"Just today. And *please,* don't follow us."

Richard stood quietly behind Angela, his dark-bearded, weathered face an almost comic mask of concern. He took his hat off now, revealing his close-cropped red hair, and held it before him as if respectfully.

"Don't worry, man," he said. "We're friends now, aren't we? Your wife just wants to talk, and she needs somebody other than you to listen to her."

"Just wait here in the village," Angela said.

"We'll be back before dark," Richard said.

"I still love you," his wife said.

"Hey, ain't this civilized?" said Richard.

The younger of the two women came out of the thatched, half-walled enclosure that housed the kitchen with his plate of scrambled eggs and refried beans, together with a cloth-covered basket of tortillas. Tom had remarked on her indigenous beauty their first morning here—her profile was right out of some pre-Columbian mural—and Angela, referring to their gardener back in Trujano, said, "Yes, wouldn't she and Antonio make a perfect couple?"

He looked down at his food without interest now, then up to see Angela and Richard negotiating the dirt street—the strewn garbage, the indolent pigs, the foraging chickens, the collapsed pariah dogs—until they reached the gringo named Charlie and his dusty pickup. They climbed into the truck bed and hung on to the wooden rack along its sides as Charlie pulled away into the scrub outside the village.

Tom waited all that endless-seeming day in their cell-like hotel room, sweating on the hanging bed through the oppressive afternoon heat, seeing rats scuttling along the rafters. He thought of sneaking out to the Plantation to spy on Angela and Ricardo, then realized the masochism, the humiliation, of that. So he waited. He even slept. When he woke the sun was low over the ocean and it was cooler. He rolled out of the bed and went to the little table with its clay basin and pitcher of water. Splashed water on his face, then buried it in the towel he and Angela had shared and that carried, just faintly, her smell like an ache in its damp folds. Lowered the towel and opened his eyes to see Richard in the doorway.

5

"Where's Angela?" he asked anxiously.

"Oh, I left her out at the Plantation," Richard said. "She's decided to stay out there a while."

"What, with you?" Tom knew the answer.

Richard looked sternly at Tom. "Your wife's kind of confused now, man. She doesn't know if she wants to stay married to you. She needs time to think."

Tom's head began to spin.

"She'll be *okay*, man. I'll look after her."

"Oh, I bet you will. You opportunistic bastard."

Richard looked hurt. "Okay, I won't lie to you, man. I *like* Angela. A lot. But I'll bring her back to you—if that's what she wants, finally."

Tom couldn't think.

"Honest, man, I didn't talk her into this. This was *her* decision."

"Oh yeah. And you had nothing to do with it, right?" There was a sick hole in Tom's gut. It was like panic.

"*C'mon*, man. You care about Angela's happiness or just your own?"

"How long we talking about?"

"A week maybe."

"A *week!* You think I can just—"

"Look. She wants you to go back to your place in Trujano and wait. She *doesn't* want you moping around here. She'll wire you from Pochutla in a couple days."

"Couldn't she have said goodbye to me at least?" Tom heard the whine in his voice.

"She didn't want to *see* you right now." Richard gripped Tom's shoulders. "She has to work things out for *herself*, man.

She still loves you, I think. She'll probably come back to you. But you gotta give her time."

He wanted to see decency in Richard's eyes. He wanted to believe that Angela would be all right with him. He just wanted her to be happy. Nobody belonged to anybody anymore.

Not until later, alone and paranoid in their rented house in Trujano, would he brood on the possibility—*the certainty!*—that Richard had lied to him, that he had Angela strung out and helpless under the Plantation's palms. What if he'd abandoned her? But that agonizing thought, that sinking sense of having left her with somebody they barely knew in his beach bum's paradise didn't strike him until he'd overcome his own sense of abandonment, his own helplessness.

"Take care of her," he heard himself say.

"I *will*, man."

And then numbed, yielding to the spirit of the age, Tom found himself *hugging* the man who was taking his wife away from him.

The afternoon bus from Puerto Bonito climbed the mountains to Pochutla, where he waited for the overnight bus to Oaxaca City. Outside the bus station two adolescent boys were selling live iguanas. People ate them here. The boys had them trussed up on the sidewalk, their snouts taped shut, their clawed feet bound for safe handling. Tom nodded gravely to the boys and the apparently older of the two caught his eye. With something like a mocking smile he nudged one of the gorgeously ugly creatures with a bare toe and said, "*¿Lo quieres, señor?*"

Tom wagged his forefinger in the sign for no and walked past them to the entrance of the stone church at the head of the square. In the dim, hushed interior he made out the dark form of a woman in a middle pew. He felt her eyes upon him as he walked past her to kneel before the gilded altar. He folded his hands, bowed his head.

Dear God, if it be Thy will, bring my wife back to me.

It was a hollow prayer. He hadn't prayed, hadn't been to Mass or Confession or taken Communion in months, in years, after marrying a Jew and neither of them going to church or a synagogue. He wasn't even sure he believed in God anymore.

Now he crossed himself and stepped away from the altar. No atheists in foxholes, he thought sarcastically.

He got into Oaxaca City at four the next morning and took a room in a hotel near the market. He was paying the night clerk when a Mexican hippie he vaguely knew, long-haired and bearded, came into the lobby with a blond gringa. She had a wan, pretty face and looked wasted. They both looked wasted.

"*¡Amigo!*" the Mexican called to him. "*¿Cómo está?*"

"*Bien,*" Tom said dully. He'd forgotten the dude's name but remembered him from being introduced by their landlord's son in the zocalo one day, and more especially from when the two came out to his and Angela's place in Trujano with samples of Oaxaca's famous magic mushrooms and they all got stoned and this middle-class Mexican made fun of the gardener as he was watering their garden—mimicked his ungrammatical Spanish, joked about his peasant mentality. In Tom's zonked perceptions, the dude had transformed from a Jesus lookalike into the devil.

The girl stood vacantly beside him. German? Californian?

"How *you* doing?" Tom asked her, without interest.

She smiled but didn't say anything.

Alone in his hotel room, Tom wrote in his journal, *When couples break up, there's one who leaves and one who's left.*

Then he climbed into the empty bed and slept fitfully until noon.

Chapter 2

He woke to a beautiful, cloudless day, hot in the sun but cool in the shade, the dry air almost bracing at five thousand feet altitude. He walked to the zocalo, had coffee and pan dulce at a sidewalk café. The few gringos he saw in the square were all of the counterculture. He waved off a sarape salesman but gave ten pesos to a pretty young female beggar while it occurred to him she might only be supporting her junkie boyfriend. He called for *la cuenta*, left a twenty peso note and a five-pesos tip on his table, then walked to the second-class bus station. He was lucky. His bus, one of a fleet of old school buses, had just started its engine. He got on and it took him the five miles south of the city to the village of Trujano.

The bus stopped in front of the adobe church. Tom got off with a couple of locals and walked the short way down the highway to the place he and Angela had rented for the winter, the "country house" of a doctor in Oaxaca. He unlocked the iron gate and entered the walled enclosure of the house and garden. Locked the gate and walked through the garden to the house and, with nothing else to do, lay down on the bed that until recently he'd shared with Angela. He tried to sleep but only lay staring at the white-plastered ceiling.

Antonio, the gardener, came by that afternoon. He was a young man of twenty just finishing high school in Oaxaca under the sponsorship of the doctor, his *patrón*. He appeared every other day or so to water the plants.

"*¡Hola!*" Antonio called.

Tom stepped outside the house as Antonio unlocked the gate with his key and walked toward him on the path between the trees and flowers.

"*Buenas tardes*," Tom said.

"*Tardes*," Antonio said, smiling. Then a frown crossed his handsome face.

"*¿Donde está la señora?*"

He was too polite to call her by name, though Angela had been tutoring him in English and they'd spent a lot of time with him otherwise, going on walks together into the *campo* outside the village.

"She's in Puerto Bonito for more time," Tom said in his limited Spanish.

Antonio looked puzzled, so Tom added, "*Ella gusta el mar.* He wanted to add that, besides liking the sea, she was working on her tan, but that exceeded his small command of the language.

"*Ah sí*," Antonio said.

He began his watering, starting with the poinsettia, the big red Nativity flower, *la noche buena*, growing near the house

11

entrance and against the wall of adobe brick topped with broken bottle glass. Tom watched him for a moment, musing on Antonio's innocence. He might have lost it, Tom thought somewhat bitterly, to *la señora*.

Presently: "*¡Adiós!*" Antonio called, and Tom from inside the house heard the clang of the gate as the gardener shut and locked it and departed, leaving him alone again with his thoughts. All he could do now was think—think and suffer his sadness in what seemed like an utter suspension of his life. He was in a kind of limbo—or was it a purgatory, assuming this break, this separation, was only temporary. Or had he lost her?

He thought of Antonio's loss, out of some kind of distancing of his own: the gardener's story of the murder of his father, the mayor of this village when Antonio was a child. His father was on a bus one day that stopped in an "enemy" village. Two *malos*, bad men, got on, walked down the aisle to where Antonio's father was sitting, and shot him dead.

So there were feuds down here, political or just personal, between families or villages (Zapotecs versus Mixtecs?), that Tom might have looked into and written about had he and Angela not been engaged in a feud of their own. And of course he was too stricken now to be interested in much of anything except what had happened to them—to *him*. He couldn't write anymore, except anguished entries in the journal he'd started as a record of their stay in Mexico. The novel he'd started lay abandoned at a hundred very rough, very first-draft pages. It was about a dropped-out journalist pretty much like himself, and he'd been happily engaged in the writing until Angela's *un*happiness intruded. That's when they decided they needed a vacation on the coast.

Now it made him sick to even think about his novel. Almost the first thing he'd done that morning was to pull the typescript out of the drawer where he'd left it before leaving for Puerto Bonito (was it only a week ago?) and consider burning it. He thought of burning everything he'd written here, including the drafts of a couple of short stories he'd done as a warmup to the novel. He was aware now of his writing as possibly the self-centred cause of their separation.

But then he could no more destroy his writing than he could destroy himself, though he'd entertained that notion too for a wild moment before dismissing it with a snort of self-derision.

Toward evening, he took a walk that had been a favourite of his and Angela's. It was across the highway and on a path to the village cemetery where there was a tree Angela liked, a gnarled old species like a giant *bonsai*. The sight of it caused him to embrace the trunk as if it were Angela herself and bawl into the sky like a child. Afterwards he felt only more sorrow and a kind of vertigo from having had the bottom drop out of his life.

Back in the house, Tom sat at his portable typewriter in the smaller bedroom he'd turned into his study and wrote a long, indulgent letter to his friend Don in New York. Don had served as best man at their wedding. He told of the apparent breakup of his marriage without, he hoped, too much self-pity. Yet reading over what he'd written he saw that, despite his effort to be fair to Angela and place whatever blame on himself, he'd filled three, single-spaced pages with little more than Poor Me and How Did This Happen snivelling.

He smoked some grass that night out of a desire to feel something of what Angela might be feeling now, to "join" her spiritually, away off in Puerto Bonito with Ricardo and no doubt getting high with him before doubtless getting it on with him. As usual, he found the experience rather unpleasant. Angela had liked getting high, and making love when high, and so they'd smoked enough marijuana and, when they could get it, hashish over the last year or so. Hash especially took him out of himself, made him fear he might lose himself. He didn't like having his senses deranged.

Still, when people passed you a joint or offered you a draw off a pipe of hashish, you accepted it because it was hip. As for dropping acid, Tom had abstained quite simply because he was scared shitless of it. He'd heard of people flipping out on it, winding up in a psych ward.

Angela, though, dissolved a tab in a glass of orange juice one morning, whereupon Tom spent the rest of that day, and into the wee hours of the next, more or less babysitting her through alternating spells of childlike wonder and abject terror.

A new age had dawned, and Tom could date his first awareness of it to the summer of 1963 in Chicago. He'd worked late at the paper and was cruising up the Outer Drive to Hyde Park in his faltering '54 Ford when, over the car radio, he heard Bob Dylan for the first time. His voice was some old guy's, he thought, until the kid who'd caught a ride with him, a student at the University of Chicago, said Dylan was his age, just twenty-two, and wasn't he great? Tom had just turned twenty-eight and felt suddenly old.

Two months later he met Angela and felt young again.

Then JFK—the president!—was assassinated. The shock

cultural
references

of that. It marked the stark beginning, Tom would decide later, of the Sixties, as he began taking notes on the changing times Dylan was singing about—as a journalist, as a writer—and collecting some of the texts of the times, Mao's *Quotations*, his so-called Little Red Book; Heinlein's *Stranger in a Strange Land*; Hesse's *Steppenwolf*; the novels of Kurt Vonnegut, Richard Brautigan, Ken Kesey.

Earlier he'd read a collection of sociological writings called *Man Alone*; Paul Goodman's *Making Do*, Jack Kerouac's *On the Road*, Joseph Heller's *Catch-22*.

He liked the new folk music, Joan Baez and Judy Collins—Dylan too, eventually, who was from his native Minnesota. Then, four years into his marriage with Angela, they saw *Easy Rider* and Tom found himself digging the movie's soundtrack and Peter Fonda's chopped Harley. The film was a paean to the freedom of the road and Tom's conversion to what was happening.

Before this, in the Navy, he'd become a jazz afficionado, collected LPs of Chet Baker, Stan Getz, Gerry Mulligan, Dave Brubeck, Stan Kenton. Cool jazz was a soothing compress on one's fevered brow, a rhythmic balm on the riot of one's young emotions. It was cerebral rather than visceral. Even when blown hot, it went mostly to your head, whereas the new electronic rock went directly to your groin, its jingle-jangling, electric twanging invited you to let go, let it all hang out, the evidence of which you saw at any of the weekend rock concerts, the "be-ins" or "love-ins" that were happening, where young women, swaying, gyrating in front of the band, might take their shirts off, baring their sweet breasts. Tom grew to love the free-floating sensuality in the air that kept him in a

15

more or less constant state of arousal and which he managed to sublimate by seeing Angela as all women, his own flower child.

Until she didn't want him anymore.

Tom had smoked more grass and was stoned out of his skull. He turned to his journal, his sole companion now, his lonely solace.

One trouble was I tended to compartmentalize my life; I compartmentalized my wife, shutting her out when I was writing, only turning to her when my day's stint was done. "You don't talk to me," she said. "You talk at me, as if I'm your student and you're my teacher. You're like my father!" I liked reading to her—from writers I admire, stuff of my own. I wanted her admiration! But what did she want? I'd like to know now. I'd like a second chance.

He went to bed then, wanting to sleep and sleep until Angela decided about their marriage—until he got her telegram and could start thinking about the rest of his life.

Chapter 3

Tom meant to wait at least three days before checking at the telegraph office in Oaxaca. There should be a wire from Angela by then. Meanwhile he had to prepare himself for what her wire might say, that she was staying with Richard or, anyway, that their marriage was over. Then what? He'd have to move—go back to the States, he guessed, find a job of some kind. Maybe even return to journalism. By noon of the second day, though, crazy with anxiety, he found that he couldn't wait any longer and took the bus into Oaxaca. There was no wire from Angela. He sent one to her:

> PLEASE DO NOT MAKE ME WAIT ANY
> LONGER. I LOVE YOU. I WANT YOU BACK BUT
> I WILL HONOUR YOUR DECISION.

Back in Trujano a group of children stared at him as he stepped off the bus in front of the adobe church; they exchanged looks and giggled. Oh yeah, he thought. There must be talk by now, village gossip. The *señor*, he is alone. The *señora*, she is gone. *¿Muy triste, no? Los gringos. Gringos jipis.*

Gringo paranoia. They'd both felt it their first days here, in this peasant village full of curiosity about them: these *norteamericanos*, these *gringos jipis.*

Almost more than their foreignness, their living in the doctor's house set them apart. The house itself, never mind the wall surrounding it, was modest enough, a small, one-story brick building with a tin roof in which there were four small rooms: a diningroom with a partitioned-off kitchen; two bedrooms (one Tom took for his study), and a glass-enclosed area that appeared to be a children's playroom.

The other houses in the village were of adobe rather than fired brick, and had thatch or tile rather than metal roofs, house and yard enclosed by a rickety fence of upright, lashed-together sticks.

Their first days here children gathered at their iron gate to stare in at them as if they were exotic animals: gringos in a cage. Then Angela, who knew some Spanish from high school and was studying it again while Tom wrote in the mornings, began to visit with the children through the bars of the gate and presently to walk with them through the village. In effect, they adopted her. Soon, with Tom tagging along, they were going with the children into the *campo* to be shown the various plants—which were useful and for what, which harmful—the kids all yelling answers at once to Angela's questions. She was a plant person. And so, despite her rudimentary Spanish, she found one level of where these people were at and could speak, on that level, their language. Tom felt left out.

One evening they went by invitation with Antonio for *cena,* supper, with him and his family. Inside the family's enclosure of upright sticks they found chickens scratching in the dust and a grunting pig lying in a dry wallow beside a tree. Antonio's mother stood under the roof over the house's entrance by her *hornilla,* the open, three-sided brick fireplace found outside most of the houses in the village. She was toasting tortillas and heating a big pot of something on a *comal,* the large, earthenware, slightly concave plate that you placed over the *hornilla* for cooking. The pot contained *pozole,* a delicious stew, they soon discovered, made with hominy and in this case chicken. There were so many things to learn here, all the names for things. You learned them partly through reading but mostly by asking.

Antonio's mother had a strong, pleasant-looking face. It was impossible to tell her age.

She shook their hands. "*Mucho gusto,*" they both told her. "*Bienvenidos,*" she said, welcoming them, and added, "*Mi casa es su casa,*" that stock expression of Mexican hospitality.

They entered the house and were in the kitchen, above which hung a single light bulb weakly illuminating the windowless interior. The floor was of dirt hard as cement from daily sweeping and dampening and generations, probably, of foot traffic. The kitchen looked to be one of only two rooms in the house and, judging from the pallet in one corner, doubled as a bedroom. A sarape hung over the entrance to what Tom guessed was the bedroom itself.

Mother and daughter, they were told, slept inside the house, Antonio and his brother in the shed across the yard.

After the meal, Antonio walked them through the dark

village loudly resounding with barking dogs to the gate of their casa—"*Para tu protección.*"

Now he walked about their walled little estate, an oasis of flowers and fruit trees, bougainvillaea and poinsettia, orange and avocado, the trunks of the trees whitewashed against the leaf-cutter ants. You saw them sometimes, in procession, each ant carrying a particle of leaf to their nest somewhere. The valley outside the village was desert but green along the river, the Átoyac, and in the surrounding mountains, in clefts near their summits, there were green clumps of pine forest called *ocotes*. "It's so beautiful here," Tom kept reminding Angela after they'd begun fighting—as if that were reason enough for them not to fight.

They had come to Oaxaca in the far south of Mexico because a favourite writer of Tom's, D. H. Lawrence, had spent time here some forty years before. Almost the first thing he did after their arrival, near the end of November 1969, was to drag Angela along on a pilgrimage to the Hotel Francia, where Lawrence and Frieda and Lawrence's groupie, Lady Dorothy Brett, had stayed upon *their* arrival in late 1926. Then they searched out the house that Lawrence and Frieda later rented in the city and where, as Tom excitedly told Angela, he wrote *The Plumed Serpent*.

Once settled in Trujano—their place found by way of a friendly shopkeeper in the zocalo who knew the doctor whose "country house" was for rent, the rent absolutely affordable— they began to revel in the region's high tropical dry season, its perfect winter climate, the nights almost freezing (good sleeping weather!), the days sandals-and-shirt-sleeves warm.

Tom woke in the cold mornings to the sound of the big black-birds—great-tailed grackles, he learned from his bird book—walking scratchily overhead on the tin roof of the house. With the sun spilling over the mountains and beginning to warm the valley, he'd slip quietly out of bed so as not to wake Angela, and go through the house throwing open the windows to let the day in, its pure air, its lovely light. He'd dress, do his morning calisthenics in the garden, then draw water from the slow tap in the kitchen to boil for instant coffee and call Angela, still sleepy in their bed and wanting sometimes to make morning love, for their usual breakfast of scrambled eggs and *pan dulce,* the delicious Mexican sweetbreads. They'd eat together in the garden, congratulating themselves on being here.

Afterwards he'd write for three or four hours while Angela practiced yoga, then read or sunbathed or studied Spanish. That she might have, after three months of this, become bored—that their isolation might have eaten into their rela-tionship—didn't occur to him then.

Afternoons, they took walks together, in or outside the village, not always with the children now, more often with Antonio. Once or twice a week, they went into Oaxaca to check their mail, visit the market, eat supper in a restaurant, occasionally see a movie. One day they took a bus to the flat-tened hilltop of Monte Albán to marvel at the ruins of that ancient Zapotec stronghold. With Antonio they visited other pre-Hispanic ruins in the three *Valles Centrales* extending out from the city: Zaachila, Mitla, Cuilápam. They bought a guide-book, in English and Spanish, that included a short history of the Zapotec and Mixtec cultures.

And all the while they were absorbing the timeless

sights and sounds, the ancient *feel* of Mexico: cries of *chiba!* from the old goatherd who, dressed in his *campesino* garb of white cotton shirt and trousers, his shirt colourfully fringed at the cuffs, a straw sombrero on his head, a machete in a leather scabbard hanging by a thong from one shoulder, herded the village goats through the dirt streets of the village every morning and across the paved highway and into the hills for the day. *Chiibaaa!* And the village women, their gray and black rebozos draped like shawls over their shoulders or wrapped round their heads so that they looked like Berbers. Oxen, pulling two-wheeled carts out of the Middle Ages, plodding along the highway or in the fields. Dogs barking in the night, roosters crowing in the pre-dawn. Turkeys gobbling, burros braying, the burdened little beasts almost lost under their loads of cornstalks or charcoal. Vultures, *zopilotes*, soaring in the cloudless blue sky until, a roadkill sighted, they converged and dropped like dive bombers to alight squabbling on the body of a dog or an armadillo or some other animal struck down by a vehicle racing toward the coast.

The loud, brassy Mexican music, often to an oompa beat by way of the Austrian influence that also introduced beer to Mexico during the brief reign of Maximilian I in the 1860s (music that reminded Tom of the country dances he'd attended in Minnesota as a farm boy). It blared through the afternoons and into the wee hours sometimes over the loud-speaker hung from a tree outside the village hall. Fireworks, exploding during the day or at night, for no apparent reason. *Borrochos*, lurching off the bus from town and collapsing beside the road to be pulled to their feet by their stoic wives or daughters and supported home. Heavy drinking was *macho*, Tom gathered, part of being a man in this culture.

And then the *smells*, pungent, spicy, stinking—wood smoke and local cooking, animal and human waste—smells of the earth and of the high, dry air and the thousands of years of human habitation. Smells out of ancient history.

Here is where he set out to write his version of the novel every journalist keeps buried within him, postponed, while he meets the deadlines of his profession. Here is where, one night after failing to make love and then bitterly fighting and at last wearily reconciling over mugs of hot, spiced *chocolate*, Angela confessed to having a "crush" on Antonio.

He ate a lonesome supper of tortillas and scrambled eggs with goat cheese, washed down with a bottle of beer. Then shots of fiery, evil-tasting mezcal that caused him to think of another writer he admired who'd spent time in Oaxaca, the alcoholic Malcolm Lowry, while he scribbled in his journal, documenting his loneliness, his misery. He wasn't aware of getting drunk or of falling asleep until he woke face down in his journal, his mouth open and slobbering over the pages. He roused himself, undressed, then dropped onto the bed where he lay, wide awake, through much of the long night.

The next morning, to kill some time before the afternoon bus into Oaxaca, Tom climbed to the *ocotes* above Trujano. Under the piñon pines, on a thick bed of fallen needles, he lay down and was dozing when he heard a rustling behind him and sat up to see a scorpion scuttling toward him. He leaped up, momentarily distracted from his sorrow. He might have been stung! Without Angela to nurse him, to get the venom's antidote from Antonio or somebody else in the village.

He hiked back down to the village having disposed of only three hours, with another three hours to wait before he could take the bus into town to check at the telegraph office for some word, at last, from Angela.

He remembered when they'd been happy here—or anyway, when *he* was happy, ignorant of her boredom and isolation, her growing infatuation. The morning they found a scorpion in their bed, which reminded them of precautions they'd heard from the doctor: throw back the covers before you climb into your bed at night; check the floor beside the bed in the morning before you step onto it; shake out your clothes before you dress.

The night Angela, reading at the dining room table, looked up to see the discarded skin of a big snake, draped over the rafter above her. They laughed at that.

And the night Angela was in the *baño*, sitting on the toilet, while Tom was in bed reading—*Great Expectations,* funnily enough—when suddenly it felt as if somebody or some *thing* was under the bed, kicking up at him through the mattress, and Angela was crying, "*What is it? What's happening?*"

Earthquake. Or maybe just a tremor, but scary enough for Midwesterners.

Four o'clock finally came, and he caught the bus into Oaxaca and checked the telegraph office in the Alameda: nothing. He walked through the market, then to various places in the city he and Angela had explored together. Ate enchiladas mole in the cheap restaurant they found off the zocalo, choked with nostalgia, then saw a movie at the Cine Rio, a Mexican western without subtitles. It hardly mattered that he understood only snatches of the rapid Spanish; the violent action was diverting enough.

That night he wrote in his journal:

I'm prepared, I think, for what her telegram might say. But why is she taking so long?

Chapter 4

There was no telegram the next day, nor the day after, nor the day after that. Each afternoon, Tom took the bus into Oaxaca to check.

That Angela might come back to him was doubtful now, but he hoped he might see her before he left Mexico—here, in Trujano, where she and Richard might come for her belongings. But then he imagined her telegram, when it finally arrived: *Don't be there when we come for my stuff. Please, just go away.* In his mind he began composing a last letter to her, like a suicide note, for her to find when she and Richard got here.

This was the year people gathered in southern Mexico for the solar eclipse. It would happen on March 7, in two days. He decided he would wait until *after* the eclipse. And then . . .

There were clothes to wash. He found the metal tub and the old-fashioned washboard that went with the house and, outside the wall, in the fenced back garden under the hot sun, scrubbed away at his dirty jeans and underwear and a couple of shirts. Villagers passed by, walking the path outside the barbed wire. The young men hooted or whistled. The older men stared. The women looked down as they passed, as if ashamed for him. Men didn't wash clothes in Mexico.

Antonio came by. He'd started to wonder about Angela, Tom knew, and there was concern on his face now. *"La Señora,"* he said, without his usual smile. *"¿Qué pasa?"*

What's happened, Tom wanted to say, is that my marriage might be over, finished, *terminado, acabado,* whatever was the correct word in this instance. But he only said, *"No sé,"* which was true: he didn't know.

Antonio looked puzzled, smiled uncertainly, then began watering the garden.

That night, sinking into sleep, Tom found himself fantasizing about the blond German or California girl he'd seen with the Mexican hippie at the hotel in Oaxaca. He imagined having her naked before him, of kissing her wan face, of having her mouth open under his for their tongues to probe for each other, of grasping her breasts and then tasting them like luscious fruits, of running his hands over her hips, over her thighs, of burying his face in her blond bush and having her turn and push her soft buttocks against him, then bend for him to enter her from behind, her breasts swaying, her hands braced against the edge of a table or the bed and him thrusting, thrusting up into her. He achieved a gigantic, throbbing hard-on, grasped it, and at once ejaculated a sticky mess over his belly with such a flood of sadness and relief, of guilt and regret. It seemed worse than masturbation, was more like adultery. But wasn't it Angela who was committing adultery these days, or was she? Was there such a thing as adultery anymore?

He was trying so hard not to feel sorry for himself.

The day of the eclipse there was a lot of traffic past the house, cars, buses, jeeps, motorbikes, all heading for Miahuatlán for the best viewing. He could write a story about their breakup, he thought. *Eclipse*. He had the title for it.

At eleven that morning there was a sudden stillness in the air. A coolness. The sunlight began to fade, to die. It was as if a dreadful storm were approaching, or a gigantic something overhead casting its shadow: the end of the world! What must have been the awe, the dread, of early humans during an eclipse? He felt some of it himself.

There was a strange, unnerving dusk for perhaps a minute. Tom stepped out of the house to see the sun like a black disk in the sky. A flock of vultures rose flapping out of a tree. Dogs began barking.

Then a rim of light appeared along one side of the disk, blinding; then more light that you dared not look at as the rim widened. There was something like a speeded-up dawn. Some vultures settled in a tree to await the renewal of the sun's warmth and the thermals that would allow their soaring flight again. Off in the village roosters crowed, heralding the day's return.

It was another day to get through. Another day of waiting.

There were no buses running, Tom discovered, so he walked the five miles through the afternoon heat into Oaxaca. He passed whole families picnicking along the road. Boys, old men, setting off firecrackers. It was fiesta, *El Dia del Eclipse*.

Again, no message from Angela. It had been ten days. That

it had been that long, that Angela had been silent for that empty length of time, abruptly struck Tom like a blow. All his abject feelings of rejection and hurt and self-pity became as nothing compared to his awful feeling suddenly, *his certainty!* that something bad had happened to her. He wanted to fly then, literally *fly* to Puerto Bonito, but since he didn't have wings and there were no planes to Puerto Bonito, he'd have to wait. He'd have to wait through all the remaining hours of that day and into the evening to take the overnight bus to Puerto Bonito.

Chapter 5

Angela knew, after less than a week with Richard Sullivan, that she'd have to leave him. She knew, really, within a day or so after his return to the Plantation after seeing Tom in Puerto Bonito to ask him to wait there while she stayed out at the Plantation for a while—Richard had talked her into it—to give her time to think, time away from her husband of five years, time to decide whether she wanted to stay married to him.

She knew what Richard wanted that morning he'd talked her into going out to the Plantation with him, after she'd confirmed what he'd picked up on, that she and Tom were a couple in trouble. He was there to take advantage of it, move in on her. Okay. Why not let him? He was attractive. She was on the Pill. And besides, she wanted to know—after being a virgin when she married Tom and being faithful to him all these years—what it would be like with another man.

She found out about fifteen minutes after Richard returned

from the village to his ramshackle hut on top of the dirt mound in the midst of the Plantation's palms. He'd told her to stay in the hut, where she'd be safe while he was gone; not to wander by herself among the Plantation's "freaks."

Right after he got back from seeing Tom he rolled a joint and they shared it. Then she allowed him to lead her to his cot, which proved much too narrow, so they resorted to a straw mat on the earthen floor where she experienced his raw urgency, his going at it as if he wanted to hurt her, which felt good, it was what she wanted, what she needed after so much frustration and anger and yearning. Then he came, too soon, and rolled off of her.

"Wow," he said. "It's been a long time."

Afterwards he was gentle with her, but already she was thinking of Tom back in Puerto Bonito. How long would he wait for her there? It was rather a comfort to know he was waiting.

In the days that followed she tried to enjoy herself. The booming ocean, the long stretch of empty beach, the palms under which you could lie all day in a hammock—it was restful, it was therapy! And the encampment of hippies, most of them Americans but including some Canadians and two or three Europeans. One guy, a Brit from Yorkshire, had mouthfuls of accent she had trouble understanding.

Everybody was young, interesting, interested in one another. They were all hip, in the hip here and now.

One day a psychedelically painted van pulled into the encampment containing two guys and a girl—from Canada, they said, though none was Canadian. One of the guys was German, the other guy and the girl American.

The swimming was marvellous. At high tide the white-tipped waves came lifting, curling, breaking to crash foaming on the yellow sand. She learned to body surf from the French couple, who warned her of the rip current in front of the coral outcrop just past the encampment. A guy had drowned last year off the outcrop, a Mexican hippie who'd panicked in the current and went under and whose body, when it washed ashore, was reverently, if crazily, buried in the sand by the Plantation community.

A week or so later the boy's wealthy parents, who somehow got word of his demise, came down from Mexico City, exhumed the body, and took it home to be given a Catholic burial in the ancestral plot. Richard told this story as a kind of joke, but Angela didn't laugh.

The days took on a pattern. Richard was up at first light every morning and made their breakfast. That was nice of him. Then he rolled their joints for the day and they shared one before eating, the first of several joints as the cloudless morning advanced to a cloudless afternoon and the temperature rose from comfortably cool to stiflingly hot and they left the hut to lie on hammocks under the palms until, desperate to cool off, they ran across the burning sand in their bare feet to plunge into water warm as a bath.

They tried once to lie together on one hammock but found it too awkward, too hot, and anyway, they were too stoned to balance themselves. After their morning meal they were never hungry enough (too hot!) to eat again until evening. By late afternoon, after bottles of warm beer and joint after joint, Angela wasn't sure where she was or who she was with. It was too weird. She was floating, in a hazy dream. She began to wish it was over.

She introduced herself to the three Canadians. They'd pulled their psychedelic van in under the palms and kept pretty much to themselves, but they were friendly enough, perhaps saw her as someone who might need some friends. The tall, handsome German fellow seemed to be their leader. The shorter guy wasn't bad looking either, was maybe with the girl, or maybe she was with both of the guys. Who knew anymore? Everything was so strange now.

How many days had passed? She didn't know. Was Tom still waiting for her in Puerto Bonito? She hadn't decided whether to go back to him yet, but she wanted to know if he was still there. Maybe he wasn't anymore. If he wasn't, maybe that would decide for her finally. Decide for them.

"Hey, you ain't thinking of going *back* to him, are you?" Richard said. "Jesus Christ, lady, you had *me* fooled."

"I'm the fool."

"What's *that* mean, for fuck's sake?"

But then he said, "*Okay*, if it'll make you feel any better, I'll go back to the Port to see if he's still there. I won't be surprised if he isn't."

"I'll go with you."

"C'mon then. He'll be gone, though, you wanna bet? After all this time?"

And when in Puerto Bonito she found that Tom was indeed gone, Angela felt not sadness so much as anger. He'd left her! Then no, she thought, they'd left each other and, yes, it was sad, but then something else struck her.

She was free.

The next day the Canadians left for home and she went with them.

Chapter 6

Puerto Bonito in the early morning looked exactly as it had three weeks ago, when he and Angela arrived here. Only everything had changed.

Tom stepped off the bus from Pochutla with three or four *Indios*, the men in straw sombreros, the women with black rebozos over their shoulders or wrapped around their braided heads, both sexes very small, almost stunted, talking in their native language. He nodded, smiled at them. One woman crossed herself and pulled her rebozo up to her eyes.

It was still cool, the sun still back of the low hills behind the town. The empty Pacific lapped calmly against the shore.

He walked down the dirt street to the restaurant, where Puerto Bonito's gringos met each morning to start yet another day in paradise. This early there was only one customer, a young longhair sitting reading at one of the tables. The two women were in the kitchen. The older one was slapping corn paste to make tortillas, the younger, pretty one feeding charcoal into the clay *hornilla*.

Just off the cement pad on which the tables rested was the yellow sand beach, pockmarked with animal and human footprints, stretching down to the sapphire bay. In a while the village fishermen would come in with the night's catch, sailing or paddling their dugouts onto the beach to carry their catch of tuna or bonito or red snapper up to the restaurant.

Tom nodded to the longhair. He nodded back, seemed to smile to himself. Yeah, Tom thought. His and Angela's story must have made the rounds by now, enlivening the dullness of the place. But if something bad had happened, would the guy be smiling?

A woman Tom knew, and liked, came out of the hotel and crossed the street. She was an old bohemian out of Taos, New Mexico, by way of New York City, who wore her long gray hair in two thick, native-style braids and adorned her ears, wrists and fingers with heavy turquoise and silver jewelry. She was deeply tanned and had a wrinkled, once-beautiful face.

"If you're looking for your wife, she's not here anymore."

A mix of fear and hope shot through him. "She's gone? Where'd she go?"

"We're not sure. Anyway, she and Ricardo didn't last long."

She motioned to a table and they sat down together. Tom remembered her name finally: Cynthia. She claimed to have seen Dylan Thomas once, drinking himself to death in the White Horse Tavern in Greenwich Village.

"What happened?"

"Oh, they only lasted about a week. Then some Canadians came down here in a wildly painted van and camped out at the Plantation. They were from some commune up there, I guess, and on their way back to Canada. Your wife decided to go with them. She and Ricardo had a fight about it—they were at Rosita's place, the Tortilla Lady's?—and he freaks out. He's got her down on the ground, trying to keep her from leaving, when Rosita comes out and whacks him over the head with her broom." Cynthia laughed. *"Tu loco!* she tells him. He jumps up and yells, "I'm not crazy!" Cynthia laughed again.

"Anyway, your wife went off with the Canadians. They were kind of strange. She seemed a little lost." Cynthia smiled sympathetically.

"Jezus!" Tom said, his dread returning. What kind of state was Angela in? What kind of weirdo freaks was she with now?

"You have any idea where they were *from* in Canada? Where they went?"

"Ricardo might know."

"He still around?"

"He's still out at the Plantation, I think."

The young longhair, still smiling to himself, sat looking down at his book. Tom strode over to him.

"You got something to tell me, man?"

"Me? What about, man?"

He was just a kid, one of your hippie nomads, here one day and gone the next. His blue eyes stared up at him, their pupils dilated.

"At ease, mate," Tom told him. "Sorry."

He returned to Cynthia, said, "Thank you," then started walking up the street toward the edge of town and the rutted road to the Plantation. The morning heat bore down on him and he realized he was hungry and wasn't carrying any water and probably would collapse before he reached the Plantation. He turned back to the restaurant.

"I was just going to have breakfast," Cynthia said. "Why don't you join me?"

He caught a ride out to the Plantation with Charlie, just as years ago, it seemed, Angela and Ricardo did as Tom sat watching them go off together.

"Been down the coast with Larry," Charlie said, "on some rich guy's yacht. Got off in San Arista—in Chiapas? We went up into the mountains on mules."

Charlie was a stocky, tough-looking guy, an army deserter hiding out in Mexico, as he readily admitted. Called himself a prospector. That was probably code for smuggler. Whatever, there was something true and solid about him. He'd be a guy to have with you in a pinch, Tom thought.

"How was it?"

"Beautiful," Charlie said. "We're going back there before the rainy season. The place is untapped!"

The road out to the Plantation was a twisting dirt track through the brush and across rocky creek beds, dry now in the dry season or with a few remnant puddles in them. They passed houses scattered up the hillsides, small, bungalow-like affairs of brown adobe with red tile roofs, mostly open under their eaves. Farther out of town were houses of mud-daubed cane with palm thatch roofs almost lost in the landscape, blended into it as if camouflaged.

"Tell me something," Tom said. "Whatta you know about Richard?"

"Ricardo? Oh, he's a fixture down here, kind of a one-man

welcoming committee. I met him the day I got here, two, almost three years ago. He helped set me up."

"Yeah, well he set me up too," Tom said.

Charlie grinned. "You mean he stole your wife? Excuse me. Don't mean to offend. Anyway, she didn't stay with him, I hear. So why you going out to see him now? Gonna beat the shit out of him?"

"I just want him to tell me where she went."

"You think he knows?"

There was a twenty-foot mound among the Plantation's palms on which sat a small, crumbling adobe hut with missing or broken roof tiles. Tom climbed to the top of the mound and walked into the hut to find Richard Sullivan, aka Ricardo, at a wooden table rolling his joints for the day. He looked up with a goofy smile, then raised his arms as if to ward off a blow.

"That's right, asshole."

"I figured you'd show up."

"Yeah, well you and I need to talk," Tom told him.

Richard seemed to have aged since Tom last saw him. He was twenty-nine, five years younger, in fact, than Tom. Angela had thought him handsome. In a couple more years, though, his cheeks more sunken, the lines in them more pronounced, he'd start to look like what he was: a tropical bum. Maybe Angela had seen that finally.

He'd attracted both of them at first, from the day of their arrival in Puerto Bonito, possessed as he was of some of Puerto Bonito's seedy allure, an allure only enhanced, initially, by Ricardo's powerful weed. Some four or five days floated by, during which—for Tom, anyhow—the gringo scene in Puerto Bonito began to pall, took on a surreal, not to say sinister, quality. He began to push for them to leave. Angela wanted to stay. That started them fighting again.

"Where *is* she?" Tom demanded now. "Why the hell didn't she wire me? I waited up there in Trujano for ten whole fucking days!"

"She wrote you a letter, man. You didn't get it?"

"When?"

"Just a couple days after you went away, man. She wrote she was *staying* with me—told you to go home. Then we had a fight, which you probably heard about, and she split."

"I never got any letter."

"Mexico, man. You haven't heard from her since? Jesus. We *both* better start looking."

"You have *any* idea of where she's gone?"

"The people she left with were from some kind of hippie commune up in Canada. I know that much."

"I heard that already. But *where* in Canada?"

"British Columbia, I think."

"*Where* in British Columbia?"

"Not sure. On some big lake, I think. How many big lakes are up there?"

"How should I know?"

"We could look at a map."

"You have one?"

"Larry. Larry's got an atlas."

"He around?"

"I saw him yesterday. He's just back from a trip with Charlie."

"I heard." Tom remembered Larry: Larry Swanson, ex-Navy diver, more of a hustler than Charlie, more than Richard even.

They found him in his shack under the scrub trees off the

beach. The beach's yellow sand stretched as far as you could see between the ocean and the scrub trees and was empty except for a couple of figures from the hippie camp. The ocean boomed and crashed against the shore.

"Hey," Larry said. "Heard you were back. Sorry about your old lady."

Almost naked in bikini trunks, wearing reflector shades, Larry could have modelled for ads in a slick magazine. His blond hair was bleached almost white by the sun, his trim body tanned to burnished copper. Angela had remarked that his looks were almost too good to be real.

"Do *you* know where the hell she went?" Tom asked him now.

"Canada, I heard. The people she went off with were Canadians, weren't they, Ricardo?"

"Yeah, from British Columbia," Richard said. "On some big lake up there. You still have your road atlas, Larry?"

Larry dug in his Navy foot locker and came up with a Rand McNally atlas of North America. Turning to the map of British Columbia, they found a number of long, narrow lakes between the Alberta border and the British Columbia coast.

"Christ," Tom said. "Could be any one of those."

"Yeah, but you go up there and ask around among the longhairs," Larry said, "and you might find her. Assuming that's where she actually went with those hippies, and she's still up there."

"Yeah," Richard said, "she could have left those people by now. Like she left us."

Us? I should never have left her here, Tom thought. I should have stayed, no matter what.

"Anyway, we better get started," Richard said.

"Huh?"

"I'm going with you."

"No way. You—"

"Look, man, I feel as responsible as you do for what's happened. Angela could be in some real trouble. She could be a fucking prisoner of those fucking Canadians!"

Larry laughed.

"She's my wife!"

"And she *left* you, man."

"Yeah, and then she left *you!*" This was crazy, Tom told himself.

Larry, a big grin on his face, said, "Maybe the two of you, the two of you *together*, could get results. Aren't two heads better than one? Hey, that's funny. Two *heads*, get it?"

"Not goddamn butting *against* each other!" Tom shouted.

"Look," Richard told him. "We got a common cause, man, a common concern. We *both* wanna find Angela and make sure she's all right. Why not join forces?"

"Right," said Larry. His face took on a dreamy look. "Two guys in search of the same woman, their mutual lost love. Sounds like an epic adventure, the stuff of legend!"

"Too much," Tom said helplessly. "This is too weird."

"Man, these are weird times," Richard said. "C'mon, let's go. Maybe we can get to the Port in time to catch the two o'clock bus to Pochutla."

41

Chapter 7

Travelling north with the Canadians she'd met in Puerto Bonito, Angela slept outside at night on top of their van. Despite the cold after sundown on Mexico's high central plateau that only got colder as they drove north, she'd declined to snuggle inside with the two men and the woman because, as she told them, she liked the loveliness of sleeping out under the stars. What she didn't say was that she wasn't that comfortable with them. They were strangers—also a little strange: what was their relationship exactly?

But then stoned on their grass, awestruck, made fearful by the awful immensity, the profound, cold distance of the stars above her as she lay on top of the van at night, she began to freak out. She was freaked out generally, though nobody seemed to notice.

They had some trouble at the border. The men's longhair appearance, their psychedelically painted van, alerted the US border guards and the van was searched. Then the men were searched. Then the women, after being taken into a room and ordered to strip by a female guard who then examined them, not excluding their private parts. There was little danger of their failing the inspection, however, because they'd made a point of smoking up their dope before reaching the border.

In El Paso Angela thought of leaving the three and taking a bus back to Chicago. She imagined Tom was there by now, moved back into their apartment in Hyde Park. She couldn't return to the apartment herself, of course. That left their friends Sue and Cliff in Evanston who, hopefully without taking sides, undoubtedly would take her in. She thought of Sue's motherly warmth and Cliff's cheerfulness and felt weepy suddenly. What she didn't consider was going back to her parents in Cincinnati to suffer their clucking concern, their reactionary judgment. They'd been leery of her marriage anyway, at nineteen, to a man ten years older than she, a *goy* and a Catholic! *Didn't I tell you?* She could hear her mother, She could see her father's impassive lawyer's face.

"Could somebody lend me some money?"

"What for?" said Klaus, the van's owner and whom she knew now to be the group's leader. She was constantly aware of his good looks, which his soft German accent only accentuated. She'd decided the woman must be with him, rather than with the other guy. The other guy seemed to be the odd man out, and in fact Angela wondered why he hadn't come onto her. Not that she wanted him to. She wasn't sure what she wanted from the German.

"Bus fare, back to Chicago."

They'd stopped for lunch and gas at a combination filling

station and general store outside El Paso. Angela bought a stamped postcard and wrote a note to Sue and Cliff. The clerk said it could be mailed from there.

"Chee-cago. Why go back there?" Klaus asked.

"It's home, I guess."

"The husband you left. He will be there?"

"It's a big city."

"Stick with us, why don't you. Come to B.C. You will love it."

The woman, a rather plain-looking blonde named Shelly, and who actually was an American, said, "The move now is away from the cities, Angela, going back to the land? And if you're facing the draft, you head for Canada. B.C. is beautiful."

" *Ja*," Klaus said. "Going back to the land now is groovy."

"It's hip," said Mike.

"Mike worked on a dude ranch in Wyoming," Shelly said with a smile in his direction. "Before that he was a rodeo cowboy."

Angela could see that now, his compact body. He had the look of a cowboy. Maybe Shelly was with Mike.

Mike said, "Yeah, I did the rodeos, both sides of the border. Rode too many broncs, fell off too many times. It was easier playing cowboy for eastern dudes."

"*Ja*, not to mention all that eastern nooky that went along with it, eh Mike?" Klaus said.

"Don't mind Closs," Mike told Angela, deliberately, it seemed, mispronouncing the German's name, which Angela had noted rhymed with mouse. "He's just jealous."

Mike had a faint drawl, Angela noticed now. It was maybe a little put on.

Klaus smiled at her and said again, "Come on, Angela. Come with us to B.C. Check it out."

"What else you got going for you, honey?" Shelly said.

"Not much," Angela admitted.

"Good," Klaus said. "We go."

They drove northwest out of Texas and into New Mexico, past empty regions of rock and sage, then up into snowy mountains and high plains. After a long day, somewhere in Colorado, Klaus exited the freeway and found a lonely wayside for the night.

Early the next morning they were off again, only stopping, when necessary, for gas or calls of nature. While refueling the van, they refuelled themselves—with junk food, mainly, as the only kind available. Drove out of Colorado and through Wyoming that day until, in darkness, they just missed hitting a deer and decided to stop.

Angela slept in the van now, as it was too cold at night to sleep outside anymore. She curled up, rather uncomfortably and fully clothed, on the front seat under the one blanket she'd been given, while the others shared the foam rubber mattress that filled the van's floor behind her. One night she heard sounds of lovemaking, muffled but unmistakable. The stirring, the occasional soft moan, disturbed her, turned her on. Who was doing it? Who cared? She felt out of it, somewhere else. Where?

Another two days flowed by, Klaus mostly at the wheel, relieved periodically by Mike or Shelly. There was little talking, a lot of dozing. Angela passed the time in reverie, remembering trips with her parents when she was a child—Carlsbad

Caverns, the Grand Canyon—during which she and her older brother, in the back seat of the family car, distracted themselves by shouting out the lines on Burma Shave signs or seeing how many states they could tot up by noting the license plates on the cars they passed. It was a way of removing themselves from their bickering parents who, up front in the car, disputed every time they came to a point of interest. Their mother wanted to stop, their father to keep driving. Then where to stop at night, which hotel or motel? Couldn't be too expensive, nor too cheap.

She couldn't wait to get out on her own. Her big brother became a terrible tease after they'd both entered puberty; but then, in high school, they became confidants, he telling her about guys, she telling him about girls. Then he went off to college and she was left alone with their controlling parents until, after taking a stenographer's course at a junior college, she went off on her own, despite her parents' misgivings, to Chicago.

The open, familiar-looking landscapes sweeping past her now. They made her nostalgic, they made her sad.

They crossed the plains of Montana and entered the Rocky Mountains. There were still patches and then fields of snow beside the highway. They crossed the Continental Divide, and then west of the Rockies, off the freeway and driving up a secondary road in the Idaho panhandle, they entered a cloudy region of narrow valleys enclosed by softly contoured, forest-covered mountains where evidently the climate was milder than east of the Divide. As if to prove that, it started to rain, slicking the road and further darkening the landscape. Close to the border, Klaus pulled off the road and drove up a lane through trees to an open field, where they parked for the night.

The next morning they crossed the border into southeast British Columbia, without incident, and soon came to a town called Marshland. Here they stopped at a bakery for coffee and sweet rolls. Then, with Mike at the wheel, they drove out of town and climbed above a flat valley, drained marshland, Klaus told Angela, hence the name of the town. The valley, sunk between the mountains, reminded Angela of Oaxaca, where Tom had been so obviously happy at first and she so restless, so confused, so unhappy finally. Already there were areas of worked-up soil in the valley, and Angela could imagine how green it would be in summer, how beautiful.

"I'm getting anxious," Shelly said. "What if Paul doesn't take us back?"

"Oh, he will," Klaus said. "We are the prodigals returned."

"Who's this Paul?" Angela asked.

"He's who we follow," Shelly said. "It's his place we're going to. It's special. *He's* very special."

"*Ja*, he is special," Klaus said. "He will tell you so himself."

"Hey," Shelly said. "Maybe you should have stayed in Mexico, Klaus. You don't sound all that glad to be going back to Ramala."

"Where else I got to go? Where else have any of us?"

"Yuh-ah," Mike said. "It's the place to be. Especially when the shit hits the fan, right?"

"What're you talking about?" Angela asked.

"Shut up, Mike," Klaus told him. "You will scare her."

"What? What'll scare me?"

"Nothing," Klaus told her. "I mean to say it is Paul who will tell you what he and his place are about. What *we* are about."

"You aren't some cult, are you?" Angela demanded. "Some doomsday cult? Waiting for the end of days? That kind of crap?"

"We wait for the beginning," Klaus said.

"Of what?"

"Something new. Something better."

"Revolution, you mean?"

"Better."

"It's nothing bad, Angela," Shelly assured her. "It's all good."

They were going up the twisting highway along the shore of Sturgeon Lake now. The lake was a long blue cleft in the mountains, two to three miles wide, another reminder of Angela's life with Tom—that picture of a Norwegian fiord he'd pasted on a wall of their apartment in Chicago. His paternal grandparents had come from Norway.

An hour or so later the highway angled down past a sign that said Sturgeon Bay. It soon ended at a ferry landing just as the ferry was leaving.

"Shit," Klaus said. "Now we wait."

"For how long?" Angela asked.

"A good hour and a half," said Mike.

"I'm getting out," Shelly said. "I need to pee."

They all got out of the van as the ferry, only half full, backed out into the lake, swung around, and began churning away toward the far shore. A logging truck came engine-braking down the hill and stopped behind their vehicle.

There was a restroom here and a restaurant across the road. Shelly and Angela used the restroom. When they came out, Klaus was waiting for them. Mike could be seen walking toward the restaurant.

"They have good ice cream there," Klaus said. "I treat you."

In the restaurant Angela looked for postcards but there weren't any.

"I'd like to write somebody," she said.

"Who is it this time, this guy Ricardo?" Shelly said dryly, but she went out to the van and came back with a box of stationary reeking of pachouli oil. Angela pulled out a sheet of the fancy paper and a corresponding envelope and sat at a table by herself. She wrote a letter to Tom while the others sat nearby licking ice cream cones. She struggled to express, *explain* herself, striking out words here and there, filling both sides of the paper. She took a second sheet and wrote a post-script. Then another. Finally she addressed the envelope to Tom, care of the Andersons in Evanston.

"Can I mail this here?" she asked the man behind the counter.

"Not here, but you can at the postoffice in Reeds Landing, across the lake."

She licked the flap and closed it, sealing off her words—of what? Regret? Uncertainty?—and immediately wished she hadn't. She wanted to tear open the envelope, tear up her letter. Had she given Tom some hope after all? *Should* she have?

Chapter 8

Four days after leaving Puerto Bonito Tom and Richard found themselves on a highway, surrounded by empty fields, somewhere in the middle of Missouri. They'd been dropped there by a farmer who'd picked them up outside Kansas City. They'd gotten as far as Kansas City by Greyhound from Laredo, before deciding to save what little money they had left by hitching the rest of the way to Chicago. This after Tom had cashed his last American Express traveller's check in Kansas City and spent most of it to send on Angela's belongings, left in Trujano and which he'd gathered up and carried with him, to their address in Hyde Park by parcel post. He'd followed that with a telegram to the young couple subletting their place asking them to hold her stuff for him—or her.

He thought of wiring Angela's parents. He thought of calling them with the hope they'd heard from her by now, would know where she'd gone and been told she was all right.

But what if they *hadn't* heard from her? What could he then say to them? That she'd left him and he didn't know where she'd gone or who she was with and that in effect he'd abandoned their daughter in a foreign country?

Surely she would get in touch with them—if not with him—eventually.

Okay, so he was a moral coward.

"It's getting dark, man," Richard said, stating the obvious. "How long we been standing here?"

They'd been standing there for almost an hour, no cars had passed them for a while, and Tom was ready to start walking. Maybe they'd come to an empty barn or shed in some field where they could shelter for the night.

"No way, man," Richard said. "I ain't sleeping in no barn."

"Tell you what," Tom said now. "Somebody comes along, *you* take the ride. I'll wait for another."

"Come *on*, man. Don't be that way."

"What way is that? Too square for you? Too uptight?"

Tom was filled suddenly with an almost suffocating rage. He took a breath and then said evenly, "It's time we split up, Ricardo. *Enough* of this hip horseshit. As if we're fucking amigos."

"We have a common cause, man, remember? A mutual love? We're on a mutual quest."

Tom stared across the dismal landscape. He'd tried repeatedly to lose Richard before this, first in Oaxaca before they got on the bus for Mexico City, then in the vastness of that polluted city before they boarded the train for Nuevo Laredo; finally on the train itself, walking the length of the cars, ostensibly to find a *baño,* but really to hide out until the train made a stop and he could jump off and watch it leave with Richard still on it. But in San Luis Potosí, after Tom stepped off the train onto the station platform, Richard was beside him, saying, "Geez, man, I almost lost you!"

With a smirk on his face.

Then, in Monterrey, where they changed to the train to Nuevo Laredo, Richard was a big help, after all, because of his fluent Spanish.

But their joining forces was absurd, it was even funny. And at the same time there was something annoyingly touching about Richard's concern. The bastard really cared for Angela.

"We could try to get along," Ricardo said.

"You took advantage of us!"

"I *did*, okay? But if it hadn't a been me, if woulda been somebody else. She wasn't happy with you, man. Face it!"

Tom kept thinking about the fact that, alone, he'd have had the fare to Chicago. He'd *be* there by now, taking the El to Evanston, where Sue and Cliff lived now, and where he and Angela had left their car rather than in Hyde Park, where it might have been stripped or stolen. He might already *be* in his car, heading for Canada.

The vehicles that passed by at intervals were occupied by people who simply stared at them. Once a pickup truck, with two men in it and a rifle strapped to the back window, slowed for the men to look them over before accelerating away. That scene in *Easy Rider*, the one where Dennis Hopper gets blown off his motorcycle after giving the finger to a redneck poking a shotgun out a pickup window at him, popped into Tom's head. He and Richard, before crossing the border, had made themselves up to look as straight as possible. Richard wore his watch cap and seaman's dungarees, Tom was in slacks and his corduroy jacket and had trimmed his beard. They'd both gotten haircuts. Maybe they still looked like hippies, though. Maybe they looked like civil rights workers.

Probably they had Yankee written all over them.

A car finally stopped for them. The driver was a plump, middle-aged guy with curly brown hair and a shaggy beard dressed in casual but expensive-looking clothes. His car was a late-model Buick convertible with the top down. Richard hopped in front, leaving Tom to climb in back.

"Unzip the cover back there, will you?" the driver asked. "Time to put the top up. Getting chilly."

He pulled his car back onto the road and tromped on the accelerator. "My name's John Snyder. Call me Jack. What's yours?"

"Tom," Tom told him.

"They call me Ricardo," Richard said.

"Ricardo. You've been south of the border, I take it."

"Mexico, yeah."

"Both of you?"

"We met down there," Tom explained.

"Ah. And now you're road buddies."

"Right," Richard said. *"Compañeros."*

Jack Snyder turned out to be an English professor currently on leave from Washington University in St. Louis. He was writing a book.

"What about?" Tom asked.

"It's sort of an extended essay. About Mark Twain and racism. What he was saying in *Huckleberry Finn*, for instance,

Huck's relationship to Jim, Huck a white boy and Jim a runaway slave, floating down the Mississippi together toward freedom. You've read it?"

"More than once," Tom said.

"What I could never figure out," said Richard, "is how floating *down* the river, into the heart of fucking Dixie, was gonna get them to freedom."

"They were heading for the mouth of the Ohio," the professor informed Richard, "then up that river to the free states."

"Oh," Richard said. "I didn't know that. I'm just a sailor."

"In the Navy?"

"Merchant seaman."

"What about you?" Snyder asked Tom.

"In the Navy," Tom said. "Joined to get off the farm."

"I was a country boy myself," Snyder said. "Born and raised in Ohio."

"I'm from Minnesota."

"Couple of hicks," Richard said.

"And proud of it," Jack said. "Right, Tom?"

An hour or so later they were driving along the Mississippi approaching Twain's, or rather Sam Clemens's, home town, Jack told them. "Look," he said, "why don't you guys stay the night at my place? My girlfriend and I are renting an old farmhouse outside of Hannibal with plenty of room. It's not every day I meet a couple of characters like you two."

"Thanks, but . . ."

"That'd be great, man," Richard said.

"What about your girlfriend?" Tom asked.

"Oh, Sandra's cool. Besides, she likes meeting new folks."

The professor's house was a weathered, two-story clapboard affair off a country road some miles downriver from Hannibal. It stood in a grove of enormous old cottonwoods that filled the air with their sweet scent and were already in full leaf. Tom saw the house and its surrounding trees as probably not all that changed from Sam Clemens's day.

Snyder parked in front of the place, and Tom and Richard followed him up some stone steps and onto a wooden veranda where there was an old-fashioned glider and a couple of modern lounge chairs.

"C'mon in," the professor said. He opened the screendoor and then the wooden entrance door into a foyer where there was an open stairway to the second floor and, to their left, an old-fashioned parlour or sitting room. In front of them stretched a hallway to the back of the house.

"Sandy!" Snyder called. "Your old man is home!"

They heard the floor creak above them, then a beautiful young woman Tom recognized as Indigenous appeared at the top of the stairs. She was barefoot, in blue jeans and a white blouse, her dark hair falling almost to her waist.

"Where have you *been*? I was worried," she said as she padded down the stairs. She only glanced at Tom and Richard.

"Doing *r*esearch, honey, where Clemens' uncle used to live. You knew that."

"You didn't tell me you'd be gone for two days!"

"I called last night! You didn't answer."

"I was out," she said.

"Where?"

"None of your business."

Snyder grinned, then nodded toward Tom and Richard.

"These are guys I picked up hitchhiking. They're staying the night, okay?"

Tom and Richard introduced themselves.

"Hi," she said, and smiled now.

"What's to eat, Sandy?" Jack asked her. "We're starved, aren't we, guys."

Sandra turned and walked down the hall. Snyder motioned for them to follow and they found themselves in the kitchen. "I have some catfish I can fry up," Sandra said. "And some left-over cornbread."

"A meal fit for Huck and Jim themselves," Snyder said. He opened the refrigerator and pulled out three Falstaffs. Grabbed the opener off a wall hook. "Let's go in the living room."

"You need any help?" Tom asked Sandra.

She gave him her smile. "Thanks. But go on with Jack. I'm fine."

Jack was full of his project, the research he was anxious to complete so he could start writing before his year's sabbatical was up. He was hoping for a grant that would allow him an extension of his leave to produce a first draft.

"There's been a lot of shit lately about Twain's supposed racism, his use of the word 'nigger,' for instance. Certain so-called critics seem to forget that Twain, along with being a man of his time, was also *ahead* of his time. They put down *Huckleberry Finn*, for godsake—maybe the Great American Novel—as ruined by Twain's use of the "n" word. Hell, Conrad used it. Faulkner. Ernest Hemingway. They were real-ists—okay, they were racists too, but who wasn't then? They were of their time."

Huckleberry Finn was a book dear to Tom's broken heart.

He'd read it three times, he told Jack. "The language. The book's ode to the river. And *Tom Sawyer*. That part where Tom and Huck and Joe Harper run away to Jackson's Island? I must have read that a hundred times when I was a kid," Tom said.

"*Tom Sawyer's* a boy's book," the professor said. "But *Huckleberry Finn*?"

Snyder went on about Clemens's—the future Twain's—association with the slaves on his uncle's farm west of Hannibal, people who even as a boy Clemens recognized as fellow human beings.

"Supper!" Sandra called from the kitchen.

After supper, Snyder still talking and Richard, when he could get a word in, trying to tell a sea story or two, Tom stepped out on the porch and sat on the glider. It was a cold lovely night, spangled with stars, shrill with spring peepers. Presently Sandra came out and sat beside him. She lit a joint, took a deep toke, then passed it to Tom. He accepted it, took a somewhat shallower toke, held it, and his head filled with that familiar, not exactly pleasant, fuzziness.

He exhaled, coughed. "I'm not a regular doper," he said, and laughed. He laughed, but he wanted to cry, thinking of Angela now.

"Neither am I," Sandy said, taking another hit.

"You at the university?" he asked tightly, holding his second toke a little longer this time.

"I dropped out when Jack started his leave. I'll go back this fall, whether he gets his grant or not."

"What're you taking?"

"Something called Native American Studies. It was Jack's idea, initially. I was what you might call ignorant of my people's history."

"Who're your people?"

"My father was Chippewa, Ojibwe, Anishinaabe, take your pick. My mother was a Catholic nun teaching on the Red Lake reservation in Minnesota. They fell in love, she left her order, left the Church. She was mostly German, I guess, from a little town in Iowa. She died having me. I've only seen her picture."

"I'm sorry."

Sandra inhaled deeply, held the joint out to Tom. He shook his head.

"My father raised me with a succession of step-mothers, some good, some not so good. I dropped out of school when I was sixteen, left the rez when I was seventeen, and I was more or less on the street in Minneapolis when Jack found me. Rescued me. He was getting his doctorate at the U then. He helped me finish high school, got me into college."

And yes, Tom thought, got *you*.

As if reading his mind, Sandra said, "He never took advantage of me. It wasn't like that. I wondered why. I started to think he maybe didn't like women."

"Then what?"

"He was too old for me, he said. He was shy! Okay, we're twenty years apart. He could be my daddy. But he isn't."

Tom was starting to shiver from the cold, or was it from sitting next to this beautiful young woman, hearing her story, feeling close to her? He thought of going into the house for his jacket, but that would interrupt this time with her, maybe end it.

"There's a sadness in you," she said. "I sense that."

"It's that obvious?" Tom said.

"Wanna talk about it?"

"No."

But then he did, surprising himself, until he realized it was Sandra's marijuana at work, her empathy and, yeah, maybe something like wanting to woo her.

He told her of the breakup of his marriage in Mexico and Richard's part in it, and how both of them now were looking for his wife to make sure she was okay and wasn't that kind of strange?

He was left feeling ashamed, disloyal to Angela, for spilling his guts to this stranger no matter how sympathetic, no matter her beauty.

Sandra touched his arm. "I hope you find her, Tom, and she's okay. Maybe you'll get back together."

"I doubt it. But I have to know she's all right. The way it happened, the *scene* down there, her going off with God knows who to God knows where?"

"And now the two of you are looking for her together."

"Yeah, far out, isn't it. Don't ask me why, but I can't hate the guy. These are far out times, I guess."

"And you're out of sync? I pick up on that, too, a little."

"Yeah, I'm too young to have been a beatnik, too old to be a hippie. I'm over thirty and not to be trusted, or so they say now."

"Jack's forty-five. But he prides himself on being one of your hip professors, turned on and tuned in to his students and the times."

"Angela's just the right age and she's tuned in for sure, I guess," Tom said. "So are you, I think."

"Not exactly. Peace and love? Nice idea, but it's turned kind of sour since Manson, don't you think? I'm for the American

Indian Movement. You palefaces can join us if you like."

She stood up. "It's getting cold out here. Let's go in and see how Jack and your friend are doing."

They were getting drunk. Tom joined them by accepting another Falstaff. Sandra went upstairs to bed and Tom was relieved when, not long after, Jack said, "I'm ready to crash, how about you guys?"

There was an extra bedroom upstairs with a double bed that Tom and Richard might share—like Ishmael and Queequeg, Jack suggested with a grin, but neither was up to that. Richard offered to toss for the bed, but Tom opted to sleep on the living room couch.

The couch was comfortable, but he lay awake for what seemed like half the night, unable to stop thinking about what had happened to him and Angela, wondering where she was now, and was she all right, and the romance of their meeting and their moving in together and how things went wrong somehow.

How had it happened? When did it start?—Angela's picking at him, his defensive anger, her increasing dissatisfaction. Was it because his low sperm count made it unlikely she could ever get pregnant by him after they decided, three years into their marriage, that they were ready to have a child?

No, that wasn't enough of an issue; they could always adopt, they told each other. Anyway, they'd started fighting before that. There was the gap between their ages, for one thing: Angela was eighteen and Tom twenty-eight when she walked into a party at his friends' Sue and Cliff's place—in Chicago's Old Town then—and he was immediately attracted to her slender, perfectly formed face and how prettily she'd tied back her long brown hair. She looked, he thought, like the beautiful young Virginia Woolf.

She'd come in with a guy in a tailored suit and a smug look on his face. He mingled with the crowd and she disappeared.

Tom found her, coming out of the bathroom as he was heading to the kitchen for another beer.

"Hi."

"Hi yourself," she said, and started to move past him.

"I'm Tom."

She stopped then and smiled. "Angela."

"Cliff says you work with Sue at the American Airlines ticket office."

"So you asked about me, huh?" Her eyes showed a glint of humour.

"I did. Coincidently," Tom said, "I work with Cliff. Well, not exactly anymore. We work for the same paper."

"You a reporter like Cliff?" she asked. "That sounds like such a glamorous job to me."

"Hardly. Cliff's on cityside now. He even gets out on the street occasionally. I'm still in the neighbourhoods section, where they start you out at the *Trib*, glued to my typewriter and telephone. Where're you from, by the way?"

"Cincinnati. Where are *you* from?"

"Minnesota. I'm what you might call an escaped farm boy."

"That's something else I have romantic notions about—farming."

"City girl."

"Country boy. And in the big city now, *huh*. How do you like it?"

"I like Chicago all right. Starting to hate my job."

"Me too!"

People kept sidling past them to reach the bathroom, so they moved to the empty kitchen and sat down at the table.

"You in college?" Tom asked. "Working part time at the ticket office?"

"Thinking about it. Working full time at the ticket office."

"What do you do there?"

"I'm a cashier. Sue books flights now, as you probably know."

She'd graduated from high school only a year and a half ago, Tom learned to his dismay—he'd hoped she was a bit older—and took a secretarial course before coming up to Chicago to get away from home, to be on her own finally. She wasn't sure what she wanted to do yet—or be. Did he?

"I want to be one of the greatest writers who've ever lived," Tom said, and laughed.

She laughed with him. "That sounds like a line from somebody."

"The young and supremely ambitious F. Scott Fitzgerald. Except Fitzgerald made it."

"And you haven't yet? You published anything?"

"Couple stories in one of the raunchier of the *Playboy* imitators. Modest payment."

"That's something, though, isn't it? Maybe I can tell people I knew you *when* someday."

"Ha!"

Then he said, "You could be a stewardess. "Like Sue was."

"Oh, that's what Alan, the guy I'm with, tells me. He's my boss, by the way. *I know.* Dating your boss is kind of like incest.

Anyway, after talking to Sue—no way. You're nothing but a glorified waitress."

"Coffee tea or me, right?"

"Right."

He liked her voice, its lovely lilt. He liked her smartness. He liked everything about her. But she was way too young for him. Just out of high school? He was trying to resist her appeal.

Then her date, her *boss*, burst into the kitchen and said sharply, "*There* you are. Let's go, Angie."

And she was gone—for good, he thought.

But then he saw her again, the following Monday on the Illinois Central commuter train, both on their way to work. She was perched on the edge of an aisle-facing bench at the front of the crowded, lurching car, balancing a book on her lap, her arms beautifully raised above her head, attempting to pin her hair back.

"Need some help?"

"Oh. Hi! I'm running late, as you can see." Smiling, she handed him her clasp, then lifted her arms again to hold her hair back. He managed to fix the clasp. Her hair was soft and smelled of shampoo.

"Thanks. It's Tom, right?" She patted the seat beside her and he sat down.

"What are you reading?"

"Baldwin. *Another Country.*"

"Whattaya you think?"

"It's good. It's angry."

"Did you know Baldwin's both a Negro *and* a homosexual? That makes him *doubly* an outsider, as somebody's said."

63

"No kidding!"

They reached the Loop, plunged underground. The train stopped at the Van Buren station. Angela stood up. Hesitated. She was as shy, he realized, as he was.

"Can I—"

"You can call me at the airlines office," she told him, then joined the crowd of office workers leaving the train.

The train went on to Water Street, the end of the line, and Tom left it to climb the stairs to Michigan Avenue. He walked as if on air into the Tribune Tower, rode the elevator to the fourth floor and strode past the City Room and into Neighbourhoods to hang his suit jacket on the rack by his desk, loosen his tie, roll up his shirt sleeves and sit down at his typewriter as if playing a scene out of some old flick about the romance of newspaper reporting. There was no romance in Neighbourhoods.

Irene Petrakis, his partner on Southwest Side News, said, "You're looking mighty pleased this morning, Tommy. Ya make out?"

"Actually . . ."

Irene was a couple of years younger than Tom, but you'd never know it. She was a native Chicagoan of Greek parentage who'd started at the *Trib* as a copygirl. She had thick reddish hair and a powerful face and the cynicism of an old hand on the paper. Tom enjoyed a flirting relationship with her, might have asked her out for something other than a drink after work but for the fact that she towered over him.

"How we doing?" he asked her. "We gonna make deadline?"

They had until noon Wednesday to finish filling their Sunday section, eight to ten pages of everything from one-line fillers to hard news to feature stories to full-page picture layouts. More often than not, for all their efforts, the advertising department brought down enough copy to override a good deal of their editorial copy—almost none of which could be held over and therefore was dead.

"That's up to you, sweetie. I'm turning in *my* eight stories a day."

Irene had just given her notice, after booking passage on a freighter to Egypt following an avid reading of Lawrence Durrell's *Alexandria Quartet* (thus declaring herself a romantic), so in two weeks Tom would be left in charge of Southwest Side News and having to break in her replacement. Assuming there would *be* a replacement for her and he wouldn't have to go it alone for a while. He wasn't ready!

Tom and Angela had their first date that Friday, going out to dinner and a movie. Saturday night they caught Miles Davis and the beautiful young Nancy Wilson at the Sutherland Lounge on the South Side feeling slightly self-conscious and not a little hip in the otherwise all-black audience. During one of Miles's tight improvisations on his muted trumpet, Angela reached under the table and clasped Tom's hand—gripped his heart.

She was sharing an apartment on 57th off Jackson Park with a nurse at Michael Reese Hospital, so they couldn't go *there*. But Tom's apartment on 51st was shared with a salesman who, during the week, was often out of town. He happened to be *in* town that week, but the following week he was on the road. Tom and Angela spent every night of that week in his apartment and he gave up drinking after work with Irene Petrakis.

A month later they found a nice little walk-up in an old

brick apartment building shaded by horse chestnut trees on 53rd Street, and moved in together.

A couple of months after that Angela's parents, unannounced, showed up for a visit after deciding, from her breezy letters home, that they'd better check on her. What they found was she was shacking up.

"She's only eighteen!" her mother yelled at Tom. "How old did you say *you* were again?"

Angela's father didn't say anything, only regarded him with his appraising eyes.

"I'll be nineteen in February, Mother," Angela said patiently, "remember?"

"So?" her mother demanded. "You going to continue living in sin together? What if you get pregnant?" She turned on Tom. "*What if she gets pregnant?*"

"We'll get married," Tom told her.

Which in fact they did, six months later and perhaps too quickly, in a "mixed" ceremony, since Angela was Jewish on her mother's side and Tom still nominally a Catholic. Both a rabbi and a priest, the most progressive they could find, jointly officiated in front of a small gathering of friends and family in her parents' back garden in Cincinnati. This was followed by a reception in the private dining room of a family restaurant. The assembly included Angela's older brother, in law school at Dayton, their father's alma mater; a couple of aunts and uncles and their spouses on their father's side from various parts of Ohio; nobody from their mother's side except her older sister, a steadfast old lefty who'd flown in from New York.

"Such bourgeois bullshit," she said to Tom, shortly after introducing herself. "Why did the two of you even bother?"

She was a handsome woman, Angela's outspoken Aunt Helen, white-haired but still with it. He liked her. He liked Angela's mother too, who had her own, more conventional strength of character. He imagined the two sisters at each other's throats occasionally.

Angela's brother had a quick, sardonic sense of humour. Tom liked him.

Herb Gilbert, Angela's tax lawyer father, took some effort; he played mind games with you, played the devil's advocate, liked to test your smarts. His conservative politics had Tom playing the liberal, if not the radical. It was fun for a while, until it got exhausting.

Tom's folks had driven down from Minnesota. Tom's younger sister and her husband sent congratulations and the gift of a silver platter from Boulder, where they lived now. His kid brother, in the army and about to be shipped out to Korea, sent a card from Fort Hood, Texas. He'd get out before the Vietnam buildup.

The bride and groom's parents, striving for some common ground, compared their struggles as young couples—during the Depression, in the case of Tom's folks, and in the years just after World War Two in the case of Angela's. The two hip clergymen got drunk together.

Four years later, still living in Chicago, Tom working now for a trade magazine that sent him out of town periodically, Angela still working at the American Airlines ticket office and attending classes part time at the University of Illinois on Navy Pier—and with the times grown ever more permissive—maybe she began to feel cheated of experience, that she'd married too young. He'd loved their living together, their intimacy. Not having to look for love anymore, able just to be himself, while she, perhaps, missed the excitement of their first times together and felt unsettled, guilty, angry at finding herself attracted to other men. As if he had ceased to be attracted to other women.

Mexico might have fixed things. Mexico offered the adventure of travel, escape from their predicament, perhaps fulfilment of their, or anyway *his*, romantic dreams. But then travel was no escape, they discovered, no solution to your problems. Your problems went with you.

Tom woke when he heard Sandra in the kitchen. He rolled off the couch in his rumpled clothes and found her making pancakes and frying bacon.

"Smells good."

She studied him. "You in shape to travel? You look a little hung over."

"I'm okay. Just took me a while to get to sleep."

"It's that couch. Sorry."

She poured him a cup of coffee.

Jack came downstairs, his hair wildly tousled and scratching his beard. "Morning," he said gravely.

Then Richard came down, his lined face with a couple of new furrows in it, and Sandra said, "You look *definitely* hung over."

"Coffee," Richard croaked.

Fuelled by coffee and bacon and Sandra's good buckwheat pancakes, they began to talk, taking up pretty much where they'd left off the night before. Tom forgot for a while that he was unhappy.

"So what're your plans, boys?" Jack asked finally. Sandy got up to clear the table. Tom started to help, but she waved him off.

"We'll hit the road again," Tom said. "Hitch the rest of the way to Chicago."

"And then what?"

"I may go back into journalism." He said that off the top of his head, knowing he probably should for a time, make some money before setting out to find Angela—also knowing that any delay in his search might result in never finding her.

Jack nodded. He seemed to know nothing of what Tom had told Sandy.

Richard said, "I'll check in with my union in Chicago. Maybe ship out through the Seaway."

Jack rose from the table. "Okay. Great meeting you guys. Keep in touch, why don't you?" He pulled a card out of his wallet. Richard took it, then handed it to Tom. "You're more likely to write, man."

"Sandy'll drive you to where you can stick your thumbs out," Jack said. "Be good, as they say, and if you can't be good, be careful."

He shook Tom's hand and then Richard's. They left him in the house and followed Sandy to the car.

She drove them across the river to the highway leading north. Pulled over, got out of the car with them, and shook Richard's hand. She gave Tom a hug.

"Find her," she said in his ear. "Maybe love will triumph."

"I won't forget you," Tom whispered back to her.

She drove away then and left them standing in the chilly morning.

"Man, you should go after that Sandy," Richard said. "Take her away from an old egghead like Jack."

"Like you took Angela away from me?" Tom said furiously.

"She took her*self* away, man. Remember?" Richard reminded him.

Chapter 9

It took three rides to make Peoria, where a young Bible sales-man picked them up on the edge of town and drove them the rest of the way into Chicago. Dropped them off in the Loop at the start of rush hour. The banks were closed, so Tom couldn't withdraw any money. They had change for the El to Evanston, and Tom used the pay phone on the station platform to dial Cliff and Sue's number. Sue answered.

"Tom! You're here at last. Cliff worked late, he's probably right behind you. I was just leaving to pick him up."

It was good to hear her voice. "Sue . . ."

"I know. Just wait. I'll be right there."

Before he could mention Richard, she hung up.

The next train pulled in and Cliff stepped out of a car onto the platform in a suit and tie and carrying a briefcase. He was one of a crowd of whitecollar types getting off the cars, sport-ing a mustache these days that made him look dashing, rather sleek. Which went along with his new post as feature editor of *Urban Bachelor*, one of the classier *Playboy* imitators. Tom felt the gap between them now since their rookie days together on the *Tribune*.

Cliff spotted Tom at once and strode smiling over to him. His smile turned quizzical when he noticed Richard.

"No, I haven't had a sea change," Tom assured his old pal with a grin. Cliff laughed, and nodded to Richard before giving Tom a hug.

"Sue says you know about Angela and me."

"Yes. I'm so sorry."

"She must have written you."

"We got a card."

"When? From where?"

"El Paso. About a week ago."

"Did she say where she was going?"

"Not exactly. She was with some people heading for Canada."

Why hadn't they stopped in Trujano for her stuff? Tom wondered now. He might have seen her then; they might have talked. They might even have reconciled. Anyway, what had been *her* take on their separation? Probably less glum than his.

"Did she sound . . . "

Cliff held up a finger that said "wait" just as Sue drove up in their Volkswagen bug. She got out of the car and walked toward them. She'd put on weight, her round, pretty face grown a little rounder, her full figure a little fuller, in marked contrast to Cliff's workout trimness. Then Tom guessed she was pregnant.

You could see bemusement in her eyes as they went first to

Richard, then to Tom.

Sue and Cliff exchanged looks.

"Richard's a friend," Tom explained. "He's looking for Angela with me. We both want to be sure she's all right."

Sue seemed about to say something when Cliff said, "Hey, we live in interesting times. Let's get going, though. I've had a rough day. We got food at home, babe?"

"I can make spaghetti," Sue said.

"Great. We can talk over dinner."

Cliff and Sue had a mortgage on a small, two-story brick house on a tree-lined street not far from the lake. As soon as they got there, Sue, with Richard's surprising help, began preparing dinner while Cliff led Tom into his study where he pulled a card—then a letter—off the bookshelf above his desk.

"Got this letter just yesterday," Cliff said.

The card, addressed to the Andersons, had a picture of downtown El Paso on it and these matter-of-fact words in Angela's neat hand:

> *Dear Friends, Tom and I had our troubles in Mexico and have split up. It was all my doing. He's probably on his way back to Chicago and I'm with friends heading for Canada. I'm all right. Hope he is. I still care for him, but I can't be married to him anymore. I'll write again when I can.*
>
> *Love, Angela*

Tom took up the letter. The envelope, addressed to him care of the Andersons, was mauve coloured and smelled of pachouli oil. No return address, but the stamp was Canadian and the postmark legible: Clarke's Landing, B.C.

He tore open the envelope, pulled out the letter. It was on fancy matching paper and had been written, with several squiggled-out words, only a week before. It was April first today, April Fool's Day, he wryly reminded himself.

March 25

Dearest Tom,

I say "dearest" because I still love you and always will. I miss you and at the same time know that we can't be together now, maybe not ever again. (Ha! That's holding out some hope for us and assuming you still have feelings for me besides hurt and anger. As for my feelings, they're sort of mixed up. Maybe yours are too.)

I am trying to understand what happened to us, why we had to separate. I guess I wanted something I wasn't getting from you, from our marriage and you kept demanding what it was when I didn't know what it was myself. Those last days in Puerto Bonito when we were stoned all the time and Richard sort of standing around, waiting to make his move—I was on a bad trip, I was "freaked out" (God, I hate that expression, but it's the way I felt, like a freak), and you didn't have a clue. No. I won't blame you anymore. That's over.

Angela

There was a P.S.

For too long I wasn't honest with myself or with you or about our relationship. It was just a lot easier to <u>repress</u>

what was too difficult to deal with. I wish I weren't so
fucked up. I wish I knew what I want.

Then a scribbled-over couple of sentences and finally:

In some ways, I'm sorry we ever went to Mexico. Maybe
if we hadn't—no, what happened could have happened
anywhere. Be happy, Tom. I'll always remember how
happy we were before things got so complicated.

Tom folded the letter and put it back in its envelope, the
cloying smell of the pachouli oil half-sickening him. He felt a
surge of anger, followed by a wave of sympathy, of admiration,
of love. Her letter was so heartfelt. She was so brave.

"Patch. She used to hate the stuff."

"The new Angie," Cliff said.

"Gotta map?" Tom said thickly. "Let's look for Clarke's
Landing, British Columbia."

"You haven't missed much," Cliff told Tom, after the two were
alone in the kitchen, having volunteered to do the dishes following the meal of Sue's delicious spaghetti and meat balls,
together with garlic bread and a tossed salad, all washed down
with a bottle of Bardolino. "The war's still on and the revolution hasn't happened yet. Some good music going down."

He nodded toward the living room where the Andersons' hi-fi
system was cranked up and there was a rocking, jingle-jangling
version of "Who Do You Love?" on the turntable.

"Quicksilver Messenger Service," Cliff told him. "California
group. They're all the rage lately."

Sue and Richard had gone to the neighbourhood

convenience store for more wine. Tom supposed she had engineered the trip to give him and Cliff some time to talk privately—and a chance for *her* to check Richard out. During the meal, they'd simply stuffed their faces and gulped wine and reminisced about their glory days—Tom and the Andersons, that is—while Richard sat grinning, his head turning from one to the other.

Back when they were both reporters for the self-proclaimed "the world's greatest newspaper," Tom and Cliff, as fellow vets, fellow would-be writers, had taken to each other right away, though they came from different worlds. Cliff, born and raised in Chicago, had lucked out as an Army draftee by serving most of his two years in France while Tom, as a Navy enlistee, hadn't done so bad either as a submarine sailor stationed in Hawaii. They'd both come to the *Tribune* after getting degrees in journalism on the GI Bill, Tom's from the University of Minnesota, Cliff's from Northwestern. As for prior journalistic experience, Cliff had spent a year on City News, Chicago's wire service that was an excellent training ground for big-city reporters, while Tom had worked the summer between his junior and senior years at Minnesota for a small-town daily south of the Twin Cities.

Cliff, a little older than Tom (twenty-eight to Tom's twenty-six then), sort of took him under his wing. Called him "Huck Finn in the city," a pleasing image, Tom thought.

Cliff stepped away from the sink, dried his hands, and went into the living room. Quicksilver had finished and he put on another record. Another rock band, a female singer this time. Her hoarse wailing was familiar, but her name escaped Tom.

"Janis Joplin," said Cliff, as he returned to the kitchen.

"Of course," Tom said.

When Sue and Richard returned from the convenience store, Richard fixed his eyes on Tom and nodded toward the door. Tom followed him outside. They stood on the porch in the chilly night air. The streetlight, just down the block, obscured the sky and any stars they might have seen.

"I've decided to ship out," Richard said.

Tom looked at him.

"Sue tells me you got a letter from Angela and probably have an idea now of where she's at. If you find her, lemme know how she is. Got something to write on?"

Tom pulled out the notebook he carried in his shirt pocket and opened it to an empty page. Handed it to Richard.

"Got a pen?"

Richard moved to the light from a window and quickly wrote something in Tom's notebook. Handed it back to him.

"That's my sister's address in Baltimore. I check in with her now and then. You might give Angela this address too, if you find her. She can reach me there if she ever wants to."

Along with his upsurge of hope, his relief to be getting rid of Richard, Tom felt twinges of something like affection for the asshole.

"I gotta say it, Ricardo. I won't be sorry to see you go."

Richard grinned and held out his hand. Tom took it. Then they hugged, causing Tom to think back to that far-off day in Puerto Bonito when he hugged this man who was taking Angela from him out of numb helplessness and sorrow and stupid trust.

"Amigos, no?" Richard said.

"*Possible*," Tom told him in Spanish.

Back inside the house, Tom looked at his watch. It was after nine already—too late, he decided, to start for Canada. Besides, he needed to wait until tomorrow, when the banks would open.

Sue and Cliff, at the kitchen table, had expectant looks on their faces.

"Richard's shipping out," Tom told them. "I'm leaving tomorrow for British Columbia."

"Wonderful," Sue said. "Who's for gin rummy?"

Cliff opened the fresh bottle of wine.

Sue made popcorn.

They played gin rummy until midnight.

Chapter 10

The next morning Tom woke in the guest bedroom to the sounds of Cliff and Sue in the kitchen. He dressed, and found them having breakfast.

"Want some scrambled eggs?" Sue asked.

"Thank you."

They heard Richard stir on the couch in the living room, and presently he appeared, looking haggard, an unlit cigarette in his mouth.

"No smoking in the house. On the porch," Sue told him.

After breakfast, Sue drove Cliff to the station to catch the El into the Loop. Tom went out back of the house, where his '64 Fairlane sat on blocks and covered with a tarp. Richard came out and helped pull the tarp off. Then, insisting on it, he did the work of jacking up the car, one wheel at a time, so Tom could pull the blocks out from under it.

"Thanks for your help," Tom mumbled.

"No sweat."

They stood there, staring uncertainly at each other.

Sue came out and rescued them.

"What's happening, guys? Don't you both have things to do? Places to go?"

"Right," Tom said. He turned to Richard. "I can give you a ride into the Loop."

"No thanks," Richard said. "Just drop me at the El."

Tom drove to the station and Richard got out of the car. He lifted his pack out of the back seat, then walked around to the driver's side.

"So long, mate."

Tom reached through the window and they clasped hands. Richard's eyes—were they a little moist?

"If things don't work out . . . I mean, you know where to find me, man. Ever thought of going back to sea?"

"No," Tom said.

Driving away, he saw Richard in the rearview mirror raise an arm and splay two fingers in the peace sign.

Tom honked his horn.

He drove to Hyde Park and spent the rest of that day and all of the next getting ready to leave. He had his car tuned up, the oil changed, and bought two new tires for the back wheels. At what had been his and Angela's apartment, he packed some things, including a box of his books, and left the young couple who'd sublet the place with the idea they might have it indefinitely.

Then he drove into the Loop, went to his and Angela's bank, and withdrew six hundred dollars, half of what was left in their account.

Back at Sue and Cliff's place in Evanston, where he would spend another night, they went out to eat supper at a local steakhouse. Afterwards Cliff left them for his study, where he had work to do on the next issue of *Urban Bachelor*. Sue made coffee, then she and Tom moved to the couch in the living room.

Sue sipped at her coffee, then placed her cup on the low table before them.

"I think Cliff's having an affair," she said quietly. She looked down at the table as if speaking to it. "Well, maybe not an affair exactly, but I think he's screwing around. It's that magazine he's working for, the *ambiance* of it, their so-called philosophy. I've been to their office. Lots of sexy young things around."

"You want me—"

"I'm pretty broad-minded, you know? Cliff and I both played around before we were married, and yes, we've had our little flirtations since then. Sex is in the air. But I'm pregnant now, in case you haven't noticed, and we let it happen, and isn't having a kid together some kind of commitment?"

She turned to him as if expecting an answer. All he could do was put an arm around her. What's wrong with us? he wondered. Why can't couples stay together? Why do we hurt each other? Why is the fucking grass always greener on the other side of the fucking fence?

"You want me to speak to him?"

"No!" Sue glanced toward his study and lowered her voice. "I'll confront him myself, if I have to. Maybe I won't have to."

"So long as he works at that magazine, he'll be tempted," Tom said. "I would be."

"Yes, and if I was surrounded by a bunch of beautiful men where I was working, I'd be tempted too. Monogamy sucks, let's face it."

"Yeah, wouldn't it be great if we could just do it with whoever turned us on?"

Sue smiled and patted his hand. "Cliff and I will work it out," she said. "Or we won't. Either he'll fess up or I'll call him on it and we'll have a big fight and get over it, or we'll call it quits." She took a breath. "Or maybe it'll pass by itself and we'll have our baby and live happily ever after. Anyway, it's our business. You have yours," Sue told him.

"I doubt Cliff wants to lose you," Tom said.

"I don't want to lose *him*," she said.

The next morning, too nervous for breakfast, Tom loaded his car, said goodbye to the Andersons, and drove out of Chicago with the sun just rising behind him and his senses as tuned up as the engine in his old Ford.

"Let's hit the beach," Navy sailors on liberty said, "and see what happens."

The road ahead rushed toward him. The road behind streamed away in the rearview mirror.

He would see what happened.

Part Two

Canada, 1970-71

Chapter 11

Driving the northwest freeway out of Chicago, jockeying the lanes, passing other vehicles while wonking and wailing, a la Bob Dylan, on a harmonica, Tom pushed his car up to seventy, to eighty miles an hour with the wild intent of reaching Clarke's Landing, British Columbia without stopping, except for gas.

He whipped past Rockford, then Freeport, reached East Dubuque—then struck due north on Highway 61 along the Mississippi, up through Wisconsin to La Crosse and over the river into his native Minnesota. By that time he'd worked out a passable rendition of "Blowin' in the Wind."

There were youthful hitchhikers outside almost all the towns he swept by, standing at the freeway entrances just off the asphalt and now along 61, their packs on the weedy, snow-patched ground beside them—couples mostly, long-haired boys and girls holding up signs that said BOULDER or

PORTLAND or SANTA FE, San Francisco being passé now, it seemed, as a hip destination. He raced by them. Didn't feel like giving anybody a ride, no matter how interesting looking; later maybe. Right now, he just wanted to go.

He thought of stopping, though, to see his folks. They'd quit farming ten years before, while Tom was in the Navy, and now owned a hardware store in the little town north of Albert Lea, where his mother grew up. But he passed the turnoff that would have taken him there, stopped for gas just south of St. Paul, then got on 494 to whip around the Twin Cities and head northwest again, toward the North Dakota border. He stopped for gas again outside Alexandria, drove on. Drove all that day and into the night, reached Moorhead and crossed the Red River into Fargo, where he had to stop for gas once more. Thought of looking for a motel, finally, but kept going.

He'd been fifteen hours on the road and thought he could keep driving forever as he raced north over the flat bed of what, ten thousand years ago, had been an enormous glacial lake. He drove through Grand Forks, then west to Devils Lake, then north again to Minot. Here he had the choice of staying on Highway 2 or continuing north, some fifty miles, to the border and, some miles beyond that, to the Trans-Canada Highway. Either way would take him to the Rockies. On his map, however, the Trans-Canada looked like the quicker way to British Columbia.

It was after eleven when he reached Minot. He'd begun to doze at the wheel. Drove through the flat town and on its northern outskirts finally stopped at a rundown-looking motel where, after twice ringing the bell in the tiny office, a Native woman parted the curtain behind the desk wearing a bathrobe and rubbing her eyes and rented him a unit.

Earlier he'd pulled off the road with the thought of sleeping in his car. But it was too cold, he quickly decided, with a punishing wind that rocked the vehicle and began seeping into it as soon as he'd turned off the engine and, with it, the heater. It wasn't spring up here yet.

He parked in front of his unit. Down the line was only one other vehicle, a pickup truck with Saskatchewan plates. He carried his duffle into his room and found a double bed made up with a faded spread, a scratched side table with an antique lamp, adjoining bathroom (sink and mirror, toilet, water-stained tub with shower), no TV. He was tired; but more than that, he was hungry, and he could use a drink.

Across the highway was a ramshackle building with a blinking HAMM'S sign and the name ROCKY'S over the entrance. Two cars were parked in front of it. Tom put his back to the frigid wind and, crabwise, crossed the highway. Pulled open the door and stepped into the place and found himself in a low-ceilinged room with an L-shaped bar running most of its length. A string of booths stood against the opposite wall and an old-fashioned Wurlitzer jukebox in one corner. Beyond the bar was a pool table at which two country ruffian types were playing. The larger man nodded curtly to him, then bent over the green felt, lining up a shot. His partner stood across the table from him, stick in one hand, beer bottle in the other, staring at Tom like a simpleton.

A women sat at the bar, a mixed drink in front of her and a smoking cigarette in the ashtray beside her. The bartender, his brown hair tied back in a ponytail, stood with his back to her, looking up at the television in its cradle above the bar. Johnny

Carson was on, his guest Jane Fonda, expressing to an amused-looking Carson her opposition to the Vietnam War. "You're full of it, girl!" the woman shouted at her. "Yeah, and I'd like to fill her with something else," the bartender commented.

At the pool table there was a click of balls and the leathery thunk of one dropping into a pocket. The woman shivered, Tom guessed from the cold draft he'd brought in, and turned to him.

The bartender turned away from the television.

"Almost closing time, friend. What'll you have?"

"A beer. Budweiser, if you got it."

"No Bud. Hamm's, Grain Belt. Hamm's on tap."

"Hamm's then."

The man pulled a glass and placed it, foaming, in front of him.

"Pretty cold out there."

"Hey, this is *North* Dakota."

Tom felt the woman's eyes on him. "Just passing through?" she asked huskily.

Her hair was frizzled blond, artificial looking. She'd looked better, Tom thought, once upon a time.

"Yup."

"You staying at the motel?" the bartender asked. "If so, that's my old lady that checked you in."

"I am."

"We call it the Assiniboine, after my wife's people."

"Emphasis on *ass*," the woman told Tom, breaking into a coarse laugh that deteriorated into a smoker's fit of coughing. Recovered, she took a drag on her cigarette and added,"It's our local passion pit."

The bartender had turned back to the television. Tom asked him, "There anything to eat here?"

Without turning around, he said, "Couple sandwiches in the cooler. Ham and cheese. Chicken salad."

"I'll have the ham and cheese," Tom said. "And a bag of chips."

The sandwich, processed cheese and canned ham between white bread, was damp and spongy. But it was edible, along with the chips and washed down with his beer.

The woman swung around on her stool and smiled. "I'm Lana."

"My name's Tom."

"Where you from, if I may ask?"

"Chicago," Tom told her.

"Chicago," the woman said. "I went there once. It's way too big, though, and it had a funny smell. What is it?"

"Industry. The steel mills in South Chicago and Gary, Indiana," Tom told her. "Their smell carries over the lake."

"What's that lake again?"

"Michigan. Makes you feel less hemmed in by the city, if you happen to live on its south shore, as I did. And you get used to the smell. You even get to kind of like it."

He felt strange, suddenly. He was in a strange place, though this bar was like any back in his native Minnesota, and this woman was of the kind he used to know, ex-farm girl or from a country town. He was an alien here, he realized, not a country boy anymore.

"Hey Rocky!" the woman called. "Another drink for this lady."

Rocky turned away from the television—another of Carson's guests had come on, somebody Tom didn't recognize—and scooped ice into a glass, poured a shot of rum into it, then filled the glass with Coca Cola. Slid the glass over to the woman, then looked at Tom.

"Another beer?"

"Okay."

Tom saw the two men rack their cues and start over. They drew close—*too* close, he thought—surrounding him.

"Tom," Lana said, "I'd like you to meet Ralph, my husband"—she inclined her head toward the taller of the two men—"and our friend Howie."

Tom nodded to the men in turn.

"Just passing through?" Ralph asked.

He was blond, like his wife, looked younger than she and had narrow, cold blue eyes. Tom met them, then looked away.

"Yeah."

"Where you headed?"

"Canada."

"Canada. Where abouts in Canada?"

"British Columbia."

"British Columbia," said Lana. "That sounds so, you know, exotic."

"Like California," Howie said.

"Exactly! Like California. Where I'd like to go someday."

"In your dreams, babe," her husband said, his cold eyes on Tom. "Why British Columbia, I wonder?"

"Why not?" Tom said. "Supposed to be beautiful. Thought I'd go out there and look around."

Ralph studied him. "You dodging the draft?"

"Why else would he be going to Canada?" Howie said excitedly.

"No," Tom said evenly. "Sorry to disappoint you," He didn't

like where this was going. "I served my time."

"What in?" Ralph asked.

"The Navy."

"Been to Nam?"

"Missed it. Finished my hitch before the buildup."

"Weren't you lucky. I did a tour. So did Rocky here. Howie, he psyched out, didn't you, Howie."

Howie nodded, smiling. "Where you from, by the way?" he asked Tom.

"Tom's from Chicago," Lana told them.

"Chicago," Ralph said. "So you're a city boy."

"Country boy." Tom said, feeling the flush on his face. "I grew up on a farm."

"So did I!" Howie thrust his hand out. "Put're there, buddy." Tom took Howie's limp hand, then dropped it.

"I hear tell there's lots of hippies out there in British Columbia," Ralph said.

"Yeah, I heard that too," said Howie.

"Hippies," Ralph went on. "Peaceniks. Fucking college kids. Rich kids."

"We don't see many hippies out *this* way," Howie said.

"Rocky's our closest approximation," Lana said.

Rocky swung around from the television. "I'm no hippie," he said. "You know that, Lana."

Ralph gazed quizzically at Tom and said, "I still have to wonder though. Here you are—an American, no draft dodger, and you're heading for Canada. You a Vet for Peace now, by any chance? Don't love your country anymore?"

"I have a friend in BC," Tom said, his hackles rising. "I'm going out there to see her."

"Oh," said Lana. "How'd she wind up there?"

"She's Canadian," Tom lied. "We met in Mexico."

"Mexico." Ralph said. I went down to Mexico one time," Ralph said. "After Nam. Went down the Pacific Coast on my Harley all the way to Zihuatanejo. Know where that is?"

"We were in Oaxaca," Tom said. "Know where that is?"

Ralph blinked. "I didn't like it. The heat and humidity— and the people! Their look, how they lived. And not knowing the language. Reminded me of Nam."

"How'd *you* like it down there?" Howie asked. "With all those gooks."

"I liked it fine," Tom said. "I liked the people better than a lot of the gringos down there." He slid off his stool. "Gotta go," he said, and turned his back on them.

"Hey, you still owe for your beer!" Rocky called after him.

"Oh. Sorry." He took a twenty out of his billfold. Rocky rang it up and started to bring him his change. Tom said, "Keep it. Buy yourselves a round." Like he was offering them a tip, a *propina*, *la mordida*, the bribe you offered cops in Mexico to let you go. He was little spooked.

The cold wind caught the door as he opened it, banging it against the building. He turned as he went out, expecting to see the three looking after him; instead they were staring up at the television and the start of a late movie.

Outside Tom thought of just getting in his car and driving through the night, taking Highway 2, instead of the Trans-Canada. The border was probably closed by now. Then he realized how tired he was.

Sometime later, through the motel's thin walls, he heard voices and laughter from across the road and two cars start up.

Then they peeled out, one after the other, in opposite directions. Presently he heard the crunch of gravel as someone—had to be Rocky—walked past his unit. The wind moaned outside, sending cold drafts through the room. He lay curled up under the blankets on the sagging bed. And slept finally.

The next morning the truck from Saskatchewan was gone and the motel looked deserted. The tavern across the road looked derelict.

He thought of driving back into Minot for breakfast; instead he drove to the border and arrived there a little past eight, the border just opened and nobody ahead of him. The guard stepped out of the station. Tom opened his window and the guard came around to it and asked to see his driver's license. Then he asked where Tom was going.

"Clarke's Landing, British Columbia. I'm visiting a friend."

The guard peered into the back of the car where Tom's duffle and a bunch of his clothes lay on the seat. "Can I open your trunk?"

Tom handed him his keys.

The guard opened the trunk, filled with Tom's box of books, his portable typewriter, and a pile of Angela's stuff that she might appreciate when he found her.

The guard closed the trunk and came around to Tom's window again. He said, "And how long do you expect to be in Canada, sir?"

"Couple weeks or so," Tom told him.

The guard studied him. "Okay," he said, after a moment. "But if you decide to *stay* in Canada, see Immigration."

And he waved Tom through.

Chapter 12

A long daydream of driving, mile after monotonous mile across the flat prairies of Manitoba and then Saskatchewan, that dryland sea streaming by him at what he figured was a safe ten miles an hour over the speed limit. He slowed to the regulation thirty through the grain elevator towns, not wanting to attract any Mounties, stopped twice for gas, and once pulled off the road to piss. Mostly he kept his foot on the accelerator, kept going.

He passed Regina, passed Moose Jaw, might have stopped in Swift Current to eat; instead he drove on as darkness, racing westward across the planet, overtook and passed him. He kept going through the black night and a sudden spring blizzard that filled his headlights with swirling, dazzling snow for another hundred miles. The snow disoriented him, slowed his driving, but stopped as he came over a rise to see the lights of Medicine Hat, Alberta, below him. He was still a hundred miles from the mountains. But he was too tired to go on.

He found a motel and checked in. Took a walk to relieve his stiffness after twelve hours of driving. Found a Chinese restaurant where he ordered chop suey and green tea. Ate as though starving. Walked back to his motel and took a shower, climbed into bed and started to read himself to sleep: *The Teachings of Don Juan*. He'd bought the paperback in St. Louis on his way to Mexico with Angela in November 1969 (he'd written his name, the place, and the date on the inside cover, as was his wont), but he hadn't looked at it till now. Now found it rather dull. It put him to sleep. He woke at 1 a.m. with the book on his chest and the bedside lamp still on. Got up to pee. Returned to bed, put out the light, and slept without dreaming until nine o'clock the next morning.

Late! He drove into the town centre, found a cowboy café, and ate a satisfying breakfast of bacon and eggs with hash browns, toast and coffee. Then got on the road again. It was a bright cold windy day.

Driving fast and steadily, only stopping in Fort Macleod to eat a hamburger, he reached the mountains by early afternoon. They appeared at first as a low, jagged wall on the western horizon. Pretty soon he was in the rolling foothills with the high peaks of the Rockies in front of him, and then he was going through a valley leading to the Crowsnest Pass in a wind that threatened to blow his car off the road. Gradually, and then all at once, he was enclosed by the mountains, their sheer stone peaks and dark-green forested slopes, under a cloudy overcast. He came to where the highway had been bulldozed through a gigantic mass of rocks and boulders, the result, according to a roadside informational plaque, of half a mountain sliding down into this valley in 1903 and burying the town of Frank. There was nothing left of the town, but you could see the great gap in the slope above where a great chunk of it had fallen away. Had Angela seen this?

Then he was out of Alberta and into British Columbia, passing isolated houses with smoking chimneys and beat-up vehicles in the yards, slag-heap evidence of coal mines, stone outcrops leaning over the road, rock and forest, more rock and more forest. It was a claustrophobic world in this gray afternoon after the sunny openness of the prairie. He was a flatlander, after all. Angela, born and raised in Cincinnati on the Ohio River among forested hills, was probably taking to these mountains.

He passed through a town that might have been in the Alps. Then a town with a mile-long strip of restaurants, motels, gas stations lining the highway. He was driving through rain when he reached Marshland, in a flat, agricultural valley walled in by mountains, which his map told him lay at the south end of Sturgeon Lake. He was through the town in a few minutes, intending to drive up the shore of the fiord-like body of water to the ferry landing at Sturgeon Bay, across the lake from Clarke's Landing, where Angela had mailed her beautiful letter to him. That he might just find her there, that his search might end this soon, was too improbable, too happy even to think about.

At the turnoff outside Marshland to Silver City a posting of the Sturgeon Bay ferry schedule suggested he might miss the last sailing of the day. The turnoff would take him to Silver City, his map told him, and from there up the Sturgeon River to the lake again and Clarke's Landing. That was the long way around, but it would get him there.

The turnoff led across the valley and up into the mountains. Up and up to the summit of a high pass as the rain turned to snow and it got dark and there were still banks of snow along the road; then down and down, having to carefully brake because the road was slippery, a little scary, his headlights stabbing a lonely path through the thick darkness and the falling snow.

The snow turned back to rain and the road levelled off, finally, taking him through a long, empty stretch in which the dark evergreens on either side of the road turned pale in his headlights and there were only patches of old, dirty snow in places. No other lights except his own, not a single house light or even the occasional, reassuring lights of another car.

Eventually the road began angling down again, down and down. He caught glimpses of a raging creek on his left, then the lights of houses on his right, along the top of a ridge.

Abruptly, he was in downtown Silver City, its streets empty, its businesses closed. It was larger than Marshland, but he was through it in about ten minutes and crossing the bridge over the Sturgeon River, then driving along its west bank, passing houses on both sides of the road that grew fewer and farther between, many of them dark—most summer cottages, he would eventually learn—until, after some twenty miles, he saw the sign for Clarke's Landing and entered what appeared to be only a hamlet.

He stopped in front of a lighted restaurant, and on entering found the place empty, except for a handsome woman cleaning the grill. "We're closed," she said. But then she gave him some leftovers—barley soup and a cold roast beef sandwich and reheated coffee. It was a little after nine in the evening, according to the clock behind the counter. He'd crossed into Pacific Time and gained an hour.

The woman moved to his side of the counter and began mopping the floor. Tom said, "I'm looking for a friend who wrote me from here. She was with some hippies, I think. There any people like that around here?"

"Nope," she said. "Not yet, anyway."

"How about up the lake?"

Tom knew from his map that Clarke's Landing was midway up the length of Sturgeon Lake. He was at the start of the lower Sturgeon River, the lake's outlet, along which he'd just driven.

"Oh, probably. Up the lake and over in the Purcell Valley, I hear."

"Where's that?"

"Shortest way from here is to go up the lake to Henderson, then over the pass. Lots of young people coming up from the States now. Kids going back to the land, as they say. You one of 'em?"

"No."

"Don't get me wrong. I kind of like their spirit."

Tom ate the rest of his sandwich and finished his coffee.

"There a place to stay in this town?"

"There's the Shore Inn," she said. "Just go past the ferry landing and turn on the road there. Couple of blocks and you'll see it on your right. Too early for tourists, so they're bound to have vacancies."

She went back behind the counter and emptied the coffee pot into the sink. Rinsed it under the tap. Turned back to him.

"The other thing, you can drive into Silver City. You'll have your pick there. Three hotels and half a dozen mo*tels*."

"Thanks, but I just came from there. I've had a long drive."

"Well, then. The Shore Inn's cheaper anyway."

Chapter 13

In the restaurant the next morning, Tom met a logger who knew of some young people of the kind he was looking for. And, yeah, they were over in the Purcell Valley.

"They like to skinny-dip in the river. They even *garden* in the nude!"

He was a smiling, shaggy haired young guy, clean-shaven, in steel-toed work boots, a red shirt, jeans held by suspenders. "Me and my buddy went over there last summer—to look at the girls, eh? Found this group on a farm, on what they called a commune. We were made to feel, you know, sort of unwelcome."

The woman from last night, who turned out to be the restaurant's owner and who'd welcomed Tom with a nice smile this morning, brought his sausage and eggs and he dug into them.

"You're from the States, eh?" the young logger said.

"Yeah."

"From California?"

"Minnesota."

"Where's that?"

Tom placed it for him by saying it bordered on Canada between Winnipeg and Thunder Bay.

The logger was from Prince George.

"Where's that?"

"Midway up the province. You a Vietnam War draft dodger, by the way? No offense, brother. I happen to work with one."

"No," Tom told him.

With directions from the logger, Tom drove up the shore of Sturgeon Lake to Henderson, a nice town on the alluvial fan of the Henderson River, then up over the moderate pass to Galena, another nice town on another lake, above which, across the water and between two mountain peaks, was a field of snow Tom guessed was a glacier. The lake was Purcell Lake, long and narrow like Sturgeon but only half its length on Tom's map, its opposite shore without evidence of habitation, the slopes above it unbroken forest. Galena looked somewhat smaller than Henderson.

Tom stopped at a gas station on the edge of town. The attendant came out and said, "Fill 'er up?"

"Yeah." Then Tom said, "I hear there's a group of young people living on a farm down the valley from here."

"Hippies, you mean? Don't know about that bunch. The bunch I know about are in an old logging camp across the lake."

The attendant had a red face, graying hair, and a beer belly.

"They stop here for gas sometimes in their old truck. The driver's a guy, usually, with another guy or a couple of girls.

The girls aren't bad looking. I'm out here filling up their vehicle, they're inside filling up on pop and potato chips, stuff they don't get in what they call their commune, I guess. That'll be eight fifty."

Tom asked how to get to where they were.

"Just drive through town toward the lake and take a right on Sawmill Road. That'll take you around, past the mill, to the bridge across the river at the top of the lake. Other side of the river look for a dirt road on your left. That's the old logging road to the old camp. That's where you'll find'm." He chuckled. "They think we don't know where they are. They're squatting, of course, on crown land."

"That government land?"

"Yup. They'll be kicked off eventually."

Might Angela be one of the good-looking girls the attendant had noticed? Or one of the naked girls the young logger and his buddy had ogled on the farm down the valley from here?

He was buzzing inside.

The river was a wide stream, rushing under the bridge, spilling into the lake. The old logging road turned out to be a narrow, rutted track being encroached upon by forest. It rose and fell, twisted and turned, following the shoreline of the lake. There were still patches of snow under the trees. The road was muddy in places, his car bottomed out a couple of times, he was afraid of getting stuck. The grade grew steep, and he lost sight of the lake until he reached an open outcrop with a fine view of the lake from some hundreds of feet above it. He stopped the car and walked to the cliff's edge. Below he could see a submerged shelf through the clear water and how it dropped off into the blue depths. Directly across the lake was the town.

In his car again he was soon braking, his automatic transmission in low gear, down a steep incline to the shore again where he entered a level clearing in which there were a couple of old log buildings and a person with his or her back to him in a straw hat, gum boots and stripped to the waist, turning over dirt with a shovel. That person turned and revealed herself to be a bare-breasted young woman. He stepped out of his car and they exchanged stares.

He'd parked beside a 1950s Chevrolet pickup truck carrying a funky little wooden house by way of a camper. Extending out into the lake on piles was a large wooden ramp near the end of which were the rusting remains of a gigantic winch. Past the ramp was a flat wooden bridge over a creek, beyond which the road turned and disappeared into the mountains. The creek, in spring flood, was roaring.

He started toward the girl, noticing now that beyond her and the log buildings was a small, neatly constructed A-frame, and beyond that, hard against the steep slope coming down into the clearing, a shack partially built of what looked like scrap lumber and salvaged sheets of tin. He recognized a privy behind the smaller of the log buildings. Behind the larger building was a lean-to shed, and over by the creek, under a big cottonwood, its leaves nearly formed, was a little popup tent of the kind backpackers use.

"Can I help you?"

A young fellow with lank, shoulder-length hair and a wispy beard stepped out of the privy.

"I don't mean to intrude," Tom said, "but I'm looking for a

friend, a girl, who might be here."

"What's her name?"

"Angela."

"Nobody here by *that* name," the fellow said. "Could she be going by a made-up name? That's the hip thing now."

"I don't think so. Anyway, I was hoping to find her here. We met in Mexico and I've been looking for her ever since. She left Mexico for British Columbia, and I got a letter from her, sent from Clarke's Landing, and I—"

"Then she might be around here somewhere. Lots of folks like us in this part of BC now. Hey," he said, "you hungry, man? It's time for lunch. You're welcome to join us."

"Thanks, but . . ."

"Maybe somebody in our group knows something. My name's Chuck, by the way."

"Tom. You sure I—?"

"Yeah, man."

They shook hands.

Passing the young woman working in what Tom saw now was the start of a garden, Chuck said, "Lunchtime, Sarah."

She turned, presenting her broad, handsome face. Her auburn hair hung in a thick braid down her back, her skin showed the beginnings of sunburn, her full breasts swung excitingly as she lifted a last bit of soil with her shovel and turned it over. The soil didn't look very good.

"This is Tom," Chuck told her.

She dropped the shovel, picked a woolen shirt up off the ground and put it on. Then she walked over and shook Tom's hand. She had a man's grip.

"Hi," she said.

"Nice meeting you."

They started toward the bigger of the log buildings.

"We're in an old logging camp here," Chuck said. "The loggers' dining hall, where we're going, is our community hall now. The other building over there was their bunkhouse, where some of us sleep. We were lucky to find this place."

"How long have you been here?"

"Since last fall. That is, we *found* this place last fall and moved in, but when winter came and we realized we'd be snowed-in and have a five-mile walk to town for supplies, we rented a house in Galena. We moved out here again this spring as soon as the road in was passable. That was about a month ago."

"Where're you folks from?"

"Oh, all over. I'm from Seattle originally. Graduated from the university and promptly got my draft notice, so me and my old lady headed north."

"No trouble crossing the border?"

"Naw. Canada's welcoming folks like us as refugees. We just piled into our truck and drove to the border and told the guard we'd be looking for land. A lot of people doing that now. We lived in Vancouver for a while."

Ah, Tom thought, thinking back to the guard's waving him through at the border despite the pile of his belongings in the back of his car and Angela's stuff in the trunk.

"Where're *you* from?" Sarah asked Tom.

"Minnesota," Tom told her.

"That's Midwest, right?"

"Right. And you?"

"Oh, I'm from a little cow town in Alberta called Foothills."

Chuck said, "Sarah's one of our token Canadians. We're mostly Americans here."

"Where's the rest of you?" Tom asked.

"In the hall by now."

"Yes, and we better get in there," Sarah said, "before the grub's all gone."

Tom found the hall filled with young men and women and some children, the women in jeans or long skirts and sweaters, the men in jeans and sweaters or sweatshirts—their uniform, it seemed.

The kids were two long-haired little boys, twins, Tom guessed, and a blond little girl, all dressed more or less alike in castoff-looking clothing so that Tom couldn't tell the boys from the little girl at first. Shoes and more gum boots like Sarah's littered the entrance. The adults padded about the hall's rough wood floor in their socks. The kids were barefoot. One guy, for comfort or maybe just to be different, wore sweat pants.

"This all of you?"

"Pretty much," Chuck said. "One of us is away on a job. And the guy we call the professor, he's in Silver City getting a tooth pulled."

So no Angela. Anyway, to have found her here, would have been too easy, Tom thought. He might never find her, he thought glumly, in this part of the world or anywhere.

"You all right?" Sarah asked.

"What?"

"You grunted, like you're in pain."

"It's nothing." He laughed, his voice cracking like an

adolescent's. "I was just noting the scene here. You guys seem pretty together."

"Appearances," Sarah said.

At the back of the hall was an enclosed kitchen with a service-counter opening through which Tom could see a man and two women working around an old-fashioned, wood-burning cookstove.

Tom followed Chuck and Sarah to the long trestle table in the centre of the hall and sat down among New Eden's adult occupants. He got some friendly nods and smiles, but nobody spoke to him.

"Come and get it!" one of the women in the kitchen called out, which caused everybody, adults and children, to line up at the counter to have their food dished out for them like in a Navy chow hall or at a church social. You got a bowl of stew and thick slices of bread. Somebody carried a big jug of apple juice to the table, and it was passed around for you to fill your glass or cup.

"We take turns doing kitchen duty," Chuck told Tom. "Women *and* men. We're trying to break the stereotypes."

"Not easy," Tom said.

"You got that right," said Sarah.

The stew was composed of vegetables, beans, and brown rice. The bread was whole grain.

"We're mostly vegetarians," Chuck said. "Of *necessity* because we don't have electricity to run a fridge and besides, we're on a limited budget. It's really hard, though. Once in a while," he confessed, "I sneak into Galena for a hamburger."

"Shame on you," said Sarah, giving Tom a grin.

"All of you can't have arrived here in your truck."

"Oh no," Chuck said. "Some people just drifted in."

"Like you," Sarah said.

The kitchen crew came to the table. Tom looked around and counted heads: nine in all, not including the children and excluding himself—three women and six men, all still in their twenties, he guessed, except for one of the women who'd been in the kitchen; she looked a little older than the others. Who was their leader? Did they even have one?

Then a guy with a head of blond curls at one end of the table caught his eye and asked pleasantly,"Who's our newcomer? I don't think he's been introduced."

"My name's—"

"This is Tom," Chuck said. "He's looking for somebody he thought might be here, and I invited him to our meal."

"I'm Joel," the curly haired guy said. "And these . . . " he prompted, and one by one the others spoke their first names for Tom to immediately forget. "You here to check us out? We welcome visitors, of course, if they aren't here just to gawk. Tell us about yourself."

"Not much to tell. I'm here from Chicago where I was a journalist."

"What brought you to Canada? You a draft resister? You doing a story on communes?" The latter said somewhat hopefully, Tom thought.

"No," he said. "I served before Vietnam and I'm not up here as a journalist. I'm looking for somebody. Her name's Angela."

He felt foolish now. Nobody spoke for a moment, putting two and two together, Tom guessed.

"What's she look like?" the boy across the table from him asked. He was the one in sweat pants, his bearded, long-haired good looks somewhat groomed, Tom thought. His name was Mark, he remembered now. "I tend to notice people, especially women."

Hoots of agreeing laughter.

"You'd notice *her*, I think," Tom said. "About five-four. Long brown hair." He cleared his throat. "Kind of angelic looking, like her name," he told them.

The boy in sweat pants said, "Your girlfriend, I take it."

"My wife, actually."

"Did you split up?" the older woman, named Helen, asked. She was sitting beside Joel. Tom guessed now they were a couple.

"Yeah," Tom said, not wanting to, "about a month ago, in Mexico. She joined a group of Canadians and left with them for some commune that I *hope* is in this area. I got a letter from her, from Clarke's Landing, but she might have been just passing through."

"You think she wants to be found?" Helen asked. "I mean, should we even be helping you?"

"I'm not *after* her," Tom said, "if that's what you're thinking. It's just . . . She was kind of lost, I think, and I don't know what kind of people she's with, and I just want to be sure she's all right."

Joel said, "There's no folks like us around Clarke's Landing. Up Sturgeon Lake maybe."

He looked around the table. "Anybody know of a commune on Sturgeon Lake?"

Blank looks, shaking heads.

"You been to Harmony Farm yet?" Joel asked. "That's down the lake from here, in the Purcell Valley."

"No," Tom said, guessing now it was the place the young logger had visited.

"Check *them* out. If your wife isn't there, David might know something. He's tree planting now, but we'll ask him when he gets back."

"When'll that be?"

"Soon, I think. He's planting on the coast. Anyway, you're welcome to stay with us till he gets back. See how you like us while we see how we like you."

"Thanks very much," Tom said, "but I'll check out this other place first. If she isn't there, I'll come back, I guess, if that's all right, and wait around to talk to this guy David."

"We won't let you just wait around," Joel told him with a smile. "We all do our share of the work here."

"Be happy to help out."

After the meal, Tom helped with the cleanup. Then, though he wanted to head right down the valley to this other commune where he might find Angela at last, find her well and happy and be relieved of his anxiety about her—or find her in need of rescuing—he was delayed by Joel.

"Let's talk," he said.

They sat at the trestle table. "You know about our movement?" Joel started. " Back to the land? Back to basics?"

"A little," Tom said.

"It's the way people used to live, you know? Self-sustaining, before modern industrial civilization took over. The rat race. I was in it. So were you, I guess, as a journalist? We've dropped *out* of all that. I was stuck in a whitecollar job in Phoenix until I wised up and headed for San Francisco with a flower my hair. The Summer of Love? But things fell apart there pretty quickly. Pretty soon we had all these strung-out folks on the Haight going hungry, getting sick. The Diggers helped. I joined them. You heard of them? We collected food and gave it away, provided medical care, places to crash. Put on street theatre, held happenings, be-ins. There was to be no private property anymore, no buying and selling. Everything free for the people! But then the scene got scary. The country, though. That's where it's at now, man. And getting *out* of the country, out of the States, before you're drafted into America's imperialistic war."

Imperialistic war. Tom was a little bothered by the incendiary sound of that. Like he was bothered by the affected spelling of America in counterculture newspapers: "Amerika." Calling cops "pigs," etc.

"Woodstock," Joel was going on. "I wasn't there, but I know people who were. I'd like to see the film when I can. *There's* our generation, man. Brought together by our music."

Tom said, "Your generation isn't mine exactly. My wife, though. She's just the right age. She's an Aquarian, in fact, in the Aquarian Age," Tom said, as if that had any significance. He ached for her suddenly.

Joel nodded. "Anyway, back-to-the-land is part of the movement now. It's part of the revolution. Of course we're on government land here, I guess, and we'll probably'll get kicked off eventually. Meanwhile, we're looking to buy some land but so far haven't found any we can afford. We need folks with money. How're *you* fixed, by the way?"

"I'm not," Tom said. "Anyway, I'm not here to go back to the land. I just want to find my wife and make sure she's okay."

"That's cool," Joel said. "But as I say, you're welcome to join us for the time being and contribute what you can to our group. We call what we're trying to create here New Eden. We've learned a lot already. We got some good people. We'll make it, I think."

"This David, who's working now, he provide your money?"

"Part of it. When he works. We all work odd jobs when we can. I don't have any money, but Helen has some from a trust fund. She comes from an old California family. We met in the Haight and decided to move to Canada before I got my draft notice. Met Judy and John, and Chuck and Annie—Annie isn't with us anymore, she's in Vancouver and moved into a communal house. Vancouver isn't a bad town, reminds me a little of San Francisco, but the move by then was out to the country. BC was a refuge, we heard, so we came up here. You were in the service, you say? Before Vietnam? If you were facing the draft now, would you resist?"

"If I was twenty again? Maybe. Back when I was twenty and where I come from you didn't question the call to serve. Like you didn't question a lot of things." Joel arched his eyebrows. "You might not *want* to go, but you went. My boyhood buddies didn't wait to be drafted, they volunteered for it. Got it over with. Me, I joined the Navy to see the world, like the recruiting posters promised. Patriotism had nothing to do with it. It got me off the farm."

"But this stupid war . . ."

"We had our own war then. The so-called Cold War that's still going on and that led to Vietnam, don't you think? America wants to save the world for democracy."

"I used to think that," Joel said. "I voted for Goldwater in sixty-four, can you believe that? But then I got wise. America's just saving the world for itself, man, saving it for capitalism, for the rich. Anyway," he said, "we're working toward a viable alternative to the straight world here. In New Eden everybody contributes to the common good, each according to his or her means and ability. We're all equal. We share everything."

"Sounds a little like Marx."

"Yeah. Ever read the Nearings, though, Scott and Helen? *Living the Good Life*? That's our bible."

"Missed it."

"We have a communal copy over there." He pointed to a shelf of loosely assembled books in a corner of the hall. "You're welcome to read it."

Outside the hall, Tom ran into Chuck. "Where do people bed down here? I might be staying around for a while."

"Great, man. You might find room in the old bunkhouse. That's where people sleep other than David in his A-frame or Sarah in her tent over there. Joel and Helen and Judy and John sleep in the hall with their kids."

He grinned. "I can put you up. That's my shack over there. Don't have no roof over it yet, just a tarp, so it gets pretty cold at night. You got a sleeping bag?"

"Yeah. You sure?"

"Yeah, man. I'm alone right now. Going without."

"We're in the same fix then."

"Wait'll this summer, though. People'll start drifting in, like you did. Lots of young folks on the road these days. Lots of girls. We *both* might get lucky."

Tom had an image of Angela on the road, drifting in

somewhere, bringing luck to some longhair like Chuck here.

"Okay. Thanks a lot. It won't be for long, I hope."

For supper that night people filed in about six. The same crew, including Helen, was on kitchen duty. Tomorrow would be Chuck's turn, he said. His and Sarah's. "Kitchen duty's a drag," Chuck said. "Have to admit it. But it only comes around once a week or so."

The fare was like Mexican this time, beans and rice with cheese sprinkled on top. It was good. Plain water to drink— untreated, from the stream coming down off the mountain. It was good too.

After the meal, the big, dark-bearded man and the small, sandy-haired woman who looked like she'd just come down out of the West Virginia hills sat down in a corner and began playing and singing. The man strummed a guitar, the woman picked at a banjo, and they made some good oldtime bluegrass. People carried their dirty dishes to the kitchen, then sat listening at the table again or on the floor, their backs to the wall. That's where Tom found a place. The woman had a high sweet, down-home voice. The man's was a bass counterpoint.

"They're good," Tom said to Sarah, who'd hunkered down beside him. "They could be professional."

"They are. Little Judy and Big John, they call themselves. We're lucky to have them."

"American?"

"Half and half. John deserted from an army post in the States after he got orders for Vietnam. Judy's Canadian, from the Maritimes. They met in Toronto, got married to give John status, then teamed up as performers."

"They're not performing anymore? Professionally, I mean?"

"They quit after they got kids."

"They play every night?"

"No. Just whenever they feel like it. Friday nights, usually. Like tonight. They have two of our three kids." Sarah gestured toward the two boys, rough-housing in a corner. The little girl was sitting quietly by herself.

"The boys are twins," Sarah told him, "as you probably can tell, Randy and Robbie."

"Who's little girl?"

"Helen's, by her first husband. They call her Brightness. Helen's with Joel now."

"I figured."

Brightness was aptly named, Tom thought. She had a bright, open, attentive little face. The boys seemed less aware of anything other than themselves, or maybe they were just being boys. What was it like for the kids here? They seemed happy enough. They had the commune's extended family looking after them, he guessed.

Sarah had turned away from him to listen to the music. Helen and one of the younger women had gone around lighting candles. Somebody lit a Coleman lamp above the musicians and you could hear its hissing now and then. Tom felt Sarah's closeness, the warmth radiating from her body. The image of her topless beauty floated into his head. Who was she *with*? She was with *him* right now, or so it seemed, and he wasn't sure what to do about it, if anything.

He missed Angela. Where was *she* now? Who was *she* with?

Chapter 14

Where Angela found herself was in some sort of semi-religious commune in the middle of nowhere. To get there they'd driven out of Clarke's Landing and north up Sturgeon Lake to a small town called Henderson. Then over a pass to another long, narrow lake and another small town (the town was Galena, on Purcell Lake, Klaus told Angela), then north again, past a pretty river valley in which there were idyllic-looking farms, to the remote south shore of yet another lake, where there was a tiny settlement composed of a dozen clapboard houses, a combined gas station and general store, and a sawmill. The mill was marked by a yard of piled logs and a smoking, conical metal structure called a teepee burner. It was for burning sawdust and scrap lumber, Klaus said.

The place was called Douglas. The lake was Heron Lake and its shores beyond the town, for as far as Angela could see, were empty. The slopes of the mountains, except for some squarish bare patches—cut blocks, Klaus said—were covered with conifers growing so thickly together they were like a green, furry robe laid over them. It was a gray, cold day.

They crossed the bridge over a creek spilling out of the lake and drove up the opposite shore, the mountains rising sheer above them, their forested slopes as yet unmarred by logging.

"The Bearpaw Range," Klaus informed her. "Grizzly country. They are lords of the wild. They have no natural enemies."

"Except us," Mike said. "If ya can call us natural."

Trees mostly hid the lake that fell below them as the road lifted above it. After some miles, Klaus slowed the van and turned down a tunnel-like lane that soon opened out to a ledge with a magnificent view of the lake and on which was a group of wooden buildings. The largest was a funky, octagonal affair of two stories on either side of which stood a pair of one-story, rectangular buildings that looked like dormitories. There was a fourth building, a kind of glass-enclosed gazebo close to where the ledge dropped off to the lake. Outside it a group of young men in overalls and young women in gray smocks like hospital gowns stood in a circle with their heads bowed and holding hands.

Klaus parked the van next to the only other vehicle in the clearing, a Volkswagen minibus, free of psychedelic markings.

None in the group seemed to notice their arrival. Then a man in a long robe stepped out of the octagonal building and seemed to float toward them.

He reached them as they were climbing out of the van. Angela was immediately struck by his eyes. They were like deep, dark pools in his narrow, handsome face. His black hair curled like a nimbus around his head. His thick mustache was tinged with gray. He looked familiar somehow.

He nodded to Mike and Shelly, who stood smiling at him, then turned to Klaus. "So. Y'all have come back, Klaus. I had a dream you would."

He had a low, resonant voice. Angela was immediately drawn to it, to *him*, despite herself.

"That is horseshit, Paul. You know we come back."

The man smiled. "It's Mustafa now, Klaus. So how was Mexico?"

"Mustafa," Klaus said. "It has a ring to it, *ja*? Mexico was beautiful. Depressing also."

"Of course," Mustafa, formerly Paul, said. Angela was trying to place his soft accent. It was Southern, but where from? "The dirt. The poverty. Like in India or North Africa, ah imagine."

"*Ja*. And all the gringo hippies down there now. They are spoiling the place, corrupting the locals. They are worse than your regular tourist because they think they go native. They go native like in a movie."

"What y'all have to remember," Mustafa said, "is that to the poor in the so-called Third World we're sorta like aliens from another planet. We invade their world and infect them with our money, our *things*, like our forebears infected the New World with measles and small pox. But then the natives gave us syphilis, right?" He laughed.

He pointed his pooling black eyes at Angela. "And who have we here? Y'all were in Mexico too?"

"My name's Angela," she told him. "And yes. I was."

"Angela. You're aptly named, darlin'. And how did *you* all find Mexico?"

Angela was put off now by his easy flattery and her

awareness of *his* awareness of his attractiveness. "I liked it. I liked the people, or anyway, the people in the villages."

"Their simplicity, right? Though a course they're not as simple as they seem. In countries like Mexico you're always on the outside and not exactly lookin' in."

Shelly said poutingly, "You haven't even said hello to me, Paul—I mean Mustafa."

"Oh, you know I love you, Shelly," Mustafa said, "as I love everybody and every thing." He opened his arms and Shelly moved into them. Then Mike stepped up and received a hug. Klaus stood by with an amused look on his face.

The place was too strange. Angela didn't know if she could stay here. But where else might she go? Shelly was friendly enough, even a little protective. So was Mike. As for Klaus, he started coming on to her and she let him; she was definitely attracted to him. She was attracted to Mustafa too, but in a way she didn't like because of *his* strangeness. He was even a little scary.

Ramala, the name he'd given his establishment, and Mustafa, the name he'd given himself, they were both so hokey. As for the routine, the setup here, it reminded Angela of a description she'd heard once of a progressive girls' school as both freely expressive and rigidly controlled. Except this place was co-ed, like a combined monastery and nunnery, the sexes housed separately in the two dorms and otherwise segregated except for group events. Alcohol and drugs were strictly forbidden. *Officially*, sex was forbidden, though that rule was secretly and regularly broken, Angela would discover.

The days were divided into "on" and "off" times. The off times, like school recesses, included a half-hour break in mid-morning and an hour-long break in the afternoon when you were allowed to go off by yourself to read or reflect. Times on, apart from assigned work periods, were given to group drumming and chanting or silent meditation during which you were supposed to "cleanse" your mind of distracting thoughts—that is, tune out your "static," the better to hear the "healing hum" of the universe, feel the comforting embrace of the cosmos. The object was to achieve detachment and enlightenment—and, for those most truly enlightened, liberation, finally, from life's many distractions including, Angela gathered, those of the flesh.

Meals were in the octagonal building in which there was a kitchen and a long, rectangular dining table on the first floor. Mustafa's quarters were on the second floor, and before the food was served there was a period of waiting before he strode down the stairs like a head of state.

How had all this been paid for? Angela wondered. The guy must have money.

After each meal the men and women dispersed to their separate quarters, and in the women's dorm Angela was soon aware of homoerotic encounters after lights out at ten o'clock, as well as furtive visits, back and forth, between the men's quarters and the women's. Didn't Mustafa know of this? It was actually something of a turn-on.

Saturday evenings were something else. After the communal meal in the hall, everyone trooped to the Chapel, the gazebo-like building overlooking the lake, to sit on cushions on the wood floor, in a half circle in front of Mustafa, who reclined in a stuffed chair. Then began a kind of encounter session called Speak Out that was a little like what Angela knew of Quaker meetings in that you were encouraged to share any good, any uplifting thoughts you might have had during the week. But then you were asked to reveal any "bad" thoughts, any shameful or otherwise troubling things out of your past, any lapses of self-control in the present—any barriers, in short, to your enlightenment.

There were to be no secrets in Ramala; you must reveal all, in open, healing confession.

The disclosures could be entertaining, if not sometimes shocking, and it wasn't long before Angela realized that Speak Out was actually looked forward to as a diversion from Ramala's otherwise dull routine, an entertainment. She was amused at first by the general eagerness for the weekly sessions, then appalled to find herself looking forward to them herself.

Mustafa's stern rule was that nothing revealed during Speak Out was to go *outside* Speak Out. "What a priest hears in Confession," he reminded his followers at the start of every session, "stays *inside* the confessional."

Of course the rule was regularly broken—by Klaus, among others, with a gossip's glee.

One evening at Speak Out, after a long, unnerving silence, an older-looking woman said quietly, "I was visited by my father last night."

"In a dream, right?" Mustafa said, as if to reassure the others. He sat comfortably back in his stuffed chair.

"No, he was *there*," the woman said emphatically. "Like he used to come to me when I was a little girl. My mother would send me to bed and afterwards my father would come to me." The woman's eyes were tightly closed and her brows knit, as if from pain or concentration.

"I . . ."

Angela held her breath.

"He'd lie down with me."

Mustafa, his face impassive, said, "Go on, Elizabeth."

"He . . . I *liked* it!" she declared, and her eyes opened. There were tears in them.

"Of course you did. Go on," Mustafa insisted.

"That's all."

"Elizabeth," Mustafa said patiently. "There's more now, isn't there. You can tell us. It's safe for you here. Let it out."

"He loved me!" the woman shouted. "And I loved my daddy!" Her face contorted into ugliness. She started to cry.

"That's good, Elizabeth," Mustafa said gently. "You feel better now, don't you?"

She was sobbing. Mustafa and everyone else were silent. Finally she stopped, and Mustafa looked around. His liquid eyes fixed on Angela and she felt herself blush. She looked away.

"Who else would like to speak?"

A boy, perhaps still in his teens, stood up. He appeared to be stoned on the proceedings or on something else. "I just got here," he said, "but I know this is where I want to be. It's so beautiful here. Everybody is so beautiful."

Nods of agreement. Supporting smiles.

Then a sweet-looking young woman began to moan, to rock back and forth, her eyes rolling up into her head. Others began to rock. And then to moan. Angela had all she could do to keep from joining in. She didn't know she had closed her eyes until she opened them to see Mustafa's eyes upon her again.

"And what of you, Angela? You're new here also."

"I'm okay," Angela said.

"You have nothing to share with us?"

"No," she said.

"In time you will," Mustafa assured her. "We all have things inside us that we must get out. Things we must speak of to be rid of them."

Angela got a sisterly smile from Shelly, who was sitting opposite her beside Mike, who was looking blissful. Klaus, sitting next to her, gave Angela a wink.

Suddenly, a pale, overweight girl sprang heavily to her feet and began howling. It was a cry, a keen, of deepest mourning, of pain and grief and rage, and it went on and on, vibrating off the glass walls and raising the hair on Angela's head. The others sat with bowed heads out of something like respect for the girl's apparent anguish.

She stopped at last, out of breath, it seemed, and the air as if rang for a moment. Then she sighed, smiled sleepily, and slumped to the floor.

Creepy, Angela thought. But she'd been moved.

Mustafa sat smiling in his stuffed chair.

Everybody clapped.

"I very much would like to fuck you," Klaus told Angela one night after the evening meal in the hall and they'd helped with the cleanup and had stepped outside to look at the half moon. It would be lights-out soon, when they would go to their separate quarters.

"We have got to know each other, *ja*? We are man and woman, *ja*?"

Angela had resisted that first blunt hit on her, but in fact

Klaus had only voiced what she'd been thinking about *him*. He was too good looking. And he had that sexy accent.

A couple of nights later they sneaked out to the Chapel, surprising someone ostensibly in meditation. That person, in fact the young woman who'd let out a primal scream at the last Speak Out, surrendered the place to them with what Angela took to be a knowing grin

"*Ja*," Klaus said after she'd left. "The Chapel has many uses. Paul pretends not to know of them."

Behind his back, Klaus always referred to Mustafa by his former name. It always made Angela laugh. Her laugh now was tinged with nervousness.

"It's like this place is founded on hypocrisy," she said.

"*Ja*," said Klaus. "Paul is a hypocrite."

"What's *with* him exactly?"

"Oh, he thinks he is some kind of holy man, a prophet. He's full of shit, of course. He makes it up as he goes along."

"Do *you*—do the others—believe any of it?"

"Shelly and Mike, they buy most of it. The others? Totally. Me, to some little extent, *ja*. To the extent I have to."

"What's that mean?"

"Mustafa, Paul, he comes up here from the southern United States somewhere. He's a phony, *ja*? But not one hundred percent. He believes his shit—some of it, anyhow—and not all of it is shit."

"But if you know he's a phony, why do you stay with him?"

"I should go back to East Germany? Let Paul, Mustafa, whatever he likes to call himself, play the prophet. He has the money for it—for this place. We help him live out his fantasy, *ja*? And he lets us stay here."

"You're from East Germany? You escaped?" Angela said. "When? How'd you do it?"

"Nineteen sixty-two. I was seventeen. I, uh, how shall I put it? I did a guard a favour."

Angela didn't ask what it was. She said, "Mustafa. Where'd he get his money?"

"Who knows? Who cares?"

They were sitting on the bench outside the Chapel now. Klaus put his arm around her. She responded by throwing a leg over him to straddle his lap and face him.

"Oh, I like this very much," Klaus said.

They kissed. His hands went under her dress and grasped her buttocks. He drew her onto the hardness under his jeans. It made her dizzy. Then he was lifting her up and laying her down on the bench and pulling her pants off past her sneakers.

"Wait," she said, and sat up, kicked off her shoes, then unbuttoned her blouse. She watched as he unbuckled his belt, unzipped his fly, and lowered his jeans. That he didn't bother to take them entirely off—there was something a little too *Slam, bam, thank you, ma'am* about that as, in the moonlight, she saw the enormity of his swollen cock and, helplessly aroused, opened herself to receive it.

Chapter 15

Tom left New Eden the next morning, his car's rear wheels spinning, barely carrying him up the steep, stony incline out of the old logging camp. Driving the old logging road was a negotiation of its bumps and ruts to where it finally came out near the bridge at the head of the lake. He crossed the bridge, passed the sawmill and drove through Galena. Then down the length of Purcell Lake to where the Purcell River flowed out of it and on down the beautiful Purcell Valley. He watched for River Road, which Joel said to follow to the first place he would come to. That would be Harmony Farm.

He soon reached it, a rundown house, a big old barn and a couple of sheds, a grove of shade trees, their leaves almost fully formed. Beyond the buildings an open meadow stretched to a line of cottonwoods along the river. There were naked children in the meadow, and a couple of tethered goats cropping the circles of grass their tethers allowed.

Tom got out of his car and walked toward the house. He heard voices behind it. Walked around and was treated to the sight of two young women playing badminton in the nude.

They stopped their playing and stared at him without embarrassment. "Hello," the woman closest to him said. She was dark, or already darkly tanned, had a thin face and long, heavy black hair partially covering her breasts. "Can we help you?"

"Sorry for intruding," Tom said, striving for nonchalance. "I'm from New Eden, up the lake? I'm looking for a woman named Angela. She here, by any chance? Or has she *been* here?"

The woman looked at him suspiciously, then across the net at her companion. "I don't think so," she said. "There's only a dozen of us here, counting our kids. Nobody named Angela."

"Okay, but if someone by that name shows up here, could you get word to us in New Eden?"

"I don't imagine you have a phone," the woman said. She still looked sceptical.

"No. But could you leave word at the co-op, say, in Galena?"

"Maybe. We don't get up that way very often." She had a New York accent, Tom decided. "But sure, if a woman by that name does show up here, we'll tell her there's somebody in New Eden looking for her. Will she know who that is?"

"She'll know."

"Okay then. She can decide if she wants to see you."

The other woman stood looking at Tom—with interest, he thought. She was blond and sunburned, beautiful and beautifully formed, her pink skin splotchy with mosquito bites.

The darker woman smiled. "How you guys doing over there in New Eden?"

"Fine, I think. I just arrived there."

"Draft dodger?"

"No."

"I'm Jane, by the way, and this is Debbie."

"Hi," said Debbie.

"Pleased to meet you," Tom said. "I'm Tom."

Back at his car, he turned and saw a tall, thin young man with a ragged red beard who looked for all the world like the reincarnated D. H. Lawrence step out of the house. He was followed by a sweet-faced young woman with an extended belly. The man was in bib overalls, the woman in a mini-dress. They stared at him. Tom flashed them the peace sign.

He went back to New Eden. Where else might he go right now? Silver City? Rent a place in Galena? His money might last a while longer here, and anyway, he seemed to be welcome in this commune, could work for his keep and maybe this guy David, when he came back, could steer him in some hopeful direction.

He met Robert Crawford, "the Professor," New Eden's dropped-out college instructor, returned to the commune after having had an abscessed tooth pulled in Silver City. He was plump, bespectacled, a professed Marxist who looked older than he doubtless was and who, in fact, hadn't so much dropped out as been kicked out of teaching—by the board of governors of a small, supposedly progressive Midwestern college for "brainwashing" his students.

"Yeah, I was accused of poisoning the innocent young minds of the sons and daughters of the local, God-fearing farmers," he told Tom with a grin, "so my contract wasn't renewed. Best thing that ever happened to me."

"I'm the son of God-fearing farmers," Tom told him, grinning back at him.

"So? What do you think of our little utopian experiment here?" Crawford asked. "Back to the land? Back to nature? It harks back to Rousseau and the Romantics of the late eighteenth and early nineteenth centuries, Coleridge and Shelley, for instance. The idea of a group of like-minded people living happily together in some ideal rural setting. Dropping out of conventional society. Living free, being free to love whoever the hell one wanted, et cetera."

"D. H. Lawrence," Tom added. "His would-be utopia he called Rananim. Nathaniel Hawthorne and Brook Farm."

"Exactly. What do you think of the idea?"

"Interesting," Tom said.

And he thought of Jack Snyder, the professor writing a biography of Mark Twain while living with a beautiful Native American woman named Sandra outside Twain's hometown. What would *they* think of New Eden?

That evening there was a communal meeting about the garden Sarah had started and what to plant in it. Robert got them off the topic for a moment by pointing out the aptness of their name for themselves. New Eden was a garden, he said, indeed maybe the Garden itself, restored, and weren't they all Adams and Eves together?

"Groovy thought, man," Mark said.

And Sarah said, "Groovy or not, we've got to feed ourselves."

She spoke of the poor soil they had to work with and the need for fertilizer.

"We're composting our kitchen scraps," Helen reminded her.

"Composting attracts bears, doesn't it?"said Judy, of Little Judy and Big John. She had a singer's lilt in her voice.

"We need a barking dog," Mark said.

"We need some good old-fashioned cowshit," Sarah said.

Everybody laughed. Tom said, "I saw a notice of cow manure for sale in Galena when I went through there the other day. We could go get a load in your truck."

"Can't use the truck," said Chuck. "There's our camper on it."

"Can it be taken off?" Tom asked, wanting to be useful.

"Doubt it," Chuck said. "It's heavy, man. We couldn't just lift it off."

"How about dismantling it?"

"That would ruin it," Joel said. "It's a work of art! Chuck and John and I built it in Vancouver."

They all went outside to study it. Tom looked for screws; instead he found the thing had been nailed together. "I think if we're careful," he told the group, "we can take it apart and afterwards put it back together—with screws this time. I've done some carpentry. We have any tools?"

"Some," said Joel. "I dunno, though. Whatta *you* think, Chuck?"

"Let's do it," Chuck said.

They started dismantling the camper the next day, and indeed, more or less destroyed it. The cedar-shingle roof had been attached to the camper's walls with toed-in nails that, from shifting back and forth while the truck was in motion, had worked themselves loose. So the roof came off easily enough. But then the camper's plywood walls, nailed to the 2x4 studs set into the truck's rack holes, wouldn't lift out; they had to be pried off the studs. That ripped out sections of the plywood because the twist nails used clung stubbornly to the studs. Finally, in working the studs out of the rack holes, two of them broke off.

"Shit," Joel said, giving Tom a look. "You sure you can rebuild the thing?"

Tom wasn't sure, but he said, "I think so. With maybe another sheet or two of plywood."

He glanced around ruefully. "Sorry," he said. "I'll pay for the plywood."

"Anyway," Sarah said, "we can get some manure now."

Tom volunteered to go with Joel for manure that afternoon. Joel drove the truck to Galena and they found the notice Tom had seen, still posted in the co-op with directions to a farm in the Purcell Valley. The heavy-set farmer there, using his tractor and front loader, filled the bed of their truck with mixed cow and horse manure from a mostly depleted pile in his barnyard. He had a definite accent that Joel said was Russian. There were a number of Russians, members of a religious sect called Doukhobors, he said, in this part of the province. The man charged them twenty dollars. Joel paid him with money he'd drawn from New Eden's communal stash.

The truck was riding low now, almost touching the frame, Tom noticed.

"We'll have to take it easy on the way back," he said.

"You're the farm boy," Joel said. "How about you drive?"

Tom pulled the truck out of the barnyard and onto the farmer's driveway leading to the road. Joel said, "Hey, man. How's *this* for scoring some good shit?"

And they both laughed.

Back at New Eden they unloaded the truck, using the commune's one shovel and one pitchfork. The shovel was a spade, more fitted for digging in dirt than in cowshit laced with straw; the pitchfork, with only three tines, was designed for pitching hay, Tom knew. Still, with Mark helping, in less than an hour they'd unloaded the truck and made a pile of manure beside the garden. Sarah came out of the hall and said, "Lovely. Now all we have to do is spread it."

"We need another fork," Mark said.

"We need a four- or five-tined fork and maybe a tiller to work the shit in," said Tom.

"Can't afford a tiller," Joel said. "Maybe after David gets back from tree planting."

Others appeared, spilling out of the hall and the bunkhouse, walking up from the lake or out of the woods. It took them the afternoon, all taking turns with the fork and shovel, to spread the manure and work it into the soil.

Joel was beaming afterwards. "Cooperative labour!" he said. "Just like in the olden days."

"Not all that long ago," Tom said. "Where I grew up, farmers still got together to thrash—thresh—their grain."

"No kidding," Joel said.

It was a vivid memory, and Tom described what it was like at thrashing time during the war—World War Two, that is— the neighbours arriving at his folks' farm with their wagons and teams, the clap-clap-clap of an old steam tractor pulling the boxy old machine that operated off the tractor's pulley to shake the heads off the bundles of oats or wheat and blow the stems—the straw—into a pile. The roaring, dusty excitement all day, men sacking up grain from the machine's bin as it continued to fill, the growing straw pile until it was big as a barn while Tom and his sister Debbie, under their mother's orders, carried soap and water to the stand outside the house for the crew to wash up afterwards. The meat-and-potatoes-with-dessert meal prepared by his mother and the men's talk around the board table set up in the front yard under the shade trees. By 1950 that was mostly gone, Tom told the others, as many farmers, including his father, had their own combine by then.

"Must've been something," Joel said.

At supper that night there was talk of building a fence around the garden—to keep the deer out.

"A deer fence?" said Clay. He was from Detroit. "Is that necessary?"

"Yeah," Joel said. "We're in what they call the bush out here. There's a lot of deer around."

"Yes," Helen added excitedly. "Have any of you seen a movie called *The Yearling*? It's about a family living in the backwoods of Florida. Anyway, the boy in the story has a pet deer that gets into his folks' garden and they have to built a high fence around it to keep the deer out."

"How high?" Clay wanted to know.

"Oh, higher than your head, I think," said Helen. "About eight feet?"

"The deer jumped over it," Tom reminded her. He'd seen the movie, read the novel.

"Yes, and wasn't the ending sad?" Helen said. "The boy had to shoot his deer, remember?"

"Part of the boy's growing up," Robert instructed. "It's a

coming-of-age story."

"Aren't we getting off the subject here?" Joel said. "I thought we were talking about building a deer fence. Who knows how to go about it?"

Only Tom and Sarah had any idea. Actually, Tom's idea of a deer fence was based on the movie. On the Minnesota farm he'd grown up on, deer weren't a problem so much as their own cows. They'd been unable to keep a garden because, sooner or later, the cows got into it.

It was Sarah, growing up in the foothills of the Rockies in Alberta, who pretty much knew how to go about it.

"We'll need some poles," she said. "Any lodgepole around here? Like what the Indians used to make their tepees?"

"Then what?" Joel asked. "Won't we need barbed wire or something?"

"Just wire won't keep deer out," Sarah said. "They'll slip through it or under it."

"How about wire netting?" Tom said. "What we called pig fence."

"Yeah," Sarah said. "That would do it."

"Wait a minute," Joel said. "How much is all this gonna cost? We're pretty short now after buying manure."

Tom said, rather recklessly, "I can probably cover it, along with the plywood we'll need for the camper. Meanwhile, we can cut the poles. We got a chainsaw?"

"We got an ax," Joel said.

They spent two full days labouriously chopping down and lopping the branches off a dozen lodgepole pines, a convenient stand of which Sarah found across the creek. Then they had the job of peeling the bark off. Luckily, they found a long-handled, chisel-like tool seemingly made for the purpose in the lean-to shed behind the hall. They all took turns at the peeling and made a big pile of strips of bark that, when dry, could be used as fire starter, Sarah said.

They tried digging the post holes with their one spade, but the ground was mostly rocks so that making post-size holes with it was impossible. What they needed, Tom suggested, was a post-hole digger, which he described as basically two spades attached on hinges and facing each other. You drove the spades, pile-driver fashion, into the ground, spread the handles apart, which angled the shovel blades and held the dirt, then lifted the dirt out of the hole. Done repeatedly, you dug yourself a post-sized hole.

"How much'll *that* cost?" Joel wanted to know.

Tom and Joel drove into Galena in the communal truck, and at the hardware store were sold an auger that the clerk said would work far better—"with all the rocks in these mountains"—than the kind of digger Tom had asked for.

Besides the auger, they bought three heavy roles of wire netting, a big bag of staples, and a couple of hammers. The total cost exceeded the hundred dollars Tom had taken from his dwindling stash. Joel contributed the balance.

After two more days of work, digging the post holes, placing the poles and then stapling the wire netting to them, they had their deer fence, complete with a makeshift gate using strips of rubber for hinges from a discarded inner tube (another lucky find in the shed behind the hall).

"Success!" Helen said, as they all stood around admiring their accomplishment. "Wasn't this fun?"

"We're doin' it, people!" Joel told them.

Candlelit evenings in the communal hall. After-dinner joints being passed around, Judy and John providing background music to the increasingly stoned conversations. Tom found himself enjoying the group feeling, being part of it. New Eden, he thought, could be a real alternative to the straight world. The Serpent might never enter here.

He usually sat on the floor, back against the wall, next to Chuck and Sarah. Those two weren't actually together, Tom realized. Who was Sarah *with*? Mark, or Clay? They both had their eyes on her. So did he, and why not? She was beautiful, like one of the sturdy farm girls Tom had failed to appreciate as a farm boy, always drawn to the "smoother," seemingly unattainable town girls. Angela was a town girl, whom he'd won five years ago and now almost certainly had lost.

"What's with Sarah?" Tom asked Chuck one evening after the communal meal. He'd stepped outside to piss. Chuck came out to do the same. "Is she *with* anybody?"

"She's taking a break," Chuck told him. "Her last old man was an Alberta biker who wound up an accessory to murder. Went to jail. Which is when she came to us."

"Too bad. I mean that's she's off men."

"Yeah. I thought we might get it on sometime, but no. We're just friends."

Another evening, during the after-dinner cleanup, Tom joined Sarah in the kitchen. She had water heating on the cook stove and was stacking the dishes.

"What can *I* do?" Tom asked.

"I'll wash," Sarah said. "You dry."

Afterwards, she said, "Wanna take a walk?"

They left Chuck, Mark and Clay playing poker by

candlelight at the trestle table and walked to the lake. Climbed up on the ramp and sat dangling their legs over the water. Dusk turned to dark. The lights of the town winked at them from across the lake.

"Galena's only two or three miles away over there," Sarah said. "If only we had a rowboat."

"Or a canoe," Tom said. "We might look for a used one."

"*We*, you said. Have you decided to join us?"

He'd thought about it. "I'd like to," he said, more or less truthfully. "But I have to find my wife—somehow—just to see how she is, where she's at, where *we're* at. You know?"

"I hear you."

She touched his face. He touched hers.

"No," she said softly. "Find your wife, Tom. See how *that* goes."

They walked to her tent and said goodnight.

Tom found the card game breaking up inside the hall and Joel and Helen putting their daughter to bed before going to bed themselves in the storeroom. Little Brightness slept on a slab of foam rubber on the kitchen floor.

Judy and John had gone on to the bunkhouse. Mark blew out the candles on the table and Chuck produced a flashlight. Outside, he pointed it toward the bunkhouse for Clay and Mark. Then Tom followed Chuck to his shack.

Chapter 16

The man named David came back from tree planting with news of the shooting of student protestors at Kent State University in Ohio and something over five hundred dollars to add to the communal stash. He arrived in a beat-up truck driven by a fellow tree planter who dropped him off, then swung his truck around and drove up out of the clearing.

David was the real leader of New Eden, according to Chuck. He reminded Tom of Charlie, the army deserter hiding out in Puerto Bonito. He had Charlie's tough, capable look about him and a compact, muscled body not gone a little beefy, as Charlie's had.

"Four students killed and a bunch wounded," David said. "Weekend warriors of the Ohio Natural Guard—the fuckers fired into the crowd. The war's come home, some say."

"Fascism!" Joel cried.

The Professor, a dreamy half-smile on his face, said, "This

138

could be the start the revolution."

"We should all be down there!" Mark shouted "Where it's happening!"

"No," Helen said firmly. "We left all that behind to live the good life up here, didn't we?"

"The so-called," said David.

He wore a hooded sweatshirt with the sleeves cut off so you could see the tattoos on his muscled forearms. One said *U.S.M.C.*, the other was of a tropical flower of some kind with the word *Phuong* under it. Vietnamese, Tom figured. The name of the flower? The name of a girl? The tattoos were like bumper stickers, declaring what and where David had been. He still had the stiff-backed posture of a Marine, but he wore a thick, handsome mustache and had let his sandy hair grow out to be tied back in a ponytail. Not a jarhead anymore. Tom felt a kinship.

In the hall after supper that night, Tom introduced himself, then got to his concern.

"I'm looking for my wife," he said. "We split up in Mexico and she joined some Canadian hippies who maybe brought her up here somewhere. She's maybe in another commune. You know of any others around here? She wrote to me from Clarke's Landing, and I figure—"

"You trying to get back with her?"

"I doubt that'll happen. But I want—"

"No idea of where she was going?"

"Not a clue. We separated under zonked-out circumstances, and I'm afraid for her now. She might be in bad shape, in a bad situation."

"What's her name?"

"Angela."

David thought for a moment. "I'd try Harmony Farm," he said. "That's the commune down the lake from here, in the Purcell Valley. The dude I planted with? He's from there and talked about a couple of the women. Didn't mention one named Angela. Still . . ."

"I went there," Tom said. "No luck. What about up Sturgeon Lake?"

"Don't know of any group on Sturgeon," David said. "But there's a weird setup on Heron Lake, *north* of Sturgeon. I was there once, when I first got here and was looking around. The head honcho's kind of spooky, strolls around in a long robe like some kind of biblical prophet and his followers come on like they got their heads up his ass."

Tom laughed. "What are they, Buddhists or something?"

"Not sure. But the place is pretty regimented, the men and women in separate quarters that look like barracks, for chrissake. I didn't like the vibes there. Didn't like their leader. Made me think of Manson."

"Jesus."

"What's *your* story?" David asked now. "No offense, ace, but you look pretty straight to me."

Tom laughed again. "You're not exactly a furry freak yourself, mate. Despite the ponytail."

"Let's take a walk," David said.

They walked to the lakeshore, then climbed the logging ramp and sat looking out over the moonlit water.

Tom said, "You and me, we're the only ones here been in the Service, I guess. I was in the Navy and you—your tattoos tell it—were in the Marines and in Vietnam, right?"

"In Nam yourself?"

"Naw. I got my discharge before the buildup."

"What'd you do in the Navy?"

"I was on a submarine."

"Atomic?"

"Diesel and electric. There was only the *Nautilus* then, on the East Coast. I was in Hawaii, out of Pearl."

"I was at Kaneohe before they shipped me out to Nam. Subs, though. They're special, right? Sleek, sinister. Hazardous duty. I guess that's part of their appeal."

"They're crowded, uncomfortable, claustrophobic. But yeah, submariners feel kind of special."

"They do have an air about them."

"Feet, farts and fuel oil," Tom told him.

David laughed. "No, I mean they have their own *esprit de corps*."

"You're right. The silver dolphins a submariner wears? They're like an aviator's wings."

"Guys on destroyers. They have it too, I guess."

"Tin can sailors," Tom said. "Surface sailors."

"Listen to us," David said. "Fellow warriors. Brothers-in-arms."

They both laughed.

"Not that I wasn't a gung-ho Marine at first," David said. "Till I got to Nam and started to wonder why we were there. I felt for the people but was scared shitless of them at the same time. But I found a girl over there."

"That her name on your arm?"

David pronounced it.

"Beautiful name."

"Yeah, well, who knows what's happened to her? I just hope I didn't leave her pregnant. That's something else we have in common, huh buddy? We've both lost a woman we loved."

"What brought *you* up here?" Tom asked now.

"Oh, I went to see a friend in Minneapolis after I got out. He was a veteran against the war. I started going to demonstrations with him, started hanging out with what the local paper called Young Radicals. Hooked up with a young radical girl for a while. Then I met a kid wanting to dodge the draft, drove him up to Canada, and here I am."

"How'd you wind up here, though? In New Eden."

"I was in Galena one day after selling my car for the money. Looking around. Didn't know what I was looking for, only knew I didn't have anything to go back to in the States. Nothing in Philly, where I grew up. Anyway, I met Joel and Helen on the street and they told me about New Eden. Sounded neat. Joel's sort of an airhead, but I like Helen, don't you? She's grounded, as they say. And how about Sarah? She's New Eden's Eve, as far as I'm concerned."

They fell silent. Tom looked out over the lake, on the almost full moon reflecting on the water, water so still it looked solid enough to walk on. Miracles happened.

David stood up, then Tom did. They climbed down off the ramp.

"So I guess you'll be going up to that weirdo's place on Heron Lake."

"Got to," Tom said.

"It's north of Sturgeon, like I said. You'll come to a little sawmill town called Douglas. The place you're after is up the lake from there. Good luck, man."

"Thanks, man."

They shook hands.

Chapter 17

Tom drove north out of Galena the next day. The road was empty for a stretch, lined with conifers through which, on his left at intervals, he caught sight of the river that flowed into Purcell Lake. What was it called again? The Alder. It was wide and slow up here, a beautiful stretch of water.

Then the trees fell away and he was going past a flat lovely valley on the other side of the river in which there were farms and fields and pastures, grazing cattle and horses. He came to a roadside filling station and stopped for gas. Had a Coke and a hotdog before driving on.

Trees lined the road again, the river veered away and disappeared and the asphalt changed to gravel. On the forested slopes were blocks of clearcut. Occasional homesteads broke the green monotony, simple frame houses sided with rough board and batten and roofed with cedar shakes, all set in clearings in which there might be a couple of outbuildings and a car or a pickup truck, or both. They were like the lonely places he'd seen coming into BC from Alberta. There he'd seen signs of coal mining; here was evidence of logging.

He came at last to a tiny settlement beside a fast-flowing creek. Just a few wooden houses all huddled together as if in defence against the surrounding wilderness, beyond which was a sawmill, and beyond that the widening expanse of what had to be Heron Lake. The one gas station in town was a weathered building with DOUGLAS SERVICE painted on it in faded letters and a pair of old-fashioned pumps out front. Tom pulled in and the attendant came out.

"Fill 'er up?"

"I'm good," Tom said. "But I hear there's a group of young people up the lake from here. Can you tell me where they are exactly?"

"I guess you're talking about our longhairs," the attendant said. He was a heavily built man with graying hair and the requisite twinkle in his eyes. "Cross the creek outside of town and drive up the lake till you come to a turnoff toward the water. Their place, I hear, is at the end of that road."

"Thanks."

"Watch out, though," the attendant said, the twinkle gone from his eyes. "They're a strange bunch, I hear."

Tom crossed the creek and started driving up the lake. He could feel his heart starting to pound. Might this be it, finally? Might he find her here? And how would she be? His hands were sweating on the steering wheel.

The road was rutted gravel, seemingly leading to nowhere. It dipped and climbed along the lake's craggy, forested shore, going on and on until he was afraid he'd missed the turnoff.

But then he came to it, a dirt track that led down through the trees as his heart started pounding again and he drove out onto a bluff overlooking the lake where there was a group of wooden buildings, two of them barracks-like, just as David had said, and a pair of vans, one new and the other old and psychedelically painted.

Tom turned off the engine and stepped out of his car. He leaned against it, looking around. He didn't see anyone at first. Then a group of young men in overalls and young women in gray shifts began filing out of an octagonal building, apparently without seeing him. They dispersed toward the barrack-like buildings, the men going to one, the women to the other.

Angela was among the women.

He called to her. She stopped, stood gaping, and he walked up to her.

"I knew you'd find me somehow."

"Your letter helped. I could read the postmark. It was a nice letter."

She wouldn't look at him. His heart had stopped pounding. "How *are* you?"

"I'm fine," she said. She looked at him now. "You?"

"Not sure."

It had been only three months since their breakup in Mexico, but she looked remarkably different. The soft beauty of her face that in the days before their breakup could turn hard and almost ugly had been restored, even enhanced. He had a clue as to why this was. He himself had developed an acid discharge during their troubles. After the breakup, that condition disappeared.

A tall, fair-haired young man with movie star good looks

came out of the octagonal building and walked over to them to stand possessively beside Angela.

"Klaus, this is Tom. My husband," she told him.

"Ah," Klaus said. "So very pleased to meet you." Tom noted his German accent and the mocking tone in his voice.

They didn't shake hands.

"Tom and I need to talk, Klaus," Angela said. "See you later."

"You are sure, Angela? I'll be close by," he told her.

"Please. I'll be all right," Angela said, smiling warmly at him. Tom tried not to feel anything.

She led him to the gazebo-like building overlooking the lake. They sat on the bench outside it.

"Your letter," he said. "It gave me some hope."

"I didn't mean it to," she said. "I'm sorry. I just wanted you to know that I still cared for you but that we couldn't be married anymore."

"That still true?"

She was quiet. Then: "You must hate me."

"Christ, Angie. I still love you."

"I still love *you!* Oh God," she said, "when you showed up here today, out of the blue, my heart stopped. And now I wish you'd stick around. That's kind of sick, isn't it?"

Some of his exasperation—his rage!—at her mixed-up, cruel honesty welled up. "Sounds like you'd like to have me in reserve," he said, tasting his bitterness.

She gave a weak little laugh. "No. Maybe. That *is* sick."

He longed to take her in his arms, to ease his turmoil. He moved toward her. She drew back. That stopped him as if he'd hit a wall.

"Anyway," he said, "I found you finally. I was really worried about you. You sure you're okay?"

"You were *worried* about me? Then how come you didn't stay in Puerto Bonito until I'd made up my mind?"

"What? According to Richard, you didn't want me hanging around there. He said you wanted me to go back to Trujano and wait up *there* until you made up your mind."

Angela simply stared at him. "He . . . I told him to tell you I needed more time to think things out. To wait in Puerto Bonito."

"He told me what best served his fucking interests! I took his word for it. I went back to Trujano and waited up there for ten of the longest fucking days of my life!"

Angela gripped his hands. "I'm so sorry," she said. I went back to Bonito finally, with Richard, but you were gone, just as Richard said you'd be."

"Of course I was gone! Just as Richard fucking knew I'd be. By your supposed request. By his goddamn, self-serving lie!"

"My God," Angela said. She looked away, then at him again. "Oh Tom, I was so bummed out after we split up. He took advantage of that. He took advantage of *us!*"

"No shit!"

Tom began to think—to wildly hope. They'd both been duped. But now they *knew*, they could start over. Couldn't they?

Angela's eyes softened. "Just tell me where you'll be," she said. "You staying in Canada? Going back to the States?"

"I'm in a commune called New Eden about a hundred miles south of here. It's in an old logging camp on Purcell Lake, across from a town called Galena."

"Maybe we'll visit you sometime."

"You and that German dude?"

"Maybe."

"How you fixed for money?"

"I'm okay," she said.

He pulled out his wallet and gave her all the bills it contained: two hundred dollars. She hesitated, then took it.

"You have more, I hope."

"I have enough to last me a while," he said. "You have more money too. I left half our savings back in Chicago for you."

"Thank you."

They stood facing each other. He saw something like love in her eyes. He tried to show some love back to her.

"I . . . I'm all right myself now. I've maybe found somebody," he told her.

"I'm glad," she said.

His ears were ringing with the tension between them.

"Be happy," Angela said.

"You too."

She looked away and Tom said, "So this is goodbye, I guess."

"I guess."

"Take care of yourself."

"You too."

He did an about face and walked back to his car without turning around for a last look at her, for maybe a farewell wave, for some signal that all was well. It was a supreme act of will, an empty, stupid gesture of stupid pride.

Chapter 18

Angela watched Tom walk away without so much as a goodbye wave and felt a part of her running after him (*Wait! Stop!*) as he climbed into his car and drove away, drove out of her life.

That he could just leave her here, in this weird, unsettling place. Okay, she was with Klaus, and he was exciting enough, but he wasn't Tom, her husband of five years, who was so safe and solid and familiar, and maybe that was the trouble. That night at Sue and Cliff's party when they first met and she saw genuineness, gentleness in his smiling, open face. That he wasn't so gentle as he seemed, that he was full of impotent rage at times, a frustrated writer, chained to the rat race—that he could be frightening, though never threatening—she soon discovered. She thought she saw some of her father in him, his manly strength without her father's conventionality, his uptightness. Yet Tom *was* conventional in his own way; uptight in his way, and a disappointment finally. No, not a disappointment so much as not what she wanted finally, what she thought she needed.

Had their five years together been a mistake, a waste of time? What *was* it, exactly, that she wanted, that she thought she needed? Was it only the excitement of somebody new? What Tom perhaps was experiencing now? At his mention of somebody else she'd felt a surprising stab of jealousy, an unwarranted sense of betrayal, a choking wad of fury!

You weren't supposed to feel jealousy anymore. Jealousy was passé. Possessiveness was out. She should be free of jealousy, free of possessiveness, free of her unhappy, unfashionable, mixed-up feelings that would never leave her, she thought helplessly. Never.

Chapter 19

Tom took his time driving back to New Eden. He might have kept going—to the border, to somewhere else. To Vancouver, maybe, or back to Mexico. Back to Chicago even—back to journalism. He would run out of money soon. He was an illegal alien here. He'd be discovered eventually, maybe deported.

When he came to the lovely valley across the river with its farms and cows in pasture, he turned off onto a gravel road that took him to the river's bank. He pulled over and got out of his car. There was a landing here, and a cable ferry just starting across from the other side with only one vehicle on it, a farm truck carrying a load of loose hay. The ferry bumped against the concrete landing, lowered its ramp, and the truck drove off. The man at the wheel, a guy wearing a wool cap, nodded to Tom as he passed. Tom nodded back.

On impulse, he walked onto the ferry and was followed by a couple of cars. Then the ferryman (actually a woman), up on the bridge, started them across the river. The river was in spring flood, pushing against the craft, straining the cables, sliding the ferry a little sideways in the current. Tom, leaning against the railing, looked upriver to where the valley narrowed and gave way to the mountains and thought, *I could live here.*

He got off on the other side and walked down a dirt road to a little settlement: a store, filling station, some houses. In the store the middle-aged woman behind the counter sold him a candy bar, asked where he was from.

"Down the valley," he told her.

"Oh," she said. "One of our refugee Americans."

The sugar rush only increased his emptiness, his lost feeling. Where to go now ? What to do?

He walked back to the landing where a logging truck, its empty bed folded back on itself, and the inevitable pickup and a couple of mud-strewn cars waited in line. The ferry was just pulling in. Its ramp clanged down and the vehicles drove onto the deck. Tom walked aboard and the ferry started back across the river.

He watched the sun descending behind the western slopes, felt the air turn chilly as the ferry floated into shadow. The gathering darkness, the evening cold flowing down from the mountains—he felt the darkness, felt the cold.

The ferry bumped ashore. He began walking toward his car. He was shivering, yet all at once he felt exhilarated; ahead lay shelter, warmth, the warmth of human company.

Two hours later he was on the old logging road approaching New Eden. The sun was long gone behind the mountains and it was almost dark. When he stopped the car and stepped out to piss, he could see his breath. But it was May, the merry month of May and the days, if not the nights, were getting warmer. It would be summer soon, the first summer of the new decade, and the world around him was green and growing and he was starting over.

Chapter 20

One evening after supper the guy from Detroit named Clay, ex-grad student in sociology, who never seemed to smile, suddenly brightened and came up with an idea. Why not spend some of the money David had just contributed to the communal stash to buy a turntable and an amplifier and then a gas-powered generator to make electricity for it? In addition, they might rig up a couple of lights in the hall.

"We're missing some great music," he told the group. "All the good rock bands now? Judy and John are fine, but I been looking at our record collection here. We got some great stuff, but we can't play it. Everything from Dylan and Baez to Judy Collins and Jefferson Airplane. Grace Slick! Steppenwolf and The Grateful Dead—the Rolling Stones! It's *our* music, and I for one miss it."

"I miss it too," Helen said, surprisingly. You would have thought her taste ran to Fifties doo-wop. "Maybe just a simple record player?"

"Me too," Janice said, which wasn't surprising. She was New Eden's newest member, whom Mark found wandering in Galena one day, wooed her, and brought her out to New Eden. Her story was she'd run away to San Francisco during the so-called Summer of Love from some hick town in Saskatchewan and been on the road ever since. She was pretty in a stray-cat kind of way—looked, Tom imagined, like any number of the attractive waifs you'd have seen in the Haight-Ashbury around 1967.

"What do *you* think, David?" Joel said. "Any objection to spending some of the money you've added to the kitty in this maybe frivolous way?"

"All of it, you mean. Anyway, I wouldn't call it frivolous," he said. "Rock was our music, too, over in Nam."

"Wait a minute," Sarah said. "There's some practical things we need around here. Like a chainsaw for cutting firewood. Like maybe a canoe for crossing the lake when we're snowed-in this winter. Tom thinks—"

"Besides," broke in Robert, the Professor, suddenly the purist among them, "I thought we were going back to basics here. Won't this be like a copout? Running a gas motor half the time just so's we can listen to the Stones? Think of the fuel cost. Think of how we'd be helping to pollute the planet. You start making compromises like this and pretty soon you're back in the System. No," he said. "My vote is no."

Everyone started talking at once.

"Quiet!" said Helen.

The pandemonium continued until Mark jumped to his feet and shouted, "Hey! Let's all shut the fuck up for a minute!"

The group went quiet. Joel said, "Thank you, Mark. Okay, let's go around the table." He started with Helen. "What do

155

you think, honey?"

"I don't like the idea of having to run a noisy motor to give us power," she said, "but really, I'm all for more music. Couldn't we get it some other way? As for electric lights, who needs them? Candles are fine, as far as I'm concerned."

"Hear, hear," said the Professor.

"If we can find a way to make electricity without a gas engine, I'm all for it," Helen said.

"Me too," said Chuck.

"I'd dig it," Mark said.

"All right," said Sarah. "But anyway, we'll still need a chainsaw before winter."

"Granted," Joel said. "But for now, music's the thing, it seems, and if I'm hearing you people right the next step is to figure out some source of environmentally OK power."

"Right," said the Professor, pulling off his glasses as if to aid his thinking. "I see two alternative sources here. One, the creek. Maybe we can rig up some sort of hydroelectric thing. Or two—how about solar power?"

"Not enough sun," Mark said.

"In the winter, maybe," Robert said. "But it's spring now, and summer's coming. Of course there seems to be a lot of cloudy days here in the mountains, but in summer won't we get enough sun? Anyway, I don't know much about it, but with solar power, or water power, or with a gas turbine, won't we need storage batteries?

"Anybody here *into* this kind of thing?" Joel asked.

"What about the *Whole Earth Catalog*?" Sarah suggested. "There must be something in *there* about alternative forms of power."

"Great idea!" said Clay.

But unbelievably, a check of New Eden's random library found *that* counterculture resource to be missing.

`"Shit," Mark said. "We could try Harmony Farm. *They* must have it."

"Anyway, we're looking at a trip into Silver City," Clay said.

"You know what this is?" Joel said excitedly. "This is anarchism in the best sense of the term! Who's in charge here? Nobody. This is group process, group problem solving."

"Hey," Sarah said now. "We're forgetting our own musicians." She turned to Judy and John. "We wouldn't be taking away from you guys, would we?"

"Don't be silly," Judy said.

"No way," John said.

Joel's eyes fell on Tom.

"What about you, Tom? You with us now? Whatta *you* think?"

And that's when Tom decided that, yes, he was with these folks. "I guess I'm for it," he said. "I don't know anything about making electricity off the grid, but with all of us turning to, I suppose we can do it, one way or another."

"All in favour . . ." Joel said.

Tom looked over at Sarah. And liked the way she looked back at him.

The expedition to seek out and purchase, if affordable, a sound system and a generator to provide power for it, set out for Silver City a couple of days later. It had been decided, after all, that some alternative, ecologically friendly form of creating power would be nice, but how long and at what cost would it take to rig up, say, a Pelton wheel, and would it even work? Now that hearing good, recorded music again was a possibility, nobody wanted to wait. The sure mechanical means for it won out.

Initially everybody wanted to go to Silver City—they were all ready for a trip to town—but there wasn't room for everybody, even in their two vehicles. So Helen volunteered to stay behind with Brightness. Then Judy and John opted to stay with their twin boys. Janice, after living on the street in Vancouver, was really digging the country, she said, and would be happy to stay too. Then Mark, though he'd been eager to go, decided to stay with Janice.

Tom took three in his car, Sarah up front with him, Chuck and David in back. Joel, driving the commune's truck, wedged Clay and Robert in the cab with him. They set out after breakfast. It was a fine May morning, a Saturday. It felt like a holiday.

They stopped for gas in Galena, then headed down the Purcell Valley, the road winding between wooded slopes and lofty crags on their left and the Purcell River, swollen with spring runoff and lined with cottonwood and birch in full leaf, on their right. They crossed several bridges over several flooded, whitewater creeks flowing toward the river, and came at last to where the Purcell emptied into the Sturgeon. Here they turned left onto the highway that took them along the south bank of that river into Silver City.

Approaching the orange bridge that would take them across the river to the town, Tom thought of his first sight of San Francisco from the Oakland side of the Bay. Silver City, in fact (population 10,000), was like a miniature San Francisco, its mostly wooden houses climbing the slopes above the

Sturgeon River that might serve for the Bay and the bridge for the Golden Gate.

They were a jolly group that, after parking their vehicles on an uphill street, all but skipped down the sidewalk, past some of the town's gawking citizens, to the town centre along Sproule Avenue.

"Invasion of the hippies, right?" Tom said jauntily.

"Yeah," Clay said. "But they're probably wondering what *you're* doing with us. You still look pretty straight, man."

"Consider me in transition," Tom said, which got a laugh.

On Sproule, they decided to split up, Joel and Clay and Robert to go down the street to Radio Shack to check out speakers, an amp, and a turntable; Tom and Sarah, David and Chuck, to head down to Silver City Industrial on River Street to look at generators and storage batteries.

"Where'll we meet? When?" Joel wanted to know.

"What about that Chinese joint across the street?" Robert suggested.

"I'm not big on Chinese," Clay said. "How about the A&W?"

"Chinese is good," said Sarah. "And a lot healthier."

"Let's take a vote," Joel said. "Those for Chinese in the Western Star?"

Everybody raised their hand except Clay.

"Majority rules," Joel said. "Meet there in, say, an hour?"

"An hour might not be enough," Sarah said.

"An hour and a half then. Two hours max."

Two hours later they were all sitting in the Western Star restaurant eating chop suey and drinking green tea and talking over what they'd found in Silver City for their project.

Joel and company had priced an expensive but necessary, Clay insisted, sound system.

The whole package, amplifier, speakers, turntable, would cost some two hundred bucks. David and his group found that a gas generator, a couple of truck batteries, wiring, receptacles, etc., would cost around five hundred.

In short, they were short of money.

"Why don't we just buy a simple record player?" Sarah said. "Like Helen suggested. You know, one of those portable jobs that closes up like a little suitcase."

"Nah," said Clay. "Those are no good. We want a decent sound system, don't we?"

"Okay, so whattaya think, people?" Joel said. "We dip deeper into the communal pot?"

"What, go back for it?" Robert asked.

"Not necessary," Joel revealed now. "Helen and I have a little savings account here—strictly for emergencies, you understand. I'm sure I can draw enough out of it to pay the rest of what we owe here."

"You and Helen have a private little bank account?" Sarah said. "Isn't that interesting."

"It isn't private anymore, Sarah," Joel told her.

"Makes you wonder, though," she said. "Who else among us has a private stash?"

"We could maybe have a meeting about it when we get back," Robert suggested. "Air the possibility that others in the commune have been holding out."

"We're getting off topic here, people," Joel reminded them.

"Yeah, Clay said. "Do we use some of Joel's private money

now or not? I say we do. Let's complete our business."

"I don't know," Sarah persisted. "Isn't there something a little disappointing about all this?"

It took them a day to rig up the generator and the storage batteries and do the wiring to supply power to the hall for the sound system and, while they were at it, a light in the kitchen to make preparing the evening meal there a little easier. David did most of the work. Turned out he knew more about mechanical and electronic stuff than anybody.

Two nights later, after enduring the sound of the generator for a couple of hours to charge the battery, David, by unanimous vote, got the honour of putting the first record on the turntable. He pulled Steppenwolf's first album out of the communal stack and dropped the needle on "Born to be Wild." Everybody started shouting along with it like it was the national anthem.

Born to be wild! Born to be wild!

A jug of red wine was opened and passed around, joints were rolled, lit, and passed around and they all got a little drunk and a little stoned. The kids got a little stoned, it appeared, simply by breathing the second-hand smoke. They were seldom put to bed until their parents decided to crash, Tom had noticed, and now the twin boys strolled around the hall with the adults, little Brightness too for a while, until she slumped to the floor with a sleepy smile on her pretty face. By that time the adults as well were lolling about, grooving on the music.

Janis Joplin's hoarse vocal straining was on the turntable, then the sweet voice of Judy Collins. When she launched into the title song of her great album of a couple of years ago, Tom, as always, sank into nostalgia.

Who knows
where the time goes?

Helen suddenly sprang up and charged into the kitchen. Presently she came out with a big smile and a huge bowl of popcorn. It was soon empty. Tom, high as a kite, had a sudden yen for something sweet. In the kitchen—*great!*—he found a jar of peanut butter and a jar of honey. He looked for shredded coconut. Shit, didn't find any. Okay, he made a pile of peanut butter balls without coconut, stuffed his mouth with one, and took the rest out to the hall. There was a communal grab for them, and they were gone.

The evening rocked on, an orgy of good music and good dope and shouted talk and spontaneous singing, as if the music they were listening to and the dope they were smoking formed the basis of who they were. It was a bonding, a celebration.

"All power to the people!" Joel yelled.

"Right on!" came the chorus. "All power to the people!"

Brightness started to cry, which caused Helen to rush over to her. "Oh honey," she told her. "Mama forgot all about you."

And she took her little daughter's hand and led her into the kitchen, where Brightness slept on the floor next to the warmth of the old-fashioned range.

Judy and John's little boys, reclining in a dark corner, had fallen asleep leaning comically against each other. Judy, some-what contritely, woke them and she and John lifted them up to carry them to the bunkhouse. "Good night, comrades," John called as they left the hall.

Things mellowed out after that under the influence of what Mark, who'd scored it, said was prime Kootenay Green.

Tom, sitting next to Sarah on the plank floor of the candle-lit hall, their backs against the log wall, her warm body touching his, was overcome by mixed emotions, lust and sorrow, his loss of Angela, together with the thrill of this other woman. He didn't know what to do about it. Then he did.

He put his arm around her. She leaned into him. After a moment, she said, "Let's go," and stood up. He stood up with her and she took his hand. Holding hands, they walked out of the hall and felt their way across the dark clearing to Sarah's tent.

Chapter 21

One evening Shelly handed Angela a note inviting her to Mustafa's quarters for "your interview." It was after the evening meal and Angela was helping with the cleanup in the hall kitchen.

The note was typewritten on fancy letterhead, the word "Ramala" embossed at the top of the sheet in black, medieval-looking script. It was signed "Mustafa" in a large, assertive scrawl.

"My interview?" Angela asked. "What *that's* about?"

"Depends," Shelly said.

"On *what*, may I ask?"

"On your individual case," Shelly told her. "That's about all I can say. We're not supposed to talk about our interviews with Paul, I mean Mustafa. They're personal."

"My *case*?"

"Your situation. Who you are and where you're at."

"Where I'm at?"

"Yeah, where you *are*, personally, spiritually, psychologically. What's holding you together and what's pulling you apart."

"He some kind of psychoanalyst?"

"He's much more than that," Shelly told her.

"Well, he won't psychoanalyse *me*," Angela said. The prospect frightened her a little.

"Oh, he'll get things out of you," Shelly assured her. "But don't worry, honey. It'll be to your benefit and strictly between you and Mustafa. To reveal anything about your interview, he says, is at your peril."

"At my peril?" Angela said. Now she wanted to laugh.

Mustafa's quarters took up the entire top floor of the octagonal building, divided into his bedroom, his study-cum-sitting room, and the only indoor bathroom on the premises. His bathroom included a shower and flush toilet (the dorms each had a shower and compost rather than flush toilets outside the dorms). The water for Mustafa's establishment was supplied by a gravity fed line out of one of the creeks flowing into the lake, the intake for which was somewhere above the buildings. It was a simple, wonderfully effective system. Who had devised it all? Angela had wondered upon her arrival here. Then she learned it was Klaus, and wasn't surprised. She didn't have to ask, by that time, who had paid for it—who had paid for this whole setup. Mustafa, Paul, had money, but where did it come from?

Mustafa sat behind his small desk and Angela stood defiantly before him now, prepared to fight or flee.

"Foist off," he said with what Angela now knew was a New Orleans accent,"when people are drawn to me, ah like to know where they're all comin' from. Where they're *at*. S'down, darlin."

Angela sat in the straight-backed chair in front of his desk. "I wasn't drawn to you," she told him. "I didn't know anything about you until I hitched a ride with Klaus and let him bring me here."

"Y'all think that was an accident?" Mustafa asked.

He was in one of his embroidered, expensive looking robes, and had something like a fez on his head. He pulled a pack of cigarettes from a drawer in his desk and offered one to Angela. She declined. He reminded her now of the avuncular old rabbi who'd prepared her for her bat mitzvah.

"How y'all like Ramala so far?"

"It's interesting," Angela allowed. "I'm not sure I like it, though."

She noticed the bookshelf beside his desk. On it were titles Angela recognized because they were among Tom's books in their Chicago apartment, books he'd acquired as a lapsed, though not completely fallen away, Catholic: *The Desert Fathers,* St. Paul's *Epistles*, Augustine's *Confessions*. And she wasn't surprised to see a copy of the Knopf hardbound edition of Kahlil Gibran's *The Prophet,* the very book Tom gave her on the anniversary of their first year together and which she'd found both beautiful and rather trite. She remembered Gibran's beautiful face on the back cover and all at once knew who Paul Thibideau, alias Mustafa, resembled—perhaps by design.

Mustafa puffed on his cigarette. "Okay, y'all maybe find it a little too strict, too controlled right now. But to hold people togetha, ya gotta have organization, *disc*ipline. Along with a common goal, ya dig?"

"And what is *your* goal?" Angela asked.

Mustafa smiled. "In a word, *transcendence*. A higha plane."

"A higher plane?"

"Look, we all come into this mortal coil with a body and a mind. With a spirit and a soul. Our body's what we're stuck with, okay? and it ages, deteriorates. Our mind, too. Body and mind, they're gonna cease to exist. We're all gonna die! But our spirit, more especially our *soul*, that's gonna live on, and so why not seek to join it, *now*, disembody ourselves—oh, yeah, it can be done, I'm sure—and in effect *leave* this mortal coil, this, let's face it, imperfect world while we're still alive?"

Mustafa's face was distorted with intensity. It was funny, a little frightening.

"You were Catholic, I guess," Angela said. "Like my husband."

"Yes, but I'm way beyond that now."

"Catholicism has this thing about the body—the flesh—versus the spirit, right?"

Mustafa, or Paul—his New Orleans accent, his faintly hip way of speaking, was serving to cancel out his made-up exotic name and the patriarchal robes he affected—waved that off and smiled again. He sucked on his cigarette, inhaling deeply, then snubbed it out in a stone ashtray. Smoke issued from his mouth and nose. "Okay, let's get down to it. Everybody has an *aura*, gives off certain vibes. You're no exception, Angela. You're sad, I think. Maybe a little lost."

His easy assumption of her state of being angered her, mostly because he was right. She stood up.

"Wait! It's nothin' to be ashamed of, darlin'. Most of my

167

people were lost when they came to me. That's why they came. S'down again. *Please.*"

Angela remained standing. "We have nothing to say to each other."

"Oh, but we *do*, hear? Y'all are fuckin' Klaus now, for instance. *No-no!* It's all right, y'all haven't transcended yet. Neither has Klaus, sad to say. You're both still of the body. Saint Augustine, for instance, he—"

"Came up with the idea of Original Sin, didn't he? Eve the temptress?" Angela said.

Mustafa smiled. "Klaus was a tempter. He was a beautiful boy, and so lost when he came to me."

An image of Mustafa with the lost, teenage Klaus popped loathsomely into Angela's head.

"He's like a son to me," Mustafa went on. "And like a wayward son, he rebelled against his father. He left Ramala and took Shelly and Mike with him. But they're back now. He's back."

"The prodigal returned, huh?"

Mustafa smiled. "We all have our stories," he said. "We've all come from somewhere. We've all had our troubles."

Angela turned to leave.

"Come back! You need to talk about your breakup, your failed marriage."

"That's none of your business!" Angel said. Tears came to her eyes. She wiped them angrily away.

"Among other things," Mustafa said, "I've done a little psychological counselling. I can see you're in distress over the breakup of your marriage. *Sit. Down.*"

She sat down. What she wanted was to lie down and curl

up. More tears came. She let them come.

"How old are you?"

"Twenty-four."

"How old were you when you married?"

"Nineteen."

"Were you a virgin?"

"No."

"So you had relations with other men before you met your husband?"

'No!"

"You were abused?"

"No!"

"So you and your husband had sex before your marriage?"

"We lived together."

"And you eventually married. Then what?"

"I got antsy after a couple of years, okay? Other guys started looking really good to me."

"Of course. Y'all married too young. And your husband was your first. We're not naturally monogamous," Mustafa told her, as if she didn't know that by now.

"Tom is ten years older than me," Angela said, "and I guess he was ready to settle down and I wasn't. I missed the excitement of when we were first together, okay? I missed the romance. Tom just liked living together."

"You were bored."

"Then we—that is *I*— decided to have a baby. I, and then *we*, thought that would solve things."

"Oh yeah. Parenthood." Mustafa laughed until it brought on a fit of coughing. "That only complicates things, darlin."

"Turned out we couldn't have a child of our own, which

was just as well, probably. And now," Angela said, "now that he's found me, I realize I *wanted* him to find me. I want him around, which is crazy because I'm with Klaus now. It's like I want *both* of them."

It was a relief to have suddenly realized it, to have expressed it. Also a humiliation to have shared it with this creep.

"Ah, what a fucked-up piece of work is a man," Mustafa told Angela. "Or a woman. Until one transcends."

"So that's what this place is about?"

"Part of it," Mustafa said. He leaned toward her over his desk, his face frighteningly intense again. "What'd y'all learn from Klaus? Or Shelly, or Mike? What'd they tell you about me—about Ramala—while ya'll were driving up from Mexico?"

"Nothing much, but I got the idea this was some kind of doomsday trip. Mike started to say something about it, but Klaus shut him up. It would scare me, he said."

Mustafa jerked to his feet. His dark eyes seemed to shoot at her. "That's it!" he cried. "What's going to happen *will* be scary—for those who aren't beyond it. *We will be.* That's the thing! That's what Ramala is about! It's what achieving *pure*, and ah mean *literal* spirituality, will do for us! Complete detachment! It'll free us from the terror, the *pain*, of what's to come! We'll be *able*, in effect, to float above it, beyond it! We'll have removed ourselves. We'll have *ascended, transcended!*"

"What's to come?" Angela asked evenly, careful not to show any alarm now.

"There's gonna be a war!" Mustafa cried. "Our bad history's gonna catch up to us. It's gonna do us in! The Nigras—excuse me, *Negroes*—in their ghettos, the Native Americans on their reservations, all the peoples of colour, they're gonna rise up! They're gonna join together. Which is only meet and just," he quickly added. "We all gotta pay for our sins. There's gotta to be retribution!"

"Why not join their cause?" Angela said. "Have you thought of that?"

"They won't have us!" Mustafa shouted. "And why should they? We done them wrong. We're tainted with the sins of our history. There's no hope for us unless we remove ourselves, lift ourselves, up and out of our physical plane, our grievous fallibility, through the achievement of pure spirituality, through mortal possession of our immortal souls!"

Mustafa slumped back in his chair. He rubbed his forehead, as if he'd given himself a headache. "It's exhaustin' though. What I'm tryin' to do here, tryin' to *teach*. It's utterly exhaustin! It's demoralizin'."

His dark eyes deepened, seemed to flow toward Angela.

"Y'all are so beautiful," he said. "Y'all know that? My God, it's no wonder Klaus is fuckin' you."

"I'd like to go now," Angela said.

"Tomorra then," Mustafa said. "After the midday meal. We'll resume."

"I'll look forward to it," Angela said and stood up from her chair, turned and walked, did not run, out of Mustafa's study.

Chapter 22

They were at their evening meal, without the need for candles anymore because of the lengthening days, when the hall door opened and a young woman, burdened with a pack and obviously exhausted, stepped inside and looked uncertainly around her.

It was Angela.

Tom sprang up from the table and rushed toward her as her face seem to break apart upon seeing him.

"I was afraid you wouldn't be here," she said.

He'd been sitting with Sarah, whose eyes he could feel behind him now. He wanted to turn around to keep his connection to her, perhaps reassure her—or himself—but he could only stare at Angela and feel his heart going out to her. "C'mon," he said.

He led her outside. The evening cold had slid down from the mountains. Angela was shivering.

"We can go in the bunkhouse," he said, motioning in its direction. "It'll be empty now, and a little warmer in there."

She followed him across the clearing without speaking, putting herself entirely in his hands, it seemed, as if he knew what to do with her now, what to do with *them*. He yanked open the bunkhouse door—it was a little warped, tended to stick—and they went inside and sat on one of the bunks. She loosened her pack and let it drop to the floor.

"What happened, Angela? How did you get here?" He meant to be gentle with her but sounded stern.

"I had to leave that place," she said. "I just walked away from it."

"You walked? Literally? Where to? That little logging town, what's its name? You couldn't get a ride from somebody, that guy you were with?"

"I didn't ask. Anyway, it was at night. Everybody was sleeping."

"You left there *at night*? By your*self* ? Out there in the middle of nowhere, in the dark?"

The thought of her walking along the wilderness shore of Heron Lake, alone and in the dark, in bear and cougar country, all the way to that tiny outpost . . . Douglas. He remembered its name, suddenly.

"Yes."

"You walked all the way to Douglas? At night? Did you get a ride from there?"

"Yes. I was lucky. It was getting light by then, and there was a truck being loaded with lumber. The driver gave me a ride to Galena."

"How'd you know where to find me?"

"You told me where you were, remember?"

Angela lay back on the bunk and closed her eyes. Tom looked around for something to cover her.

"Angie, did you walk all the way out here from Galena too? How did you know where we were?"

"I found a gas station open. The nice attendant there knew where you were. He gave me directions."

An image of the station's red-faced attendant, eyes twinkling, popped into Tom's mind.

"Aw honey."

"I'm so tired," she said.

"Let's find you a bed."

"Don't *you* have a bed? Can't I share it?"

"Not exactly."

He'd been with Sarah lately, in her tent, without having actually moved out of Chuck's shack. Could they go there?

"I don't have a place of my own yet," he told her.

"Why not?" Her slightly accusatory tone irked him a little. She closed her eyes again.

He looked around. There were three double bunks in the place, all being used but not all of the bunks taken. Who bedded down in here now? Clay and Robert, Tom reminded himself, Mark and Janice. He could guess that the one double over which a cloth had been hung, for privacy, was Janice's—or Mark and Janice's. That left Robert and Clay, who instead of sharing a double had each taken a double, leaving a top bunk vacant on the one and a bottom on the other. Tom could guess that the bottom bunk, on which Angela was lying now, was Robert's—he couldn't see him climbing the ladder.

Angela sat up. "What's that smell? Smells like skunk."

"Packrat," Tom said.

"What's that?"

"A kind of wood rat. There was one in here when the group took over this place, I hear."

He was aware now of *her* smell, strong, sour-sweet, composed of exhaustion, he supposed, emotional turmoil, maybe a residue of her German boyfriend—*ex*-boyfriend, maybe.

She said dully, "I shouldn't be here. I don't know *where* I should be."

"What happened?" he asked again. "Weren't you with that German dude? You have a fight?"

"Sort of. He wouldn't leave with me."

"Why did *you* leave?"

"I had to," she said. "They wanted my soul."

"They what?"

She had tears in her eyes. He put his arms around her. She responded by grabbing onto him as if afraid he was going to let go.

"I'm here, Angie," he told her. "I'm here for you now."

"Please," she said. "Can we make love?"

But she was all sharp edges in his arms, and then her smell—it was something of a turnoff.

"Not now," he said.

She jerked away from him, lay back on the bunk.

"Wait," he said. "I'll be back."

He went out and across the clearing to Chuck's shack, where he'd left his sleeping bag after moving in with Sarah. Chuck wasn't there, thankfully. He found his bag and carried it to the bunkhouse. It was dark in there now. He found a candle and a box of matches, lit the candle and placed it on the floor by the unused lower bunk. Then he realized it needed a mattress. Incredibly, he found one, rolled up in a corner. It was dusty, mouldy, chewed into by mice, but it would have to serve. He carried it to the bunk and placed it on the bare boards. Then he unfurled his sleeping bag and laid it on the mattress.

He went over to where Angela was lying.

"I've made a bed for you."

"I need to wash," she said.

"There's an outside shower behind the hall," he told her. "Kind of primitive. Just a five-gallon pail with holes in it. We heat the water for it in the kitchen."

"Can't I bathe in the lake?"

"It's freezing cold."

"I don't care."

He walked with her to the shore and stood by as she got out of the Mexican wool poncho they bought one day in the Oaxaca market, then the Mexican blouse and sandals bought there another day, finally her panties and the wool socks and jeans bought when they were still happily (maybe not so happily) living in Chicago. Naked, she waded, without cringing, into the lake and rubbed the frigid water on herself, then plunged in and sprang out of it, gasping. She came shivering out of the lake, Tom threw the poncho over her and they raced back to the bunkhouse. It was still empty. It occurred to Tom that the others might be allowing them this privacy.

He led Angela to the bed he'd made. Unzipped his sleeping bag and opened it for her. She climbed into it. He made as if to tuck her in.

"Can't we lie together at least?"

"There isn't room."

"I'll make room."

She unzipped the bag all the way and pulled it over her, then opened it for him. "See? Come on."

He lay down next to her and she covered them. The bare mattress stank of mould. The bunk was narrow and they lay stiffly together at first, finally snuggled up out of old familiarity. It was like coming home again. It was as if they'd never been apart.

Chapter 23

But they *had* been apart, and by the next morning some of his hurt and anger, some of hers, returned to plague them.

During the night, though, it had seemed they might reconcile, that things might be that simple. Snuggled up together, as if nothing had ever come between them, Tom began to feel his old, untested love for Angela. He fell asleep, then woke to find himself pushing against her soft buttocks and her pushing back. They made love then, for the first time since Mexico, since a lot of days before their separation on that hot, unhappy morning over four months ago now in Puerto Bonito. Doggy style at first. Then face to face, fused, her legs wrapped around him. She moaned, called him "Baby," a lovers' term he'd never heard from her before, one she had to have picked up from another lover. Then all he wanted was to get *off* in her, while Angela met him with something like his own grim determination. It was exciting, at first. But then she stopped

participating, just lay back and took it, so it more like mastur-
bating than lovemaking.

And so the spell was broken, the magic gone.

In the morning Tom went looking for Sarah. He found her in
the garden, not topless this time, though it was a hot day and
felt like summer.

"Look who's here," she said. She was making shallow
trenches in the turned-over soil with a hoe, then dropping
seeds into them at intervals and covering them over.

"You all right?" he asked.

"I'm fine," she said. "How are you?"

"Okay."

"Just okay? Not perfectly reconciled? Not on a second
honeymoon?"

Her sarcasm was rather flattering.

"We have what you might call unresolved issues," Tom told
her. "Some bitter shit still between us."

"You obviously love each other."

"I guess. Anyway, Sarah, I'm sorry if . . ."

"It's all right," she said, "David's been hitting on me for
some time. We finally made it last night. I've maybe found my
true love."

"Good for you," Tom said.

"So you're off the hook," Sarah told him, and pulled a
packet of seeds from the bag slung over her shoulder.

"What's that you're planting?"

"Lettuce, carrots, broccoli. Lots of squash. I've planted
corn, too, but I doubt we'll get a crop. The soil's too poor
here. We need more compost. And something to sweeten the

soil—bone meal, phosphate or potash."

"The manure should help."

"Wanna give me a hand?"

"Sure," Tom said.

"See those poles? You can help me set them for the beans."

She'd cut saplings in the woods along the lakeshore with the communal ax, chopped them into lengths of eight feet or so and lopped off their branches. Now she had him make four tripods with the poles, tying each together with twine.

"Follow me," she said, and together they carried the poles to a corner of the garden, where she spread the poles of a tripod and pushed the butts into the turned-over soil.

"Can you set the rest?"

"Yup."

`"Not too close," she instructed. "Space them a couple of feet apart."

She watched him place the next tripod. Allowed a smile. "You never had a garden on your farm?"

"Never could. Didn't I tell you? The cows always got into it."

"That's what a fence is for."

"They always broke *through* the fence. This one should keep the deer out, though."

"We'll see," said Sarah.

Angela said, "I saw you working in the garden with Sarah. You looked like a couple."

"Are *we* a couple?"

"We used to be."

"Christ. You think we'll ever be again?"

"I'm here. Maybe we're in a place now where we can live

together without owning each other."

Tom thought about that, then couldn't help mentioning what was bothering him. "You called me *baby* last night when we were making love," he said. "Where'd you learn *that* little term of endearment—from Ricardo or that German guy at the ashram or whatever the fuck it is?"

"Stop it."

"We started *out* making love last night, but it turned into something else, wouldn't you say?"

"Can you just stop it?"

He took a deep breath, blew it out. "Dammit," he said, and felt such a wave of his old helplessness and such an ache of frustration and love.

Chapter 24

New Eden wasn't anything like Ramala, Angela was relieved to discover. There was the discipline of communal work, taking turns at cooking, the cleaning up afterwards, looking after the children who, apparently without formal agreement, were obviously a communal responsibility. Not that Judy and John didn't attend to their twin boys, nor Joel and Helen to little Brightness.

But it was something the way people here seemed to be managing together, free of Mustafa/Paul Thibideau's paranoid creed and Ramala's private school-like regimentation. Here people were more or less like-minded, she guessed, fellow dissidents, peace-and-love advocates, dedicated to the back-to-the-land thing, but free and easy too. She thought she was going to like it here. She and Tom might even make it here together—or maybe they wouldn't, and would it matter? She didn't know. She was content for the moment not to know.

June came, and the weather turned cold and rainy. "Monsoon June," a cheerful clerk in the Galena co-op called it. When the rain periodically stopped, the sky remained overcast and wisps of cloud rose from the slopes as if the mountains were breathing and you could see their breath. Cloud stretched in columns along the slopes and the air had all the chill and dampness of the clouds. It was as if they were living in the clouds.

It was a wonder anything could grow in such weather. And yet every leafy and needled tree, every plant, was burgeoning. And despite its poor soil, green shoots from the seeds they'd planted began popping up in the garden.

"What we have here is interior temperate rain forest," Robert told them, as if from his college lectern. "It's dryer to the east, I gather, under the west slope of the Rockies, and desert between here and the coast. The coast now. That's coastal temperate rain forest, where in winter they get rain, instead of snow."

"Sounds miserable," Clay said.

Sarah said, "I lived on the coast for a while, and I'll take Alberta's snow and cold any day. At least the sun shines there in the winter, especially when it's forty below."

"It never gets anywhere near that cold in this part of the province," Joel said. "Judging from last winter. Hell, it barely got below freezing."

"But no sun, remember—for a month at a time," Helen said.

"I did some skiing last winter," David said. "Above Silver City? Up there, above the clouds, you had sun."

"Let's all go skiing this winter!" Sarah said excitedly.

"Who knows how?" Helen asked. "Anybody?"

"Let's you and I go then," Sarah said to David.

Her being with David now had Tom feeling twinges of jealousy. But she wasn't his anymore. Never had been, really. And anyway, he was back with Angela now, more or less; and they had sex, more or less dutifully, almost every night when he imagined she was Sarah. That was funny. Making love with Sarah those few times, he'd imagined she was Angela. He remembered a line from some novel or movie where the man, or was it the woman, after they'd made love says, "I'll tell you who *I* was thinking of, if you'll tell me who *you* were thinking of."

It was like that.

Then one night Angela said, "I imagine you think of Sarah when we're making love, right?"

No surprise. Angela's intuitiveness, her astuteness, was a marvel. He was happily, or was it unhappily, reminded of it now.

"Why don't you just go to her sometimes?" Angela said. "I won't mind."

"She's with David now. You wanna go to him? We might switch."

"Wouldn't that be fun?"

And they both laughed.

"Feels good, doesn't it," Tom said.

"To laugh, you mean?" said Angela. "Yes."

David went off again, hitching to the north end of Sturgeon Lake to seek work with a Quaker building contractor he'd heard about who made a practice of hiring Americans.

Exiles, he called them. Refugees. Sarah showed no signs of missing him.

Soon after David's departure, a guy named Peter drifted in. He was from LA, he told them, and not much else. Pitched a tent behind the bunkhouse, from which the smell of marijuana began to waft, and pretty much stayed in it. Showed up for meals, then returned to his tent. Hardly said a word. Exuded mystery. Attracted the women.

Janice went to him, with Mark having to shrug it off. Then Sarah, with David not around to do anything about it. What would he have done? Helen expressed some interest but claimed not to have acted on it. Judy, of Little Judy and Big John, showed no interest at all.

That couple, in fact, suddenly decided to leave after getting a letter from their old agent with the offer of a gig in Vancouver and more to come if they wanted them. Within a couple of days they'd packed up their instruments, their few other belongings, collected their twin boys, and were gone.

Meanwhile, Angela began visiting Peter—at first just to get to know him, she told Tom, maybe find out where he was at. Was he just shy? Or was it a pose, the clever ploy of a woman-izer. Neither, she decided. She decided he'd been damaged in some way, and that made him all the more interesting to her.

She got him to take walks with her. He got her to smoke grass with him. Their smoking grass together, when he learned of it, almost more than what followed, made Tom sick with jealousy.

When it happened, he was more or less prepared for it. Or so he told himself.

"Peter and I have started making it."

"Oh? Big surprise. But why tell me?"

"I wanted you to know."

"*Why*, for godsake?"

"Because you're my husband! And I still love you. I want to be honest with you."

They were alone in the bunkhouse, after the midday meal in the hall for which Peter hadn't shown up—neither had Janice.

"He's with Janice now, don't you think? You next in line, Angie?"

A cartoon image popped into Tom's mind of the stoned, stiffly erect Peter, supine in his tent, and the two women lined up outside to take their turns impaling themselves on him.

"Please, it's not like that."

"What's it like then?"

"I don't know yet. All I know is I want to be with him now."

"Okay, but can you tell me something? What the *fuck* is his big attraction?"

She burst out laughing. "Apart from the obvious, you mean? He's not *you*, for one thing. He's different. He's sweet and gentle. He's . . ."

"Dead from the asshole up, in other words."

"You'd say something like that. Peter wouldn't."

"Good Christ! Maybe Peter should hold a workshop for the rest of us poor blokes. Share his goddamn fucking secret for attracting women to him like bees to fucking honey!"

"It's probably only temporary," Angela said.

"I thought we were back together!"

"Oh, we *are*," she told him. "But this . . . Can't people love more than one person at the same time?"

Tom wrote in his journal some days later:

Angela still with Peter and this morning, after days of
overcast and cold rain, the sun came out and all at once
it didn't matter. I'm almost happy to be here. Chicago.
What's there for me? What's here for me? Better here than
there, I suppose.

Here, for instance, was the waif-like Janice, who wasn't
with Mark anymore—Mark had gone off somewhere—and
probably wasn't with Peter anymore either. Angela was with
Peter. Sarah, New Eden's freest of free spirits, was very much
with David again, since his return to New Eden after failing to
find work with the Quaker contractor. Janice, meanwhile, was
pretty and appealing. Tom started coming on to her. And why
not? They both were available, why not to each other?

They sat talking by the lakeshore one evening, perched
atop the old logging ramp. It was toward the end of June now
and felt like summer finally, though the lake was too cold
yet for swimming. They watched the full moon rise over the
mountains and cast a stream of light on the water.

"Full moon . . . and empty arms!" Tom sang, that old song.

Janice gave a cynical little laugh. "Yes. It's almost too much,
isn't it."

They talked through the night, fuelled by a pea-size ball
of hashish Janice had scored in Galena that they smoked in
her little hash pipe while the moon crossed the sky, finally
faded, and birds began singing and it was getting light. They
sat with their legs dangling over the water. Tom looked at his
watch—it was four a.m.—and remembered early mornings in
Pearl Harbor standing deck watch on his tied-up submarine

at the start of another beautiful day in Hawaii. Remembered walking barefoot through the dew-wet pasture at the start of a summer day on his folks' farm in Minnesota to get the cows for the morning milking.

Janice talked about the summer of 67 in San Francisco, the so-called summer of love, and of finding herself pregnant afterwards and having her baby the next spring in Vancouver, virtually on the street. She talked of leaving it, wrapped in her head scarf, on the doorstep of a St. Vincent de Paul mission and how all she felt was relief.

"Wow. How old were you?"

"Sixteen."

That made her only twenty now, he figured.

"Wasn't it kind of hard, though, giving up your baby?"

"It was hard *having* it."

She was a little hard herself, Tom thought, which only made her more interesting, more attractive somehow. She also had talent, wrote little poems, could draw, played passable guitar, had a sweet, sad-sounding voice. Wrote her own sad, sweet songs.

"Ever been to Vancouver, Tom?"

"No. I hear it's nice, as cities go."

"Reminds me a little of San Francisco. I'm thinking of going down there for a while. Wanna come?"

"When?"

"Soon. Come with me, why don't you."

She gave him her crooked little gun moll's smile, and Tom felt that sinking thrill, that mixture of fear and excitement that used to strike him whenever an attractive woman other than Angela came onto him—that temptation like a threat he'd

188

always resisted as a faithful husband. With Sarah it had been easy to yield, easy after he was sure he'd lost Angela and felt free. He was free again now, wasn't he?

"What'll we do for money? You been holding out on the group?"

"We all hold out a little, right? What about you?"

"I've got some stashed, yeah. The way things are with Angela and me now, I've been thinking of taking off"

"Take off with me, then."

"I . . ."

She turned abruptly away.

"I'm not twisting your arm, you know."

"It's not . . . I mean you still hung up on Mark? Or with Peter—that is, when Angela isn't with him?"

"Mark went straight on me for doing it with Peter. As for *him*, Angela can have him."

Tom thought for a moment, then told her, "I've had my eyes on you all along, actually." Which wasn't a lie, actually, nor completely true.

"Really?" Janice said. "What a coincidence."

Chapter 25

They left New Eden after breakfast a couple of days later. No fuss. No group meeting necessary. "We're all free here," Joel told them. "How long will you be gone, by the way?"

"Ten days or so," Janice told him. That long? Tom asked himself.

Angela wore an odd little smile when he said goodbye, suggesting what? That she was happy for him? Pleased to see him go? An hour later, standing with Janice on the roadside outside Galena, Tom felt unwell, finally threw up his breakfast.

"Having second thoughts?" Janice asked sourly.

"Sorry. Indigestion, I guess."

They'd decided not to take his car. Much simpler and cheaper to leave it in New Eden and hitchhike, Janice convinced him (Angela herself drove them to Galena; how hip was that?). Presently they got a ride all the way to Silver City from a friendly old couple who beamed upon them as young lovers.

In Silver City they were again lucky to catch a ride with a tired-looking trucker going as far as Osoyoos, a town on a lake in the desert region of the province that eventually appeared, spectacularly, a thousand feet below them, before the winding road took them steeply down, the trucker engine-braking his rig, past farms and orchards to the valley bottom and over a causeway across the lake into the town. They climbed out of the truck by the public beach with a "Thanks for the ride!" shout to the driver, then wolfed down a lunch of pop and hot dogs at a snack bar on the sand. The beach was crowded with adult sunbathers, the water full of splashing youngsters. The sun was hot and the water warm, they discovered, after taking their shoes off and wading into it.

"We should hit the road," Tom said after a while. "We don't want to be hitching in the dark."

"Whatever," Janice said.

They sat on a bench watching the children in the water, Tom waiting patiently for Janice to move. At last she stood up, shouldered her pack, and they walked to the western edge of town and stuck out their thumbs. Soon enough, a longhair couple in a Volkswagen minibus stopped for them, and they tooled along for hours until, going over the Hope-Princeton pass, the van's air-cooled engine overheated. Loose fan belt, as it turned out, which the guy managed to tighten. By then it was dark, and they drove through the darkness while Janice dozed with her head on his shoulder and Tom felt protective of her while thinking of Angela.

They got into Vancouver about ten that night and were dropped off on Hastings. Janice led them past derelicts and panhandlers to a rundown hotel she knew about with a cavernous lobby in which a number of the old and not-so-old guests, more probably residents, sat dozing or staring into space in a variety of ratty, upholstered chairs.

They rented a room on the fourth floor and took the ancient lift to a creaking wood hallway smelling of disinfectant. They were tired but more than that, hungry; so, after dropping their packs in their room, they went out on the street again, to another place Janice knew of, an all but empty greasy-spoon café where they sat in a booth and ordered hamburgers and coffee, and where, as they waited for their food, Janice lay her head on the table only to have the man at the till dash over and shout, "No! No *nodding out* in here!"

They were asked to leave. That forced them to walk the street until they found another greasy spoon where junkies were allowed, it seemed, and they stuffed themselves with corned beef hash and eggs.

Wearily, they trekked back to their hotel, took the old elevator to their room, and dropped onto the sagging bed without showering, though Tom dutifully brushed his teeth; Janice didn't bother. Somewhat dutifully, too, he snuggled up and began stroking her.

She pushed him away. "No. I'm too tired."

Lying beside her then, listening to the incessant coughing of the other occupants through the hotel's thin walls, he wondered what he was doing here. Presently Janice began to snore, ever so lightly, as if controlling it in her sleep. He fell asleep himself eventually.

Janice woke in the night wondering who she was with. Tom. She was with Tom, but was he with her? He was still with

Angela, she guessed, no matter his effort to be with her. His making the effort rather endeared him to her. She imagined being with Angela. She imagined being with both of them.

All her life had been a longing, an estrangement, a hole that had never been filled. There was so much that simply eluded her, avoided her, didn't interest her or disappointed. Sometimes she just wanted to wrap herself around something, another person, a tree! Sometimes she just wanted to sleep. Sometimes she didn't want to wake up. Sometimes . . .

"Tom?" she said.

But he didn't wake. She snuggled up to him. He was warm, so warm! She sank into his warmth and once more into sleep.

In the morning Tom got up, took a shower, dressed and sat reading one of the books he'd brought with him. Janice stayed in bed., turned away from the sun streaming in through the dirty window. Below them Hastings Street was busy, noisy with city traffic that he wasn't used to anymore.

The book was *Trout Fishing in America,* the title of which had attracted him because of its suggestion of Hemingway when he came upon it in Barbara's Bookstore on North Wells Street in Chicago after work one day in 1967. He was attracted as well by the cover, the mustachioed, long-haired Richard Brautigan and his toothy girlfriend, both dressed in duds maybe out of a Salvation Army store, both hip and funky looking as they posed for a photographer late one afternoon in San Francisco's Washington Square. (You knew of the location and time of day from the author's self-conscious opening to his little novel.) Tom had bought the book as a product of the times and, slim though it was, hadn't read more than the first few pages till now. Now he laid it aside once more.

"Jan, you awake? Let's get some breakfast."

"Lemme sleep!"

"It's ten o'clock already. It's a new day."

And shouldn't they be enjoying it—as shouldn't he be enjoying this adventure with this other woman? But he kept thinking of Angela, missing her like a severed part of his body, though in New Eden they'd been together only tenuously lately, and she was doubtless in the arms of Peter now. Damnit! Janice was smart and appealing and he was with *her* now, but already he wished he was back with Angela—however tenuously.

"Come *on*, Janice" he said again. "You gonna lay in bed all day? It's depressing."

"Oh, all *right*," she said, and sprang naked out of the bed, which knocked Angela out of his head for a moment.

"Wanna . . ."

"I want some breakfast," she said. "And I need to score."

They walked down Hastings, where a few of the homeless lay curled in doorways, Janice striding ahead and obviously at home in this part of Vancouver. They came to the café they'd been ejected from the night before.

"No nodding out on the table this time," he joked.

She gave him her crooked little smile.

They had French toast and coffee, then Janice led him to Gastown and a bar where, without much delay, she connected with a clean-shaven dealer in cut-off jeans and a sweatshirt, maybe a college student in support of his education. Tom stood by as Janice negotiated for an ounce of hash.

She turned to Tom. "You got twenty bucks?"

Walking away from the guy, Tom said, "Really, Jan, we spend our money this way. we'll be broke soon."

"So? We're on vacation, aren't we? We gotta have dope."

She led him to a park, where there was a gathering of young people, one guy playing a guitar, another whonking on a blues harp, people swaying to the music. "This is more like it," Janice said. "Reminds me of Golden Gate Park."

She'd forgotten her hash pipe but lit a cigarette, dropped a speck of the hash on the burning end, and they took turns inhaling the smoke. A couple of hits and pretty soon it seemed to Tom that the cries of the gulls circling overhead were almost threatening. But then he started to dig the music and saw a girl of surpassing beauty and felt an almost sickening rush of desire. He wanted her—*here. Now.* If only life were that free.

A long time later, or maybe not so long, they were back on Hastings and in a bathhouse where, after sweating in the steam room and then showering together, they lay on the cot in one of the private little booths. Janice watched Tom harden, then allowed him to enter her. She squirmed a little, sucked in her breath once or twice. "Just fuck me," she said, and so he did; it was pleasurable enough, a temporary release.

The next couple of days they simply wandered the streets, Janice leading him here and there, on her home turf, it seemed, Tom feeling increasingly out of it. He was ready to go back, back to New Eden, which was all the home he had now, however unhappy. He missed Angela! Didn't matter she was with somebody else. It didn't matter that *he* was with somebody else.

They walked the streets every day until exhausted, until

they had to stop somewhere. Every stop, though, cost money. You couldn't just sit in a café without ordering at least a cup of coffee. And they had to eat occasionally, which cost money. Their fleabag hotel cost money. Sometimes they just sat on the curb for a while. Once a cop came by and told them to move on.

Tom thought of the park they'd visited their first day. They could sit on a bench there in the shade or even lie down on the grass—for free and without hassle. "Too far," Janice said. "I'm too tired."

Their third day, or was it their fourth, they wound up going back to their hotel for a nap. When they woke, it was dark and the city coming to nocturnal life, but all they could afford of its diversions now was a trashy double feature in a foul-smelling theatre. It stank of poor maintenance, stank of the clientele, bums off the street, drunken men and some women, sleeping it off until the last feature ended and the house lights came on and an attendant appeared to empty the place out.

"We're almost broke," Tom said to Janice as they left the theatre. "We can hardly afford another night in our hotel."

"Not to worry," Janice said. "I know a woman on Denman Island I used to stay with. She'll put us up."

"Where's Denman Island?"

"You'll see. C'mon. I'll show you how to survive down here."

Chapter 26

They took a bus to Horseshoe Bay the next morning and caught the ferry to Nanaimo, on Vancouver Island. Hitched up island to where they took a cable ferry across the narrow channel to Denman Island. Found the woman Janice knew still living in a weathered frame house she shared with young wanderers as they drifted in—as Janice had drifted in one day in 1968 after having and then abandoning her baby. The woman, named Annette, currently had three, nonpaying boarders, a guy and two girls, who showed up, one by one, that afternoon and disappeared into various parts of the house.

Janice and Tom sat with the woman on her porch after she'd fed them toast and scrambled eggs. She watched them eat with a benevolent smile on her hard face.

She was Dutch, early middle age perhaps, still spoke with an accent and listened, perhaps fondly, as Janice chattered on about this and that with sardonic wit as if afraid to stop talking. Annette was a surrogate mother, Tom guessed, to kids like Janice, refugees of the peace-and-love movement that hard drugs and Manson and the Hell's Angels had darkened. Was Annette herself a refugee? If so, she seemed to have found a place for herself, a *purpose*, among all these young people striving to prolong their youth. She was prolonging her own youth, he thought, or trying to. How old was she, really? How old was Janice again? Twenty, he recalled, and here he was, at thirty-five, her "old hippie," as she'd introduced him to this woman. They were all refugees.

"You seem happy now," Annette told Janice. And to Tom she said, "What about you? How did you two get together?"

"We met in a commune," Tom said, and fell back on his stock description of himself as a dropped-out journalist. Added he'd been married and was now more or less separated.

"Your wife, where is *she* now?"

"She's in the commune too."

"Ah. I see," Annette said.

They stayed the night, Janice sleeping on the living room couch, Tom on the floor after they'd first tried sleeping together on its narrow width. The next day they ferried over to nearby Hornby Island to visit a commune Annette said they would find there. Janice was for skipping it, but Tom, still the journalist, the aspiring writer, wanted to check it out. How might it be different from New Eden—or that pseudo-religious asylum Angela had escaped from?

They arrived in time to witness a gleeful squirt-gun fight, boys against the girls, running through the rooms of a big old farmhouse that now accommodated about a dozen members of the counterculture.

The house, the weathered outbuildings, especially the barn, its hay lofts above the walk-in basement with its double row of stanchions for some thirty cows—all was familiar to Tom, reminded him of the farm he grew up on in Minnesota. He climbed the ladder to the beam over one of the lofts and walked across it, suffering vertigo for a moment and nearly falling. He swung from the rope attached to the hayfork, as he used to as a boy, impressing Janice and one of the young women of the commune.

Later, Janice off somewhere, Tom was invited to take a sauna with this girl in the small cement-block building next to the barn that he recognized as the old milkhouse. They were joined by another couple, the guy rather straight looking, probably an ex-jock, the girl with long raven hair and alabaster skin.

The sauna was heated with a propane stove on top of which was a small pile of rocks. It wasn't long before the rocks began radiating heat and the guy dipped water from a pail and splattered it on the rocks. Steam filled the air with a loud hiss. The place grew hot, the air stifling.

"*Hunh*," was the appreciative chorus from the four of them.

Boards had been laid across what had been the milkhouse's cooling tank to make a bench, and the raven-haired beauty now sat on it and the guy leaned over her and began massaging her thighs. She smiled up at him. Tom noted his half-engorged penis and wondered, were they partners or just enjoying some extracurricular activity? He felt twinges of puritanical judgment, some envy of the guy.

The girl he was with—they were standing now, eyeing each

other's bodies—began to lather him with soap. She ran her hands up the inside of his thighs, gave his balls a playful little tweak. His penis began to swell.

"We always soap each other up like this," she said brightly. "Fun, huh?"

"It certainly is."

Then it was his turn to soap her. Emboldened, he lathered up the length of *her* legs, inside and out, then travelled up under her arms and over her breasts. She grinned at him the whole time.

They stood there, covered with soap.

"Now what?" Tom asked.

"We wash off."

"Where?"

"Next door in the pump house. We've rigged a shower in there."

They went next door and turned on the shower. The water was icy cold. The other couple had disappeared.

He moved as if to embrace her. She backed away, smiling.

"What about your friend?"

"She's off with somebody else, maybe."

Anyway, he was stricken now with his old, anguished, interfering jolt of ambivalence, of Catholic morality, of something like the old panic at the possibility of being unfaithful. This girl probably picked up on it.

"What's your name again, by the way?" she asked.

"Tom. What's yours?"

"Susy."

They shook hands.

He took a walk by himself in the nearby woods. Fog was coming in from the ocean, the trees dripped with moisture. There were giant slugs on the ground, fat as sausages. Where was Janice?

Back in the house a number of the women were preparing supper. The one seemingly in charge asked Tom if he was staying the night. She had a nice smile, was girl-next-door attractive, exuded female warmth. He imagined being with her, imagined joining this commune, where things seemed more playful, less complicated than in New Eden.

"Not sure," he said.

Janice suddenly appeared, said, "*There* you are. Where were you?"

"Where were you?"

"Let's go," she said.

They took the ferry from Hornby to Denman, then the ferry from Denman to Vancouver Island itself where, on the highway going south, there was little traffic and nobody stopped for them. The summer solstice was hardly a week away and there were hours of daylight left, but the sun was gone and it was cold. So cold and damp they could almost see their breath.

"Bummer," Janice said. "Okay, let's go back."

But it was Tom who wanted to go now. "We'll get a ride," he said. "Look, here comes another car."

The car slowed, the driver obviously looking them over, then sped away.

"I'm freezing!" Janice said.

"Let's warm up," Tom said, and started straddle hopping. "Remember doing these in high school gym class? We did 'em in Navy boot camp too. They get your blood flowing."

Janice made a face. "I hated gym." But she started hopping too.

The road grew deserted. The cold increased. They started walking. A car passed them, then stopped.

"Run!" Janice cried. "Before he changes his mind!"

The driver was a courtly looking guy with silvery hair. "How far you kids going?"

"Nanaimo," Janice said, breathless.

"Well, I can drop you off in front of my place. It's only about ten miles down the road, however."

"That'll be fine," Tom said

Janice hopped in beside the driver and said, "Thank you, kind sir." Tom climbed in back, and they started down the road. The man said, "Where you folks from?"

"The interior," Janice told him.

"Oh? Been on the road a while?"

"We hitched down from Silver City," Tom said. "We live on Purcell Lake."

"Purcell Lake," the man said. "Beautiful country. The Purcell River Valley? Beautiful."

He told them about a bicycle trip he and his wife took one time, from Silver City to the Purcell River, up the valley to Galena, then over the pass to Sturgeon Lake and back down to Silver City. Camped along the way. Visited the hot springs.

"That was a great little trip," he said. "Sort of our second honeymoon."

One thing led to another and Tom mentioned he'd been in the US Navy, in the submarine service.

"Really? I wrote the script for a submarine picture once.

After the war. World War Two, that is. During the war, the submarine force was the so-called Silent Service."

"Why was that?" Janice asked.

"The Navy wanted to keep its sub operations secret," Tom said, "especially in the Pacific."

"Right," the man said. "Especially after Pearl Harbor."

Turned out he'd been a screenwriter for MGM before being blacklisted, which caused him and his wife to emigrate to Canada in 1953.

"So what brought *you* up here?" he asked Tom. "I guess you aren't dodging the draft."

"We're back-to-the-landers," Janice said. "Or anyway, *he* is."

"And you aren't? Oops, here's my driveway." He pulled in and stopped.

Janice hopped out of the car. "Thanks for the ride, mister."

Tom got out and walked to the driver's window. The man rolled it down and they shook hands.

"Thanks a lot. Nice talking to you."

"Same here," the man said, then waved as he pulled down his tree-lined driveway and disappeared.

They crossed the road and stood waiting for another car. None appeared. It was getting dark. Getting colder. "This is shitty," Janice said.

Then here came the man in his car again, driving across the road to them. He cranked open his window.

"I thought you two might still be here. How'd you like to have supper with my wife and me? Afterwards I'll drive you to where it'll be easier to get a ride."

Chapter 27

His wife was a chubby, sweet-faced woman with an English accent. Her name was Cheryl. His was William. "Call me Bill." They were Bill and Cheryl McElroy.

"My war bride," McElroy told them. "We met in a London pub. I was an army corporal, just arrived in England, waiting to be shipped over to France. This was *after* D-Day, but the war hadn't been won yet. I told Cheryl if I survived the war—I survived the Battle of the Bulge, in fact—I'd marry her."

"And he was true to his word," Cheryl said, smiling fondly on him.

The meal was overdone roast beef with boiled potatoes and carrots, washed down with imported English ale. "Meat and two veg," Bill called it. "Learned to like it over there." Tom liked it and so did Janice. She cleaned her plate and accepted another helping.

"I'm aware of your back-to-the-land movement," Bill said.

"Pretty interesting. Your counterculture is interesting. Not sure of the drug aspect, though. Can't see it as all that much different from what alcohol does for you."

"It's totally different," Janice said.

"I'm not into drugs much myself," said Tom.

"Oh?" Bill said. "Do I detect a generation gap?"

He talked about movies, about some of the stars he'd known ("I could tell you stories"), and how the blacklist made writing for the movies, even under a pseudonym, too tough to make a living.

"People like Dalton Trumbo managed. A few others," he said. "I got out before I was called before the House Un-American Committee."

"Were you actually a communist?" Janice had the temerity to ask.

Bill smiled. "No, but like a lot of us in those days, people who grew up during the Depression, I had leftist leanings. I wrote a screenplay once about Joe Hill, but it got buried. You know about Joe Hill?

Tom nodded. "A little."

Janice said, "I know the song by Joan Baez."

"Actually it's from a poem by a Brit, written around 1930 and set to music by an American some time later. Joe Hill was a hero of the Wobblies, the Industrial Workers of the World, a minstrel of the people, years ahead of Woody Guthrie and Pete Seeger, not to mention Joan Baez."

"Pie in the sky. That came out of one of his songs, didn't it?" Tom said.

"That's right. *The Preacher and the Slave*, which ends 'There'll be pie in the sky when you die.' Great song."

Cheryl had the dishes done before either Tom or Janice noticed. "Sorry," Janice said. "Tom and I could have done them."

"No bother, my dears." Cheryl looked at her husband, who looked back at her. "Would you two like to stay the night?" she said. "It's getting rather late to hitchhike. You can have our son's room."

"Great idea!" McElroy said. "Stay the night and have breakfast with us. We haven't had any young people around since our son emigrated to Australia. You'll have an easier time hitching in the morning."

Tom looked at Janice.

"Thank you so much," she said. "But we'd like to get going, wouldn't we, Tom. I have a friend we can stay with in Nanaimo."

"Oh? Then let me drive you there," Bill McElroy said.

"No-no," Tom said. "That won't be necessary."

"I'll drive you to Qualicum Beach then. That's halfway to Nanaimo and it should be easier to get a ride from there."

"You people have been too kind," Janice said.

"Nonsense," said McElroy.

"I'll ride along," his wife said. "I'll just get my coat."

Qualicum Beach was something of a retirement community, McElroy said, as he drove through to the other side of town. He pulled into a gas station, still lit up, where they might catch a ride with someone stopping there. Tom and Janice climbed out of the car, thanking the old couple for their hospitality.

"Good luck, kids," Cheryl McElroy said out her rolled-down window.

"Keep the faith," McElroy told them out of his. "My

generation had our go. It's up to you young people now."

And drove away. Janice walked to the station's south entrance and onto the highway. Tom followed.

"Nice folks," he said.

"Yeah, maybe a little *too* nice," Janice said. "Made me nervous."

"Why?"

"I'm sorry, but when people come on too nice like that I can't help wondering what they're really like."

"Like old Bill's probably an asshole underneath it all, and Cheryl's—"

"Maybe."

Tom let that pass. "Who we staying with in Nanaimo, by the way?"

"Nobody. I just made that up."

It wasn't long before a Volkswagen minibus came rapping toward them and they stuck out their thumbs. It went past them, slowed, then stopped. They ran toward it as a side door opened for them to climb in. Inside they joined a motley group of what looked like fellow hitchhikers. The driver was a beardless young guy in a baseball cap.

They trundled off, the vehicle's headlights stabbing ahead onto the empty road. Nobody said anything until an array of blinking red lights turned on behind them.

"Fuck," the driver said. He turned around to his passengers. "Everybody straight?"

By some miracle, everybody was.

He pulled over. The cop car pulled up behind them and an RCMP constable in Mounty uniform stepped out and wrote down their license number. Then he was beside them, tapping on the driver's window. The driver rolled it down.

"Good evening," the Mounty said. "May I see your driver's license?"

He took it to his cruiser. Then he was back.

"Okay," he said. "The reason I stopped you is your left taillight is out." He peered into the back and sniffed. "Get it fixed as soon as possible," he told the driver. "Good evening."

He strolled back to his cruiser, turned off the blinking lights, swung out, and sped off down the highway.

"My taillights are both working," the driver said. "It's what I'm driving. The cops have a thing for VW buses, it seems."

"They're seen as hippie wagons," the guy beside Tom said. His hair hung to his shoulders, his handlebar mustaches drooped past his chin.

"Guess so," the driver said. "Maybe I should grow my hair a little longer to go with my vehicle."

"Do it, man!" the mustachioed guy said.

They pulled into Nanaimo. Tom and Janice, along with the mustachioed dude, piled out. The VW continued on.

"Know of a place to stay in this town?" Tom asked the guy

"There's a hotel over in the next street. Or you can stay in my place," he said, "if you don't mind crashing on the floor. I only have one bed and me and my old lady more or less fill that up."

Janice pulled at Tom's sleeve. "C'mon. Let's find the hotel."

The hotel was a grand old establishment gone a little to seed, handily near the bus station where, in the morning, they could buy tickets to Vancouver by way of the ferry to the mainland. Their room smelled musty, but the ornate bed was a commodious four-poster. They undressed, got under the covers. After a while Janice moved close to him. He turned toward her and they kissed. It was sweet. He was truly with her, all of a sudden; he could imagine some future with her.

"I'm on my period," she said. "Otherwise . . ."

"I don't mind if you don't."

She was sweetly responsive. Held him tight, her arms and legs wrapped around him. She moaned. He came. She breathed in his ear, "I love you, Tom."

"I love you too," Tom told her.

Later Janice said, "Ugh. The bed's all wet." She threw back the covers to reveal a patch of blood on the sheet. "Ha! The maid'll think you took my cherry."

"Shall we leave her a note?"

"Yes! I'll write it."

Janice hopped across the room to the little desk, pulled out the top drawer, and found a ballpoint pen and sheets of the hotel's stationary.

"How convenient," she said. "We're in a class hotel."

She sat naked at the desk and wrote a note, then showed it to Tom with an impish grin. In a neatly printed hand, Janice had written:

Please excuse the stain on the bed sheet. Has it happened to you?

A sister

"Cute," Tom said. "Shall we also leave a tip?"

"Of course! A dollar should do."

She took a towel from the bathroom and placed it over the wet blood stain and they got into bed again. She was soon asleep, snoring a little, until Tom nudged her and she rolled over. He snuggled up to her and felt such a jumble of emotions. Who did he love?

He was awake at first light and eager to be off, but Janice slept on—and on and on. He dug through his pack for the other book he'd brought with him—*Slaughterhouse Five*—and instead came up with his journal. He hadn't written in it lately.

Where am I? My abiding emotion, it seems, is one of homesickness. Where's home? Fog outside the window of this hotel in this faraway town as I wait for the girl I'm with to get up so we can get going. To where? Where might I feel at home?

Janice opened her eyes, then closed them again. She rolled over, turning her back on him.

"We should get going," Tom said.

"Lemme *sleep*." But then she threw the covers off and sat up. "What time is it?"

Tom looked at his watch, though he didn't have to. "After seven."

"When's our bus leave?"

"Seven-thirty, I think. We can make it if you get up now."

"Turn around then."

"What?"

"Turn around. I don't want you to see me this morning."

"Why?"

"I feel ugly, is why. Like I usually do in the morning, particularly a morning after."

"After what—making love?"

"Whatever. I feel ugly now, okay?"

"You're beautiful," he told her, seeing the acne scars that Janice usually hid with makeup.

"You see my face?" she said angrily. "I'm like a leper. I should wear a sign, *Unclean.*"

"You're beautiful," he said again

"Cut it! C'mon, let's get out of here."

They just made it to the bus. It took them to the ferry landing and onto the ferry. They ate breakfast in the crowded diner, then went out on deck to watch the gulls gliding beside them as if stationary, riding the vacuum within the vessel's flow of air as it churned toward the mainland.

It took an hour and a half to reach the mainland. The bus rolled off the ferry and took them to the Vancouver depot where they'd started for the Island two, or was it three, days ago? They walked to Hastings Street and found a hotel cheaper even than the one they'd stayed in before. It was a flop house, reminding Tom of two-bit places he'd known as a sailor.

The bed, though, was surprisingly comfortable. Tom lay listening to the coughing coming through the hotel's walls. He looked up at the stained ceiling, saw figures there, faces, which whiled away the time, for a time. He was half-asleep when Janice said, "Let's drop some acid."

"You got the money for it? I don't."

"I got the money. C'mon, let's hit the street."

They went to the bar in Gastown where they'd bought the hash, saw a different guy this time, long-haired, furtive-looking, who sold Janice a tab of acid for fifteen bucks. "You weasel. That's exorbitant," she told him. But she paid it.

They pooled what was left of their money and found they

had just enough for another night in their flophouse hotel and maybe a greasy spoon breakfast in the morning. Then they'd really be on the street.

"We've got to head back," Tom said. "Today. Otherwise we won't have the money for bus fare to Silver City."

"I'm not interested in going back."

"I won't leave you here," Tom told her.

"Then stay with me. We'll get by."

"*You* will, maybe. I'm not used to being on the street."

"Course not. Country boy. Go on then. I'm staying."

"What'll you do? Panhandle?"

"I'll busk. I've done it before."

"How? You don't have your guitar."

"Then I'll sing. Sing my little heart out, *a cappella*. I'll sell matches. I'll be the little match girl."

"Be serious, Jan. You've got to go back with me."

"No! I didn't realize how sick I was of New Eden till we got down here. This is where I belong."

"I won't leave you," he repeated.

"I know." She touched his face, gave him her crooked little smile. "C'mon then. Let's go back to the hotel and trip out, then fuck like rabbits."

"We should check out."

"Later. First things first. Or aren't you interested?"

In their hotel room, Janice took over. She cracked open the can of orange pop Tom bought in the lobby and poured it into a paper cup from the bathroom. Dropped the tab of LSD into it. "All right, drink half of this," she told him. "I'll drink the rest."

Tom took only a swallow or two.

"That's enough for me. I've never dropped acid before. I'm a little scared of it."

"Too late, Jack. You're on your way."

She downed the rest of the pop. Grinned at him.

"Now what?"

"We wait. Wanna get naked in the meantime?"

Pretty soon they were writhing on the bed together. Tom stayed inside her afterwards, soon hardened again, and it was during their second go that he found himself fascinated by Janice's acne-scarred face as she stared up at him, wide-eyed, silent, as if he was violating her. That caused him to pull out and back away. He sat back on his knees. She sat up, pushed back against the headboard, still staring at him as he grew aware of the singular shape of her face, of the bones under her now almost transparent skin. He saw her ancestry, the high-cheeked evidence of her Slavic forebears. Her maternal grandmother was from Romania, she'd told him. He watched as the scars on her face deepened, became miniature canyons that he imagined going into to explore their mystery.

"You're beautiful," he told her, without any ambivalence.

"And you're stoned," she said.

A long time later he was up and dressed and sitting in the room's single chair, waiting for Janice to come down. She lay uncovered on the bed, watching the flashing neon light outside their window, until he pulled the blanket over her. She kept exclaiming about the light. Tom grew impatient. How long did this stuff last? They should get going.

He closed his eyes. When he opened them again it was the next morning. He was stiff from sleeping in the chair all night,

Janice was sick.

"You *can't* be sick. We gotta go."

"I'm *sick*, I tell you. I ache all over. Leave me alone."

She turned her back on him and pulled the covers over her head.

Tom went out to check on the bus fare to Silver City. It would cost sixty bucks for the two of them. They had maybe half of that left. He could pawn his watch, he thought. It was the gold Bulova he'd had since high school, a graduation gift from his folks.

When he left the bus depot to look for a pawn shop, it was raining. He ducked into a doorway to wait for it to let up. A cop appeared, filling the doorway. "What are you doing there, sir?"

"Staying out of the rain," Tom said.

"Come with me, please." The cop took his arm and pulled him toward a cruiser that Tom hadn't noticed before. The cop's partner stepped out and opened the car's back door. Tom was pushed inside.

I'm screwed, he thought. All he had for ID was his Illinois driver's license. He was an illegal alien. He was going to be deported.

But the cop didn't ask for an ID, probably because Tom looked like a person without one. Instead he was forced to sit behind the barrier between the car's front and back seats, looking out at people passing freely by, many bent under umbrellas, while his description was called in, he guessed. He couldn't hear what was said, but he had an image of himself with his mane of wild hair now and his ragged beard.

While they waited for what Tom imagined was a rundown on him from police headquarters, the cops chatted with each other, then chatted with him. He turned on what he hoped was some charm, talking gaily of how rainy he was finding Vancouver and the coast generally, and how he much preferred the interior, where it didn't rain so much. He was in Canada visiting friends, he said, in the Kootenays.

The car radio squawked unintelligibly, and the cop who'd picked him up off the street said, "Okay. You can go."

"Thank you," Tom said. *Pigs*, he thought as he climbed out of their squad car, then smiled to himself at how readily the term had come to him. They'd hassled him on a slow day out of boredom, he guessed. Hadn't treated him badly, only laid their authority on him.

It had stopped raining. He found a pawn shop after asking a man on the street who in turn asked for a handout. Pawned his cherished watch, which had cost his folks more than a hundred dollars back in 1955—for $50—then went back to the bus depot and bought two one-way tickets to Silver City.

At the hotel, he half-expected to find Janice gone, half-wished, in fact, that she might be; but no, she was still in bed, still with the covers over her head, apparently sleeping.

"Okay," he told her. "I got us bus fare to Silver City. We can leave tonight."

She threw back the covers and gave him a sullen stare. "How'd you manage that, may I ask?"

"Peddled my ass, of course."

"Oh sure." She grinned at him. "Tender meat off the farm, eh?"

"How I was seen sometimes when I was a sailor."

She reached for her pack and rummaged through it. "Oh no, where's my stash?" she cried. "I thought I had a joint left over!"

"You smoked it, remember? Anyway, I wouldn't smoke in here," he said. "The sign says no smoking. And that would include grass, I should think."

"You should think," she said. "Who talks like that, some educated queer?"

She was sitting up in bed now, clutching her pillow, looking ugly. "Seriously, where'd you get the money?"

"Hocked my watch."

"Oh," she said. "You shouldn't have done that."

"Well, I did. And now we can get out of here."

"You mean *you* can get out of here."

"No, I mean *we* can get out of here. You're really at home down here, aren't you. In some fleabag like this or out on the street."

"Right. I'm completely at home." She smiled. "We got enough for a meal, by the way? We got enough to stay a couple more days?"

"We got enough for a meal and to see us through till this evening. Bus leaves at six."

"Okay, but I'm not going back just yet. Maybe not ever."

"Oh, c'*mon*, Janice. Stop this, for chrissake."

She bristled like a cornered animal.

"Don't you know who I am, *what* I am?" she shouted. "I'm a parasite! A leech! I've been a leech all my life, ever since I left home, mooching on people, moving in with them until I'm asked to leave or it's become obvious I *should* leave. I'm a tart, haven't you noticed? Doing what I have to do to survive in this jungle. I look after myself, Jack. I feed my appetites and don't give a damn about anything or anybody else. I'm not a quote-unquote contributing member of the commune or society or anything! I do my tart's little shuffle and get what I want until people are on to me and I have to move. Well, they're on to me in New Eden."

She was an actress, Tom realized, along with having a way with words. Her bitter little smile showed glints of pleasure in her own performance. She was too much. She was something else.

"You're okay in New Eden," he told her. "You contribute."

"Nah. I don't pull my weight, haven't you noticed? I don't even try. Anyway, I'm tired of the effort, tired of putting on a *show* of pulling my weight, of fitting in with the quote-unquote group. I'm a loner, always have been."

"That's a copout," Tom said. "*No se puede vivir sin amar.*"

"What's that?"

"You can't live without loving—or without love, as some people might translate it. It's a Spanish saying. I got it from *Under the Volcano* by Malcolm Lowry, who got it from Somerset Maugham, who got it from a sixteenth-century Spanish friar. I looked it up."

"You would. You're such a scholar. I tried to read *Under the Volcano* once. It was too complicated, too sad."

"Like life. Some funny parts in it, though."

"Like life, yeah. I live without loving, without love, more often than not," Janice said.

"Really? *We* have love, don't we, Janice? You said you loved me that night in Nanaimo."

"Yeah, well. I was swept up by the moment." She grinned at him, her crooked gun moll little smile.

"I'm not gonna leave you," he insisted.

"No? You'll be sorry," she said. "Anyway, I'm starving all of a sudden. Let's eat."

217

Chapter 28

It was a twelve-hour bus ride through the night to Silver City. Tom alternately read and looked out the window. He finished *Trout Fishing in America* and started *Slaughterhouse Five*. Janice had given him the window seat, saying she wanted to sleep. Instead she dug a frayed notebook out of her pack and started writing in it.

"Your journal?"

"My notes, diary, whatever."

She flipped through the pages. "It's more grab-bag than diary. I write my songs in it, bits of poetry. Wanna hear something?"

"Sure."

She opened to a page. "My face in the mirror," she read "Not me. What others see."

She looked up at Tom, as if defiantly.

"Nice."

"Wanna hear another?" She turned the page. "A butterfly. Its wings spread wide. Transformed."

"That's good,"Tom told her. "Like Haiku."

"Not exactly. Doesn't follow the rules."

"Yeah, but you give us an image, a flash of insight."

"You got that?" She snuggled against him. He put his arm around her.

The bus moved across the flat farmland of the Fraser Valley. Then it was climbing into mountains, the slopes rising sheer above the road, covered with both needled and leafy trees, tangled shrubbery, thick pelts of moss, all incredibly green in the setting sun. The Coast Range's temperate rain forest, Tom told himself, lush as tropical jungle.

It turned dark and Janice slept, her head on his shoulder, while he sat awake, feeling tender towards her. Perhaps she *was* a little ill, he thought, ill psychologically, ill at the prospect of going back to New Eden where, according to her jaundiced view of herself, she'd worn out her welcome.

Presently the driver turned the bus lights out and Tom closed his eyes.

They got into Silver City a little after six in the morning. Ate breakfast in the bus depot since nothing else was open. Hitched, in two stages, to Galena. Walked the five miles into New Eden.

Angela was the first person they saw as they came down into the clearing. She was in shorts and a halter, beautifully tanned, picking greens from the garden, and when she looked up at them, at *him*, his heart overflowed.

He went to her, aware of Janice's discreet removal of herself, of his abrupt, self-centred dismissal of her, full of guilt

219

and remorse and desire.

Angela was shy at first; they both were shy. She took his hand finally, and they walked to the bunkhouse, found it empty, stripped and climbed into a lower bunk together. They entwined, connected, and he sank, dissolved, inside her. She was all, she was everything, he was enveloped, he was overcome as he fell, finally, into a sweet swoon of renewal.

Chapter 29

It didn't last, of course. After a couple of days Angela went back to Peter, and Tom, as soon as she'd have him again, went back to Janice. She'd moved into Sarah's tent (Sarah and David were sharing his A-frame now) and, when she felt like it, allowed Tom to spend the night with her. There were times when she *didn't* feel like it. There were times when Peter too needed to be alone, or perhaps wanted a change of partners, which occasionally brought Tom and Angela together again.

One night he had *both* women, first Janice, who afterwards turned moody and sent him away, then Angela, whom Tom found alone in the bunkhouse after Peter, in some kind of similar funk, had sent *her* away and put her in a such state of ardour that Tom could hardly satisfy her. *Shades of Henry Miller!* he thought wondrously, *going from Anais Nin to his wife June!*

As for Janice, one night she told Tom, "The trouble is I'm in love with both of you. Could we try a threesome?"

Tom said quickly, "I doubt Angela would go for it." Would *he*?

"Just kidding," Janice said. Was *she*?

A day or two before this Janice and Angela had found themselves alone in the hall. They'd done the kitchen cleanup after the midday meal and afterwards sat down at the trestle table with cups of tea. The others were outside somewhere, enjoying the day.

Angela took a sip of her tea and asked, "Did you have a good time in Vancouver?"

"We had a time," Janice said.

"What's that mean, that you *didn't* have a good time?"

"I mean all during our trip," Janice said, "I knew Tom wasn't really *with* me, though he tried to be. I resented it at first. Then I appreciated his trying."

"How do you feel about Tom now?"

Janice glared at Angela. "What is this, some kind of cross-examination? I love him. Despite that he doesn't really love me. He loves you."

"What do you love about him?" Angela really wanted to know.

"Oh, lemme count the ways," Janice said. She relaxed. Angela saw her starting to enjoy this. "He's a nice guy, or tries to be. He's got a nice body, and he appreciates yours. What do you love about Peter, by the way?"

"He isn't Tom," Angela said at once. "He's a mystery."

"Don't you think Tom is? Don't you think you and I are, even to ourselves, for godsake? We're *all* a mystery,"

Janice declared.

Angela thought about that.

"How do you like it here, by the way?" Janice said. "This back-to-the-land thing. I mean, do you think you'll stay? With or without Tom?"

"I don't know. I don't think Peter's going to stay, and if he leaves, I'm not sure I'd go with him."

"I wouldn't," Janice said.

"Why not?"

"I'd stay with Tom. There's no future with Peter."

"You don't think so?"

"I know so. I've got his number."

Angela wondered what that might be, but she let it pass. "I'll always love Tom," she said, "but I've found I can love other men too. I think living communally like this, surrounded by other people, being allowed to be intimate with someone other than your partner when there's a mutual attraction . . . that might be a solution to strict monogamy, trying to make it strictly as a couple."

open marriage

"It's called open marriage," Janice said. "Being free to fuck whoever you want, in other words."

Angela laughed. "I guess. That's not all of it, though."

"I'm bi-sexual, myself," Janice said. She stood up and came around to Angela's side of the table and gave her a hug.

Angela stiffened, despite herself.

"Whatever," Janice said. "I'm your friend, you know."

"And I'm yours," Angela said, not sure she meant it.

July brought warm, then hot weather. Swimming weather. Swimming nude in the lake became a daily, anticipated event,

223

an expression of freedom, a gleeful liberation from any shreds of clinging puritanism. Each late afternoon there'd be a jolly communal strip, then a whooping run off the fifteen-foot height of the old logging ramp into the cold, breathtaking, invigorating water. Even Peter took part, surprising Tom with the fitness of his body. Sarah, of course, was a vision of full-bodied female beauty, and Helen—for someone practically middle aged—was a revelation. As for Angela, Tom tried not to notice her familiar form because he'd lost her—mostly anyhow, to a guy who was ignoring her to frolic with the other women, women who no longer visited him in his tent—or did they? Wasn't he supposed to be with Angela now? The prick didn't deserve her.

And so the summer rocked on. "Rocked," as in sex, drugs, and rock and roll. Tom participated while feeling estranged, the odd man out, unhinged, hanging on, as Angela grew more and more obsessed with Peter and, what's more, insisted on telling him about it.

"Do me a favour, will you? Stop telling me about your fucking affair with Peter."

"You're the only one I can talk to!"

They were on a walk together after the evening meal. Angela had suggested it, and Tom had wondered why.

"You can't talk to the other women? Compare notes, for chrissake?"

"Hardly. They're not interested in him anymore."

"You can't talk to *him*?"

"Not like I can talk to you. You're my closest friend."

"But not your lover anymore."

"You're still that, too, if you want to be."

"Oh yeah? Whenever you happen to feel like it."

They'd crossed the bridge over the creek and started up the logging road. Now she stopped, took a breath. "I'm finding that I can love more than one person at the same time. I mean sexually. Peter's another person. He's not bitter, for instance, like you are now. He's not mean and nasty and judgmental, which you can be sometimes. I thought writers were supposed to be accepting, open to the universe."

"Writers are *human*, goddamnit! Like everybody else! Anyway," Tom told her, "I'm not a writer anymore. I never was, in fact."

"That's another thing about you. Your self-pity."

"I . . ."

"Let's just stop this now."

"Fine. I suppose I should be happy for you. I guess I am, actually."

"Are you? Really?"

"Yes. And no."

Tom took to hiking alone up the mountain, to be by himself, to be alone with nature. Back in Minnesota, a farm boy, the nearby woods had been his escape from the farm. Here the mountains were becoming his escape from New Eden.

In the long afternoons while the others lolled about, reading, napping, making love, perhaps even doing a little work, he'd make himself a sandwich in the communal kitchen, fill a bottle with water from the creek, then start up the gradual, relentless, switch-backing ascent of the old logging road. The road was washed out in places, the forest invading, and there were any number of overgrown skid trails, faint animal paths, that provided interesting detours, took him into secluded places where he might stop to eat his lunch and enjoy what appeared to be untouched wilderness—until, here and there, he'd find evidence of the mining that had preceded the logging in this country: the unravelling end of a steel cable sticking up out of the humus; an abandoned shovel, its handle disintegrated, its blade rusting away; a discarded ore car, lying on its side, almost lost in the vegetation.

He flushed deer occasionally, whitetails, their "flags" of alarm familiar to him from those he used to see in the woods around his folks' farm. Mule deer, which he saw in the higher elevations, were new to him, their markedly long ears and black-tipped tails, their stiff-legged, hopping way of running.

One day, after an hour and a half climb, he reached a level area called a bench, where there was an old log landing. Saplings were springing up amid lupine, thimbleberry and wild strawberry on ground once cleared and flattened by a bulldozer. To one side of the landing was a big slash pile containing some good firewood, Tom noted. Nearby lay a broken length of chain and a dented and rusting fuel container. The magnificent view was of the long, glistening expanse of Purcell Lake from maybe four thousand feet above it, the rounded mountain tops across the lake almost at eye level, while above and below the landing were the clearcuts you could otherwise only see from across the lake.

A light plane flew by, heading up the lake at exactly his altitude, and Tom waved at it. The pilot, who'd obviously seen him, responded by wagging the plane's wings.

Beyond the landing, in an overgrown clearing overlooking the lake, he found a collapsed log building by a rushing stream. A prospector's old cabin, he thought, or a trapper's. The stream was lined with more thimbleberry and growths of the prickly devil's club. In front of the ruined cabin were a number of flat rocks that had been fitted artfully together to form a three-sided fireplace— the rocks still black where flames had licked them long ago, the remaining bed of ashes hardened into a cement-like slab.

This became his mountain refuge, his retreat from New Eden, where he could sit propped against the stone fireplace, could read or write in his journal and look down on the lake far below and at the mountains across the lake where the snow was finally gone from the pair of rocky peaks.

He'd had a secret place something like this in the woods near his folks' farm in Minnesota when he was a day-dreaming boy. He'd felt trapped on the farm. He felt trapped now in New Eden. In the military you spoke of the Outside. That was civilian life, what you'd left behind after joining the service. The military was the Inside, an enclosed, regimented society that for some was a refuge from the Outside and for those drafted into it a kind of minimum-security prison. Convicts spoke of the Outside. Monks, cloistered nuns. New Eden was Inside, a refuge, a retreat from the Outside straight world.

He made a note one day in his journal:

I'm in a state of suspension here, as if awaiting orders to my next duty station. Funny: we left the outside world to be free of it and in some ways have only imprisoned ourselves inside this one. We've made a prison of each other.

One day Tom saw a gigantic bear, humped and tawny coloured, a *grizzly*, he knew at once, plodding up the logged-over slope just below him, plodding *toward* him, unaware of him because of the updraft. He felt a stab of fear, looked frantically around for a tree to climb—but there wasn't one close by, and Tom knew better than to run. The bear kept coming. He'd heard so much about grizzlies, how dangerous they were, how hikers or hunters sometimes disappeared in high country. The common assumption was they'd encountered a grizzly.

Tom stood perfectly still as the bear lumbered past him, so close he heard the crack and crunch of its heavy tread, actually smelled its wildness. Then, slightly upwind of Tom now, it smelled *him,* and stopped. It turned toward him and *woofed.* Stood up to its full, gigantic height, looking this way and that, as Tom held his breath. Bears were near-sighted, he'd read somewhere. Yet it caught his eye for a moment and Tom looked quickly away. He'd read that you must never look directly into the eyes of a dangerous animal; the animal is threatened.

This animal slunk down into a crouch now, as if preparing to charge. Tom had read what to do if charged by a grizzly; you were to drop to the ground and curl up, knees and head tucked into your chest, hands locked behind your neck. The idea was the animal might leave you after a couple of angry bites. It was an idea that seemed utterly insane now. If charged he'd act on instinct. He'd run!

That he might die here, horribly, painfully, killed in the wild by this beast of the wild. Probably eaten by the beast. His remains never found. These thoughts banged in his brain and he braced himself. Thought of Angela. She'd be all right, he hoped. All right in New Eden with Peter or someone else or by herself. All right without him. That was a comfort somehow.

He was even in a funny way accepting of how he might die now. There would be something elemental about it, primal, in tune with the natural world of which he and everyone was a part. He was aware of the triteness of this revelation. But it was a revelation nonetheless.

The bear woofed again, and Tom began slowly to back away. By way of an experiment he began to talk to it, as if it were only a threatening dog. "It's okay, big fella. I'm not going to hurt you. You going to hurt me?"

The bear remained in its crouch, its enormous face, its intent, near-sighted eyes, its cylindrical snout, all pointed at him. Tom kept backing away until, almost stumbling over a fallen branch, he turned slowly around. Started slowly down the slope, angling in the direction of the old logging road, his shoulders hunched, the back of his neck bristling, fear shooting up into his mouth. He turned around, half-expecting to see the bear coming after him now, but it was nowhere in sight. He stopped to listen. Heard nothing. He was sweating, but his heart stopped pounding as he made his difficult way over fallen timber, through thickets of second growth, bushwhacking—that was the word for it, he remembered. He reached the old logging road, finally, and from there it was an easy walk back down to the lake and New Eden.

By that time he'd shrugged off his encounter with the grizzly, and in fact felt exhilarated! The encounter might have been fatal but it had not been, had not even come close, and he was filled now with an awareness of life, the wondrous gift of life, and what matter where it was going for him, with or without Angela. Whatever happened now, it would be all right, he thought. It would be all right.

Chapter 30

High summer. A succession of hot, sun-filled days that turned wonderfully cool after the sun went down. The mornings were cool, building gradually to the hot afternoons.

Their garden, despite its poor soil, was producing a harvest of greens that would have wilted in the heat but for the pails of water they took turns hauling from the lake. Then David, or was it Joel, suggested they might harness the creek for irrigation, as they *hadn't* done to produce hydro-electricity and might yet accomplish; that idea was again rejected as too expensive, and anyway, too complicated. Piping water from the creek, though, seemed simple enough.

So, with a couple hundred yards of relatively cheap plastic pipe and some clamps and couplings, they soon had a line from the creek to the garden—the screened intake lodged in the creek some fifty feet above the clearing—that provided enough gravity-flow pressure to operate a sprinkler and, in addition, run water to the hall. The creek was clear of silt now after the spring runoff, but still, the intake had to be cleaned periodically of fallen leaves and conifer needles were sucked onto the screen. That called for wading into the cold, rushing, actually refreshing water.

By August the corn they'd planted had tasselled out and ears began to form, but whether they'd actually get a crop, given the poor soil, was debatable. Sarah and Tom, both country types, doubted it. They'd have garlic, though, and onions. And in the fall they'd have a crop of squash. And turnips and potatoes. which could be left in the ground till freeze-up—and even later, if they got an insulating dump of snow before the ground froze.

"We'll need a root cellar, though," Sarah said, "or most of our vegetables will rot."

"Too bad we can't freeze them," Helen said.

Joel said, "No, no freezers, even if we had the electricity for one. Aren't we trying to get off the grid here? Better we should can our vegetables. Like our grandfolks did. Anybody know how to can?"

Sarah did. "We'd need jars, and a canning kettle. How's about digging a root cellar instead?"

The majority agreed, and the next day they started digging, taking turns with their one shovel and, glory be, the pick they found in the shed behind the dining hall. The digging was hard enough; every swing of the pick or probe with the shovel struck a rock, or a root, so it took until the evening to produce a hole roughly the size of a grave and considerably less than six feet deep.

The second day they struck water.

231

"Now what?" Joel said. They stood staring at the water oozing up into the hole.

"Make a well out of it?" the Professor suggested.

"Anybody know how?" Janice asked.

"We could maybe line the hole with rocks," Tom offered, remembering the abandoned well on his folks' farm that his father and the hired man eventually filled in before he and his sister Debbie, as children, fell into it.

"How we gonna do that," Mark asked, "while the fucker's filling with water?"

"Yeah," Clay added. "Who's for getting down in that mud?"

"I know what," Sarah said. "Why didn't I think of it before?" She pointed to the slope behind Chuck's shack. "We dig into the bank there. Like we're digging a mine shaft."

"Worth a try," David said.

They moved to the least rocky part of the slope behind Chuck's shack and, taking turns, one person with the pick, another with the shovel, started digging. They were lucky at first. The slope here was mostly gravel; but then they struck what the Professor called glacial till and the going got increasingly rough.

At lunchtime Helen and Angela left to make sandwiches for the crew. Peter showed up at some point and took a turn at shovelling. Janice took a turn. Work continued till suppertime, and after supper, David suggested they go back to work. "We got another couple of hours. We could finish the digging by dark."

Tom, though exhausted, was willing to work with David, but nobody else was. The consensus was to finish the job tomorrow.

The next day, though, only half the crew showed up, including Joel and David and Sarah, Tom and Angela and Chuck. Peter had stayed in his tent. Where was Janice? Chuck developed a blister and excused himself.

The rest kept gamely at it until they'd burrowed maybe ten feet into the slope.

"Isn't that enough?" Joel wondered.

"I doubt it," Sarah said, "though this isn't forty below Alberta. Anyway, we'll need timbers to shore it up, I think."

"I think we should dig some more," David said. "Spend another day at it."

The consensus was no. They spent the next day gathering poles, boards, whatever they could find to place over the ceiling and along the sides of what they now called their walk-in root cellar. The shoring up pleased everybody, but their work wasn't finished. They'd have to close the entrance somehow, Sarah said, to keep the cellar above freezing during the winter.

"We'll figure something out," Joel said.

By this time it had become obvious there were two groups in the commune: those who did most of the work and those who did as little as possible. Joel didn't want to make an issue of it, not yet anyhow. "Those serious about making it here will sort themselves out. Slackers will start to feel unwelcome and go away."

"You think so?" Helen said. "Sooner or later, some people will have to be asked to leave."

"Meanwhile," Tom broke in, surprising himself, "summer's almost over. Winter's coming. I didn't grow up on a farm for nothing. We gotta prepare for it. other than keeping our vegetables from freezing."

"I know that. We will," Joel said.

Tom had walked in on Joel and Helen having a discussion in the otherwise empty dining hall and inadvertently joined it.

"We need some solid people," Helen said.

"We have them," Joel said. "David and Sarah. You and me." He looked at Tom. "You too, Tom."

"Then there's Clay," Tom said. "And Peter. Mark's okay, when he's here, but he's often away, chasing tail. Robert tries, but . . ."

Clay would rather read, Tom thought. Robert? He was learned and funny, all intellectualized head on an out-of-shape body, totally urban, pretty much useless in what he called "this wilderness."

Angela. She hadn't been mentioned. Or Chuck, both of whom did their share. Peter? Peter would be gone, Tom thought—he hoped—as soon as the summer was over. Janice?

"Getting back to preparing for winter, we need firewood," Tom said.

"We have *some*," Joel said. "Behind the hall—left there, I guess, by the loggers."

"Not much."

"Right. So I guess you're right."

"We'll need a chainsaw"

"We can't afford one now."

"There must be used ones around. Cheaper than a new one."

"Time for another meeting," Helen said.

A meeting was held that evening after the meal. Joel opened with a little speech about their communal ideal of self-sustainment in perpetual conflict with their periodic and undeniable need for more money than Helen's trust fund provided— at least *some* money, now and then, for necessities they couldn't produce themselves and might never produce. Certain foods, for instance, beans and rice, sugar and tea and coffee, the odd treat, the odd indulgence, such as beer or wine, going to a movie once in a while at the drive-in down the valley or the theatre in Silver City, not to mention the basic tools they needed for working the land, for survival in this brave new world they were making. "For a start," he said, "we need to gather firewood for the winter. Tom? You want to speak on our need for a chainsaw?"

All eyes turned to Tom.

"Wait a minute,"Clay said. "Tom just got here. Is he some kind of expert all of a sudden?"

Tom had risen from the table as if he were back in Catholic school and Sister Superior had called on him. He felt the flush on his face, a twinge of anger.

"I'm new here, yes," Tom said, "but where I come from we burned wood and coal to keep us warm in the winter. We don't have a coal furnace here, and anyway, we probably couldn't afford to buy coal. But we have a wood stove in the hall and another in the bunkhouse. David has a stove in his A-frame, Chuck one in his shack. We can either buy firewood—assuming somebody could haul a couple loads in here and get out again—or, with a chainsaw, we could cut our own wood. We got the manpower—excuse me, the people power—and lots of trees around us. Either way's gonna cost us money. But buying a chainsaw, I think, will be cheaper in the long run than buying wood."

"Tom's right!" Sarah agreed. "We'll have to buy gas, and oil to mix with it, though. And chain oil, but that would be way cheaper than buying firewood."

"How much firewood do you think we'll need?" Helen asked.

Nobody knew for sure, but Sarah said, "I know it doesn't get as cold here as in Alberta. Or in Minnesota, right, Tom?"

"True, it doesn't get that cold here," Joel said, "but we get lots of snow. We did last year, anyhow."

"Did we ever," Chuck said.

"And that's another thing," said Sarah. "We'll be snowed in unless we get a boat—a canoe—so we can cross the lake for groceries."

"Why not leave the truck at the start of the logging road, off the plowed road into town?" David suggested.

"What, and slog all that way through the snow every time we need to go to town?" Clay said. "Besides, leaving the truck there it might get stolen or towed away as abandoned or some other shit."

"This ain't Detroit, Clay," Joel told him.

"Anyway," David said, "we have several stoves, and I guess we're gonna need several cords of wood to keep 'em going."

"How much is a cord again?" Joel asked.

"A pile of stacked firewood four-foot wide, four high, and eight feet long," Sarah told him.

"Sounds like a lot," Joel said.

"Enough for one stove, maybe," David guessed.

"But do we have the money for a chainsaw right now?"

Sarah asked. "Not to mention a canoe."

"Ah," Joel said. "That's the hassle."

Janice had remained silent through the discussion, a fascinated look on her face.

The upshot, as Sarah pointed out at the meeting after breakfast the next morning, was that somebody, or some bodies, would have to find a job.

That led to a discussion about who would go looking for work, and who would stay and gather firewood. Of course they'd need a chainsaw to gather firewood, which Joel thought they could come up with the money for after all, but what about a canoe and all the other stuff they'd need for winter? Where might a couple of them find immediate work?

The mill, David said. "One thing, though," he added. "Assuming the mill is hiring now, they'll ask for your social insurance number, or have you apply for one. What you might do is apply for work under a phony name and use that name to apply for a SIN."

"Perfect," said Joel. "Circumvent the system. Okay— assuming the mill's hiring, who's willing to apply there?"

The sudden silence caused everybody to laugh.

David said, "I hope to go tree planting again, sign on with the Harmony Farm crew, so I should keep myself open for that. Anyway, who's able-bodied enough here?" he asked. "Work at the mill is assembly line. Who's had that kind of experience?"

"I worked one summer on the line at the Chrysler plant in Detroit," Clay said. "Hated it, but I guess that makes me a candidate."

"I'll go," Tom said, suddenly excited at the prospect of

outside work.

"I'm with Tom," Mark said.

"Hold on," Joel said. "Don't forget the firewood we'll have to gather. Can we spare all three of these guys to go work at the mill?"

"I doubt they'd all be hired," David said.

"But what if they are?" Joel asked. "That would make a huge hole in our work force."

"Okay," Mark volunteered. "I'll stay back then."

"Good of you," Clay said—with some sarcasm, Tom thought.

"Just one guy getting a job there might do it," David submitted. "The mill's union and pays pretty good, I hear."

At this point Helen said, "I move that the three of you—Mark you stay in for the moment—draw straws to see who goes."

"Don't have any straws," Joel told her.

"Okay," Helen said, looking annoyed. "I'm thinking now of a number between one and ten. Mark?"

"Seven," Mark said.

"Clay?"

"Five," said Clay.

"Tom?"

"Three," Tom said.

"Tom wins!"

Chapter 31

The following Monday Tom drove in his Fairlane to the Galena sawmill and was directed to the office. There he was given an application form by a pleasant older woman who reminded him of his mother. He filled it out under the name of Joseph Harper (his private little joke: Joe Harper, friend of Tom Sawyer and Huck Finn in *The Adventures of Tom Sawyer*). For an address he put General Delivery, Galena, B.C.. Sure enough, the form asked for his social insurance number. When he told the woman he didn't have one, she said, "That's all right," and gave him a form to apply for one. Then she sent him out to the yard to see the foreman. "Ask for Nick."

Nick turned out to be a beefy, middle-aged Russian who looked Tom over and said, "Okay, I put you on green chain, starting tomorrow. Be here two-thirty. You got work boots? Gloves?"

Tom reported for work the next afternoon after first buying

leather gloves and expensive steel-toed boots at the general store in Galena. (After a quick meeting, the funds for them had been released from the communal stash, making quite a hole in it, Joel remarked.) At the mill he was issued a hardhat, given a few minutes' instruction, then put to work. Starting pay was minimum wage, but after a couple of shifts, on probation, he could join the union (required, actually). Then his pay would jump to the starting scale. Shifts were seven days on, then three days off. He was put on afternoons, 3 to 11. His next shift would be days, starting at seven in the morning.

The work was physically hard and demanded deftness. He was slow and awkward at first, earning the impatience of his fellow workers, until he got with the stream of boards coming off the conveyor and could grab one board after the other to make a load on his cart. They came in waves of the various sizes and grades. More than once the pile on his cart tipped over, and he had to *start* over. That brought shouts of laughter from those around him at first; later a round of curses. Despite his gloves, he developed blisters, eventually calluses.

"You gonna make it, boy?" Nick asked him his third day. He was a nice guy, Tom decided, if slightly threatening, like the chief of the boat on his submarine.

"I'll make it," Tom told him.

"Some guys, never," Nick said.

The apocryphal story was of a guy who, despairing of ever learning his job, one day climbed onto the conveyor leading to the chipper, the machine that chopped scrap lumber into bits, and allowed it to carry him into oblivion.

It was funny, almost believable, given the frustration of his first couple of shifts. Near the end of his first seven days, however, he found he could lose himself in the work's rhythm and come out of it—as used to happen on the farm, despite his longing for escape—rather pleasantly exhausted and pleased with his ability.

By that time he'd become an accepted member of the crew—they were mostly his age or younger, he guessed—and was enjoying the camaraderie. He could pretend he was one of them—maybe he *was,* just another working-class bloke. "Bloke." This was Canada, after all, a member of the British Commonwealth. This was *British* Columbia.

At the end of each shift, the crew headed straight to the Galena pub for pitchers of beer. They all, except Tom, drank as hard as they worked. Tom would join them for a quick glass or two, following which, to their cries of derision, leave the bar and drive back to New Eden.

It was like going from the real world back to the Land of Oz.

He found a buddy at the mill, a compact little Québécois named Adrien, ex-logger, longtime faller, who'd developed nerve damage, "faller's hands," after some ten years of working with a chainsaw. He'd had to quit falling, he said, before losing the use of his hands.

Tom told Adrien he had some French on his mother's side, which caused Adrien to break into the language until Tom stopped him.

"Sorry," he said. "My mother's great-grandparents were French-Canadian, but she spoke only English."

"Too bad, eh?" Adrien said.

"I know a little Spanish," Tom told him.

"How so?"

"My wife and I spent last winter in Mexico. A lifetime ago."

"First Mexico and now Canada, eh? You've left the States behind?"

"I guess."

The way Adrien used his body for emphasis when he spoke, how he stressed his words, reminded Tom of his maternal grandmother.

"The war, eh?"

"That and the general rat race. I used to go to work in a suit and tie."

"And now you're a hippie?"

"Sort of," Tom said.

Chapter 32

Angela was with Peter in his tent. It was mid-morning and the sun was beating down on it. They'd smoked some grass, made love, and she was wanting to talk now. *He* hardly ever talked when they were together, mainly listened, and she was beginning to wonder now if he even bothered to listen. She talked too much, she knew, probably bored him, maybe wished he was with someone else. Did it *matter* who he was with? If anybody, it must be Sarah he preferred, voluptuous Sarah, Sarah the freest of free spirits. But Sarah was with David now. Janice? She was with Tom now, but she'd been with Peter too, though not very much. How come? Those two had seemed made for each other, both outsiders, essentially loners, both passive, it seemed to Angela. Or were they? Passive-aggressive? Angela thought, remembering her college course in psychology.

"I try to stay cool," Peter told Angela, and she tried to match his coolness while wanting more from him, *more*—and there were hints of more. He was a secret she wanted to know. A good part of why she was with him, she'd come to realize, was to learn his secret. It would not be the same as what Janice called his number.

They were lying side by side now. He'd begun playing with himself to work up another erection. She began to help him. When he climbed over her, she was ready for him, but instead of his usual, gentle insertion, he crawled forward and presented her with his stiff penis.

Without thinking, she took it into her mouth. He laced his fingers in her hair and said, "Ah. That's right, baby. Ahhh," and she remembered the few times she'd done this with Tom, how it had happened on impulse at first, surprising both of them.

He grasped her head now and thrust into her throat. She gagged, coughed it out. "I can't," she said.

"Sorry. I won't do that again."

"No. I mean I can't do this with you."

"Why not? I would've done *you* afterwards. Shit," he said, and collapsed beside her.

She grasped his penis, to make amends. He pushed her hand away.

"It's what I especially like," he said. "I thought we'd reached that point."

"I'm sorry," Angela said. But she wasn't.

"I thought you *liked* being with me. I thought—"

"I do! It's just . . . it's something I've hardly ever done. I can't . . ."

"Do it with anybody but your husband? Aren't we all past that bullshit? Aren't we free? Isn't being free what we're about here?"

"I don't feel that free," Angela said.

His tent was suffocating, suddenly. She sat up. "My God, it's too hot in here. I can't breathe."

She unzipped the tent flap and threw it open to see Tom, between shifts at the mill, a pack on his shoulder, heading out of New Eden's clearing for another of his solitary hikes up the mountain. She almost called to him. She wished she was going with him.

Chapter 33

Toward the end of August Joel and David pulled into the clearing one day with a canoe in back of the truck. It was a used aluminum fifteen-footer Joel had seen advertised on the bulletin board at the co-op in Galena. The price listed was $100, but Joel got it for $90, cash, after pointing out the canoe's several dents and scratches.

Now they had a means for fishing on the lake, rather than just from the dock, as well as crossing the lake to Galena this winter when the old logging road doubtless would be blocked with snow. Anyway, the steep grade out of the old logging camp, once covered with snow, would be too slippery for either of their vehicles to climb.

Except for the canoe, they'd be snowbound.

There was urgent talk now of preparing for winter, gathering firewood, buying a chainsaw. Talk but no action. For one thing, they didn't yet have the money to buy a chainsaw.

Meanwhile, the weather was perfect, the days went beautifully by, winter seemed far off.

Then it was Labour Day, summer officially over, and there was the quickening feel of fall in the air. It was back to school for the kids in and around Galena, and the town seemed full of them when Tom, off day shift at the mill, stepped out of the pub after the requisite beer or two with his fellows and headed back to New Eden.

In New Eden, the subject of tree planting came up again. David suggested they bid on a couple of the contracts they'd find listed at Forestry headquarters in Silver City.

"You're landed, aren't you?" David asked Joel.

"Yup. Helen too."

"Good. There should be no hassle then. We can bid for a contract under your name."

A couple of days later Joel and David drove into Silver City. At the regional office of the B.C. Forest Service they found that most of the contracts still open for bids looked rather forbidding: thousands of trees to plant in remote areas by a crew of at least a dozen, David figured. One contract, though, a comparatively small one—120,000 Douglas fir and ponderosa pine seedlings on a recently logged site in the Trout River watershed beyond Silver City—looked doable, he said. Joel asked for an application, and he and David took it to a restaurant to do some figuring.

"We'll need food for a crew of six or so," David said. "Won't have to camp in the bush or stay in a motel or rent a house because it says we can bunk in the warehouse at the ranger station."

Joel filled out the application, including his social insurance number and a figure he and David hoped would be the low bid, and signed it. Then they drove back to New Eden.

The next day it started raining, and didn't stop for three days. When it did, there was no sun anymore, only columns of low cloud along the lakeshore and layers of cloud wreathing the slopes. You could see your breath in the mornings. Swimming was over for the year, and people complained of the cold at night. They started drawing on their dwindling supply of firewood to warm the hall during the evening and to take the chill out of the bunkhouse at bedtime. It began to rain again, a steady drizzle that kept on and on—day after day. Winter was definitely coming. They should start firewood gathering; everybody knew that, but nobody wanted to work in the rain.

"It's not gonna rain forever," Joel said. "We had some nice weather in October last year."

"I don't think we should *wait* till October," David said.

Robert, the Professor, cleared his throat. "It occurs to me that we might have a problem getting wood. Thanks to Tom, we'll have the money soon for a chainsaw, but does anybody here know how to use one? And does anybody know how to go about *getting* firewood off these mountains? Where to find it, for instance? What's the best wood to look for?"

"Can't be that hard," Chuck said. "All these trees . . ."

"You don't cut *live* trees and burn green wood. I know that much," David said.

Joel said, "There must be a lot of dead stuff lying around. And anyway, cutting live trees wouldn't be environmentally hip."

Tom spoke up at last. "I know of somebody who might

248

advise us. Somebody I work with at the mill who used to be a faller."

Everybody turned to him.

"I start a new shift the day after tomorrow," Tom said. "This guy's on the same crew with me, so I'll see him then. If he's agreeable, we could meet him after work one day."

Two days later, Joel and David met Tom and Adrien in the Galena pub after they came off shift. Adrien said, "Of course! I give you a hand. I'd love to see your setup, eh? I still have my saw. I'm not supposed to use it anymore because of my hands, eh? But I could lend it to you, and show you how to handle it so you don't cut your legs off."

"Great," Joel said. "We were going to buy a saw, but if we can use yours . . . When could you start?"

Adrien looked at Tom. "Our shift ends Wednesday, eh Tom?"

"Right. I could bring you out to New Eden then," Tom said. "You could stay with us for the three days we're off."

"*Tres bien*," Adrien said. "Hey, you got any nice hippie girls out there for this French lover?" Then, as if in apology, he added, "You guys really hippies? You don't look that much like the ones I see in Montreal or Vancouver."

"Weekend hippies there," David said. "Students. We're maybe the real thing," he said, winking at Tom.

"Yeah, we're serious," Tom said. "Dedicated back-to-the-landers. New pioneers." He and David grinned at each other.

Adrien said, "We have some fun, eh?"

By the following Thursday it had stopped raining. The day promised to be lovely, not summer warm anymore but autumn warm. The firewood gatherers, with David at the wheel and Adrien in the cab beside him, left New Eden in the communal truck right after breakfast. Joel, Mark and Tom stood in the truck bed, which held Adrien's heavy chainsaw, a container of chain oil, a can of mixed gas, jugs of drinking water and a bag of sandwiches prepared by Helen and her kitchen crew. In low gear they switchbacked up the logging road to where they began to see frost on the bracken and thimbleberry.

"They were logging up here till about ten years ago," Adrien said. "Did it with horses at first. The road out of the camp? That was originally a skid road then—for hauling the logs out to the mill with horses."

"Then later they must have used logging trucks," Joel said.

"*Oui*, the last contractor kept a truck in the camp for hauling loads off the mountain. But that first grade out of the camp? It's too steep for a truck with a load on. So you got that platform and winch for dropping logs into the lake to tow to the mill."

Ah, Tom thought. He had an image now of the working camp, saw the tugboat pulling rafts of logs to the mill.

Adrien cut the first tree down for them. "Can't numb my hands any more than they are already, eh?" It was a standing dead larch—a snag, he called it—one of the better firewood trees. "The way it's leaning," he said, "it'll fall against that big fir over there and maybe hang up. You don't want that to happen because then you have to cut the live tree holding it up and it's kind of dangerous, eh? Both trees could come down on you."

He eyed the snag, then pointed to a narrow opening

between the fir and another tree, a *live* larch, Adrien said, "There. I drop it between those two."

They watched him cut a wedge out of the snag—the under-cut, he called it—that left an overhang in the trunk aimed at the opening between the trees.

"Stand back now," Adrien ordered. He yanked the starter rope, his saw erupted into an angry whine, and he started cutting from the other side of the undercut and slightly above it. The saw bit into the wood and the chips flew against his legs. When virtually through the trunk with the tree standing fast, Adrien stepped back and turned off the saw. He inserted a plastic wedge into the cut and whacked at it with the flat side of his ax The tree began to lean, there was a resounding *crack,* Adrien jumped aside, and the tree fell over with a mighty *whump*—right where it was supposed to.

"Neat," Mark said.

Adrien fired up his saw again, and went along the fallen tree snipping off its branches. Then he turned to his spectators. "Okay, now we buck the tree—cut it to lengths. Some people cut to stove length and split their wood on site, but a lot of oldtimers cut to truck length and haul the wood out to be cut and split and stacked by their shed. You get more loads in a day that way. Who wants to try bucking?"

Tom moved, but David was ahead of him and picked up the saw.

"Okay," Adrien said, "you see how the tree fell against that rock? Gravity's pulling on it, eh? So you cut from the top where the saw won't bind, and then from the bottom where it'll pinch otherwise."

"I get it," David said, revved the engine and, lifting the saw above his head, cut an eight-foot length off the fallen tree. Then another, and another, until he reached the rock. Then, behind the rock, he placed the saw blade under the leaning trunk, cut upwards through it, and the two ends dropped to the ground.

"*Bien!*" Adrien told David. Then:"Okay. Now you gotta be careful cutting a log on the ground, cause you hit the dirt or a rock, you dull the saw, eh? So what you do, you start a series of cuts along the log, eight-foot lengths, remember, not too close to the ground. Then you roll the log over and finish your cuts."

Tom made the topside cuts without mishap. Then Joel and Mark rolled the trunk over and took turns making the final cuts. They threw the log lengths down onto the road, then loaded them into the truck.

Larch and birch made the best firewood, Adrien said. But *dead* birch, fallen or standing dead, was no good because the wood turned soft and fibrous, punky, inside the bark's air-tight casing.

"You gotta cut it green, then score the bark or split it up right away and let it dry for a year, or anyway, till spring," Adrien told them. As the scored birch dried, he said, the bark tended to peel away from the wood. The bark made good fire starter. Along with larch and birch, fir was okay. Cedar was too soft but good for kindling. Pine was soft, pitchy, burned hot but too quickly. Some of the best wood for burning, though you could hardly fill your woodshed with it, was Douglas maple, a scrub tree found growing in scattered clumps in moist ground. Within the clump there were usually three or four snags, some a foot or more in diameter but most so slender they wouldn't need splitting, all with their bark peeling off and the wood so hard and seasoned that pieces knocked together sounded like struck bowling pins.

They moved up the mountain to the old landing Tom had found with its pile of slash. It must have been there since the last logging on this mountain years ago, Adrien said. Much of the pile was filled with dirt and debris, collapsing down to compost, but there was still a lot of firewood left in it, he said. They cut the ends off the trees protruding from the pile, then dug through it, lifting or pulling out more wood that could be cut into eight-foot lengths and loaded into the truck.

They got a couple of loads off the slash pile and more loads, above and below the old landing—two or three loads a day, taking advantage of the good weather, for the three days Adrien and Tom were off shift from the mill. Then Joel and Mark and Chuck took turns bucking the wood into stove lengths and splitting it, while everyone else, men and women working together, stacked it.

There were various lengths, various stacks, needed to supply the various stoves—the two (including the cookstove) in the hall, the one in the bunkhouse, David's stove in his A-frame and Chuck's in his shack. Peter and Robert, who otherwise might have been in the way, forming a somewhat odd couple, made themselves useful by gathering fallen branches in the surrounding woods and breaking them into sticks to provide kindling.

A week later, when Tom and Adrien were off shift again at the mill, they, along with David, made repeated trips up the mountain and brought down load after load of eight-foot logs until Adrien, looking at the logs piled beside the hall and mentally transforming them into pieces of split firewood, said, "We got enough, I think."

The slash pile had supplied only a fraction of their firewood. The rest they'd found, here and there, on the slopes above or below the logging road, the easiest, of course, being snags or deadfalls they could cut to truck length above the road and throw down to the truck, the hardest being wood cut below the road that had to be carried *up* to it.

This latest pile, cut to stove length, split and stacked, would add another couple of cords to the wood already stacked in the lean-to shed in back of the hall. They'd more than fill the shed now, which would hold about six cords, Adrien thought. After the shed was filled, they could stack the additional wood under a tarp.

"Hey, that wasn't all that hard," Mark said a couple of days later, "with all of us working at it."

"Cooperative labour, people," Joel reminded them.

"Many hands make the work lighter," added Sarah. "That's what my grandmother used to say."

Chapter 34

The next day Joel went into Galena for their mail and came back with a notice from Forestry that they'd won the Trout River contract they'd bid on.

"A hundred and twenty thousand trees," Clay said. "That's a lot of planting. How long will it take us?"

"With a crew of six or so, about a month," David said. "Twenty days, if the weather's good and we each plant about a thousand trees a day."

"A thousand trees a day!" Joel said. "Is that possible?"

"Highballers can do twice that. Depending on the terrain."

"Okay." Joel looked around. "Who wants to go planting?"

"I'll go," Mark said.

"And I," said Robert.

Looking at Robert, David said, "Planting's hard, Professor. A lot harder than cutting firewood."

"I'd like to try it," Robert said.

"Me too," said Tom.

"What about your mill job?" Joel asked.

"I'll quit. Couldn't get out to it in the winter anyway, unless I paddled the canoe across the lake every morning. Every night for graveyard shift? Nobody's going to plow our road, right? We'll be snowed in, remember?"

Peter raised his hand now and said, "I'll go too," surprising everyone.

"You sure, Peter?" David asked.

"Yes," he said firmly. 'I want to be included."

Which is when Angela came on board.

A couple of days later, after Tom told him he was quitting work to go tree planting. Adrien looked down at his boots for a moment, then said, "I like to join you guys, if you'll have me. I'm ready for a change, eh?"

They found their foreman in the office. "Boys, you quit like this without notice, you forfeit pay," Nick told them. "Your whole shift." He looked at them like a stern father.

"So?" Adrien said, shrugging and throwing up his hands. He turned to Tom. "Let's go, eh?"

Tom drove them to the Galena pub for a beer. They ordered a pitcher and filled their glasses. "Be nice out in the bush this time of year," Adrien said. "When it ain't raining. You think they take me on, Tom?"

"Hell, yes," Tom said. In New Eden, an impromptu meeting was called, there was a show of hands, and Adrien was roundly accepted, not only as a member of the planting crew but, following Helen's enthusiastic nomination, as a provisional member of the commune. Adrien grinned, and blushed, through the remnants of his tan.

They left for Trout River the following Sunday, supplied with foam rubber mattresses and sleeping bags, canteens, dried and canned food—David, Mark, Robert, Angela and Peter, Tom and Adrien, all piled into the cab and in the back of the communal truck over which a canvas top had been fitted. Tom left his Fairlane in New Eden for occasional runs by the home crew into Galena. The home crew included Joel and Helen, Clay, Janice, Sarah and Chuck, who would finish the splitting and stacking of New Eden's winter wood.

It was a sixty-mile drive, past Silver City and then east over the Bearpaw Range to Trout River near the west slope of the Rockies. The Forest Service headquarters was on the edge of town. The ranger in charge took them into the combined shop and warehouse behind the office and showed them a space on the floor upstairs where they could lay their mattresses and sleeping bags. The planting site was a clearcut above the river, some fifteen miles out of town.

Tree planting, Tom soon discovered, was as hard as any farmwork, like a combination of mountain climbing and pick-and-shovel labour. In fact, you used a pick-like tool with a flattened blade called a mattock. Grasping your mattock, and with a canvas bucket holding two hundred seedlings strapped to your shoulder—plants three to six inches long, not including their roots—you struggled up the mountain, through brush and over rocks, stopping every three strides to "scalp" with your mattock a patch of ground of the sticks and stones and vegetation in front of you before driving the blade into the ground to its haft. A quick, back-and-forth tilt of the blade and you had a V-shaped hole in which to plant a tree. Tuck in the roots, close the hole, stamp the ground around it, then take three more strides (approximately eight feet) and plant another tree. Another eight feet, another tree, and so it went until your bucket was empty. Then it was back down the mountain for more trees out of the boxes stashed in the back of the truck.

The mountain was rocky. Driving your mattock into its shallow soil you often hit a rock, jarring your arm. Do that enough and you developed planter's elbow.

"Takes time, though," Adrien told them. "Like faller's hands, eh?"

That first day Tom planted three hundred and fifty trees, and was exhausted. By the end of the week, in better shape, he was planting at least five hundred a day. Adrien and David were already planting a thousand and more each day, and that's what Tom set himself grimly to match. He was fuelled not so much by their example as by the sight of Angela and Peter, planting together as a couple. They were doing surprisingly well; rather, Angela was doing well, better than Peter, who seemed not to have a competitive bone in his skinny body.

Robert didn't make it. He was so stiff after the first day, he could hardly get out of his sleeping bag the next morning. Their second day he dropped so far behind the others they lost sight of him, and David went looking for him. He found the Professor, far down the slope, barely able to swing his mattock anymore but still gamely at it, gray and sweating. David took his bag of trees and told him to go back to the truck.

The next morning, by consensus, he was excused from planting that day. That evening, after a meal of rice and canned clams prepared over the two-burner propane camp stove the Forest

Service had lent them, Robert announced he was quitting. They were sitting around the smelly oil stove in the middle of the warehouse that barely heated the building's cavernous space (on the mountain every day, they felt the approach of winter as soon as the sun went down). Robert looked appealingly around him.

"This is more than I can take, comrades," he said. "I've had my nose in books most of my life. I'll have a stroke."

"Hey, how about being our cook?" Mark said. "We can't live on rice and canned clams, and taking turns at cooking is a bummer after planting all day."

"I'm afraid I can't cook," Robert said.

"You mean you don't want to," David said.

"I mean I can't cook. You'd find that out right away."

"It's okay," Joel said. "You can go back to New Eden. One of us will have to take you, though."

"I can hitchhike."

"Maybe one of the rangers is headed for Silver City," David said. "Or could take you to Trout River so you could catch a ride from there."

"What are my chances, do you think?"

"Fairly slim, I suppose," David acknowledged. "People in Trout River probably do their shopping in Columbia, not way over in Silver City."

"There a bus service?" Robert asked.

"No way," Adrien said.

That's when Mark offered to drive Robert back to New Eden in the communal truck. They'd leave first thing in the morning so Mark could be back by the evening. He'd miss a planting day, but so what? They couldn't leave the Professor standing out on the highway.

The two left at first light the next morning. The others were up shortly after, including Peter, who walked carefully down the stairs and vomited on the warehouse floor. He'd come down with something and was excused from planting that day. The remaining five, David, Angela, Clay, Adrien and Tom, in a Forestry van, drove to the site and planted that day in a cold drizzle, nevertheless managing to empty their boxes of seedlings.

Tom and Angela planted together. It was a little tense at first; Tom felt it, if maybe Angela didn't. But then they relaxed and planted well together. They even talked a little, both carefully avoiding contention. It was nice. Tom plunked seven hundred in the ground, Angela some five hundred. Adrien, not surprisingly, planted his thousand; David not quite a thousand. They quit in the late afternoon after the drizzle turned to rain and arrived, drenched and shivering, back at the warehouse to find Mark returned from New Eden.

"Who's for the hot springs?" David asked. There was a hot springs, the ranger had told them, some miles up a dirt road outside of town.

"Who isn't?" Angela said.

Peter, though up and feeling better, declined. Angela looked at him, hesitated, but he waved her off. They left him huddled by the stove.

With Tom and Angela in the truck cab, David at the wheel, and Mark and Adrien in back under the canvas top, they drove to the hot springs and afterwards treated themselves to dinner in the hotel restaurant in Trout River.

It was still raining when they got back to the warehouse, making them wonder if they'd be able to plant in the morning.

Peter was upstairs, no doubt asleep, and Angela went up there to join him in their shared bedroll.

"Who'd like a drink?" David asked.

He produced a bottle of Irish whiskey and passed it around. Everybody took a hit, then another. They sat around the stove on empty tree boxes, soaking up the stove's welcome heat. They were quiet for a while, letting the alcohol do its work. David was especially quiet. He was like that sometimes, Tom had noticed.

Mark lit a joint and passed it around. Adrien took a toke. David waved it off and pulled at his whisky. "My drug of choice," he told them. "I tried opium in Nam but avoided most of the shit over there. Not like some guys. You were wise, you stayed sharp."

He took swig out of his bottle and passed it around again.

Mark, perhaps loosened by the whiskey, asked what Tom himself was thinking. "What was it really like over there, David?"

David looked down and didn't say anything. Then he said, "The people hid from us. Going through the villages we'd find them empty. They were as scared of us, I guess, as we were of them. And we were scary, all right. We were fucked up. All locked and loaded, all pumped up out of fear and paranoia. It was like you were outside of yourself, watching what you did. Watching what *we* did, which wasn't always good. I was a long way from Philly."

David took another pull from his bottle, then capped it. "I'm hitting the pad," he said. "Good night, folks."

"Good night," the others said. And presently followed David up the stairs to their sleeping bags on the floor above.

The next morning it had stopped raining, but they knew everything would be wet and dripping in the bush. They put on Forest Service slickers, prepared for discomfort. By noon, however, the sun was out and they were sweating in their slickers; by mid-afternoon, they were planting with their shirts off, including Angela.

That was the day when Tom, with a bag slung under each shoulder and forging ahead of everybody, planted all the way up the slope to where it levelled to a plateau and a grove of birch and aspen that might have been part of a flat, Midwestern forest. Except it was on top of a mountain, at least a mile above sea level.

Through a break in the trees he looked down on the river valley far below, the river hidden by trees, and on the slope he'd just climbed, in eight-foot stages, emptying the two bags slung under his shoulders that together had held eight hundred Douglas fir seedlings. He stood on top of the world, feeling suddenly at home, a flatlander no longer.

He walked to a thick aspen, took out his Buck folding knife, and carved his initials, *T. W.*, into the soft bark, and the date, *20 October 1970*, putting the day before the month, Navy style. Then he yelled across to the opposite slope as if calling the cows back home in Minnesota. "*Come boss! Come baaas!* and heard his voice, like a confirmation, come back to him.

Chapter 35

But then seeing Angela and Peter planting together, seeing them together every day, so obviously a couple, then having to watch them go to bed together every evening—it was a sickness inside him, a goad. It crammed him with the energy to charge up the mountain every day, to plant as many or more trees than even David or Adrien did. His wife and her lover were too close. They were rubbing their affair in his face! New Eden was too close. Out on the slopes, in the mountain air planting trees, he came to realize how hothouse, how smothering, New Eden was. Out on the slopes he might have breathed, except for Angela and Peter. They'd brought New Eden with them.

Meanwhile, there was a lovely succession of warm fall days, fine planting weather. But they were on a burned-over slope now that was a jumble of blackened, fallen timber they had to climb over or crawl under, accumulating soot, so that they looked like coal miners after a day of planting.

Then it turned cold and rainy, and they began wearing sweaters under their Forest Service rain jackets. Near the top of a slope one day and into snow, thoroughly chilled and with trees still in their bags, they decided to quit. At the Forestry station, they were given the weekend off. Gratefully, they piled into the communal truck and drove back to New Eden.

The big news when they got there was that something called the War Measures Act had been declared by Canada's prime minister after some kind of insurrection in Quebec. French separatists had kidnapped a couple of officials, killed one of them, and now the military had been called out and the police given authority to break into houses and arrest people without bail. Civil liberties had been suspended. Word of this had come over the CBC via Joel and Helen's transistor radio.

"Fascism," the Professor declared, "ever waiting to rear its ugly head."

Helen said, "How do *you* feel about this, Adrien?"

Adrien shrugged. "I'm French-Canadian, eh? But I'm no separatist."

"Oh, and something *else* happened," Joel announced, as if by the way. He looked at Tom, then looked away. "It's about your car, Tom. We had an accident."

Only now did Tom notice that his car was missing. "Oh?"

"It was the weather," Joel said, "and Clay—"

"I'm so sorry, man," Clay said.

"What *happened*, for Godsake?"

What happened was that Clay, starting for Galena for groceries one rainy day, failed to make it up the steep grade out of the clearing in Tom's Fairlane. Attempting to back down for another try, he slid off the road. Tom's car lay below the road now. A tree had stopped it from rolling into the lake.

"Shit," Tom said. "I only got liability insurance."

"Hey! Maybe it'll cover my injuries," Clay said. then added when he caught the look on Tom's face, "Just kidding, man."

Clay had suffered a bump on his head and a couple of bruises. Tom noticed the bump now. It wasn't bad.

"We thought of getting a tow truck," Joel offered, "but the cost would have been a minimum of fifty dollars."

"You couldn't afford that?" Tom asked. "We can't afford it now?"

"Our stash is about empty," Joel said. "Helen's trust payment is late."

Tom walked to where his car had gone over the bank. There it was, down near the water, nearly upside down against a tree. Really, it was a miracle Clay hadn't been badly injured.

He scrambled down to it. The car had rolled once, maybe twice; its body was caved and dented, the windows cracked or broken, oil and coolant still spilling from it. His good old faithful Ford, the car he and Angela had bought together at the happy start of their marriage. Totalled, just a pile of junk now.

He climbed back up to the road, swallowing his loss, his anger, where the others waited for his reaction. Angela left Peter to stand beside him.

"Fuck it. It's just the best car I ever had."

Chuck said, "Karma, man."

Janice said, "It was just some material thing, Tom. Now you're free of it."

She was right, of course, and he felt a rush of warmth toward her, though she wasn't with him anymore; she was with Chuck now, it seemed. And, yeah, he felt himself letting go, letting go of his car, letting go of a lot of things. Having nothing left to lose. That was freedom, maybe. Like the song said.

They had the weekend to rest up. Angela and Peter went off together. So did David and Sarah. Mark hung out in the communal hall, catching up on his reading. Adrien, however, took a look at the pile of logs behind the hall, still waiting to be bucked up, then split and stacked, and started his chainsaw. Tom, thinking of Angela and Peter balling away in Peter's tent, was as fired up as the whining saw. He threw his shirt off, told Adrien, "Let me do the cutting. You got your faller's hands, remember?"

Tom started bucking the logs, cutting them into stove lengths, and Adrien began splitting. Chuck, looking guilty, came out of the hall and started stacking wood outside the lean-to, which was already full. Then Janice came out, wanting to take a turn at the splitting. Adrien let her, being patient with her awkwardness at first.

Then David and Sarah appeared, Sarah with what looked like a post-coital flush on her face. David took the saw from Tom. Sarah joined Chuck in stacking and Adrien took over splitting again from Janice. David finished bucking, shut off the saw, and turned to stacking. Tom finished the splitting. The others finished the stacking. The result was at least another cord to add to the five cords or so in the lean-to.

Adrien said, "We keep warm this winter, eh?"

After the supper that night, Peter announced he wasn't feeling well again. He didn't think he could plant anymore.

Sarah said, "I'll take his place."

David turned to Peter, not quite disguising his sarcasm. "Thanks for all your help, Peter. Hope you feel better."

Peter shrugged, extracted himself from the table, and walked out of the hall. Angela started to follow, but he waved her off.

Tom saw the pain in her eyes.

They went back to planting, in fine weather again, though the mornings were cold and frosty before the sun rose over the mountains and warmed them at their work. Then the weather turned cloudy, grew freezing cold in the high elevations, and they tried working with gloves. But pulling seedlings out of your bag with gloves on proved awkward. So they suffered numb fingers.

Then it was raining again, a cold, persistent drizzle that made planting an endurance test each day as they struggled up the slippery slopes, plunking their trees into the wet, rocky soil. Snow was sometimes in the air, and in fact they usually found snow as they neared the top of whatever slope they were working. They fell into pairs, David and Sarah, naturally; Mark and Adrien. That left Tom with Angela. They worked fine together, as they had before. Didn't talk much, as before.

By the second week in November the weather had deteriorated to such an extent they thought of quitting; thought of stashing trees, burying whole bunches of them, as they'd heard some crews did when the going got tough.

But then, in a final, heroic push, three days of exposure to the cold and wet, they completed their contract, plunked the last of their 120,000 trees into the rocky ground and returned to New Eden to learn that Peter was gone—gone where nobody knew for sure. He'd left without leaving even a note for Angela. Tom watched her walk to the lakeshore and stand looking out over the water. It was all he could do not to go to her.

Over-written
throughout.

Not enough
events

too much detail
about mundane event
e.g. tree planting

Chapter 36

A week after the planting crew's return to New Eden, Tom woke one morning and looked out the window by his upper bunk to see the ground covered with about a foot of snow. The trees were caked with it, the sky was a whitish gray. It looked like more snow was coming.

Angela stirred in the bunk below him.

"What do you see, Tom?"

"Winter," he said.

She threw her covers off and stepped to the window. She'd been sleeping in her clothes.

"Brrrr," she said. "Let's make a fire."

There were still coals from last night in the old cast-iron stove that stood in the middle of the bunkhouse. Tom raked them forward into a pile, placed some kindling on them, then some larger pieces on top of the kindling, and finally a ball of crumpled newspaper on top of the wood. He closed the stove door and opened the vent and the damper. Presently he heard the muffled roar that told him the paper had burst into flame creating a rushing draft up the stovepipe chimney. He opened the stove door again to see the kindling on fire, the flames licking at the larger wood. Closed the door and let the fire burn full blast for a minute, then closed the vent to a quarter inch and adjusted the damper.

Angela hunched over the stove, though there was no heat coming yet. She straightened, hugging herself, looking unhappy. Tom longed to hold her.

"Do you mind if I go back to bed for a while?"

"Why should I?"

That sounded a little snarky—to her, too, he guessed—and she looked away. Then she moved to her bunk and got under the covers. She turned her back to him. He turned his back on her. *Damn it*, he thought. Damn *us*.

The bunkhouse was quiet. People had begun sleeping in with the dismal weather outside and no light until half the morning was gone; no sun, only a leaden sky with winter coming. Well, winter was here at last; here was the first snow and to Tom it was heartening for some reason. Let the others sleep in, if they wanted. Sleeping in was depressing. It was an admission you had nothing to get up for in the morning.

If nothing else, Tom got up to write in his journal, to document this particular time in his life, this place where he'd begun to feel as alienated, really, as he'd felt in Chicago while writing pedestrian copy for the self-proclaimed world's greatest newspaper.

What's to happen now between Angela and me? Now that
Peter's gone, after what appears to have been little more

*than a summer vacation for him, while Angela gave him
the gift of herself. Did he give any of himself to her? Will
she stay here in New Eden? Will I?*

Adrien was up. Then, one by one, the rest of them were
up and gathered around the stove. The stove was throwing
some heat, finally. People dressed by the fire. The men stepped
outside to piss in the snow. The women took turns using the
outhouse. Then they all trooped into the communal hall,
where Helen and Joel and Helen's little girl slept on foam-rub-
ber mattresses, Brightness on the floor of the partitioned-off
kitchen, Joel and Helen in the pantry. The cookstove heated
the kitchen and the pantry too, when Brightness's parents
didn't have the door closed for privacy. The hall itself was
more or less heated by the wood stove positioned near the
north wall, its chimney elbowed out the side of the wall. There
was no fire in it yet. Joel was just starting to make one.

"We're out of rice," Helen told them after everyone was
seated at the trestle table with bowls of her hot oatmeal—por-
ridge, Sarah called it—before them. She and Sarah, by unspo-
ken agreement, did most of the cooking now. They didn't
seem to mind, and it was a relief to everybody else. "We're out
of beans too," Helen said. "And sugar and tea and coffee—our
staples, in other words. Somebody's gotta go into Galena
for groceries."

"You think our truck can get out of here now?" Robert
asked. "After this snow?"

"The tires are pretty bad," Joel said

"That's the thing, eh?" Adrien said. "This snow is the kind
you mostly get here, wet and slippery, good for making snowballs, eh? A bitch to drive in, though, even with good tires. We

try to get out of here with the truck, we could slide off the road like Clay did with Tom's car."

Tom didn't need to be reminded.

"Okay, so we cross the lake in our canoe," Mark said. "That's why we bought the sucker, right?"

Joel looked out a window. "The lake looks fairly calm now. Who wants to paddle across it this morning? Mark?"

Before Mark could speak, David said, "I'll go."

Tom said, "I'll go too."

Mark looked a little miffed. "You guys know how to paddle?"

Chapter 37

They set out a half hour later, armed with peanut butter and jelly sandwiches, a jug of water, forty dollars from the communal pot, and Helen's list. They were dressed in sweaters and jackets they could strip off once they'd warmed up paddling There was a wind and some chop on the lake but nothing to worry about. They carried the canoe down to the water and Tom, allowing David the helm, scrambled to the bow, knelt, and took up his paddle. David shoved them off, jumped aboard, and began stroking with his paddle while also working it like a tiller to keep them on course. Tom simply paddled, shifting sides periodically to relieve the ache in his arms. He was out of shape already, despite tree planting. The canoe seemed hardly to move through the water.

Paddling steadily, the wind in their faces, it took them some forty minutes to make the three-mile crossing. They pulled into the shore below the town and tied up at the wooden pier.

The wind was gusting now. The canoe started banging against the pier. "We'd better pull it out of the water," David said.

They got back in the canoe and paddled in the near surf along the shore to the lakeside little park. Pulled the canoe up under some trees, then walked past the cement obelisk in the park with its bronze plaque honouring the American adventurer who'd founded the town during the region's silver rush at the turn of the century. Walked up Galena's main street to the co-op store and dug out Helen's list.

Rice, lentils, peanut butter, honey. Maple syrup. Olive oil and vinegar. Whole wheat flour. Beans, both black and white. Potatoes, carrots, onions and garlic. What else? Cabbage, broccoli, romaine lettuce, though the greens would soon spoil—or freeze—in what had turned out to be their unsuccessful root cellar. They'd failed to make an adequate door for it.

"Beer!" David said. "I don't see beer on the list."

"Or wine," Tom said. "You think we're allowed?"

"Whatta you think?"

"What about dope? If Mark and Clay had anything to say about it, *that'd* be on the list."

"Well, it isn't." David said. "Anyway, a little beer, a little wine, they're staples, wouldn't you say?"

"We got the money for it? This is quite a list Helen has given us."

At the checkout they were still a couple dollars short after the pretty young clerk had rung up their purchases.

"As far as I'm concerned, we can eliminate the broccoli," Tom said.

"I happen to like broccoli," David said, and fished a wad of bills out of his jeans.

"Don't tell anybody," David said, "but I keep a private little stash. Call it the individual in me."

"Haw, so you've been holding out," Tom said with a grin.

"So? How much're *you* hiding, buddy?"

Exactly $300 US, Tom reminded himself, rescued out of the tackle box in the sprung-door trunk of his wrecked car, along with his typewriter, which miraculously, in its hard plastic case, hadn't been damaged. The money, his "escape" fund, as he now thought of it, was stashed in the zippered folder in which he also kept his journal. It was all he had left of his half of their savings, his and Angela's. Her half, $600, still resided in their Chicago bank.

"Maybe more than you," Tom admitted.

At the government liquor store they debated whether to buy wine or beer; decided that wine would be easier to carry and maybe last longer. Decided on gallons of both red and white to accommodate folks' different tastes and carried the jugs, along with the groceries, loaded in their packs, to the canoe.

There were whitecaps on the lake now.

"Looks bad," Tom said. "Think we should wait to cross?"

"I don't think so," David said. "It's gonna be dark pretty soon, and this ain't gonna stop. We wait, we could be here all night and maybe tomorrow too. Where would we stay, with what's left of our money? We know how to handle a canoe. We'll be all right."

They put the canoe in the water and pushed off, Tom at the helm this time. Instantly, they were pitching and rolling in the swells and taking in water. David, in the bow, was showered with cold spray. They needed to bail but didn't have a bucket. Once they drifted parallel to an oncoming wave and nearly capsized.

"Sorry!" Tom called from the stern, wrestling with his paddle to head them obliquely into the next wave. He'd felt a stab of fear.

David, in the bow, craned his head around. "Steady as she goes there, sailor."

They learned to lean in unison, left or right, to counter the canoe's roll. It was a balancing act. Tom's fear became exhilaration.

Then it started to snow, the wind driving it into their faces. The light began to fade.

"We should turn back!" Tom yelled to David.

"Forward!" David yelled back. "Just keep paddling!"

The wind lessened, but the snow increased, falling fast and furious, wet and blinding. It grew dark, and then there was only the sound of their paddles in the water, the feel of the water's coldness, under and around them, the cold sting of the falling snow on their faces. Tom could barely see David's hunched figure in the bow.

"You keeping us in a straight line, buddy?" David called.

"I think so. I took our bearing before we pushed off."

Tom began to sweat from paddling, from nervousness. Stories of being lost in the woods came to him, and how unconsciously you walked in a circle, to the right or left, depending on whether you were right or left-handed, and wound up where you started. With the two of them paddling, though, one thrusting off the starboard gunnel, the other off the port, they were maybe staying on course.

"We should turn back," Tom said again.

"Yeah, well the trouble now is where's *back*?" David said.

They stopped paddling, let the canoe drift. The lake was perfectly calm now, the snow still falling in the darkness.

"Listen!" David said. "You hear waves breaking on a shore?"

Tom opened his mouth, thereby opening his ears (a trick he'd learned from his father their first time deer hunting together), but heard nothing except David's snort. "Fuck. I guess we're stuck out here, buddy. I hear there's a current in the lake. We might drift all the way down to where there's rapids at the head of the river."

"That's fifty miles away, isn't it?" said Tom. "Anyway, not much we can do now except ride it out till daylight and hope the snow has stopped so we can see where the hell we're going."

"Let's keep paddling," David said. "It'll keep us warm anyhow. And hey, maybe we'll get lucky and make it to shore—*some* fucking shore."

Tom felt the lake's coldness seeping up through the aluminum hull of the canoe. "Good idea." He dug his paddle into the water, felt David do the same.

They paddled for hours, it seemed, paddled until they had to rest and let the canoe drift again in the darkness, in the falling, invisible snow pricking their faces. Then began paddling again, pacing themselves, a stroke and then a pause, a stroke and a pause, resting their paddles against the side of the canoe and their aching arms for a moment. More strokes and more pauses until, throwing his paddle in the canoe, David said, "Fuck it. We're probably somewhere in the middle of this fucking lake, just going around in circles."

Tom felt him turn carefully around in his seat. "Where's the wine? Ah. Here's a jug."

Tom heard the gurgle of wine leaving the bottle, the smack of David's lips.

"Here, man, have a snort. Stretch out your hand," and Tom received the bottle from David in the darkness. He took a swig. It was the dry red, and not a very good one: harsh and sour. They passed the jug back and forth a couple of times, rocking the canoe.

They were quiet, until David said, "This reminds me a little of Nam. Hunkered down like this in the fucking dark and not knowing where the fuck you are. Only it was warm over there, *usually*. Hot as hell, in fact. What I wouldn't give now for some of that In-Country heat."

They drank more of the wine and it seemed to warm them at first. Then Tom started to shiver. He flapped his elbows like a rooster flapping his wings. Tried standing up to relieve the stiffness in his legs, causing the canoe to tip wildly and David to yell, "Si-*down*, for chrissake!"

At which point, incredibly, there was a flash of lightning, an almost immediate clap of thunder, and David dove to the bottom of canoe—his turn to nearly capsize them.

"Jezus!" Tom yelled.

He felt David rise carefully from the canoe's bottom. "Sorry, man. Old reflex. Shit! Now I'm wet. There's water in the bottom of the canoe."

"Yeah, and we don't have anything to bail with."

"We have our caps."

They actually managed, carefully bending over and then kneeling, to scoop the water out of the canoe with their caps. Then, very carefully, they resumed their seats. In the cold darkness the falling snow was almost warm now. The cold was in the air and in the water, encircling them, seeping up through the aluminum canoe.

"We gonna sit here freezing our asses till it gets light?" Tom said miserably.

"We could cuddle up," David said. "Don't worry, man. I'm only queer for women."

Carefully, so as not to rock the canoe, they lay down together. David opened his jacket, Tom opened his, and they made a kind of tent over themselves. David pressed against Tom's back. Tom, a little nervously, felt his warmth. "Too bad you ain't a beautiful woman," David said. Tom laughed, a little nervously, feeling twinges of a sailor's homophobia.

He must have dozed because he was startled when David said, his voice muffled under the tent of their jackets, "We got lost like this one time on night patrol."

He didn't say any more, until Tom was startled awake again.

"Didn't know where the fuck we were. Then it started to rain. Pretty soon we were all shivering. When it gets cold in the tropics, man, it's *cold*."

"I know," Tom said, his own voice muffled under their jackets, remembering winter nights on the sub base in Pearl Harbor, standing deck watch on his boat in a foul weather jacket.

"And we couldn't cuddle up like this. We had to spread out and stay quiet. All I could do was fantasize. Count the days left on my tour. Think about girls, about a snake maybe crawling up on me. My boyhood days in Philly."

"You a tough kid?"

"You might say that."

There was another flash of lightning, another clap of

thunder, and Tom felt the involuntary tensing of David's body. He drew away a little.

David said, "We could freeze out here, man. Die of fucking hypothermia!"

Tom, getting sleepy again, thought of the risk of not waking up. Just in case, he made what he hoped was a good Act of Contrition, soundlessly mouthing the words: *Oh my God, I am heartily sorry for having offended Thee* ... He couldn't remember the last time he'd prayed. Then he did. In Mexico, after losing Angela.

In New Eden as the day waned and the wind picked up and the lake grew choppy, people started to worry. It was getting dark.

"Why are David and Tom so late? Something's *happened*," Helen decided. "I know it!"

"Aw, they did their shopping, then went to a pub," Mark said. "I would."

"So? It's dark now. Can they cross the lake in the dark?" Helen wondered.

"I think so," Joel said. "It's a straight shot from Galena, isn't it?"

"The dark, she's confusing," Adrien said.

It started to snow. The darkness thickened. They heard thunder!

"Now I'm *really* worried," Helen said.

Angela was not so much worried as angry. *At first.* Had they lingered in some bar and were out on the stormy water now risking their stupid lives, making everybody worry? Then she was terrified, imagining them lost in the dark, out on the wind-whipped lake, the canoe in danger of capsizing and then—the worst imaginable!—actually rolling the two of them into the lake to tread the cold water until hypothermia overcame them and they drowned. They might have drowned already!

"They're maybe staying over," Sarah told them. "Let's hope they are."

She and Angela locked eyes for a moment.

Janice walked over to Angela and sat next to her. "If I had any religion, I'd pray," she said.

"I'm praying," Angela told her. "For whatever it's worth."

They were probably all right, she told herself. They were capable guys, both of them. Tom was capable. He was all right. They both were all right. Probably they were staying the night in Galena. But what if they weren't? Then they were crossing the lake in the snow and darkness and they were finding their way. But what if they weren't? You had to believe that they were all right, either safe in a hotel or miserable and stupidly trying to cross the lake and making everybody worry.

They gathered in the hall for supper, as usual. A supper was prepared and eaten, as usual. There was the after-meal cleanup, as usual. Then what? There was nothing left to do but wait.

They waited, through the evening and into the night. Little Brightness was put to bed, but everybody else stayed up. Sarah didn't go to David's A-frame; Angela didn't go to the bunkhouse, nor did any of its other occupants. They all just sat around the trestle table or paced the hall or looked out the lake-facing window into the dark. Once, twice, Angela and then Sarah led the group out to the shore to call across the water. Then Adrien—why hadn't they thought of this before?—suggested they make a fire. They made a big fire, a bonfire! and stood around it until it seemed useless to keep piling wood on it. Called out over the water. Felt utterly helpless and hopeless and finally—how else could they feel?—*resigned*.

Not Angela. Not until she saw their bodies. Not until they were found. Not until she saw Tom's body, his cold body laid out and him gone forever for her to miss forever. She was missing him already. No! Not yet. You couldn't miss somebody until they were gone. And he wasn't gone. Not yet. He was maybe lost, but he wasn't gone, and he'd be found. They'd both be found. They'd both show up finally because they *had* to. She could not accept that they would not, she could not allow the dread that kept insinuating itself, that was making her sick with apprehension.

"We gotta try to drive out of here," Mark said. "Walk out, if necessary."

"We'll have to report them missing," Helen said.

"What, go to the cops?" Clay shouted. "No way!"

"Anyway," Joel said, "there's nothing we can do now until daylight."

It was a long night.

It was a long night. Tom tried not to sleep, in case he didn't wake up. He thought of those left in New Eden, how they must be wondering, worrying about them. He thought of Angela and how she must be worrying. They'd make it, though. There was no doubt in his mind that they'd make it, that he'd make it back to her. Provided they didn't freeze to death. He would stay awake, he'd make sure they both stayed awake. They'd keep each other awake. It was a matter of time. It was just a matter of staying awake through the night that would end eventually, everything ended eventually, if only it wasn't so cold and if only . . .

He opened his eyes and it was light. He didn't know where he was. Then he knew. He was lying cold in the bottom of the cold canoe on the cold lake, surrounded by cold air. Cold was the operative word. The canoe was gently rocking, water softly slapping against the metal hull. They and the canoe were covered with snow, but it had stopped snowing.

Tom slid away from David, grasped the gunnels of the canoe and sat up; looked around to see that they were close to a shore—not the shore they'd meant to cross over to but the shore they'd started out from. They were far down the lake, though, opposite Bear Creek, once a mining camp like Galena and now a semi-ghost town. He recognized it from the crumbling brick stack poking up out of the remains of the old smelter.

It was a bright cold day, the new snow glistening on the shore, smoke from the chimneys in the town's few occupied houses lifting straight into the air. They were drifting slowly past the town, definitely in a current and approaching the bottom of the lake and the rapids at the head of the Purcell River.

David raised his head and rubbed the sleep out of his eyes. "Where are we?"

"Off Bear Creek. We didn't make it across."

Far behind them, up the opposite shore, Tom thought he recognized the headland behind which was the old logging camp. "New Eden's beyond that point, right?"

"Yeah," David said. "Hungry?" He dug through the packs, fished out a jar of peanut butter, and they both scooped out gobs of it with their fingers. Washed it down with lake water scooped up with their hands.

Then, plunging their paddles into the water, they headed for the distant headland across the lake, Tom steering them in a diagonal course more or less directly toward it. Some three hours later, weary from paddling, hungry, they rounded the point and were in sight of the old logging ramp jutting out over the water, and then of the old logging camp itself. Then here came their New Eden comrades, rushing out to greet them with cries of relief and exaltation.

Chapter 38

Tom and David's long night on the lake would become legend in the minds of New Eden's nostalgic veterans in years to come.

Canoeing across the lake became routine, as the need arose for fresh supplies or to check general delivery at the Galena post office for their mail, notably for the arrival of Helen's monthly trust fund payment. In pairs they took turns crossing the lake. Even the Professor and Helen took their turns, who might have been excused because of their age. As a matter of fact, they all got pretty good at it. For a start, they became better judges of the weather.

Bathing became a problem, though. It was much too cold to swim in the lake now, and so they took turns sponge bathing in the rusty old washtub used to do their laundry. They filled the tub with water from the creek via the line they'd rigged to the hall and heated it on the cookstove. Adrien warned that the line would have to be drained before it got much colder.

They'd lose their water, but they'd lose it anyway if they allowed the line to freeze.

"What if we just let it run?" Joel asked. "You know, through the hall and out back somewhere."

"We can try that, I suppose," Adrien said.

But the first night the temperature dropped to twenty degrees Fahrenheit, the flow of water dwindled, then stopped. It actually thawed during a couple of sunny days, then froze again—permanently—the ice in it bursting the plastic pipe in places.

"Next year we listen to Adrien. We drain the line," Helen said, and they all laughed at the absurdity of hindsight.

Now water had to be hauled from the creek in pails to be heated on the cookstove, and of course bathing had to be organized. To avoid confusion and concentrate the labour, it was decided to restrict bathing to once a week. And to speed up the process, Wednesday and Saturday night bath groups were formed. Couples bathed together, taking turns in more or less the same water, only draining some of it out in order to add more hot.

Tom chose Saturday to bathe, which corresponded to bath night on the farm when he was growing up. Angela bathed with him, as if they were a couple again. They weren't, not quite, not yet, but maybe they would be eventually, Tom thought, *hoped*. The morning he and David showed up, alive and well after all, and not so incidently with the needed supplies they'd been sent across the lake for, they'd been welcomed as rescuers, as well as the lost and found. The women took over (momentarily lapsing into traditional roles), and made a breakfast for everybody. It was a communal feast, a heroes' return celebration.

Afterwards David went off with Sarah to his A-frame, and Tom followed Angela to the bunkhouse. He thought they might make love, as they had—ecstatically, unforgettably!—on his return to New Eden after his extramarital trip to Vancouver with Janice. But: "No. Please, I'm so *relieved* that you and David are all right, that you made it back to us. But I—I don't *feel* that way with you. Not yet, anyway."

It was her hard honesty, her failure, her refusal to soften what might be hurtful. Or was it just that she didn't care?

"Let's get to know each other again," she said.

"Have we *ever* known each other?" he asked.

Tom wrote later in his journal: *Anyway, we're together here, Together in this group, in a kind of family. We have the closeness, the intimacy of family, including something like family bath night once a week on the farm.*

"I must smell," Angela would say after a week without a bath. And Tom would say, "Yes, you smell like you. I kinda like it."

The fact was they all got used to one another's smells, which naturally ripened between bath nights and weren't unpleasant so much as interesting. In fact, they were all so familiar with one another's bodies that nobody bothered to hang a cloth on bath nights in front of the service counter into the kitchen, where the baths were taken. Privacy was for squares.

Elimination, though not a problem, was definitely a discomfort involving the cold, smelly outhouse and the waiting in line for it every morning; as for urination, both men and women did it by simply stepping into the woods or behind the hall or back of the bunkhouse. Tom was used to this; he was sixteen before they had inside plumbing on his folks' farm.

Gas for the generator became an issue. They were using far too much and spending too much money for it because of running the generator every day to store power for the lights in the hall at night and to operate the record player. It was decided to make do with candles in the hall and use the record player only once a week. Friday became music night in New Eden, something to look forward to.

Yet their gas had to be rationed—no more than ten gallons of it a month. Alcohol was limited to a gallon jug of cheap red wine (the majority preference; forget the white) that had to last the two weeks between paddles across the lake to Galena. Dope was confined to a twenty dollar score of marijuana once a month—hash was deemed too expensive. Mark made their dope runs; he knew a dealer in Galena. Friday nights the group sat around listening to their records and getting stoned—the Stones, appropriately enough, were a favourite on the turn-table. Friday nights was when they felt most together.

One night in the hall, Mick Jagger aptly moaning "You Can't Always Get What You Want," people sitting at the trestle table or lounging against the walls, Mark stood up and addressed the company. He was a little stoned, a little drunk. They all were.

"Hey! Bathing's a hassle now, right? What we need is a sauna like the one my Finnis . . . my Finnish uncle has in his cabin in Wisconsin."

Mark pronounced it *sou-na*. A sauna, Mark told them, would provide a way to heat themselves up to the point where running naked through the snow and jumping into the freezing lake might become thinkable, even enjoyable.

"A sauna's a great idea," Tom said, following Mark's pronunciation. Everyone concurred. They'd have to scrounge around, though, for building material. There was a stack of old boards behind the hall, but hardly enough for an addition to the hall. Other than that, there was an abandoned tarpaulin in the toolshed.

Robert, the Professor, said, "Rather than a sawna—excuse me, *sou-na*—how about making a sweat lodge like Native Americans used—*still* use, I think. They're basically like a sou-na and pretty simple."

"How simple?" Joel asked.

"You make a circle of poles stuck in the ground, bent and lashed together for a frame, which is then covered with birch-bark or hides. The tarp we have might suffice."

"Let's do it!" Mark shouted.

The next day the sun came out, loosening the snow on the trees, which fell in clumps from their branches. Nature seemed to be smiling on them.

Everybody turned to. They needed poles first of all, and they got them by tramping through the soft snow to the creek and cutting down a number of slender willows with Adrien's chainsaw. They trimmed off the branches, then found a level spot between the bunkhouse and the lake and cleared the snow off the ground with their one shovel. The ground beneath the snow wasn't frozen, they were happy to discover, and with a heavy crowbar they found in the shed (it was amazing how many tools had been left in there), they made a circle of holes into the ground and set the poles in them like so many fence posts.

"Okay," said Robert, who seemed to have taken charge. "Now we bend the poles together and tie them."

"With what?" Joel asked.

Mark said, "With twine or light rope or wire even. But where we gonna find that?"

"We'll have to go to town," Helen said.

"Oh no. Not another paddle across the lake," Janice moaned.

"There's the twine we bought last spring for the garden project," Chuck offered.

"We still have some?" Joel asked.

"Yeah, we bought a roll of it at the hardware store in Galena, remember, Sarah?" She nodded.

"Splendid," Robert said. "We should have enough then."

"Where'd you put it?" David asked.

"I'm trying to remember," Chuck said.

"Jesus, you don't know?"

"It's in the shed, "Sarah told them with a smile. "Where else?"

It wasn't easy bending the poles and lashing them together, but they managed it finally. A couple of the poles popped out of their holes while being bent and had to be reset. Bent and lashed together, the poles made a rough circular frame. "Our own little geodesic dome," Joel remarked. He'd done very little except watch the proceedings. "Now what?"

"We cover the dome with the tarp," Robert said.

"That's it?"

"It'd be nice if we had something more to throw over it," Mark said. "It's gotta be fairly tight, to hold in the heat we'll produce."

"How do we heat it, by the way?" Joel asked.

"Same as in a sauna," Mark said. "We heat rocks, then throw

water over them."

"What, make a fire inside the lodge?" Joel said. "What about the smoke?"

"Obviously we make a fire *outside* the lodge," Robert said. "Heat some rocks, then carry them into the lodge."

"That would work," Mark said.

"You've made a sweat lodge before, Professor?" David said to Robert.

"God, no. I've only read about them," he admitted.

The tarp was just big enough to cover the pole frame, with a little left over that they weighted down with rocks. Then someone found a couple of what looked like old horse blankets, mouldy and smelly, in the toolshed, and they were piled on top of the canvas. Then the tarp was cut to make a flap entrance and cedar boughs cut to carpet the damp ground inside. Everybody stepped back to admire what they'd accomplished.

"Now all we need is a good snowfall to further insulate the thing," David said.

"This has been great," said Joel. "Another cooperative effort. Wasn't it great?"

"It's the way the world has to be run someday," Helen said.

"Don't hold your breath," said Janice.

The next day it hadn't snowed, but nobody wanted to wait. Mark took over. He built a fire outside the lodge and heated several rocks in it until they were smoking, practically glowing. Then he carried them, one by one with the shovel, into the lodge and made a pile of them in the centre of it. Tom and David laid blankets on top of the cedar boughs, close around the heated rocks. Sarah brought a pail of water from the creek.

"Couldn't find a dipper," she told them. The cedar gave off a nice smell, and the lodge was getting warm already.

"Okay," Mark said. "She's ready."

They announced it in the hall. Everybody stripped and ran out into the snow, hooting and laughing as if it was still summer and they were going for a dip in the lake. One by one they pushed through the lodge entrance and arranged themselves around the heated rocks. The flap was closed and they found themselves in inky darkness.

"Where's the pail?" Mark said. "Oh, here it is," and he must have cupped his hand in the pail and thrown water on the rocks because there was a hiss of steam and the air grew nice and hot.

"Ahhh," Robert said in the dark.

Mark threw more water on the rocks, more steam filled the lodge, and the air grew suffocating, almost scalding.

"Nice," Chuck murmured.

"Hmmnn," said Janice.

"Another hit!" Joel ordered.

The rocks hissed, the salty smell of sweat filled the lodge, and sweat began to ooze, began to pour out of Tom. It ran into his eyes, dripped off his nose.

"Who's . . . ready for the lake?" he gasped.

"Not. Yet," Sarah croaked.

Tom stood it until he thought he might faint, then declared, "I'm going." He bumped past the other bodies in the dark toward where he guessed the entrance flap might be. Found it after half-circling the lodge. Opened it.

"Close the flap! *Close it!*" came a chorus of voices.

He slipped out, the air like cold metal on his moist flesh,

the snow seeming to burn his bare feet, and ran toward the lake. By the time he got there, he wasn't that hot anymore and the water didn't look that inviting.

"Keep going!" David said as he swept past him to hop over the water as if trying to walk on it before plunging in. "Whoof!" he said, then lay back with a wacky grin on his face. "C'mon in!" he hollered. "The water's fine!"

Tom forced himself in up to his genitals, which contracted till they hurt, splashed some freezing water on himself, then waded back to shore. He tried rolling in the snow. That wasn't so bad. He stood up and, what the hell, threw himself into the lake only to spring up like a Jack-in-the-box and struggle to shore. The water took his breath away. He thought his heart would stop. His skin felt on fire. He beat his chest and gave a yodelling Tarzan yell.

"Yeahhhh!" David responded, and charged out of the water and they both sprinted for the hall as the rest of the crew, full-breasted Sarah in the lead, swept by and plunged into the lake. Janice started in, splashed water on herself, then waded back to shore. "Too cold!" Angela was the last to go in. But she went in.

Inside the hall, nobody put their clothes on for a while. Instead they stood around talking excitedly, openly admiring one another's pink bodies. "Let's have an orgy!" Mark cried, causing a burst of nervous laughter followed by an awkward silence. They were suddenly shy with one another.

"God, I'm *hungry*," Robert announced, causing another, a different, burst of laughter. "I've never been so hungry!"

He found his clothes and got into them. Then everybody got into theirs. Helen started for the kitchen.

"I'll need some help," she called over her shoulder.

Janice and Angela and Sarah followed her while the others moved restlessly about the hall like athletes coming down after a big game.

Chapter 39

Tom and David stayed up talking in the dining hall one night after the others had gone to bed. They sat across from each other at the trestle table, a lighted oil lamp between them.

"Relating's what we mostly do here, have you noticed?" David was saying. "And guess what a good part of it takes the form of."

He spoke quietly, so as not to wake Joel and Helen and little Brightness, sleeping in the kitchen area.

David was looking ever more hip these days, all vestiges of the squared-away jarhead gone. He'd let his thick, brownish hair grow long enough to tie back in a ponytail. Sported a full, luxuriant beard. He and Sarah were a solid couple now. Tom couldn't help envying him a little. She'd gone ahead to David's A-frame.

"Whatta we got," David went on, "to hold us together here? What shared beliefs or whatever? Just getting naked together ain't enough."

"We're pretty together politically, I guess," Tom said. "All more or less estranged from the establishment. Disaffected. We have that in common."

"Yeah, we're all here trying to form some kind of hip alternative to established society, some kind of refuge from the straight world that none of us can fit into, and I'm all for it, I'm not about to enslave myself to a shit job and a mortgage and all the rest of it, but the way things are going—let's face it, buddy, New Eden is a hothouse and we're just playing. *Playing* at revolution."

"Hothouse is right," Tom said. "I picked up on that a while ago. And, yup, here we are, a bunch of individual egos, all trying to live communally while insisting on doing our own thing at the same time. It's kind of sexy, though," Tom added. "You gotta admit that."

"Oh yeah. But sex can cause problems. Ever read *Mutiny on the Bounty*?"

Tom had—and in Hawaii, appropriately enough.

"And yeah," he said. "I never got to Tahiti but I can imagine how it—or Hawaii, for that matter— must have looked to guys off the old sailing ships after months at sea. The beauty of those islands. The beauty of their half-naked women."

"Remember what happened *after* the mutiny, after they reached Pitcairn's Island and burned and sank the *Bounty* so nobody'd be tempted to sail back to civilization and give their hideout away?"

"You mean when there weren't enough women to go around?"

"Right. When they were all stuck out there on that rock in the middle of the Pacific and the men outnumbered the women. What happened?"

"They started killing each other."

"Exactly," David said.

Tom laughed. "You think that can happen here?"

"Naw, but jealousy can happen, despite that it ain't supposed to anymore. Hearts can get broken, like what happened to Angela, I guess, after Peter left—like what's happened to you, if you'll excuse me saying so, brother. Think about it. What we got here is the problem of a bunch of freedom-loving freaks all trying to live together like in some kind of—"

"Extended family?" Tom suggested.

"Family, hell," David said. "Extended *marriage*. Marriage blown up all out of fucking proportion! That'll break us up, finally."

"You think so?"

"Okay, we have this *idea* of the good life," David said. "That book by the Nearings that Joel likes to call our Bible? But how viable is *that* for the mass of fucking humanity? Most people live in cities now, with all the comforts of civilization. Most people *like* the comforts of civilization, and in fact they're pretty helpless without them."

"I grew up on a farm," Tom said, "so I don't have any romantic notions about going back to the land, actually. And yet here I am. And dammit, the truth is I can't live in a city anymore and wear a suit and tie and work a nine-to-five like I did in Chicago. I could have stayed in the Navy. I think about it sometimes. I made first class, I might have made chief if I'd shipped over, but the Outside looked pretty good to me after a four-year hitch."

"I was a gung-ho Marine myself," David said, "as you

might imagine. But Nam knocked that out of me. You and me, brother, we're truly on the Outside now, I mean *outside* the Outside, and I'm okay with that. But *this*, what we're doing here, it's like temporary, man, not a fucking solution."

"I'm too old to be a hippie," Tom said. "If that's what most of us are here. Too straight, when it comes right down to it. Hell, I'm older than anybody here except Helen, maybe, and the Professor."

"Robert's over forty," David said. "Helen's pushing that age."

"I'm thirty-five," Tom said.

"And I'm twenty-five," David said. "So what?"

"So I'm over thirty and not to be trusted, supposedly, but I married a woman ten years younger than me and therefore have felt closer to her—to *your*—generation than to mine. And, yeah, I guess I believe in revolution, some *kind* of revolution, and maybe the communal, back-to-the-land thing—"

"If there's to be any revolution," David said. "In the States, I'm talking now. It'll happen in the cities. Because that's where the action is, man, the protests, the riots. That's where people are beating at the gates of the fucking establishment."

"So what are we doing up here?"

"Waiting, I guess," David said. "Sitting around here just *waiting* for the revolution."

Tom thought about it. Thought about those waiting for the Second Coming or Armageddon or the resurrection of the dead and life everlasting.

"Look," David continued, "we ain't just dropped out of the society here, we've dropped out of what's happening. Okay, this is kind of hip, kind of sexy. But how long do you think people will put up with living like we're back in the nineteenth fucking century? No, we're all up here waiting, waiting for things to change down in the world, hopefully change for the better, so we can all go back there."

Tom considered that.

"I'm serious, man!"

"Hey," Joel called now from the kitchen area. "Give it a rest, you guys. We're trying to sleep over here."

"Sorry!" Tom and David called together.

Tom lowered his voice. "Still," he said, "aren't there some basic values in what we're doing, or *trying* to do, things like living cooperatively, growing our own food, being close to nature?" Tom heard himself echoing Helen and Joel's idealism and, come to think of it, not a little of his own by now, trying to convince himself, as much as David. "We're looking *after* ourselves, aren't we? Or trying to, working toward sustaining ourselves without being tied to the system, to some horseshit job having nothing to do with who or what we are, that only sustains the system? Capitalism. There must be some other way."

"Sure," David said. "But the trouble—"

"Please!" It was Helen this time. "What you two are talking about is pretty interesting but now's not the time. Go away! Let us sleep!"

Tom and David looked contritely at each other and stood up. David blew out the lamp, and they found their way in the dark hall to the door and stepped outside. It was clear and cold, the sky filled with stars.

David moved away from the hall entrance and said, lowering his voice. ""What I was about to say in there—thank Christ Helen interrupted us—is what's *really* holding us together? What *supports* us while we play at going back to the land? Helen's fucking money! Her ain't-we-lucky trust fund! Tree planting? Who's willing to do that? Farming? Who wants to do *that,* finally? Farming's hard fucking work, as I'm sure you know. So's tree planting, as we both know."

"Here's the thing, though," Tom said. "There's something fine about people working together. The way farmers used to get together to harvest each other's crops or put up each other's barns. There's pleasure in that, satisfaction. Hell, I even think there's something noble about it."

"Oh, sure," David said. "And there was something noble about scared shitless, pumped-up, misguided grunts working together to stay alive and kill or be killed in the hell of a fucking war."

The stars were unusually bright, their light on the snow vaguely illuminating the entire clearing. The dark shape of the bunkhouse stood across from them, and off to their right was David's neat little A-frame. Behind that, hard against the looming slope, was Chuck's slapped-together shack.

"Enough of this," David said. "Let's hit the pad. We can continue our discussion some other time."

"Goodnight then, amigo."

"G'night, brother. Tomorrow's another day."

"Another day in New Eden," Tom said.

"As we wait for the revolution," said David.

And they both laughed as David headed for his A-frame to sleep with Sarah and Tom crossed the clearing to the bunk-house to sleep alone.

Chapter 40

Tom felt his way to the double bunk he shared with Angela. She was asleep, he thought, in her lower section. He undressed, started to climb to the upper.

"That you, Tom?"

"Yeah. Sorry if I woke you."

"Lie with me," she said. "There's room, I think."

"You sure?"

"Yes."

He lay down with her on the narrow bunk. It was just possible when they snuggled together, spoon fashion. She felt so good. He began to caress her.

"Don't."

"Why not?"

"I . . .I don't feel that way about you."

He rolled away from her and sat up, slamming his feet against the floor.

"You think you ever *will*?" He heard the bitterness in his voice.

"Don't be angry, Tom," she said. "Give us time. *Please.*" She sounded weary. He was weary too, so weary of their struggle.

"Good night then," he said, and started to climb again to his upper bunk.

"Don't go," she said. He looked for her face, but it was lost in the darkness.

"Why not, for godsake? What you said hurt. I don't want any more hurt."

He wanted, in fact, to suffer the hurt. He wanted *her* to suffer. He climbed to his bunk and got into his sleeping bag. He lay stiffly inside it, feeling her presence just beneath him. How much had the others in the bunkhouse heard? Who gave a shit? He tried to sleep. Thought he heard a sob. He felt like crying himself. Finally, swallowing his hurt, his bitterness, his stupid pride, he climbed down off his top bunk, off his high horse, to Angela again in the lower bunk.

She made room for him at once, sliding over and then wrapping herself around him as he stretched out. She was so warm against him. She kissed his neck.

"It's nice just cuddling," she said. "Let that be it for now."

"Okay."

"*Dulces sueños,*" she whispered in his ear.

"Sweet dreams to you," he said.

The sweetness was in the warmth of her familiar body. What he'd lost. What maybe he'd found again.

Chapter 41

Angela woke in the night and thought she was with Peter for a moment. He was still an ache inside her. The hurt of his leaving without saying goodbye, without even a note, as if sneaking off. The humiliation, her helpless infatuation in the face of his utter, finally infuriating detachment. She'd given him her love! Had he given any of his to her?

She had Tom's love; she knew that. She had the *backing* of his love, which she'd perhaps never lost for all the anguish of their breakup and her interludes with Richard and then with Klaus and finally with Peter—and of course Tom's involvement with Sarah, which she hadn't witnessed, which inadvertently she'd broken up. And then his involvement with Janice, which she *had* witnessed, more or less benignly, while she was with Peter. And yet . . . free love, open marriage: could it ever work? She and Tom, throughout their unfaithfulness, they'd remained faithful.

That morning at the Tortilla Lady's, when she told Richard she was leaving and he went crazy, tried to stop her, wrestled her to the ground—she was almost disappointed when Rosita broke them up by whacking Richard with her broom. She'd felt her power then, thrilled to it!

That was something Tom had never understood about her, her need for struggle, the adrenalin rush of confrontation! Tom avoided confrontation. You might call him passive, or passive aggressive. Those easy terms! Her need for confrontation, did it have to do with recognition? She'd never got it from her father—or her mother, for that matter—and not enough from her husband, not enough to assuage her craving for it. There were things they'd never worked out together. Then their isolation in Trujano, the only gringos in the village. Antonio! His sweet innocence. She'd come that close to seducing him. Peter. He'd been so cool, so detached, so seemingly indifferent! She'd longed to break through to him—for herself, at first, and then for *him*, after she realized his coolness was an avoidance, his detachment a fear of letting go, of feeling! He was nursing a hurt, she thought, and she'd tried to find it. But he was too distant, too protective of himself, too controlled! She'd longed for him to lose control—longed to see his fire.

They might have made it finally. But then he left.

She moved to roll over and Tom, in his sleep, rolled with her. He snuggled against her back as she'd snuggled against his. His body was so familiar; they fit so well together.

"Nice," he said sleepily.

"You awake?"

"Sort of. This bunk is too narrow. Reminds me of the berth we had on the train from Nuevo Laredo to Mexico City, remember? We had to hang on to each other to keep from falling out of it."

"At least we aren't on a swaying train here," she said.

"I liked it. It was like being on a ship at sea."

"I liked it too."

"I'll make us a double bed tomorrow."

"You can do that?"

"Sure. I can measure and cut. I can swing a hammer. I'll take these upper and lower bunks apart and make a double bed."

"You're so clever."

"I'm also very sleepy."

"So am I. Now," she said.

"Good night then, sweetheart."

"Sweetheart. You haven't called me that since we broke up."

"We back together?" he asked.

"Maybe."

They lay wrapped together and presently she wanted him. She wanted him inside her, *now*. But he was asleep. She backed into the familiar warmth and feel of his body, his good, familiar smell. Peter's had been a smoker's smell, and something else, something vaguely suggestive of ill health. He'd been indifferent to his health as he'd been indifferent to everything, it seemed. She was too sleepy to think about it anymore, too comfortably adhered to this man who, for better or worse, she was with again. She began sinking into sleep, into the confusion of love—her love for Peter, for Tom, had she loved Klaus at all? Richard? No, not Ricardo, he was an act of desperation, she thought as she began sinking, dissolving into the easeful darkness behind her closed eyelids.

Chapter 42

It snowed some more. Then snowed again, covering the sweat lodge and insulating it so well they were able to parboil themselves within minutes, after which the plunge into the lake was a breathless, refreshing delight—a liberation!—so that letting it all hang out, of having a down-and-dirty orgy was a definite temptation, a running joke, a gorgeous, unfulfilled fantasy.

If only they were evenly divided. But the odds were eight to four, in favour of the women, which might, in a true utopia, allow the women to take on a couple of men each. And just to spice things up, couldn't there be a system of rotation? More fantasy! Anyway, even if the group got it on after one of their stimulating plunges into the frigid lake, in the hall or in the bunkhouse, the likelihood was that the pairings off, even in the looseness and excitement of the moment, would happen more or less conventionally. So Tom would wind up with Angela, Joel with Helen, Chuck with Janice (she'd been sharing his shack lately), and David with Sarah, leaving Clay and Mark and Robert and Adrien looking on—unless (why not?), they got a turn.

The Problem, as they started calling it, was mostly solved when Mark, and then Robert, the Professor, decided to leave. They left together one sunny day between Christmas and New Year's after David agreed to ferry them across the lake. Mark filled his backpack with his few belongings, Robert filled a couple of suitcases with his (Mark left his dozen or so records as a gift to the commune), and they piled themselves and their luggage into the canoe. David pushed them off and took the stern paddle, Mark the bow. The Professor settled, somewhat precariously, amidships. He turned once, rocking the canoe, to wave and call goodbye to the group on shore. Mark raised an arm and gave the peace sign without turning around. For a ladies' man, Tom thought, he'd fared rather badly in New Eden, losing Janice to himself and then to Chuck. But then he was a guy with other worlds to conquer, and he had his youth and good looks to pave the way.

As for the Professor, he'd doubtless go back to teaching; or maybe he wouldn't. Tom had liked them both, was sorry to see them go. Vaguely, or maybe not so vaguely, he felt left behind.

David was back in a couple of hours, after leaving the two in Galena to seek a ride to Silver City where, separately or together, they would take a bus back to what the Professor called civilization. Later, in a letter from the Professor, the group learned he was in Toronto, teaching in a college with status as a Canadian landed immigrant. As for Mark, when last heard from, he was in Montreal and about to embark, as a passenger on a freighter, for Naples.

Chuck was the next to leave. He and Janice had broken up, mostly because of her attraction to Adrien. Adrien had been mooning around Janice for some time, without actually making a move; but then Janice made the move. She'd had the hots for him all along, she told Tom, as perhaps she'd had the hots for him once upon a time. Chuck was . . . well, Chuck was nice enough, easy to be with. But Adrien . . ."

"What about him?" Tom asked.

"He's *real*," Janice said. "There's nothing phony about him."

"Was there something phony about me?"

She only smiled.

Chuck stepped aside with forlorn grace and willed Janice and Adrien his shack. Tom took Chuck across the lake and said goodbye to him in Galena. Chuck had been his first New Eden friend. Where would he go? What would he do?

"Back to Seattle, I guess. I'll drop you a line sometime."

But he never did.

There was a cold snap after New Year's. With it came the sun, after weeks of gray overcast. They had bright, sub-zero, prairie-like winter days.

The lake froze around its edges and out into the little bay past the old logging ramp. That made it impossible, without breaking through the ice on the way to open water, to take a cleansing dip after heating themselves to the point of collapse in the sweat lodge. They went back to sponge baths in the washtub in the hall kitchen, taking turns as before.

Then the weather warmed, there was a two-day fall of wet, heavy snow that piled onto the roof of the sweat lodge and it collapsed.

"So much for that," Clay said.

He was the only one in the group now without a partner. Adrien and Janice had each other, Sarah and David, Joel and Helen—and Tom and Angela once more, out of long familiarity, if nothing else.

One night at supper Sarah, whose heart was as big, it seemed, as her bosom, suggested to the other women that they give Clay a break.

"I think we women might take turns with him," she said. "It isn't fair he doesn't have a partner."

"I couldn't do that," Janice said. "Not anymore." She and Adrien had been acting like honeymooners since Chuck's departure, spending most of their time in Chuck's—now their—shack. Tom was happy for Janice, happy for Adrien. Now he waited for what Angela would say.

"Count me out," she said.

Helen said, "I'm not much for it either, assuming Clay would be interested in an old lady like me. But why don't you go ahead with it, Sarah?"

David was silent.

Clay sat back in his chair with a sleepy looking smile on his face. "Whatever you folks decide."

Sarah said, "Okay. Bad idea, I guess. Sorry, Clay." She looked at David, who looked back at her.

"Ah well, I still have Betty Five Fingers," Clay said, and mimicked jacking off to an explosion of laughter.

It turned cold again, hardening the snow and making it good for sliding down the steep road into the clearing. Tom found a sheet of metal roofing, bent one end of it to a forty-five degree angle, and they had what he called a tin toboggan. "Used to make these on the farm," he told the others.

The thing worked so well they had fun with it for the next several days. It made a track, which became an icy chute down the steep grade into the clearing and all the way to the bridge over the creek. It got so you had to bail out of the toboggan before hitting the bridge or plunging into the creek. "Whee!" They all took turns at it. "Wheeee!"

Then the weather warmed to barely freezing again, softening the snow so that it grew too sticky for tobogganing but perfect for making snowballs. They had a couple of gleeful, stress-relieving snowball fights.

Then the ice along the shoreline grew mushy, finally broke into rafts that drifted off into the lake. For trips to Galena now they were able to launch the canoe directly into the water again, whereas before one paddler had to crouch in the canoe while the other pushed it across the ice and jumped in before the ice collapsed and they were floating.

The warmer weather, though, brought a heavy gray overcast that continued through the rest of January. The lack of sun began to get to them; everybody complained of it, complained of being confined to the logging camp's ramshackle buildings, complained of being enclosed by the sky, by the lake, by the grim trees, by the steep mountains all around. Their claustrophobic world was the camp's small clearing and the strip of stony shore in front of it that past the creek abruptly ended in a rock abutment jutting into the lake. To venture out of the clearing and into the woods or up the steep logging road was a labour of wading through the soft snow. They needed snowshoes, cross-country skis! The unrelieved grayness was like a shroud.

Then seeing the same people every day, being confined with them, crowded in with them, became an encroachment, an oppression! You couldn't move, it seemed, in either the hall or the bunkhouse, without bumping into somebody, having to *avoid* a collision. The same voices every day. The same faces. The same, finally annoying traits of character. They were like inmates, incarcerated. The lake, the trees, the mountains, were like the clamps of a vise.

Tom, having served on a submarine, had some tolerance for it. Squeezing past your shipmates, ducking through compartment hatches, negotiating the boat's narrow, constricted passageways—that was a submariner's world. Even when running on the surface, you remained confined within the boat's steel hull, below her narrow, often-awash deck, unless you were on bridge watch or otherwise allowed topside on the conning tower for a breath of fresh air and a view of the sea. Here there was no such relief, no pulling into port finally, no liberty.

There were arguments now as to who got to cross the lake, when necessary, for supplies. Before there'd been no problem: by informal agreement, people took turns. Now Joel had to draw up a list, and still there were disputes. Everybody wanted to go to town. Nobody wanted to wait their turn. When would this winter be over?

Chapter 43

The winter wore on. February came, bringing more snow. And then more and more snow until it was thigh deep in New Eden's clearing by the lake and who knew how much deeper in the mountains above them?

It was more snow than Tom had ever seen in Minnesota or Sarah in Alberta or Janice in Saskatchewan, though Adrien said they got snow like this in Quebec. As for the rest of them, Clay from Detroit and the others from such balmy, if rainy or foggy places as San Francisco and Seattle, it was depressing, even frightening.

And there was no escape unless, after digging the canoe out of the snow (it had disappeared; they'd have to find it) and several trips across the lake, they managed to transport themselves out of here. And then what? Find a house to rent, if they could afford one, for the rest of the winter? They talked it over, decided it would be giving in to panic; decided, after all, they couldn't afford it. All they had was Helen's trust fund, which anyway went mostly for food. In fact, they were almost out of food. They'd have to dig the canoe out of the snow and cross the lake for supplies as soon as the weather cleared.

"We'll just have to tough it out, people," Joel told them, as if they didn't know. They'd just have to grin and bear it and put up with one another until spring.

"Yeah," Clay said, "if we haven't killed each other before then."

What they had to avoid, Adrien told them, was cabin fever. Cabin fever was what you could get during the long gray winters in these mountains. It could drive you crazy.

Janice was the first to freak out.

"I'm getting out!" she declared one day as they sat around the trestle table, trapped inside the hall as more snow piled up outside. "I can't breathe!"

It took the three of them, Adrien and Tom and Joel, to keep her from dashing outside, inadequately dressed for the elements, with the idea of wading through the snow all the way to Galena. She might have died of exposure.

Clay stood by; as did David, both willing to let her go, apparently.

Then Clay lost it. He got into an argument with Joel a day or so later, over something or other, upon which Sarah sought to mediate, upon which Clay turned on her, calling her a sexual tease—upon which David stepped in and offered to punch Clay out and Joel withdrew, along with Helen and little Brightness, into the pantry.

"You people don't know what I've been going through!" Clay cried. He was like a puppet on strings now, jerking back and forth. "People are after me!"

"What're you talking about?" David asked. "Who's after you, man?"

"The FBI!" hollered Clay. "Other people! Urban guerrillas!"

"What, like the Weathermen?"

"Yes! I was involved with them. In Detroit. Now they're after me! The *FBI* is after me!"

"Calm down," David said. "How much were you involved?"

"I hung out with them, sorta. I was doing research for my MA thesis."

"Which I guess they didn't know about," Helen commented.

"Of course not! Anyway, they got raided, and thank God I wasn't with them at the time. Some got away and I think made it into Canada. Now they—and the FBI—must be looking for me! They probably think I betrayed them, or I was an FBI plant. They'll *kill* me if they ever find me!"

"Did you? Betray them, I mean?" David asked.

"I thought about it," Clay admitted.

Joel and Helen had come out of the pantry. Brightness peeked out. Joel yelled at her to stay in there and close the door.

"Anyway, you're safe here with us, man," David told him.

"You think so?" Clay didn't look relieved.

Tom, like everyone else, had thought Clay's somewhat sour personality had to do with his going without. He'd had occasional bursts of exuberance, like when he got them to create a sound system to play their records. But otherwise he'd been glum, and now it was obvious he'd been looking over his shoulder his whole time here.

They knew he'd been a grad student in sociology at Wayne State in Detroit, but little else about him until now. Now they learned he'd joined, "for research purposes," what he thought were somewhat radical members of the Students for a Democratic Society but who turned out to have split off from SDS. In fact, they were a Weathermen cell and Clay thought, hot ziggedy, what a research boon!—until he learned of their plan to bomb an Army recruiting station in Highland Park and thought briefly of making an anonymous phone call. But then the group's communal house was raided and those inside arrested. Those not home at the time scattered, fled—as Clay himself did when he heard about it, in a panic, not taking a chance on driving over the Ambassador Bridge to Windsor and being turned back, instead crossing Lake St. Clair in an uncle's motorboat one dark night and hiding in the woods along the Thames River till morning, then hitching west until he reached British Columbia. But he'd never been sure he was safe here.

He'd actually liked a couple of the group's members, especially the earnest young woman who called herself Emma (after the anarchist Emma Goldman; her real name was Amy). He was mostly *with* their politics (carried around a copy of Mao's Little Red Book by way of a credential); but then their talk of sabotage, of violent revolution, had made him nervous. They were scary, in fact, and for sure had him pegged now as a spy, an infiltrator, their betrayer. He was especially scared of the creep with the wispy goatee who'd struck him as a psychopath and might be in Canada now looking for him. He was more worried about *that* guy finding him than the FBI tracking him down and hauling him back to the States for questioning if not prosecution.

"Aw, those guys sound like amateurs," David said. "Not to mention dumb. *You* were dumb. Anyway, I doubt you have much to worry about. The FBI has bigger fish to fry."

Clay seemed to dismiss that; then his eyes turned shifty. "*You* guys could turn me in."

"Relax," David told him. "Who do you take us for?"

Joel was silent.

Helen said, "Don't worry, Clay. We're all revolutionaries here."

The next day dawned bright and clear—at last!—and after the communal breakfast of cornmeal mush (they were out of oatmeal), everyone helped to dig out the canoe. Then Tom and Adrien (whose turn it was), with a list from Helen and all the cash out of the communal kitty, set out to paddle across the lake to replenish their larder.

It was the first of March. Spring was still a long way off, but there was a definite suggestion of it in the air. The air was like chilled wine, Tom told himself, excusing the cliche, and it felt good to be on the lake again, digging his paddle into the cold, clear water, straining the muscles in his arms and breathing the fine air with the sun almost warm on his shoulders. He began to sweat, and stopped paddling to take off his jacket. Adrien, in the bow, felt the canoe's increased drag and turned around.

"Good idea." He laid his paddle across the gunnels and peeled off his own jacket. "Feels like spring, eh?"

"It's coming."

After forty-five minutes of steady paddling they reached the pebbly shore below Galena and tied the canoe to the town dock. They walked up the main street and into the coffee shop next to the hotel. They ordered coffee and a couple of fat donuts. "Why not?" Adrien said.

"Guilty pleasures," Tom said.

They moved on to the co-op and, referring to Helen's list, bought a huge supply of staples. The usual stuff, only more than usual: two bags each of whole wheat flour and brown rice, bags of navy and black beans, brown sugar, tofu, tea and instant coffee. Maple syrup. Honey and peanut butter (for, among other uses, making those delicious peanut butter balls that everybody craved when they were stoned). Oatmeal and cornmeal. Apples, because they would keep; cabbage and broccoli, because *they* would keep. And some luxuries: chunks of bulk chocolate. A tin of Fry's Cocoa. Jug of red wine.

All of which filled their packs and a couple of boxes supplied by the co-op that would take two trips to carry to the canoe.

There was no money left for dope. But then, they'd all been straight for most of the winter.

"No money either for gas for the generator," Adrien said. "Too bad."

"That means no music," Tom said. "Hell, I'll spring for gas. Gotta have music." He still had some money in his secret stash—not much, but he'd brought it along.

Adrien said, "Guilty secret, eh?"

They carried their groceries and a can of gas to the canoe. This being Canada, they risked leaving the loaded canoe tied to the dock to go back uptown for a quick beer in the hotel pub. They deserved it, they told each other. One beer, maybe two. Then they'd paddle across the lake to make it back to New Eden before dark.

They should have skipped the pub. That way Tom might have avoided what immediately became another complication in his life—his and Angela's.

Chapter 44

Tom and Adrien were in the pub, sitting at a table with a pitcher of beer between them, when who should walk in but Richard Sullivan. *Ricardo.* Small fucking world.

His eyes swept the room and found Tom. He came over, a grin on his weathered face. Tom didn't get up to greet him. Didn't invite him to sit down, but he joined them anyway.

"How'd you . . ."

"I got paid out in New York my last voyage and stopped in Chicago on my way back to Mexico to visit your friends. Sue and Cliff? They told me they had a letter from you. That you'd found Angela and she was okay, but it didn't sound like you were back together."

Sue and Cliff: they were supposed to be friends. Mentioning his letter, whose bitter contents no longer described his situation. Hadn't they guessed that Richard would go after Angela? Maybe they hadn't. Or maybe they had, Tom thought sardonically.

"Sorry to disappoint you, Ricardo," Tom said now. "But we got back together after all. You made this trip for nothing, ace."

Richard shook his head. "No, man, I didn't! I wanted to see you guys anyway. And believe it or not, I'm really glad you're back with Angela. Glad *one* of us is back with her."

Adrien, lounging back in his chair, looked to be enjoying this. Richard turned to him. "Hi, my name's Richard. I'm a friend of Tom and Angela's, though they might not think so. They've probably told you about me."

"I'm Adrien," Adrien said. "And no, they haven't."

He held out his hand for Richard to shake.

Tom said, "We better start back, Adrien. Unless we wanna paddle in the dark."

"Paddle?" Richard said.

"We're across the lake," Adrien said.

"Yeah," Tom said. "We paddled over here in our canoe for a load of supplies to take back to our people."

Richard's seamed face broke into a big smile. "Hey, you think I could go with you? You're in some kind of commune, right? I'd like to see it. Say hello to Angela."

"I'm not sure she'd want to see *you*," Tom told him.

"Why not, man? No hard feelings, right?"

"Speak for yourself. You beat her up before she left you, I heard."

Richard threw his head back. "I didn't *beat* her, man. I took hold of her to try to talk some sense into her, and I—"

"You knocked her down!"

"We fell!"

"Is that how it went? Not what I heard."

"What'd you hear, man?"

"*Enough*, goddammit!" Tom shouted. He was filled with rage now. Oaxaca, Puerto Bonito, it all came back in a sickening rush. How he'd been so dumb. So numb. How Richard had been so devious.

"Good thing the Tortilla Lady was there to whack you with her broom, asshole. You went a little crazy, I hear."

"Not true!" Richard jerked to his feet, spilling the pitcher of beer off the table and knocking over his chair. "I just lost it for a second. I didn't hurt her!"

Tom became aware now of the bartender and some other guy standing on either side of them. "Take it outside, fellas. No fights in here."

Richard looked confused. "Who's fighting?"

Adrien said, "Let's go, Tom."

Richard followed them outside. The weather had changed. There was a dark buildup of clouds in the west and the air had turned cold. Tom took a breath.

"I'm sorry, man," Richard said. "Give Angela my love. I'll stick around for a few days in case she's willing to see me."

"Okay," said Tom. He'd calmed down, was finding as he had before, when they were on the road together, that he couldn't hate the guy, that there was something genuine about him. "Anyway, Ricardo, we don't have room for you in the canoe. It's a two-person craft, and we're loaded."

Richard brightened. "Wait a minute. I got a rental car. Could I drive there?"

"Not until the snow's gone," Tom was pleased to inform him. "The only way to reach our place now is by canoe."

"No shit?"

"The snow won't be gone for at least another month," Tom added happily. "You still be around then?"

"You know I won't."

"Too bad."

"Look, man, I know you ain't that glad to see me. But I mean you no harm. I'm really glad that you and Angela are back together, I really am. But I came all this way and I'd like to see her. Make things up with her. I care for her. I care for both of you. We got along all right on the road, remember?"

Tom remembered Richard's self-serving lies. How would Angela feel about him now? Something sick in him wanted to know.

"Stay in Galena tonight," Tom told him. "If Angela is okay with it, we'll paddle over tomorrow and meet you."

"Far out, man! You'd do that for me?"

"Be at the pub here about noon tomorrow," Tom told him. "If we don't show up, that'll mean she didn't want to see you."

"Fair enough," Richard said.

Adrien looked from one to the other of them, grinning. "You guys, eh?"

Chapter 45

Angela's mouth dropped. "He's *here*?"

"He wants to see you. You wanna see him?"

"How did he find us, for godsake?"

"Same way I found you. More or less."

"What's *that* mean?"

"I wrote a letter to Sue and Cliff. *After* I'd found you and was sure we'd never get back together. Richard showed up at their place, off his last ship, and they—don't ask me why—told him where I was and, inadvertently, where you were, and now he's here, I suppose with the same notion I had—that maybe he could get back with you, or anyway, see how you were because the guy does care for you, after all."

"I suppose he does," Angela said, "in his way. He's kind of lost. More lost than I was."

"You don't have to meet him," Tom said. "I told him if we didn't show up in Galena by noon tomorrow, you didn't want

322

to see him."

Angela looked thoughtful for a moment. "Still . . . wouldn't that be kind of cruel? I mean, he's come all this way. Oh, I don't know what I mean. I don't know what I should do. What should I do, Tom?"

"I can't tell you."

"Of course you can't." It was like an accusation.

"What do you *want* to do, Angie? Honestly."

Angela closed her eyes—what she did when she needed to concentrate. When she opened them, she said, "All right. We'll go see Richard together."

"You sure you don't need to see him alone?"

She shot Tom a look.

They woke the next morning to dark overcast, to wind and rain and the sound of the lake crashing against the shore; looked out to see it covered with whitecaps.

"So much for meeting Ricardo," Tom said. "We can't cross in this kind of weather."

"Won't he know that?" Angela asked. "You think he'll wait?"

"Maybe. Anyway, we'll cross when we can. If he's gone when we get to Galena, so be it. Be just as well."

It stopped raining later that morning and, as often happened now after a gloomy start, the day turned warm and sunny.

Joel, or rather Helen, decided it was a day for spring cleaning. There were groans of protest.

"What we *have* is a winter's accumulation of filth," she told the group. "Just look around."

They were in the hall, at their midday meal—stir-fry again, brown rice with mixed vegetables and tofu that they were all thoroughly sick of. Looking around they saw piles of dirty laundry and untidy stashes of people's personal shit, scattered throughout the hall. There were similar piles in the bunk-house. Both places were starting to stink.

"For a start, we should do our laundry," Helen said. "We've let it go long enough."

"Oh God," said Janice. "What, by melting snow on the stove? It's enough of a chore just to keep *ourselves* clean. It'll take us days, it'll—"

"Yes it will," Helen said. "Like it did our grandmothers, with *their* large families. It's the way it is for us here. It's how we've chosen to live, right?"

"There's another way," Sarah said. "But of course that would insult the purists among us."

"Who's a purist anymore?" Janice wanted to know.

"There's a laundry in Galena," Sarah went on. "Aren't Tom and Angela going over to see this friend of theirs? Couldn't—"

"He's not exactly a friend," Tom said.

"I mean couldn't we load the canoe with our laundry and have them do it while they're in Galena anyway?"

"Great idea," said Joel.

Helen looked from Tom to Angela. "You guys up for that?"

"Sure," Tom said.

David stood up from the table and walked to a window. "The lake's calmed down. You could get started."

"But isn't it too late now?" Angela wondered. "Can we cross the lake and do the laundry and get back before dark?"

"There'll be a moon tonight," David said, "unless it's cloudy."

"Let's go, Angie," Tom said. He was eager to be off, eager to meet Richard and get it—whatever "it" might be—over with.

The canoe was quickly loaded with New Eden's dirty laundry and Tom and Angela set off.

"This could be fun, actually," she said. "A little holiday for us. Why haven't we done this before?"

They crossed the lake in good time, tied up to the dock below Galena, and carried the laundry up main street to Wash and Dry, the laundry across from the donut shop. All but one of the half dozen machines were in use, though the place was empty. They were loading the available machine when a couple came in.

"Hi. How you folks doon?" the man said. He was a handsome young black man. The woman was a pretty blonde. Both were smiling.

"We're good," Tom told them. "You?"

"We're fine," the man said, "but kinda lost. You know of a place, one of your communes called Harmony Farm?"

"Yeah. You're close. It's just down the lake from here, along the river."

Tom gave them directions. The man looked around for something to write on. The woman produced a notebook from her shoulder bag.

"I'm Chris, by the way. This is Star."

They shook hands.

"You folks part of that scene?" Chris asked.

"No, we're across the lake," Tom said.

Star, still smiling, said, "You by yourselves over there?"

"No, we're in *another* commune," Tom said.

"Groovy. What's it called?"

"New Eden."

"New Eden. Neat."

"Where you guys from?" Angela asked Star.

"Toronto. Before that, New Yawk."

"Yeah," Chris said, "Liz and me—Star here—headed up to Canada after I got out of basic and they was sending me to Vietnam. We both into the back-to-the-land thing now, know what I'm saying? Like you folks, I guess."

"Like a lot of people," Tom said.

"Yeah! That's where it's at now, right? Star said. "The city sucks now. Right?"

"Right," Tom said.

Star, he thought, formerly Elizabeth-something. It was a hippie thing to do, change your name to sound vaguely Native American out of some vague identification with the continent's first people. Sandra, the beautiful native girlfriend of Jack, the Mark Twain scholar who'd picked him and Richard up off the road, what was *her* take on this kind of well-meaning, romantic appropriation? How were *they* doing? he wondered now. How was *she* doing?

"We should go look for Richard," Angela said to Tom, "do our laundry later. It's almost two o'clock."

"We'll put your laundry in," Star said. "Ours will be done soon."

"Really? That would be so nice," Angela said.

"No problem," Chris said. "Go meet your friend or whoever. We'll load the dryers for you too, soon's *our* stuff is done."

"That would be great," Tom told him. He began digging in his pockets for change.

"We got it," Chris said. "We all brothers and sisters, right?"

"Right," Angela said.

"Owe you a beer," Tom said.

"I be back in about an hour, though," Chris told them. "Otherwise you might find your clothes on the floor."

"No, Chris," Star said. "This isn't New Yawk."

"Right," he said. "This somethin' else."

Tom turned before going out the door. "See you around."

"If not, you folks keep the faith," Chris told them.

Richard wasn't in the hotel bar when they got there. Tom was relieved, Angela too, she said. They sat at a table and Tom ordered a beer and Angela a glass of wine. Then they realized they were hungry and ordered hamburgers and fries and a salad to share. When they'd finished eating, almost an hour had passed and Tom had assured himself that Richard was gone—gone for good and good riddance.

"Time to check on our laundry," he said.

"So we missed him," said Angela. "I'm a little disappointed, actually."

But then, outside the bar, there he was, standing on the sidewalk across the street and looking off across the lake, no doubt for the sight of their canoe. He didn't see *them* until he turned and his worn face crinkled up into a grin. Old Ricardo. Tom was almost glad to see the asshole.

"*There* you are!"

He strode over to them, gave Tom a quick hug, then turned to Angela and gave *her* a hug, a long one that Tom took in stride.

Richard had arrived at the bar promptly at noon, he said; waited an hour, then walked down to the pier. He was casting a last look across the lake before giving up, before driving out of town—"and out of your lives," he said, waving his arms dramatically, "forever!"—when he turned and saw them.

Tom suppressed a laugh. They stood looking at one another.

"Our laundry," Angela said.

"Oh yeah," Tom said. "We have laundry to pick up."

They walked to the laundry and found their clothes in the dryers, the dryers stopped, their clothes dry.

Richard helped them fold and pack their laundry in the plastic bags they'd brought. They stepped outside to find it had clouded over, the light fading, with little chance they'd have the moon.

"Shit," Tom said. He looked at Angela. "We might be crossing the lake in the dark."

"Oh no," said Angela. "We could get lost, like you and David did."

"We were in a snowstorm that time, Angie, besides being in the dark. We can make it."

"Look," Richard said. "Why not stay over? I'm in the town's funky old hotel. It's like out of a Western movie, man. Stay over with me. I'll be leaving in the morning, I promise. Tonight can be our farewell."

Angela looked at Tom. Tom said, "We don't have the money, Ricardo."

"My treat, man. C'mon! We'll paint the town."

Tom looked at Angela again. She shrugged, smiled.

"Okay," Tom said, surrendering. "Better safe than sorry, I guess. The lake's pretty big and no fun to be on in the dark."

"Great!" Richard said. "God, am I glad we got to see each other again. We're amigos, right? Let's make up for what happened in Mexico."

Chapter 46

The evening started out all right. They took a walk along the lake together. Tom and Angela pointed across to the shallow indentation on the far shore and the opening in the trees that marked New Eden's clearing. They couldn't see the buildings, of course, nor the clearing itself, but even in the fading light Tom thought he could make out the old logging ramp, jutting over the water. He wished they had set out. They might have made it across before dark after all.

Nobody talked about Mexico at first. Instead, Tom and Angela described what communal life in New Eden was like, both striving to be funny about it.

"It's like an extended marriage," Tom said. "With all the difficulties of marriage— compounded."

"Sweetened a little by free love, though, huh?"

"No comment," Angela said.

Richard told some funny sea stories. Tom was reminded of

their first days together in Puerto Bonito when Ricardo was playing the old hand, showing them around, becoming their supposed friend. Hell. Maybe he *was* their friend. It was water under the bridge now anyhow. Let it be, he thought. He and Angela were back together again. Their breakup in Mexico was history.

They had supper in the Mexican restaurant outside of Galena, the one recently started by a draft dodger from California and his Latina girlfriend. It was mainly frequented by the American exiles in the area. The food was more Tex-Mex than true Mexican but pretty good nonetheless. It evoked some memories. Then driving back to Galena, they got into it.

They were all a little drunk by then, or anyway, Tom and Richard were after shots of tequila and bottles of Dos Equis before getting into Richard's rental car.

Angela, who'd had only one drink, insisted on driving. Richard hopped in beside her, leaving Tom to sit in back and stare at the two of them up front together like a couple.

Tom said, speaking to the back of Richard's head, "There's something that bothers me, Ricardo. That day in Puerto Bonito when you came back from the Plantation and said Angela wanted me to go up to Trujano and wait *there* till she made up her mind about our marriage. Why the fuck did you lie to me that day?"

"Tom . . ." Angela started to say.

Richard cranked his head around and said, "Okay, I lied to you, man, I admit it now. But I—"

"You lied to *both* of us!"

"That's enough," Angela said.

"No!" Tom said. "Let's have it out finally."

Richard swung around in his seat to face him. "So whatta we do about it, man? Have a fistfight or something like a couple of schoolboys?"

"Yes!" Richard's smiling face was infuriating. "Let's go at it, you son of a bitch! Stop the car!" he told Angela.

"I won't," she said. "This is stupid."

"No! This is necessary! Stop the car, Angie, *please*." He took a breath. "Me and Ricardo, we gotta do this."

Angela pulled abruptly off the road and skidded to a stop. "Go ahead then. Fight each other like stupid machos, like schoolboys."

Tom and Richard were already out of the car, facing each other, squaring off in the car's headlights like bare-knuckle prize fighters. It was actually funny, in retrospect. Tom swung at Richard's hilariously contorted face, Richard blocked it, then punched Tom in the nose. He reeled back, clutching his nose, feeling blood gushing between his fingers as Angela honked the car horn and yelled out the window, "STOP IT NOW! GET BACK IN THE CAR!"

Richard dropped his arms. "Angela's right, man," he said. "Let's stop this."

"Goddamn you!" Tom said. He stood holding his bleeding nose.

Angela got out of the car and gave Tom her handkerchief. They stood there, in the car's headlights, until she said, "C'mon, guys. Let's get back in the car. It's cold out here."

Tom sat in front this time. Angela drove them to Galena and parked in front of the hotel and they sat in the car without talking. Tom felt his nose. It was throbbing and already swollen but had stopped bleeding. It was probably broken.

"Somebody say something," Angela said.

"I'm really, really sorry," Richard said. "For everything."

Tom didn't speak. Angela said, "It's all right, Ricardo. It is, isn't it, Tom?"

Tom didn't say anything. Richard opened his door and stepped out of the car. He stood waiting as Angela and, finally Tom, got out and joined him on the sidewalk. Angela gave Richard the keys.

"Guess I'll be gone when you two get up tomorrow," he said.

"We could have breakfast," Angela offered.

"Naw, I better just get going." He turned to Tom, his face working. "So long, man. We might have been true friends. Maybe . . . "

"Yeah," Tom said. "Anyway, I won't forget you."

"I won't forget either of *you*." Richard turned to Angela. "So long, *mi amor perdido. Podríamos haberlo logrado.*"

"Goodbye, Richard."

"Hey, I got most of that," Tom said to Richard, abruptly angry again. "Your lost love. You and Angela might have made it."

"Let's not go there," Angela said. "*Please*. Water under the bridge."

"You're right," Tom said.

"Yes," said Richard.

Together they walked into the hotel lobby, small and wood-panelled under a low ceiling of pressed tin, furnished with a couple of ancient upholstered chairs around a scarred, knee-high round table. The lobby was empty except for the night clerk behind the desk, an old guy who rented them rooms that Richard insisted on paying for. It wasn't much: something less than they'd have paid at the motel. The register indicated they were the only guests that night.

They climbed the wooden, creaking stairs to their respective rooms, Richard to his on the second floor and Tom and Angela to theirs on the attic-like third, a quaint little room under the eaves. The hotel had been built, according to a plaque in the lobby, in 1897. It was a relic of the town's silver boom and a romantic place to stay, Tom and Angela told each other as they snuggled together under the down quilt on the surprisingly comfortable old bed. It had a curlicued brass head like Tom's old bed on the farm back in Minnesota.

The next morning Richard was gone. But he'd left them a note at the desk.

Dear Angela and Tom,

I'm really sorry for the trouble I caused and wish you both the best of everything.

I won't go down to Puerto Bonito anymore. Too many bad memories there. Going to Chiapas this time with Larry or maybe Charlie. After that? Wish I knew. I'll probably ship out again though I'll be tempted to go over the side some night. I really liked you people, both of you, and it's just too bad we couldn't of made it. What do the French call it, a manage a twa or however the hell you spell it? We maybe could have tried that.

Ricardo

Chapter 47

The winter hung on, through most of March, with intermittent, bright promises of spring followed by more snow, more cold. And yet the days were growing longer, the snow receding from the lakeshore and bare ground beginning to show in New Eden's clearing and in the surrounding woods. Birds, other than the croaking ravens, began to be heard and sometimes seen, birds Tom identified from a field guide he'd picked up at some point in the used bookstore in Galena: varied thrushes, their call in the woods a single long whistle that reminded him of a London bobby's; Clark's nutcrackers, their rasping, abrupt call; Steller's jays, their harsh calls including a perfect imitation of a hawk's screech. These birds soon disappeared. Why, and where did they go? They'd migrated upslope, Adrien informed him, into the higher elevations—proof, he said, that spring was advancing.

The robins stayed, after arriving when snow was still on the ground and the air still freezing at night. They began to hear sweet trilling in the woods that Tom eventually identified, after finally seeing the nondescript little bird, as the call of the Swainson's thrush.

Then one whole weekend there was a pure blue sky above the pure white snow on the mountain peaks and the blue lake and the dark green conifers that were soon to brighten, soon to show the paler green of their growing tips.

One morning Tom stood on the dock and watched a snow shower, a white squall, touch down on the far side of the lake and move slowly over the water toward him. There was still sunlight on this side. Then the sunlight abruptly vanished and he was struck by a stinging white flurry like miniature hail that disappeared as suddenly as it had come, leaving a dusting of the white stuff on the ground and sifting down through the trees to form droplets on the lower branches. And the sun returned.

Then winter returned one dark, cold, blizzard-y day that dropped a two-inch layer of new snow on the ground and frosted the trees white—until the next day, when a hot sun caused the snow to fall in clumps from the trees and the snow on the ground to form puddles. The sun began to shine every day, and across the lake the snow-line gradually retreated up the mountains.

Joel called a communal meeting to decide whether they should go tree planting again. A mood of excitement swept through the group. The long winter was over! Spring had come! They could drive out of New Eden now and go to work and make some money.

But then March, which had come in like a lamb, confirmed

the old saying by going out like a lion. Winter staged a last assault. They had a final, stupendous dump of snow, six, eight, ten inches of the stuff before it stopped. Then a cold snap, close to zero Fahrenheit. The migrant birds vanished. Only the dark ravens still croaked and clucked in the woods.

"We need music!" Clay cried.

"No gas for the generator," Joel said.

"We need groceries," Helen said.

They'd had boiled rice for breakfast, since they were out of oatmeal, out of bread, out of almost everything.

Time for a trip to town. Helen's trust fund payment, money for groceries, must be waiting for them at the Galena postoffice. But there was no using the truck yet—the road was still snow covered, the grade out of the clearing too steep—and as for using the canoe, the lake was too choppy. They'd have to wait until it calmed. They'd have to live on rice, pretty much all they had left to eat.

And then the weather changed again—radically. A wind came up, the temperature rose, and it began to rain; there were days of rain that, seemingly overnight, dissolved the snow and made the road as slippery with mud as it had been with snow. The clearing became a field of mud, a morass that your rubber boots sank into to the ankles. Angela, crossing from the bunkhouse to the hall one morning, lost a boot in the mud, then the other, and made it to the hall barefoot, laughing. The wind and the rain were exciting at first, spring's counter-assault on winter. But the fact was they were still trapped in New Eden, the road out impassable, the lake too choppy to cross, the rain so depressing as to invite a meltdown.

Which soon came. David and Sarah headed for his A-frame, David declaring, "We might as well fuck these days away." Adrien and Janice were in Chuck's old shack. The others, holed up in the hall, began to tear at each other like caged rats in a confinement experiment.

It started with Joel and Helen launching into an epic fight, shouting insults at each other concerning Helen's bossiness and Joel's mooching on her while pretending to be the leader when in fact *she* was. *Really*? Joel yelled. Who did the organizing? Who got people up and doing?

"David!" Helen shouted. "More often than not. And Tom and Adrien, while you're still wondering what to do."

"And what do *you* do?" Joel shouted back. "Besides contributing your trust fund?"

"That's just it, asshole. I contribute my trust fund. It's what's kept us together! And how about all the cooking I do? And who looks after Brightness?"

"I wish to God we'd never met!" Joel was beside himself now. "You're too old for me! I coulda found somebody younger!"

"Like Sarah, for instance?" Helen shouted. "You've wanted her all along, haven't you, and you made a play for her one time when you thought I wasn't looking, didn't you."

"Like you made a play for David? Like you balled Peter?" Joel shouted back.

"I never balled Peter! I only thought about it!" Helen hollered.

As if on cue, David and Sarah entered the hall in time to hear enough of Joel and Helen's altercation to join it, then get into it with each other. There were a number of angry, interesting revelations. Helen had actually got it on with David; David, for his part, had made it with Janice, once or twice, despite his considering her a flake; and what of Janice and Adrien? Where were *they* in all this? Tucked away in their shack, Tom was happy to note to himself, safely out of hearing, while Helen was screaming, "Stop it! Let's just stop it now! This is crazy!"

Everyone went quiet. Clay, their resident sociologist, had sat through the clamour with a smile on his face, doubtless taking mental notes. Three-year-old Brightness had played quietly in a corner, as if deaf to it all.

Tom and Angela left then for the bunkhouse. They'd been through this with each other too many times.

That night, the rain still pelting down, they woke at the same time in the double bed Tom had made for them, both, it turned out, incredibly horny. They had raw, completely satisfying sex. Afterwards they lay entwined and Tom, anyhow, was sinking into sleep when there was a low, distant rumble that quickly increased to a roar punctuated by a sound as of cracking rocks and snapping trees. The bunkhouse began to shake, the very ground to shake, and then an enormous *something* struck the outside wall, shattering the window next to Tom and Angela's bed and moving the bed across the floor while showering glass and stones and rocks and mud over everything. A cold draft struck them, smelling of earth and tree resin, and Angela was shouting as when the earth had moved that time in Oaxaca.

"What's happening? Is it an earthquake?"

"Jesus Christ!" Clay called from the other side of the bunk-house. "What was *that*?"

Avalanche. The word popped into Tom's head. "Avalanche!"

he yelled. "We might be buried!"

Clay, with a flashlight, came out from behind his curtain as Tom and Angela piled out of their dislodged bed. They were all naked, but nobody thought of clothes. Tom and Clay walked in bare feet across the stones and mud and broken glass on the floor and tried the door. It was badly askew, but they managed to open it, at least partially. Clay pointed his flashlight into the clearing.

"What do you see?" Angela called.

What they saw was disaster—not an avalanche but a landslide, an immense, overwhelming deluge of mud and rocks and sticks and stones, piles of dirty snow, whole uprooted trees—all come down off the mountain in the rain.

Chuck's shack—oh my God, Chuck's shack, with Adrien and Janice in it—had disappeared.

Adrien had been concerned about the shack being so close to the mountain, Tom remembered now, his mind gone cold with the reality of what had happened. Spoke of the danger of avalanche or a mud slide; spoke of building another place for him and Janice not so close to the mountain.

And David's A-frame? It had been built, intentionally or by happy accident, farther away from the slope, and now stood to one side of the slide's main flow. Nevertheless it had been pushed off its foundation, nearly toppled over. In the beam of Clay's flashlight they saw David and Sarah drop out of the small sleeping loft window that served now as an escape hatch. They were somehow half-clothed and apparently unhurt. "Hey!" David yelled, blinking into Clay's light. "You guys okay?"

"We're fine!" Angela cried. "But Janice and Adrien . . . they're—"

339

"Their place is buried!" Tom yelled.

Clay played his light on the hall. The slide had stopped just short of it.

Chapter 48

The survivors gathered in the hall. Joel and Helen, in a daze, had just tumbled out of bed. Little Brightness was crying. Someone lit the lamp on the trestle table.

"What in God's name *happened*?" Joel asked. "Felt like the whole mountain came down on us."

"That's pretty much it," David told him. "Chuck's shack is buried."

"Oh God," said Helen. "Adrien and Janice . . ."

"They're buried with it."

"We gotta dig them out!" Helen shouted. "They could still be alive!"

"I doubt it," David said dully. "If they haven't been crushed, they must have suffocated by now. Anyway, we can't do anything till it gets light."

Sarah said quietly. "We'll need an earth-moving machine."

"This is too unreal. I can't believe this has happened!"

Helen cried.

Clay had been pacing back and forth. Now he swung around at them and shouted, "How we gonna get any kind of machine, for fuck's sake? We're fucking stranded out here in the boonies. We're helpless!"

"*No,*" Tom said, finally rousing himself. "We have the canoe, remember? We can cross the lake to Galena, find somebody with a machine that can make it out of here."

Joel, who'd been standing with his mouth open as if in comic astonishment, said, "In any case, we'll have to report this, people. That'll involve the police and—"

"Oh sure, bring in the fuzz!" Clay hollered. He was rubbing his forehead as if to obliterate his thoughts, his eyes threatening to pop out. "And here's us, squatting on government land like the fucking hippies we are, and how many of us are legal? We'll be busted! Deported! As for *me,* I'm fucking wanted in the States!"

"Calm down," Sarah said.

"Hold it. *Hold it,*" Joel said. "Let's not panic, for God's sake. We gotta think this out."

"What's to think? We're all fucked," Clay declared. "*I'm* fucked."

They wound up all sitting at the hall table, reduced to silence until, at first light, they stepped outside and saw the full extent of what had happened. An entire section of the steep slope above New Eden had given way and slid down into the clearing. The word "awesome" came to Tom. The word "tragic." It was tragic that Chuck, in his ignorance, had built his shack so close to the slope. Tragic that Adrien, who knew better, had postponed moving Janice and him away from it.

There'd been reports of avalanches that winter, the deaths of back-country skiers.

It had stopped raining. The sky was clearing, but there was a wind, whipping up the lake.

Tom turned to David. The sight of the lake's rough water was serving to focus his faculties, sparking surges of take-charge capability. "You think you and I could make it across the lake and get an earth-mover out here while the rest start digging, by hand? Maybe there's an air pocket under that mess, or a hole up to the surface. Maybe Adrien and Janice are still alive."

"No," said Clay. "They're *dead*, let's face it. Let's just *forget* about digging them up and get the hell out of here, scatter, disappear!"

"Jesus, Clay," Joel said, "what kind of dude are you?"

"A *fugitive from justice*, that's what. And I'm for just walking away, *forgetting* this silly, failed, fucking attempt at whatever the fuck we were trying to do here and moving on. Starting over. Staying free. Who'll ever know what happened here, except what they can see?"

"What happened here, *besides* the slide, will come to light someday," Joel said. "People will show up here, maybe some company will decide to log here again and resurrect this camp. They'll clear away the rubble and guess what they'll find?"

Right, Tom thought. Joel was sounding like a guy in charge, finally.

"Whoa," David said, coming out of an apparent slump. "This is crazy. We all know what we gotta do. We gotta do the right thing. Dig through the rubble for Adrien and Janice. Report what happened, as Joel says. They *may* still be alive.

Miracles fucking happen."

"But if they haven't been *crushed*, they've suffocated," Helen said. "You said so yourself."

"Yeah. Well anyway, we're wasting time." David looked at Tom. "The lake looks too rough for canoeing, but maybe we can get out with the truck. Wanna try it?"

When they reached the truck, David said, "Go ahead, farm boy. Drive us out of here."

Tom backed the truck to the bridge at the far end of the clearing, then started off in first, quickly shifted to second, then floored the accelerator so they were going at about forty when they started up the steep rise out of the clearing. The truck wasn't a four-by-four but its rear wheels had positive traction, the next best thing. They swooped up the incline, nearly made it to the top, but then the rear wheels started spinning. Tom shifted quickly into reverse and let the gear provide braking as they rolled crazily back down into the clearing.

"Jezus!" David said. "Lemme try it."

They changed places and David backed to the bridge. Then he gunned the engine, spinning the wheels on the level, reached the rise at something like Tom's speed only to have the ruts their first attempt had created slow their progress so they made it only halfway up before starting to spin again. David managed to shift into reverse but then applied the brakes causing the truck to spin out of control. They went off the road and over the bank, rolled and crashed against a tree in a repeat of what had happened to Tom's car. The tree stopped the truck from rolling into the lake. It rested now, on its side against the tree, almost directly above the wreckage of Tom's car.

David was all right, but Tom's head had hit the side window, creating a spider web pattern on the glass and causing an egg-size swelling to instantly form on his right temple.

After that there was nothing anyone could do except wait for the weather to change. They all sat around the hall table again, immobilized, staring at one another. Outside, the sky clouded over and threatened rain again. The lake remained too rough to risk crossing in the canoe.

Sarah was the first to move. She went outside, climbed the pile of rubble to where Chuck's shack—the disintegrated remains of it, the *remains* of Janice and Adrien—might be and began lifting rocks and pulling at uprooted timber. David joined her. Soon everybody was on the pile, even Clay, all madly lifting and pulling at it, Joel working with their only shovel, David swinging their only pick.

Tom started to help, then felt dizzy and nauseous, which caused Angela to declare he might have a concussion and should go lie down. He went into the bunkhouse, drafty now because of the ruined door, the missing window, the partially collapsed wall, and lay down on their damaged bed. But even clothed and under the covers he was cold, and he didn't have the energy to make a fire. He went back outside and found the others sitting dejectedly on the slide now.

"It's no use," Joel said to Tom. "We need a machine."

"Those poor guys," Helen said, tears in her eyes. "It must have been terrible for them."

Tom looked away and an image of Janice swam into his head, filling him with a kind of sorrowful love for both her and Angela. He saw Adrien, his big French nose, his big smile, his competence, his friendship. It was starting to sink into him.

345

It was starting to sink into all of them. They were gone. New Eden was gone.

Clay stood up. "Let's do what I said."

"Just walk away, huh man?" said David.

"That's right. It's what *I'm* going to do."

"You would," Sarah said. "Go ahead, Clay. You have our blessing."

Nobody else said anything. After a long silence, Helen said, "I think we should cast the *I Ching*. No—I'm serious! That or have a meeting."

"We're having a meeting right now, Hel," Joel told her.

Angela reached over and took Tom's hand. He should say something, he thought. But he couldn't think of anything to say.

"Why are we all just sitting here?" said Sarah. "We all *know* what we should do. *Have* to do."

"I know what *I* have to do," Clay said, and climbed down off the slide and strode over to the bunkhouse and through its half-unhinged door. Nobody else moved. They all just sat there, waiting to see what Clay was actually going to do.

What he did was come out of the bunkhouse carrying his backpack. He stopped, hitched the pack onto his shoulders, then looked pointedly over at them. Then he started up the muddy, rutted road out of New Eden. He didn't wave. He didn't look back. Nobody called goodbye to him.

Chapter 49

The foul weather continued, whipping up the lake, pelting them with more rain, rain mixed occasionally with snow. They gathered in the hall, trapped by the weather, trapped together in something like mourning for Janice and Adrien, for themselves, hardly speaking, only finding some comfort in one another's glum company.

"The good thing," Joel offered after a long, thick silence, "is we're still together, people. We're really, truly together now. We have to *stay* together. We're family. More so than ever."

"Cold comfort," Helen said.

"Ever the optimist," said Sarah.

"Bullshit," David said.

Tom looked around. There were David and Sarah, Joel and Helen and little Brightness, himself and Angela. All that was left of the New Eden experiment, their half-assed alternative to the conventional, military-industrial, war-mongering, racist, greedy capitalist, environmentally destructive, enslaving and finally stultifying society they'd all turned their backs on. Dropped out of. Left behind to go back to the land, to live the good simple life in this friendly, hardly foreign country with the hope that things might change someday in their native land, in the straight, uptight world. David had pegged it. They'd all been waiting. Waiting for the revolution, *some* revolution, some true, radical change for the better.

He thought back and counted, counted the names of those who'd left New Eden, who'd copped out. Big John and Little Judy with their twin boys; Robert and Mark and Chuck and Peter—those you might say had reverted to type, dropped back into straight society. And now Clay was gone, running scared, and Adrien and Janice lay entombed under part of a mountain.

There'd been sixteen of them. Sixteen! And now they were only seven, the unhappy few, reduced to less than half their number in the long ago of last summer.

The second day after the slide dawned dark and gloomy. Then it began to clear. By noon the sun was out. Tom and David walked to the lake and looked out over the water, toward Galena, to what they could see of the town and the clearings above the town. The lake was calm.

"We could cross now," David said.

"Yeah"

The sun was warm on Tom's shoulders. It was April now, the deciduous trees still bare but the snow gone from the lakeshore, gone in the woods around the clearing, gone from the lower slopes, only still shining on the peaks.

David stood staring out at the lake. Then he turned and walked back to the hall. Tom watched him open the door and meet Angela, coming out. He said something to her. Tom waved to Angela, motioning for her to join him.

"What did David say to you?"

"He said something strange. 'I have to think of Sarah now.' What's *that* mean?"

"I can guess."

Angela stared at him. He watched her come to the same conclusion.

"That's right," Tom said.

"You're not . . ."

"No. We can't just walk away like the others seem ready to do."

"Not all of them," Angela said. "Not Joel and Helen. Not Sarah."

"Sarah will go along with David. I'm surprised at *him*, though."

"How can . . ."

"It's complicated," Tom said. "To get help to dig in the rubble for what's left of Adrien and Janice (their images, what their remains might look like, flashed in his brain), then have the authorities come out here and start asking questions and discover who's legal and who isn't and didn't we know we've been squatting? It'll open up a huge can of worms—for all of us."

"What else can we do?"

"We can do what the others seem ready to do—what they're probably *going* to do."

"We won't, though, will we, Tom. You and I, we won't just

leave, if that's what the others do. But where will that leave us?"

"Holding the bag," Tom said.

They went into the hall and found the others staring morosely at one another across the trestle table. Brightness, her spiky golden braids come undone, looked vacantly out from the kitchen holding a slice of her mother's bread smeared with peanut butter and jam. She took a bite, dirtied her pretty face.

"We've made a decision," David said. It seemed he was in charge now. Joel and Helen were silent.

"We've talked it over and decided that the best thing all around is just to split."

"You haven't talked it over with us," Tom said.

"Okay, we're talking with you now. I guess you still think we should call in the man. But that would get all of us, or at least *some* of us, in trouble. Clay was right to take off. Look, Joel and Helen are legal, official landed immigrants, but they could lose their status. Sarah's a Canadian citizen. Me, I don't have any status, and neither do you guys, or do you?"

"No, we came up here as visitors and never got legal." Tom looked at Angela. "But we've decided to stay, right, Angie? Or anyway, I have. I'm planning to emigrate."

"You think we could now?" Angela asked.

"Yeah, you two could blow your case," Joel said. Helen nodded.

"Look, we gotta stick together in this thing," David said. "Otherwise we fuck things up for everybody, *including* Joel and Helen."

"You guys do what you have to," Tom said. "Angela and I will do what *we* have to."

"No! Don't you see, man? We're all implicated. Suppose the four of us disappear and you and Angela *do the right thing*, so called. Don't you think the fuzz'll start checking and find out there was a bunch of us living out here, all us back-to-the-land freaks, and don't you think they'll try to round us up as some kind of accessories? No," David stressed. "We all gotta come forward, or we all gotta walk away."

"We haven't *murdered* anybody," Tom said. "Jesus."

"Yeah, but we're all subject to some goddamn form of hassle now. I say we just walk away."

Tom was getting a headache. Angela looked stricken. The others looked relieved, in some crazy way, as if David had solved things.

Tom threw up his hands. Angela gave him a look of—what? Contempt, he decided, then disappointment. Then she turned away from him.

351

Chapter 50

As they were packing up the next morning to leave—to go where? Together or individually?—a Forest Service pickup rolled down the incline into the clearing and a young guy in a green Forest Service uniform stepped out of the truck and looked around.

"What have we here?" he said. "You've had a slide, I see. Not surprising, given how saturated the slopes are now after all this rain. Looks like it ruined your nice little A-frame there. You folks been squatting, by the way?"

Joel started to speak, but David cut him off. "We didn't know we were squatting, sir. Anyway, we've just been camping here. We were just leaving."

"Oh? And how were you going to do that? I see a truck off the road there. And the wreck of somebody's car below *it*. Those your vehicles?"

And that's when Angela spoke up, filling Tom and maybe

the rest of them with guilt and shame and finally admiration.

"Something terrible has happened!" she cried. "We've lost two of our friends! They're buried under that slide!"

Chapter 51

After that, it was out of their hands. The Forest Service guy called the RCMP on his truck radio, reporting the slide and the probability of fatalities, and then called for an excavator to come dig for the bodies.

A pair of Mounties arrived about half an hour later in a four-by-four van, both tall, athletic-looking men, the older one slender with a pencil mustache, the younger big and beefy with a boy's face. They began asking questions. David took over as spokesman, claiming they had just arrived in Canada to look around for land and had used the old bunkhouse and dining hall for a couple of days. Then the slide happened, burying two of their members who happened to be sleeping in an old shack nearby.

The cop with the mustache smiled. "Is that right? That new-looking A-frame part of the old camp? Your fenced-in garden there? Actually, we've known about you people for some time. You've been squatting on crown land, did you know that? You would have had a visit from us, regardless of what's happened here."

The excavator arrived. They heard it coming for quite a while before it appeared, a backhoe on tracks that trundled over the edge of the steep incline into the clearing and rolled down it like an army tank.

Now the Forest Service guy, who'd introduced himself as Ian, took over. He asked to be shown where the two persons might be buried. David led him to his A-frame, which had been pushed aside by the edge of what Ian called the slide's "toe," then up onto the slide itself, a twenty-foot-high pile of debris stretching to the gap in the steep slope above that was like a big bite out of it. David said, "Their shack was about here, I think. Or maybe there," pointing ahead of where they stood. "The slide probably pushed it forward."

"No doubt," Ian said. "This was way too close to the slope, by the way. Bad place to build. Well, better get started."

He motioned to the machine operator, then climbed down off the slide. The machine trundled forward and the operator, a young guy wearing a bright red toque, began to dig skilfully into the rubble. The machine's hydraulic arm bent to the operator's will, its shovel became his clawlike mechanical hand as, with each manoeuver, he lifted rocks or a single boulder, an uprooted tree or a pile of mud and gravel, up and then over to one side, the weight of each load tipping the machine forward and raising its backside, until the shovel dropped its load onto an accumulating pile of debris.

While this digging was going on, New Eden's survivors were questioned by the police. They showed what identification each had—driver's licences, for the most part—and told what they knew about their buried comrades. Nobody knew of any next of kin.

It took a half-hour or so for the shovel to reach the wreckage of Chuck's shack. The operator plucked daintily now at the splintered boards, the crumpled tin, nuzzled the earth and rocks until, like evidence of a crime, a human arm appeared.

The operator shut down his engine then and they all, including the Mounties, began to dig in the debris with shovels, finally with their bare hands until, carefully, almost reverently, they exhumed the poor, broken bodies of Janice and Adrien. They lay together like victims of the volcanic eruption that destroyed ancient Pompeii, Tom noted to himself. Adrien might have known what was coming. His body lay across Janice's as if he'd tried to shield her.

"They were crushed," the older cop said. "Died instantly, I'd say. Better that than suffocation."

The bodies of the deceased were lifted into the bed of the Forest Service pickup. New Eden's survivors were loaded into the police van. Both official vehicles, equipped with four-wheel drive, the pickup following the van, made it up and out of the old logging camp without difficulty and drove to Silver City.

In Silver City the survivors were turned over to Immigration and the bodies of Adrien and Janice transported to a mortuary. At Immigration, in a process that took hours, the survivors were questioned individually by stern-faced officials. Finally they were put under house arrest in the city's vintage hotel to await their fate.

Two days later a story appeared in the *Silver City Miner* under the headline TRAGEDY STRIKES HIPPIE COMMUNE. The subhead read: Members Under Investigation.

The story included the news that an inquest had determined the cause of Adrien and Janice's death to be accidental, "the result of a natural disaster," and that no next of kin had been located.

That same day New Eden's survivors received Immigration's decisions. Joel and Helen and little Brightness, as landed immigrants, would be allowed to stay in Canada. Sarah too, of course, as a national.

David and Tom and Angela, without status, without gainful employment—illegal residents, in short—were ordered to leave the country (so much for the government's supposed leniency toward American "refugees"). They were not to return until, and unless, they met Canada's qualifications for immigration. These included a certified job offer, sufficient funds, and preferably post-secondary education. There was an age restriction, but they were all young enough, including Tom at age thirty-five, to pass that particular restriction should they seek to return.

Chapter 52

Two days later the four of them, David and Sarah, Tom and Angela, sat around a table at an outdoor café in Spokane, Washington. The café was in a park along the Spokane River. It featured an old-fashioned carousel on which children, clinging to wooden replicas of various animals and watched by smiling adults, were going round and round. The carousel's sprightly music, the children's excited cries, the warm spring sunshine—all served to lift the four's spirits.

"We can get married," Sarah said to David. She'd followed them into what she called their expulsion from Canada. "That way I can sponsor you to get landed."

"I'm not sure I want to go back to Canada," David said. "Not sure I want to get married."

"Oh," said Sarah. "I see."

"I don't mean I don't want you with me, babe," David said quickly, then turned to Tom and Angela. "Why don't we all head down to Mexico? You two've been there, right? Could be the next good place."

"I'd love to go to Mexico," Sarah said.

Angela said, "I don't think so. It wasn't a happy place, finally, for Tom and me." She looked at Tom.

"We could give it another try," he said. "It wasn't the country, Angie."

"Anyhow, New Eden was fun while it lasted, huh folks?" David said. "We'll have our fond and not-so-fond memories."

"Let's not talk about it," said Sarah.

"We learned some things, though," Tom said. "At least I did."

"What'd you learn?" David asked.

"That living communally is a struggle," Tom said. "Like human relations in general, for that matter. But it can probably work, and maybe what'll *have* to work— eventually."

"Come the revolution." David said. "That pie in the sky."

"You don't believe in revolution?" Angela asked.

"I believe that change, even a possible change for the better, is frightening to people," David declared. "People don't *really* want things to change because, let's face it, things aren't that bad—not *yet*. In fact, things are still pretty good down here— here in the States, I mean, despite the war and racism and all the rest of it. Things will have to get a hell of lot worse before anything truly radical happens. The rich and powerful will increase their riches and power, and the fucking government and the police will back them because they're in the fucking pocket of the rich and powerful. Not that things won't fall apart eventually. *Nobody's* in control, actually."

Tom said, "That might be what saves us, finally."

"What *I* think," Sarah said, "is you just live your life. While you have it. Life is short, after all."

"Yes," Angela said. "And life is good, after all."

"Not for everybody," Tom said.

David and Sarah took a bus to Phoenix the next day. David had friends there—a guy he was in Nam with, Hispanic, shacked up with a gringa. Short of going to Mexico, they might settle there, not in the city but out in the desert where it was flat and open, without trees closing you in, where it was maybe too hot in the summer but warm in the winter and without snow.

"Keep in touch," Tom told them.

"Come visit us sometime," David said.

Tom and Angela saw them off. Then they turned to each other—and to whatever lay before them.

After

Chapter 53

Tom woke to find himself alone in their bed. He climbed down from the loft, padded through the dark cabin and found Angela outside on the glider on their front deck. She was wrapped in a blanket, looking up at the stars.

"Here you are. You all right?"

"The baby woke me. It started kicking like crazy."

"Lemme feel." She opened the blanket and presented her swollen belly. He placed a hand there, felt a small movement. He put an ear to her belly, heard the rapid little heartbeat.

"Won't be long now, I guess."

"I have a feeling it's going to be early," Angela said.

It was August 1976. The Vietnam War was history, the Sixties was history, and they were back in Canada, in British Columbia again, homesteading in the beautiful valley along the Alder River north of Purcell Lake.

They'd succeeded in emigrating to Canada after a couple

of years in Chicago during which Tom worked as news editor for the little FM radio station his old friend Cliff, after leaving *Urban Bachelor*, served as manager. It was a good job, good working with his old friend again, good being back in Chicago at first. But then they both began to long for what they'd left behind, for some realization of New Eden's dream.

Nixon's landslide victory did it. They began the process of returning legally to Canada, and they were *back* in Canada, living and working in Silver City, when Nixon resigned following the Watergate scandal. All that was in another country.

With money saved from Tom's job as a reporter for the *Silver City Miner* (Angela's job as a teller at the Bank of Montreal paid their rent, bought their groceries), *plus* a surprising "loan" (really a gift) from Angela's parents, they bought land—ten acres for which they paid eight thousand dollars, cash. They built a little two-room cabin including a sleeping loft with the help of their neighbors, the Kalnikoffs, a Doukhobor couple whose children were all grown and gone and who'd sort of adopted them.

They were among those called "new people" in the valley, Vietnam War draft dodgers, back-to-the-landers, all US citizens of one sort or another, all self-imposed exiles from their native country. Some who'd evaded the draft would go back in a year or so, after President Carter's pardon. Tom and Angela would apply for Canadian citizenship when they became eligible after five years as landed immigrants.

They and their kind were only the most recent settlers in this region. Before them had come miners and loggers from the States and elsewhere in Canada, homesteaders from Europe and the States, folks fleeing persecution or seeking religious or political freedom—US Quakers, Doukhobors from Russia. And of course, long before them, were the Sinixt and Ktunaxa, the region's displaced native peoples.

They'd learned of all this from their reading, from talking to their neighbours. They'd collected a library of regional history.

They'd learned about the Doukhobors from the Kalnikoffs, that their name meant "spirit wrestler," that they were pacifists and how, after being persecuted in Russia, they'd immigrated to Canada at the turn of the century—settling first in Saskatchewan and then in British Columbia—with the help of Quakers in Canada and none other than Leo Tolstoy back in Russia. In Canada, as in Russia, they lived communally, and as in Russia they suffered persecution for resisting authority—refusing to send their kids to public school, refusing military service, refusing to pledge allegiance to the British Crown as they'd refused to acknowledge the Russian tsar.

They were assimilated now, no longer lived communally; but peace and toil remained their core beliefs. Tom and Angela could relate.

Tom worked on the cable ferry now, did odd carpentry jobs, had begun to think about writing a novel loosely based on their New Eden experience. He had his journal for raw material. Otherwise he might return to the novel he'd started—and abandoned—that long-ago winter in Oaxaca.

There was no rush, however. He'd lost the itch of literary ambition.

Angela welcomed him under her blanket.

"The nights are getting chilly already."

"Makes for good cuddling," Angela said.

Bundled warmly together, they listened to the crickets, in

full voice lately, heralding the end of summer. Time to start firewood gathering, Tom thought. He meant to have their woodshed full before the baby came, their miracle baby. And after the first snowfall he'd hunt along the river bottoms with his father's old Winchester 30-30 carbine, a gift from him; and with luck he'd shoot a fat buck and feel a hunter's mixed emotions—of regret for having taken a life along with the primitive joy of the kill. He would provide meat for him and his mate.

"Lots of stars tonight," Angela said. "We hardly ever saw them in Chicago."

"I couldn't live there again. I couldn't live in a city anymore."

"Me neither."

As to how, and where, Angela should have their baby, Tom had been for playing it safe and driving her in their pickup, when the time came, to the hospital in Silver City. Angela, though, was for natural childbirth, and when they learned that Marie, Steve Kalnikoff's wife, happened to be a midwife, they'd arranged for her to come when Angela went into labour. The miracle was that Angela had gotten pregnant—against all expectations. His low sperm count notwithstanding.

They had a phone, among other modern conveniences, and Tom called home now every couple of hours during his shifts on the ferry.

"Oh!" Angela said. "Did you see that meteor?"

Tom, snuggled close to his wife, enjoying her warmth and the chilled night air and the overarching sky full of stars, said, "Missed it."

He'd had something else on his mind. "You ever think about going back to Mexico, Angie?"

"Oh, we were so unhappy there. We *went* there

unhappy, remember?"

"You did, maybe. I didn't."

"I know. You had your writing."

"And we had each other, I thought, until we started fighting."

He remembered the line from Lowry's *Under the Volcano* that struck him after their breakup: "Oaxaca. The word was like a breaking heart."

"Anyway, we should go back there someday. Happy."

Another meteor flashed. It was that time of year. They were having a meteor shower.

"I think it would be good for us," he went on. "Like getting back on a horse after it's thrown you."

"Maybe," she said. "For a getaway in the winter sometime. We could skip Puerto Bonito, though. Richard wasn't going back there, remember? We shouldn't either. I wonder how he's doing now, by the way."

"I still wonder that about all the people we knew back then, even—"

"Peter, you mean? I still think about him."

"I still think about Janice."

"I still think about Klaus. Did he go back to Germany? Ramala's no more, and Mustafa, that is Paul What'shisname, didn't he wind up at the Esalen Institute?"

It was all so long ago. Their former loves, the New Eden experiment, those they'd shared it with—that failure, that adventure. They could look back on it now with a certain fondness. Helen and Joel and little Brightness. Where were *they* now? No longer in Canada, they guessed. The Professor. Mark. *Clay*, for godsake. Was he still on the run? David and Sarah. They'd corresponded for awhile. When last heard from, they had a place on Lake Chapala in Mexico.

"Peter and I were on such a head trip together," Angela said. "It almost wasn't sexual."

"I suppose Janice and I played some of that game ourselves."

His wife drew away from him a little. "I wonder if you realize I'm not that innocent young thing you married anymore. Who you thought you had to take care of and came looking for after we split up because you thought I might need you. And maybe I did. But I'm my own person now, buster. I can take care of myself."

"I thought we were taking care of each other."

"Oh, we are, honey," she said. "I'm just mouthing off."

She lay her head on his shoulder as Tom considered that there would always be this little tension between them, this taut linking of two individuals who, despite their love, had to work to accommodate each other. That was true of most couples, he guessed.

"Remember that note Richard left us?" Angela said. "It was kind of sweet, actually."

"Yeah, especially his suggestion we try a *ménage à trois*."

"He wasn't a bad man, really."

"Maybe. Old Ricardo. A little conniving, though, eh? A little devious?" The "eh" made Tom smile to himself. He was starting to sound like a Canadian.

He thought now of Adrien, his French-Canadian friend. He thought of Janice, whom he'd loved in his divided way. If you weren't just snuffed out at the end, he hoped they were together.

Not that he believed in an afterlife anymore. But who knew for sure? He still said his prayers at night.

There was the natural world, its birds and beasts and trees and flowers, its rivers and oceans, the weather, the seasons, the living planet itself! The vastness of the universe, its marvellous order! It was a mystery. It was all a mystery.

As for revolution, true revolution, something more than just a shift in power, some genuine change for the better. Some social-political-economic system not given to, not orchestrated by, the rich and powerful and their greed. Some saving integration with the natural world, some happy accommodation to the complexities of human relationships. Some grand righting of all the wrongs in the world. Did he still believe that was possible?

He thought of New Eden, that failed utopia. Their attempt in New Eden to drop out of straight society and how they'd all been on some kind of vacation from it, some kind of postponement of having to *grow up* as the society dictated. Sure, they'd resisted for a time; he and Angela were still resisting, he told himself, still waiting, in their modified way, for the revolution that might be just a dream, like the dream of heaven. Meanwhile, they were in the here and now and weren't they lucky, after all, to be where they were and to have each other?

"What're you thinking?" Angela asked.

"Oh, nothing. What life might be like for our kid, I guess. Him or her."

"I'm thinking about what it will be like for us—as parents. Speaking of which, I guess *my* parents will come out here for a visit after the baby is born."

"Mine too, I suppose."

"Now that we aren't hippies anymore," Angela said, and they both laughed.

Another meteor appeared, a spectacular one, a fireball, large and remarkably slow as it streamed in a shallow trajectory across the sky before breaking in two, one part dropping off toward the earth while the other streamed on—until both winked out.

"Wow," said Angela.

"Is that some kind of portent?" Tom said, and laughed alone this time.

"I'm sleepy," Angela said. "Let's go back to bed."

Tom, not wanting to move, said, "We've come through, though, haven't we, Angie? After all we've *been* through?" He was reading Lawrence again, his sequence of poems about his turbulent relationship with Frieda; had read parts of it to Angela.

"We'll see!" she said brightly, and threw off the blanket and stood up. Her nightgown bulged wonderfully where the baby was.

Tom looped the blanket over his arm and followed Angela into the cabin. She began labouring up the ladder to the loft. Time to move our bed downstairs, he thought.

"*Cuidado*," he called up softly to her.

And stood by, ready to catch her if she fell.

#

Printed in Canada